"Can we just say I'm tired of playing games and leave it at that? I want to be close to you because I like you for yourself. So do you want the same thing or have I misread the signs?"

"No, you haven't," she admitted. "But you said just this afternoon that I was a complication you didn't need."

"Overanalyzing is second nature to me. It has saved my skin more often than I care to count. But in this case I took it too far."

"Maybe not," she said judiciously. "Maybe you simply realized there was no future in a relationship with me."

"Never counting on the future is another by-product of my job. The only certainty is the here and now."

He took a step toward her, then another, until he was close enough to inhale the scent of her skin. "What do you say, Emily?" he asked hoarsely. "Will you take a chance with me?"

Dear Reader,

Harlequin Presents® is all about passion, power, seduction, oodles of wealth and abundant glamour. This is the series of the rich and the superrich. Private jets, luxury cars and international settings that range from the wildly exotic to the bright lights of the big city! We want to whisk you away to the far corners of the globe and allow you to escape and indulge in a unique world of unforgettable men and passionate romances. There is only one Harlequin Presents®, available all month long. And we promise you the world....

As if this weren't enough, there's more! More of what you love.... Two weeks after the Presents® titles hit the shelves, four Presents® EXTRA titles join them! Presents® EXTRA is selected especially for you—your favorite authors and much-loved themes have been handpicked to create exclusive collections for your reading pleasure. Now there's another excuse to indulge! Midmonth, there's always a new collection to treasure—you won't want to miss out.

Harlequin Presents®—still the original and the best!

Best wishes,

The Editors

Catherine Spencer
THE GREEK MILLIONAIRE'S SECRET CHILD

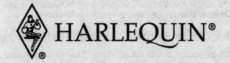

HARLEQUIN®

TORONTO • NEW YORK • LONDON
AMSTERDAM • PARIS • SYDNEY • HAMBURG
STOCKHOLM • ATHENS • TOKYO • MILAN • MADRID
PRAGUE • WARSAW • BUDAPEST • AUCKLAND

Recycling programs
for this product may
not exist in your area.

ISBN-13: 978-0-373-12823-5
ISBN-10:   0-373-12823-1

THE GREEK MILLIONAIRE'S SECRET CHILD

First North American Publication 2009.

www.eHarlequin.com

Printed in U.S.A.

All about the author...
Catherine Spencer

Some people know practically from birth that they're
going to be writers. **CATHERINE SPENCER** wasn't one
of them. Her first idea was to be a nun, which was clearly
never going to work! A series of other choices followed.
She considered becoming a veterinarian (lacked the
emotional stamina to deal with sick and injured animals),
a hairdresser (until she overheated a curling iron and
singed about five inches of hair off the top of her best
friend's head, the day before her friend's first date) or a
nurse (but that meant emptying bedpans. Eee-yew!).
As a last resort, she became a high school English teacher,
and loved it.

Eventually, she married, had four children and always,
always a dog or two or three. How can a house become a
home without a dog? How does an inexperienced mother
cope with babies if she doesn't have a German shepherd
nanny?

In time, the children grew up and moved out on their
own—as children are wont to do, regardless of their
mother's pleading for them to remain babies who don't
mind being kissed in public! She returned to teaching,
but a middle-aged restlessness overtook her and she
looked for a change of career.

What's an English teacher's area of expertise? Well, novels,
among other things, and moody, brooding, unforgettable
heroes: Heathcliff, Edward Fairfax Rochester, Romeo,
Rhett Butler. Then there's that picky business of knowing
how to punctuate and spell, what the rules of sentence
structure are and how to break them for dramatic effect.
They all pointed her in the same direction: breaking the
rules every chance she got, and creating her own moody,
brooding, unforgettable heroes. And where do they
belong? In Harlequin Presents® novels, of course, which
is where she happily resides now.

CHAPTER ONE

EMILY singled him out immediately, not because his father had described him so well that she couldn't miss him, but because even though he stood well back from everyone else, he dominated the throng waiting to meet passengers newly arrived at Athens's Venizelos Airport. At more than six feet of lean, toned masculinity blessed with the face of a fallen angel, he could hardly help it. One look at him was enough to tell her he was the kind of man other men envied, and women fought over.

As if on cue, his gaze locked with hers. Locked and lingered a small eternity, long enough for her insides to roll over in fascinated trepidation. Every instinct of self-preservation told her he was bad news; that she'd live to rue the day she met him. Then he nodded, as though he knew exactly the effect he'd had on her, and cutting a swath through the crowd, strode forward.

Given her first unobstructed view, she noted how his jeans emphasized his narrow hips and long legs, the way his black leather bomber jacket rode smoothly over his powerful shoulders, and the startling contrast of his throat rising strong and tanned against the open collar of his white shirt. As he drew closer, she saw, too, that his mouth and his jaw, the latter firm and faintly dusted with new beard shadow, betrayed the stubbornness his father had spoken of.

When he reached them, he asked in a voice as sinfully seductive as the rest of him, "So you beat the odds and made it back in one piece. How was the flight?"

"Long," Pavlos replied, sounding every bit as worn and weary as he surely must feel. Not even painkillers and the luxury of first-class air travel had been enough to cushion his discomfort. "Very long. But as you can see, I have my guardian angel at my side." He reached over his shoulder, groped for her hand and squeezed it affectionately. "Emily, my dear, I am pleased to introduce my son, Nikolaos. And this, Niko, is my nurse, Emily Tyler. What I would have done without her, I cannot imagine."

Again, Nikolaos Leonidas's gaze lingered, touring the length of her in insolent appraisal. Behind his chiseled good looks lurked a certain arrogance. He was not a man to be crossed, she thought. "*Yiasu,* Emily Tyler," he said.

Even though her sweater and slacks pretty much covered all of her, she felt naked under that sweeping regard. His eyes were the problem, she thought dizzily. Not brown like his father's, as she'd expected, but a deep green reminiscent of fine jade, they added an arresting final touch to a face already possessed of more than its rightful share of dark beauty.

Swallowing, she managed an answering, *"Yiasu."*

"You speak a little Greek?"

"A very little," she said. "I just exhausted my entire vocabulary."

"That's what I thought."

The comment might have stung if he hadn't tempered it with a smile that assaulted her with such charm, it was all she could do not to buckle at the knees. For heaven's sake, what was the matter with her? She was twenty-seven, and if not exactly the most sexually experienced woman in the world, hardly in the first flush of innocent youth, either. She knew well enough that appearances counted for little. It was the person inside that mattered, and from everything she'd been told, Niko Leonidas fell sadly short in that respect.

His manner as he turned his attention again to Pavlos did nothing to persuade her otherwise. He made no effort to embrace his father, to reassure him with a touch to the shoulder or hand that the old man could count on his son for whatever support he might need during his convalescence. Instead he commandeered a porter to take care of the loaded luggage cart one of the flight attendants had brought, and with a terse, "Well, since we seem to have exhausted the formalities, let's get out of here," marched toward the exit, leaving Emily to follow with Pavlos.

Only when they arrived at the waiting Mercedes did he betray a hint of compassion. "Don't," he ordered, when she went to help her patient out of the wheelchair and with surprising tenderness, scooped his father into his arms, laid him carefully on the car's roomy back seat and draped a blanket over his legs. "You didn't have to do that," Pavlos snapped, trying unsuccessfully to mask a grimace of pain.

Noticing, Niko said, "Apparently I did. Or would you have preferred I stand idly by and watch you fall on your face?"

"I would prefer to be standing on my own two feet without needing assistance of any kind."

"Then you should have taken better care of yourself when you were away—or else had the good sense to stay home in the first place, instead of deciding you had to see Alaska before you die."

Emily was tempted to kick the man, hard, but made do with a glare. "Accidents happen, Mr. Leonidas."

"Especially to globe-trotting eighty-six-year-old men."

"It was hardly his fault that the cruise ship ran aground, nor was he the only passenger on board who was injured. All things considered, and given his age, your father's done amazingly well. In time, and with adequate follow-up physical therapy, he should make a reasonably good recovery."

"And if he doesn't?"

"Then I guess you're going to have to step up to the plate and start acting like a proper son."

He favored her with a slow blink made all the more disturbing by the sweep of his lashes, which were inde-cently long and silky. "Nurse and family counselor all rolled into one," he drawled. "How lucky is that?"

"Well, you did ask."

"And you told me." He tipped the porter, left him to return the airport's borrowed wheelchair, then slammed closed the car trunk and opened the front passenger door with a flourish. "Climb in. We can continue this conversation later."

As she might have expected, he drove with flair and expertise. Within half an hour of leaving the airport, they were cruising the leafy green streets of Vouliagmeni, the exclusive Athens suburb overlooking the Saronic Gulf on the east coast of the Attic Peninsula, which Pavlos had described to her so vividly. Soon after, at the end of a quiet road running parallel to the beach, Niko steered the car through a pair of ornate wrought-iron gates, which opened at the touch of a remote control button on the dash.

Emily had gathered Pavlos was a man of considerable wealth, but was hardly prepared for the rather frightening opulence confronting her as the Mercedes wound its way up a long curving driveway, and she caught her first sight of...what? His house? Villa? Mansion?

Set in spacious, exquisitely landscaped grounds and screened from local traffic by a stand of pines, the place defied such mundane description. Stucco walls, blindingly white, rose in elegant proportions to a tiled roof as blue as she'd always imagined the skies to be in Athens, even though, this late September afternoon, an approaching storm left them gray and threatening. Long windows opened to wide terraces shaded by pergolas draped in flowering vines. A huge fountain splashed in a central forecourt, peacocks preened and screeched on the lawns, and from somewhere on the seaward side of the property, a dog barked.

She had little time to marvel, though, because barely had the car come to a stop outside a set of double front doors than they opened, and a man in his late fifties or early sixties appeared with a wheelchair light years removed from the spartan model offered by the airport.

The devoted butler, Georgios, she presumed. Pavlos had spoken of him often and with great fondness. Behind him came a younger man, little more than a boy really, who went about unloading the luggage while

Niko and the butler lifted Pavlos from the car to the chair. By the time they were done, he was gray in the face and the grooves paralleling his mouth carved more deeply than usual.

Even Niko seemed concerned. "What can you do for him?" he muttered, cornering Emily near the front entrance as Georgios whisked his employer away down a wide, marble-floored hall.

"Give him something to manage the pain, and let him rest," she said. "The journey was very hard on him."

"He doesn't look to me as if he was fit to travel in the first place."

"He wasn't. Given his age and the severity of his osteoporosis, he really ought to have remained in the hospital another week, but he insisted on coming home, and when your father makes up his mind, there's no changing it."

"Tell me something I don't already know." Niko scowled and shucked off his jacket. "Shall I send for his doctor?"

"In the morning, yes. He'll need more medication than what I was able to bring with us. But I have enough to see him through tonight." Struggling to preserve a professional front despite the fact that Niko stood close enough for the warmth of his body to reach out and touch hers, she sidled past him and took her travel bag from the pile of luggage accumulating inside the front door. "If you'd show me to his room, I really should attend to him now."

He stepped away and led her to the back of the villa, to a large, sun-filled apartment on the main floor. Consisting of a sitting room and bedroom, both with

French doors that opened onto a low-walled patio, it overlooked the gardens and sea. Still in the wheelchair, stationed next to the window in the sitting room, Pavlos leaned forward, drinking in the view which, even swathed in floating mist as the storm closed in, held him transfixed.

"He had this part of the house converted into his private suite a few years ago when the stairs proved too much for him," Niko said in a low voice.

Glancing through to the bedroom, Emily asked, "And the hospital bed?"

"I had it brought in yesterday. He'll probably give me hell for removing the one he's used to, but this one seemed more practical, at least for now."

"You did the right thing. He'll be more comfortable in it, even if he won't be spending much time there except at night."

"Why not?"

"The more mobile he is, the better his chances of eventually walking again, although…"

Picking up on the reservation in her voice, Niko pounced on it. "Although what? You said earlier you expect him to make a reasonable recovery. Are you changing your mind now?"

"No, but…" Again, she hesitated, bound by patient confidentiality, yet aware that as his son, Niko had the right to some information, especially if her withholding it might have an adverse effect on Pavlos's future well-being. "How much do you know about your father's general health?"

"Only what he chooses to tell me, which isn't very much."

She should have guessed he'd say that. *There's no need to contact my son,* Pavlos had decreed, when the hospital had insisted on listing his next of kin. *He minds his business, and I mind mine.*

Niko pinned her in that unnerving green stare. "What aren't you telling me, Emily? Is he dying?"

"Aren't we all, to one extent or another?"

"Don't play mind games with me. I asked you a straightforward question. I'd like a straightforward answer."

"Okay. His age is against him. Although he'd never admit it, he's very frail. It wouldn't take much for him to suffer a relapse."

"I can pretty much figure that out for myself, so what else are you holding back?"

Pavlos spared her having to reply. "What the devil are the pair of you whispering about?" he inquired irascibly.

Casting Niko an apologetic glance, she said, "Your son was just explaining that you might not care for the new bed he ordered. He's afraid you'll think he was interfering."

"He was. I broke my hip, not my brain. I'll decide what I do and don't need."

"Not as long as I'm in charge."

"Don't boss me around, girl. I won't put up with it."

"Yes, you will," she said equably. "That's why you hired me."

"I can fire you just as easily, and have you on a flight back to Vancouver as early as tomorrow."

Recognizing the empty threat for what it really was, she hid a smile. Exhaustion and pain had taken their toll, but by morning he'd be in a better frame of mind. "Yes, sir,

Mr. Leonidas," she returned smartly, and swung the wheel-chair toward the bedroom. "Until then, let me do my job."

Niko had seized the first opportunity to vacate the premises, she noticed, and could have slapped herself for the pang of disappointment that sprouted despite her best efforts to quell it. The faithful Georgios, however, remained on the scene, anxious and willing to help wherever he could. Even so, by the time Pavlos had managed a light meal and was settled comfortably for the night, darkness had fallen.

Damaris, the housekeeper, showed Emily upstairs to the suite prepared for her. Decorated in subtle shades of ivory and slate-blue, it reminded her of her bedroom at home, although the furnishings here were far grander than anything she could afford. Marble floors, a Savonnerie rug and fine antiques polished to a soft gleam exemplified wealth, good taste and comfort.

A lady's writing desk occupied the space between double French doors leading to a balcony. In front of a small blue-tiled fireplace was a fainting couch, its brocade upholstery worn to satin softness, its once-vibrant colors faded by time. A glass-shaded lamp spilled mellow light, and a vase of lilies on a table filled the room with fragrance.

Most inviting of all, though, was the four-poster bed, dressed in finest linens. Almost ten thousand kilometers, and over sixteen hours of travel with its inevitable delays, plus the added stress of her patient's condition, had made serous inroads on her energy, and she wanted nothing more than to lay her head against those snowy-white pillows, pull the soft coverlet over her body and sleep through to morning.

A quick glance around showed that her luggage had been unpacked, her toiletries arranged in the bathroom and her robe and nightshirt laid out on the bench in front of the vanity. But so, to her dismay, was a change of underwear, and a freshly ironed cotton dress, one of the few she'd brought with her, hung in the dressing room connecting bathroom and bedroom. And if they weren't indication enough that the early night she craved was not to be, Damaris's parting remark drove home the point in no uncertain terms.

"I have drawn a bath for you, Despinis Tyler. Dinner will be served in the garden room at nine."

Clearly daily protocol in the Leonidas residence was as elegantly formal as the villa itself, and the sandwich in her room, which Emily had been about to request, clearly wasn't on the menu.

The main floor was deserted when she made her way downstairs just a few minutes past nine, but the faint sound of music and a sliver of golden light spilling from an open door halfway down the central hall indicated where she might find the garden room.

What she didn't expect when she stepped over the threshold was to find that she wouldn't be dining alone.

A round glass-topped table, tastefully set for two, stood in the middle of the floor. A silver ice bucket and two cut-crystal champagne flutes glinted in the almost ethereal glow of dozens, if not hundreds, of miniature white lights laced among the potted shrubs lining the perimeter of the area.

And the final touch? Niko Leonidas, disgracefully gorgeous in pale gray trousers and matching shirt, which together probably cost more than six months' mortgage payments on her town house, leaned against an ornately carved credenza.

She was sadly out of her element, and surely looked it. She supposed she should be grateful her dinner companion wasn't decked out in black tie.

"I wasn't aware you were joining me for dinner," she blurted out, the inner turmoil she thought she'd conquered raging all over again at the sight of him.

He plucked an open bottle of champagne from the ice bucket, filled the crystal flutes and handed one to her. "I wasn't aware I needed an invitation to sit at my father's table."

"I'm not suggesting you do. You have every right—"

"How kind of you to say so."

He'd perfected the art of withering pleasantries, she decided, desperately trying to rein in her swimming senses. The smile accompanying his reply hovered somewhere between derision and scorn, and left her feeling as gauche as she no doubt sounded. "I didn't mean to be rude, Mr. Leonidas," she said, her discomfiture increasing in direct proportion to his suave assurance. "I'm surprised, that's all. I assumed you'd left the house. I understand you have your own place in downtown Athens."

"I do—and we Greeks, by the way, aren't big on honorifics. Call me Niko. Everyone else does."

She didn't care what everyone else did. Finding herself alone with him left her barely able to string two words together without putting her foot in her mouth. Resort to calling him Niko, and she'd probably manage to stuff the other one in next to it.

"At a loss for words, Emily?" he inquired, evil

laughter shimmering in his beautiful green eyes. "Or is it the prospect of sharing a meal with me that has you so perturbed?"

"I'm not perturbed," she said with as much dignity as she could bring to bear. "Just curious about why you'd choose to be here, instead of in your own home. From all accounts, you and Pavlos don't usually spend much time together."

"Nevertheless, I *am* his son, and the last I heard, my choosing to spend an evening under his roof doesn't amount to trespassing. Indeed, given the present circumstances, I consider it my duty to make myself more available. Do you have a problem with that?"

Hardly about to admit that she found him a distraction she wasn't sure she could handle, she said, "Not at all, as long as you don't interfere with my reasons for being here."

"And exactly what are those reasons?"

She stared at him. His eyes weren't glimmering with laughter now; they were as cold and hard as bottle-green glass. "What kind of question is that? You know why I'm here."

"I know that my father has become extremely dependent on you. I know, too, that he's a very vulnerable old man who happens also to be very rich."

She sucked in an outraged breath at the implication in his words. "Are you suggesting I'm after his money?"

"Are you?"

"Certainly not," she snapped. "But that's why you're hanging around here, isn't it? Not because you're worried about your father, but to keep an eye on me and make sure I don't get my hooks into him or his bank account."

"Not quite. I'm 'hanging around' as you so delicately put it, to look out for my father because, in his present condition, he's in no shape to look out for himself. If you find my concern offensive—"

"I do!"

"Then that's a pity," he replied, with a singular lack of remorse. "But try looking at it from my point of view. My father arrives home with a very beautiful woman who happens to be a complete stranger and whom he appears to trust with his life. Not only that, she's come from half a world away and signed on to see him through what promises to be a long and arduous convalescence, even though there's no shortage of nurses here in Athens well qualified to undertake the job. So tell me this: if our situation was reversed, wouldn't you be a little suspicious?"

"No," she shot back heatedly. "Before I leaped to unwarranted conclusions or cast aspersions on her professional integrity, I'd ask to see the stranger's references, and if they didn't satisfy me, I'd contact her previous employers directly to verify that she's everything she purports to be."

"Well, no need to foam at the mouth, sweet thing. Your point is well taken and that being the case, I'm prepared to shelve my suspicions and propose we call a truce and enjoy this very fine champagne I filched from my father's cellar. It'd be a shame to waste it."

She plunked her glass on the table so abruptly that its contents surged over the rim with an indignation that almost matched her own. "If you think I'm about to share a drink with you, let alone a meal, think again! I'd rather starve."

She spun on her heel, bent on making as rapid an exit as possible, but had taken no more than two or three steps toward the door before he caught up with her and slammed it closed with the flat of his hand. "I regret that, in looking out for my father's best interests, I have offended you," he said smoothly. "Trust me, I take no pleasure in having done so."

"Really?" She flung him a glare designed to strip paint off a wall. "You could have fooled me. I'm not used to being treated like a petty criminal."

He shrugged. "If I've insulted you, I apologize, but better I err on the side of caution."

"Meaning what, exactly?"

"That my father's been targeted before by people interested only in taking advantage of him."

"He might not be quite so susceptible to outsiders if he felt more secure in his relationship with you."

"Possibly not, but ours has never been a typical father-son relationship."

"So I've been given to understand, but I suggest the time's come for you to bury your differences and stop butting heads. He needs to know you care."

"I wouldn't be here now, if I didn't care."

"Would it kill you to tell him that?"

He gave a snort of subdued laughter. "No, but the shock of hearing me say so might kill *him*."

What was it about the two of them, that they held each other at such a distance, she wondered. "Do either of you have the first idea of the pain that comes from waiting until it's too late to say 'I love you?' Because I do. More often than I care to remember, I've witnessed the grief and regret that tears families apart because time ran out on them before they said the things that needed to be said."

He paced to the windows at the other end of the aptly named garden room whose exotic flowering plants set in Chinese jardinieres must give it the feel of high summer even in the depths of winter. "We're not other people," he said.

"You're not immortal, either." She hesitated, conflicted once again by how much she could say, then decided to plunge in and disclose what she knew, because she wasn't sure she could live with herself if she didn't. "Look, Niko, he'll probably have my head for telling you this, but your father's not just battling a broken hip. His heart's not in very good shape, either."

"I'm not surprised. That's what comes from years of smoking and hard living, but nothing his doctor said was enough to make him change his ways. He's a stubborn old goat."

That much she knew to be true. Pavlos had discharged himself from Vancouver General against medical advice, and insisted on flying back to Greece even crippled as he was, because he refused to put up with the nursing staff's constant monitoring. *They don't let a man breathe,* he'd complained, when Emily tried to talk him into postponing the journey. *I'll be carried out feetfirst if I let them keep me here any longer.*

"Well, the apple doesn't fall far from the tree, Niko. Where this family's concerned, you're both pretty pigheaded."

He swung around and surveyed her across the width of the room; another long, searching gaze so thorough that a quiver shafted through her. He probed too deeply beneath the surface. Saw things she wasn't ready to acknowledge to herself. "Perhaps before *you* start leaping to unwarranted conclusions," he purred, advancing toward her with the lethal grace of a hunter preparing to move in for the kill, "you should hear my side of the story."

"You're not my patient, your father is," she said, backing away and almost hyperventilating at the determined gleam in his eye.

"But isn't modern medicine all about the holistic approach—curing the spirit in order to heal the body, and such? And isn't that exactly what you've been advocating ever since you walked into this room?"

"I suppose so, yes."

"How do you expect to do that, if you have only half the equation to work with? More to the point, what do you stand to lose by letting me fill in the blanks?"

My soul, and everything I am, she thought, filled with the terrible foreboding that unless she extricated herself now from the web of attraction threatening to engulf her, destiny in the shape of Nikolaos Leonidas would take control of her life, and never give it back again. Yet to scurry away like a frightened rabbit was as alien to her nature as taking advantage of Pavlos. So she stood her ground, pushed the irrational presentiment out of her thoughts and said with deceptive calm, "Absolutely nothing."

"Really?" He leaned toward her, dropped his voice another half octave and latched his fingers around her wrist. "Then why are you so afraid?"

She swallowed and ran her tongue over her dry lips. "I'm not," she said.

CHAPTER TWO

SHE was lying. The evidence was there in her hunted gaze, in her racing pulse, so easily and unobtrusively detected when he took her wrist. And he intended to find out why, because for all that he thought he'd remain unmoved by whatever he discovered when he went to meet their flight, the sight of the old man, so brittle and somehow diminished, had hit him with the force of a hammer blow to the heart. They spent little time together, had long ago agreed to disagree and shared nothing in common. But Pavlos was still his father, and Niko would be damned before he'd let some hot little foreign number take him to the cleaners.

Oh, she'd been full of righteous indignation at his suggestion that she wasn't quite the selfless angel of mercy she presented herself to be. He'd hardly expected otherwise. But he'd also seen how indispensable she'd made herself to Pavlos; how successfully she'd wormed her way into his affections. His father had never been a demonstrative man, at least not that Niko could remember. Which had made the way he'd clung to Emily's hand at the airport all the more telling.

If his assessment of her was correct, redirecting her attention would be simple enough. After all, a millionaire in his vigorous prime was surely preferable to one in his dotage. And if he was wrong…well, a harmless flirtation would hurt no one. Of course, when his father figured out what he was up to, he wouldn't like it, but when was the last time he'd approved of anything Niko did?

"You're very quiet suddenly," she said, interrupting the flow of his thoughts.

He looked deep into her dark blue eyes. "Because I'm beginning to think I've judged you too hastily," he answered, doing his utmost to sound convincingly repentant. "But I'm not entirely without conscience. Therefore, if one of us must leave, let me be the one to go."

Ignoring her whimper of protest, he released her, opened the door to leave the room and found himself face-to-face with Damaris. He could not have orchestrated a better exit. Timing, as he well knew in his line of work, was everything. "*Kali oreksi*, Emily," he said, standing back to allow Damaris to carry in a platter loaded with olives, calamari, dolmades, tzatziki and pita bread. "Enjoy your meal."

He was over the threshold before she burst out, "Oh, don't be so ridiculous!"

Suppressing a smile, he swung around. "There is a problem?"

"If having enough food to feed an army is a problem, then yes."

He shrugged. "What can I say? Greeks love to eat."

"Well, I can't possibly do justice to all this, and since I have no wish to offend your father's housekeeper when she's obviously gone to a great deal of trouble…"

"Yes, Emily?"

She grimaced, as if her next words gave her indigestion. "You might as well stay and help me eat it."

He stroked his jaw and made a show of weighing his options. "It would be a pity to let it go to waste," he eventually conceded, "especially as this is but the first of several courses."

For a moment, he thought he'd overplayed his hand. Skewering him with a glance that would have stopped the gods of Olympus in their tracks, she waited until Damaris mopped up her spilled drink, then took a seat at the table and said, "Try not to gloat, Niko. It's so unattractive."

He wasn't accustomed to female criticism. The women he associated with were so anxious to please, they'd have swallowed their own tongues before issuing such a blunt assessment of his shortcomings. That she suffered no such hesitation appealed to him in ways she couldn't begin to imagine. He devoted his entire life to challenging unfavorable odds. And took enormous pleasure in defeating them.

Collecting the wine bottle as he passed, he joined her and topped up their flutes. Nothing like dim lights and good champagne to set the scene for seduction. Raising his glass, he said, "Here's to getting to know one another all over again."

She responded with the merest tilt of one shoulder, took a dainty sip, then helped herself to a little tzatziki and bread.

"Have more," he urged, pushing the tray of mezedes closer.

She selected an olive, but ignored her champagne.

"You don't care for Greek food?"

"I'm not very familiar with it."

"There are no Greek restaurants in Vancouver?"

"Hundreds, and I'm told they're very good. I just don't eat out very often."

"Why is that? And please don't tell me you lack opportunity. Suitors must be lined up at your door, wanting to wine and dine you."

"I'm afraid not. Shift work tends to put a crimp in a nurse's social life."

Right. And you're such a dedicated professional that you never take a night off!

He shook his head in feigned mystification. "What's wrong with Canadian men, to be so easily discouraged? Are they all eunuchs?"

She almost choked on her olive. "Not as far as I know," she spluttered. "But then, I haven't bothered to ask."

"What about your colleagues? As I understand it, hospitals are a hotbed of romance between doctors and nurses."

"The idea that all nurses end up marrying doctors is a myth," she informed him starchily. "For a start, half the doctors these days are women, and even if they weren't, finding a husband isn't particularly high on my list of priorities."

"Why not? Don't most women want to settle down and have children? Or are you telling me you're the exception?"

"No." She nibbled a sliver of pita bread. "I'd love to get married and have children someday, but only if the right man comes along. I'm not willing to settle for just anyone."

"Define 'the right man,'" he said—a shade too abruptly, if her response was anything to go by.

She dropped her bread and stared at him. "I beg your pardon?"

"By what standards do you judge a prospective husband?"

She reached for her glass and took a sip while she considered the question. "He has to be decent and honorable," she finally declared.

"Tall, dark and handsome, too?"

"Not necessarily." She gave another delicate shrug, just enough to cause her dress to shift gently over her rather lovely breasts.

He wished he didn't find it so alluring. "Rich and successful, then?"

"Gainfully employed, certainly. If we had children, I'd want to be a stay-at-home mom."

"If you had to choose just one quality in this ideal man, what would it be?"

"The capacity to love," she said dreamily, her blue eyes soft, her sweet mouth curved in a smile. Outside, the wind tore at the palm trees with unusual strength for September. "I'd want love more than anything else, because a marriage without it is no marriage at all."

Annoyed to find his thoughts drifting dangerously far from their set course, he said flatly, "I disagree. I'd never let my heart get the better of my head."

"Why not? Don't you believe in love?"

"I might have once, very briefly, many years ago, but then she died of a blood clot to the brain. I was three months old at the time."

"You mean your *mother*?" She clapped a distressed hand to her cheek. Her eyes glistened suspiciously. "Oh, Niko, how very sad for you. I'm so sorry."

He wanted neither her sympathy nor her pity, and crushed both with brutal efficiency. "Don't be. It's not as if she was around long enough for me to miss her."

The way she cringed at his answer left him ashamed. "She gave you life," she said.

"And lost hers doing it, something I've been paying for ever since."

"Why? Her death wasn't your fault."

"According to my father, it was." Her glass remained almost untouched, but his was empty. Needing something to deaden a pain he seldom allowed to surface, he refilled it so hurriedly, the wine foamed up to the brim. "She was forty-one, and giving birth at her age to an infant weighing a strapping five kilos put her in her grave."

"A lot of women wait until their forties to have children."

"They don't all die because of it."

"True. But that's still no reason for you to think Pavlos holds you responsible for the tragedy that befell her. After all, she gave him a son and that's not a legacy any man takes lightly."

"You might be a hell of a fine nurse, Emily Tyler, but you're no spin doctor."

Puzzled, she said, "What do you mean?"

"That nothing you can say changes the fact that my father didn't care if he never had a child. All he ever wanted was my mother, and as far as he's concerned, I took her away from him."

"Then he should have seen to it he didn't get her pregnant in the first place—or are you to blame for that, as well?"

"After twenty-one years of marriage without any sign

of a baby, he probably didn't think precautions were necessary. Finish your wine, woman. I don't care to drink alone. It's a nasty habit to fall into."

She took another cautious sip. "I still can't believe that, once his initial grief subsided, having you didn't bring Pavlos some measure of comfort."

"Then you obviously don't know much about dysfunctional families. My father and I have never liked one another. He has always resented me, not just because I cost him his one true love, but because I remained wilfully unimpressed by his wealth and social status."

"I'd have thought he'd find that commendable."

"Don't let misplaced pity for the poor motherless baby cloud your judgment, my dear," Niko said wryly. "I rebelled every step of the way as a child, took great pleasure in embarrassing him by getting into trouble as a teenager and flat-out refused to be bought by his millions when I finally grew up. I was not a 'nice' boy, and I'm not a 'nice' man."

"That much, at least, I do believe," she shot back, leveling a scornful glance his way. "The only part I question is that you ever grew up. You strike me more as someone with a bad case of defiantly delayed adolescence."

This wasn't playing out the way he'd intended. She was supposed to be all willing, female compliance by now, ready to fall into his arms, if not his bed, not beating him at his own game. And his glass was empty again, damn it! "When you've walked in my shoes," he replied caustically, "feel free to criticize. Until then—"

"But I have," she interrupted. "Walked in your shoes, I mean. Except mine were twice as hard to wear.

Because, you see, I lost *both* my parents in a car accident when I was nine, and unlike you, I remember them enough to miss them very deeply. I remember what it was like to be loved unconditionally, then have that love snatched away in the blink of an eye. I remember the sound of their voices and their laughter—the scent of my mother's perfume and my father's Cuban cigars. And I know very well how it feels to be tolerated by relatives who make no secret of the fact that they've been saddled with a child they never wanted."

Flushed and more animated than Niko had yet seen her, she stopped to draw an irate breath before continuing, "I also learned what it's like to have to work for every cent, and to think twice before frittering away a dollar." She eyed his shirt and watch disdainfully. "You, on the other hand, obviously wouldn't know the meaning of deprivation if it jumped up and bit you in the face, and I don't for a moment buy the idea that your father never wanted you. So all in all, I'd say I come out the uncontested winner in this spontaneous pity party."

He let a beat of silence hang heavy in the air before he spoke again, then, "It's not often someone spells out my many shortcomings so succinctly," he said, "but you've managed to do it admirably. Is there anything else you'd like to tell me about myself before I slither behind the wheel of my car and disappear into the night?"

"Yes," she said. "Eat something. You've had too much to drink and are in no condition to drive. In fact, you should be spending the night here."

"Why, Emily, is that an invitation?"

"No," she said crushingly. "It's an order, and should

you be foolish enough to decide otherwise, I'll kick you where it'll hurt the most."

She probably weighed no more than fifty-four kilos to his eighty-five, but what she lacked in size, she more than made up for in spirit. He had no doubt that, given her knowledge of male anatomy, she was more than capable of inflicting serious injury. Which should have deterred him. Instead the thought of fending her off left him so suddenly and painfully aroused that, for the first time, he questioned the wisdom of his plan of attack. *She* was the one supposed to be at *his* mercy, not the other way around, but so far, she remained utterly indifferent to his charms. He, on the other hand, was anything but impervious to hers.

Damaris came back just then to serve spinach-stuffed breast of chicken and ziti, a welcome diversion, which allowed him to wrestle his wayward hormones into submission and redirect his energy into more productive channels. "Why did you allow my father to coerce you into letting him travel, when he's clearly not up to it?" he inquired casually, once they were alone again.

"I did my best to dissuade him," Emily said. "We all did. But the only thing he cared about was coming home to Greece, and nothing anyone said could convince him to wait. I think it's because he was afraid."

"Of dying?"

"No. Of *not* dying in Greece."

That Niko could well believe. Pavlos had always been fanatically patriotic. "So you volunteered to see him safely home?"

"It was more that he chose me. We got to know one another quite well during his hospital stay."

An hour ago, he'd have rated that little morsel of information as yet another sign of her ulterior motives. Now, he didn't have quite the same enthusiasm for the task. Emily the woman was proving a lot more intriguing than Emily the fortune hunter.

To buy himself enough time to reestablish his priorities, he switched to another subject. "What happened to you after your parents were killed?"

"I was sent to live with my father's sister. He was thirty-six when he died, and Aunt Alicia was eleven years older. She and Uncle Warren didn't have children, but they were the only family I had left, so they were more or less stuck with me. It wasn't a happy arrangement on either side."

"They mistreated you?"

"Not in the way you probably mean, but they never let me forget they'd done 'the right thing' by taking me in and would, I think, have found a reason to refuse if they hadn't been afraid it would reflect badly on them. Of course, the insurance settlement I brought with me sweetened the deal by defraying the cost of putting a roof over my head and keeping me fed and clothed for the next nine years."

"What happened then?"

"The summer I graduated high school, I applied to the faculty of nursing, was accepted and moved into a dorm on the university campus at the end of August. I never went 'home' again."

"But at least there was enough insurance settlement left to pay your tuition fees and other expenses."

She shook her head. "I scraped by on scholarships and student loans."

Caught in a swell of indignation he never saw coming, he stared at her. Whatever else his father's sins, he'd never tampered with Niko's inheritance from his mother. "Are you telling me they spent money on themselves, when it should have been held in trust for your education?"

"No, they were scrupulously honest." She started to add something else, then seemed to think better of it and made do with, "The settlement just wasn't very large to begin with, that's all."

Something about *that* answer didn't sit right, either. Wasn't the whole point of insurance to provide adequate recompense to beneficiaries, especially minors? But although the subject bore investigation, he decided now was not the time to pursue it and asked instead, "Do you keep in touch with your aunt and uncle?"

"A card at Christmas about covers it."

"So they have no idea you're here now?"

"No one has," she said. "My arrangement with Pavlos was strictly between the two of us. If my employer knew what I'd done, I'd probably be fired."

Which wouldn't matter one iota, if Niko's first impression of her was correct and she'd set her sights on a much more rewarding prize. What she earned in a year as a nurse wouldn't amount to pocket change if she married his father.

Wondering if she had any idea how potentially damaging her revelation was, he said, "Then why take the risk?"

"Because your father was alone in a foreign country without friends or family to look after him when he was released."

"He had a son. If you'd thought to contact me, I could have been there within twenty-four hours."

"Maybe," she said gently, "he didn't want to bother you."

"So he bothered a perfect stranger instead, even though doing so might end up costing her her job. Tell me, Emily, how do you propose to explain your absence from the hospital?"

"I won't have to. I took a three-month leave of absence and scheduled it to coincide with his discharge."

"A noble gesture on your part, giving up your holiday to look after my father."

"Well, why not? I had nothing else planned."

Except setting aside an hour a day to polish your halo! Struggling to hide his skepticism, Niko said, "All work and no play hardly seems fair. We'll have to see what we can do to change that."

A sudden gust of wind rattled the French doors, making her jump. "Just being here is change enough. If the weather ever clears up, I'm sure Pavlos won't begrudge me the odd day off to see the sights."

"Count on both," he said, recognizing opportunity when it presented itself. "And on my making myself available to act as tour guide."

"That's nice of you, Niko."

No, it's not, he could have told her. Because whatever *her* motives, *his* were anything but pure. And because he'd meant it when he said he wasn't a nice man.

They passed the remainder of the meal in idle conversation, interrupted only by intermittent bursts of rain at the windows, but before coffee was served, she'd run out of things to say and was wilting visibly. Even he, unscrupulous bastard though he undoubtedly was, felt sorry for her. The long transatlantic flight would have been tiring enough, without the added strain of looking after his father. So when she set aside her napkin and begged to be excused, he made no attempt to stop her, but left the table himself and walked her to the foot of the stairs.

"Good night," she murmured.

"Kali nikhta," he returned. "Sleep well."

She was perhaps halfway to the upper landing when a brilliant flash of lightning arrowed through the night. Almost immediately, the electricity failed and plunged the house into darkness.

He heard her startled exclamation and the click of her high heel hitting the edge of the marble step as she stumbled to a halt. "Stay put," he ordered, well aware how treacherous the staircase could be to the unwary. Once, when he was still a boy, a new housemaid had slipped and broken her arm—and that had been in broad daylight. But he'd grown up in the villa; could quite literally have found his way blindfolded anywhere within its walls, and was at Emily's side before she, too, missed her footing.

Just as he reached her, a second bolt of lightning ripped through the night, bleaching her face of color, turning her hair to silver and her eyes into pools as huge and dark as those found in undersea caverns. "What happened?" she whispered, clutching the bannister with one hand as she teetered on the edge of the stair.

Instinctively he pulled her close with an arm around her shoulders. They felt slender, almost childlike to the touch, but the rest of her, pinned warm and sweet against him, was unmistakably all woman. "The lights went out," he said, resorting to the absurdly obvious in an attempt to deflect her attention from the fact that his body had responded to hers with elemental, albeit untimely vigor.

She choked on a laugh. "I pretty much figured that out for myself."

"I expect a power pole was struck."

"Oh," she said faintly, aware as she had to be of her effect on him. Blatant arousal was difficult to hide at such close quarters. "Does it happen often?"

Were they talking about the same thing, he wondered, as his mind fought a losing battle with his nether regions. "No, especially not at this time of year."

"I ought to make sure your father's all right."

"No need," he said, hearing footsteps and noticing the shadow of candle flames flickering over the walls at the rear of the downstairs hall. "Georgios is already on the job. But if it'll ease your mind any, I'll see you as far as your suite, then go check on him myself. Do you know which one you're in?"

"Only that it's blue and cream, with some gorgeous antique furniture, including a four-poster bed."

He nodded, recognizing her description, and keeping one arm looped around her waist, steered her the rest of the way up the stairs, turned right along the landing and felt his way along the wall on his left until he made contact with her door. Pushing it wide, he directed her inside.

The logs in the fireplace had burned down, but enough of a glow remained to fill the room with dim orange light. Enough that when she looked at him, their gazes locked, held prisoner by the sexual awareness, which had simmered between them from the moment they'd first set eyes on each other.

He hadn't meant to kiss her this early in the game, had planned a much more subtle attack, but when she turned within the circle of his arms and lifted her face to his, it was the most natural thing in the world for him to tighten his hold until she was once again pressed against him. The most natural thing in the world to bend his head and find her mouth with his.

CHAPTER THREE

EMILY had been kissed before, many times, but always with some part of her brain able to rate the experience objectively: too slobbery, too bland, too aggressive, too many teeth, too much heavy breathing, not enough tenderness. More often than not, kissing, she'd concluded, was a vastly overrated prelude to romance. Until Niko Leonidas came on the scene, that was, and felled her with a single blow.

Except "blow" was no more the right word to define his effect on her than "kiss" adequately described his action. What he did with his mouth transcended the ordinary and surpassed the divine. Cool and firm, it yet seared her with its heat. Though undemanding, it somehow stripped her of everything—her independence, her focus, her moral compass, even her sense of survival.

Apart from one rash, distinctly forgettable experience, she'd chosen to remain celibate because sex for its own sake held no appeal, and she'd never come close to being in love. But she'd have let him take her there on the floor, if only he'd asked. Would have let him hike up the skirt of her dress and touch her as no other man ever had. For as long as his kiss held her in its spell, she would have let him have his way with her however he wished.

Obviously he did not wish for a fraction of what she was willing to give. Because releasing her, he stepped back and said, rather hoarsely to be sure, "I'll go look in on my father and see about getting some candles up here."

Weak as water, she clutched the back of a nearby chair and nodded. She couldn't have spoken if her life depended on it. Although he'd put a respectable distance between them, she remained trapped in his aura. Her body still hummed. Her breasts ached. Moisture, warm and heavy, seeped between her thighs.

When he turned away, she wanted to cry out that she didn't need candles, she only needed him. But the words remained dammed in her throat and he was gone before she could free them. Dazed, she lowered herself to the chair and waited for him to return.

A brass carriage clock on the mantelpiece marked the passing minutes. Gradually its measured pace restored her racing pulse to near-normal and brought a sort of order to her scattered thoughts. What kind of madness had possessed her, that she'd been ready to give herself to someone she'd known less than a day? He spelled nothing but trouble.

I won't let him in when he comes back, she resolved. I'm out of my league with such a man and don't need the heartbreak an affair with him would bring.

But when a discreet tap at her door signaled his return, all logic fled. Heat shot through her, giving rise to a single exquisite throb of anticipation that electrified her. She couldn't get to him fast enough.

Pulling open the door, she began, "I was beginning to think you'd abandoned—!" then lapsed into mortified silence at the sight of Georgios standing there, a lighted silver candelabra in one hand, and a battery operated lantern in the other.

"Niko asked me to bring these, *thespinis*," he informed her politely, "and to tell you that Kirie Pavlos is sleeping soundly."

Rallying her pride, she stood back to let him pass into the room, and mumbled, "Thank you."

"*Parakalo.*" He placed the candelabra on the dresser and handed her the lantern. "I am also to tell you that he has been called away."

"At this hour of the night?" She made no attempt to hide her disbelief.

He nodded. "*Ne, thespinis.* He received an urgent phone call and will most likely be gone for several days."

Oh, the louse! The cowardly, unmitigated rat! Swallowing the anger and humiliation threatening to choke her, she said scathingly, "It must have been some emergency to drag him out in the middle of a storm like this."

Georgios stopped on his way to the door and shrugged. "I cannot say. He did not explain the reasons."

"Never mind. It's not important." *He* wasn't important. She was there to look after the father, not chase after the son.

"Thank you for the candles and flashlight, Georgios. Good night."

"*Kalispera, thespinis.* Sleep well."

Surprisingly she did, and awoke the next day to clear skies and sunshine. Last night's storm was as much a part of the past as last night's kiss.

Pavlos was already up and dressed when she went

downstairs. He sat on the veranda outside his sitting
room, gazing out at the garden. A small empty coffee
cup and a phone sat on a table at his side. A pair of bin-
oculars rested on his lap.

Catching sight of her, he pressed a finger to his lips,
and gestured for her to join him. "Look," he whispered,
pointing to a pair of fairly large birds. Pretty, with
bluish-gray heads, pearly-pink breasts and brown wings
mottled with black, they pecked at the ground some
distance away. "Do you know what they are?"

"Pigeons?" she ventured.

He grunted disdainfully. "Turtle doves, girl! Timid
and scarce, these days, but they come to my garden
because they know they're safe. And those over there at
the feeder are golden orioles. Didn't know I was a bird
fancier, did you?"

"No," she said, noting the spark in his dark eyes and
his improved color. "But I do know you look much
better this morning. You must have had a good night."

"Nothing like being on his home turf to cure a man
of whatever ails him. Not that that son of mine would
agree. Where do you suppose he is, by the way? I
thought he might at least stay over, my first night back."

"No. He was called away on some sort of emergency."

"Gone already, eh?" He squared his shoulders, and
lifted his chin, a formidable old warrior not about to
admit to weakness of any kind. "Off on another hare-
brained escapade, I suppose. Doesn't surprise me. Never
really expected he'd stick around. Ah well, good
riddance, I say. You had breakfast yet, girl?"

"No," she said, aching for him. He could protest all
he liked, but she saw past his proud facade to the lonely

parent underneath. "I wanted to see how you were doing, first."

"I'm hungry. Now that you're here, we'll eat together." He picked up the phone, pressed a button and spoke briefly with whoever answered. Shortly after, Georgios wheeled in a drop-leaf table set for breakfast for two, and equipped with everything required for what she soon realized was the almost sacred ritual of making coffee. It was prepared with great ceremony over an open flame, in a little copper pot called a briki, and immediately served in thick white demitasses with a glass of cold water on the side.

"No Greek worthy of the name would dream of starting the day without a *flitzani* of good *kafes*," Pavlos declared.

Possibly not, and she had to admit the aroma was heavenly, but the strong beverage with its layer of foam and residue of grounds took some getting used to. She found the fruit and yogurt salad topped with almonds and drizzled with honey and a sprinkling of cinnamon much more enjoyable.

In the days that followed, she also found out that Pavlos had little faith in doctors, rated physiotherapists as next to useless and had no qualms about saying so to their faces. He could be fractious as a child when forced to suffer through the regimen of exercises prescribed to strengthen his hip, and sweet as peach pie if he thought Emily was working too hard.

While he napped in the afternoons, she swam in the pool, walked along the beach or explored the neighborhood, taking particular pleasure in the shops. In the evenings, she played gin rummy or poker with him, even though he cheated at both.

One morning, she was wheeling him along the

terrace after his physiotherapy session when he asked, "Do you miss home?"

She looked out at the flowers in brilliant bloom, at the peacocks strutting across the lawns, the blue arc of the sky and the stunning turquoise sea. Soon the rainy season would come to Vancouver, its chilly southeasterly gales stripping the trees of leaves. People would be scurrying about under a forest of umbrellas where, just few weeks before, they'd been lying on the beaches taking in the last of summer's sunshine. "No," she said. "I'm happy to be here."

"Good. Then you have no excuse for wanting to leave early."

She thought not, either, until the beginning of her second week there, when Niko reappeared as suddenly as he'd left.

"So this is where you're hiding," he said, coming upon her as she sat reading in a wicker love seat on the patio—except they called it a veranda in Greece. "I've been looking everywhere for you."

Though startled, she managed to hang on to her composure enough to meet his glance coolly and reply with commendable indifference, "Why? What do you want?"

Uninvited, he sat down beside her on the sun-warmed cushions. "To ask you to have dinner with me tonight."

The nerve of him! "I don't think so," she said, projecting what she hoped was an air of cool amusement. "You're likely to take off at the last minute and leave me to foot the bill."

"The way I did the other night, you mean?" He grimaced. "Look, I'm sorry about that but—"

"Forget it, Niko. I have."

"No, you haven't. I haven't, either, and nor do I want to. Spend the evening with me, and I'll try to explain myself."

"Whatever makes you think I'm interested in anything you have to say?"

"Because if you weren't, you wouldn't be so ticked off with me. Come on, Emily," he wheedled, inching closer. "Be fair, and at least hear me out before you decide I'm not worth your time."

"I usually play cards with Pavlos in the evening."

"Then we'll make it a late dinner. How is my father, by the way? I stopped by his suite before I came to find you, but he was sleeping."

"He still tires easily, but he's better since he started physiotherapy."

"I'm glad he's on the mend." He glanced at her from beneath his outrageous lashes, stroked his finger down her arm and left a trail of shimmering sensation in its wake. "So what do you say, sweet thing? Do we have a date?"

Resisting him was like trying to trap mist between her hands. "If that's what it takes for you to leave me to read in peace now, I suppose we do. But I won't be free much before ten, after your father's settled for the night."

He edged closer still, a long, lean specimen of masculine grace, handsome as sin, dangerous as hell, and kissed her cheek. "I can wait that long," he said, "but I'm not saying it will be easy."

He took her to a restaurant on the water, about a fifteen-minute drive from the villa. She'd pinned up her hair in a sleek chignon, and wore a black dress she'd bought on sale in a boutique just a few days earlier, and high-heeled black sandals. Simple but beautifully cut, the dress had a narrow draped skirt, strapless bodice, and a shawl lushly embroidered with silver thread. Her only accessory was a pair of dangling vintage silver earrings studded with crystals.

All in all, a good choice, she decided, glancing at her surroundings. Unlike the bougainvillea-draped tavernas she'd seen in the neighborhood, with their paper table-cloths and simple, sometimes crudely constructed furniture, this place gave new meaning to the term stylish sophistication. Crisp linens, a single perfect gardenia at every place setting, deep, comfortable leather chairs, a small dance floor and soft music combined to create an ambience at once elegant and romantic.

They were shown to a window table overlooking a yacht basin. Tall masts rose black and slender against the night sky. Beyond the breakwater, moonlight carved an icy path across the sea to the horizon, but inside the room, candles cast a warm glow over the stark white walls.

Once they'd been served drinks and he'd chosen their meal—noting no prices were listed on the menu, she'd left him to decide what to order—Niko leaned back in his chair and remarked, "You look very lovely tonight, Emily. More like a fashion model than a nurse."

"Thank you. You look rather nice yourself."

Which had to be, she thought, mentally rolling her eyes, the understatement of the century. The superb fit of his charcoal-gray suit spoke of Italian tailoring at its best, and never mind the gorgeous body inside it.

He inclined his head and smiled. "I like your earrings."

"They were my mother's. She loved jewelry and pretty clothes." She touched her fingertip to one crystal pendant, memories of her mother, all dressed up for an evening out, as clear in her mind as if they'd taken place just yesterday. "I still have all her things—her dinner gowns and shoes and beaded handbags."

"Do you use them?"

"Not often. I don't have occasion to."

His gaze scoured her face, meandered down her throat to her shoulders, and it took all her self-control not to shrink into the concealing folds of her shawl. "What a waste," he murmured. "A woman as beautiful as you should always wear beautiful things."

"My mother was the beauty, not I."

"You think?"

"I know," she said, nodding thanks to the waiter as he presented a tray of appetizers. *Mezedes*, she'd learned, were as integral to the evening meal as the main course itself. "And my father was incredibly handsome. They made such a glamorous couple."

"Tell me about them," he said, resting his elbow on the arm of his chair, wineglass in hand. "What were they like—beyond their good looks, that is?"

"Crazy about one another. Happy."

"Socialites?"

"I suppose they were," she admitted, remembering the many times she'd watched, entranced, as her mother prepared for a gala evening on the town.

"What else?"

She stared out at the yachts rocking gently at their moorings. "They wrung every drop of enjoyment from life. They'd dance in the sitting room after dinner, go swimming at midnight in English Bay, dress up in fabulous costumes for Hallowe'en, decorate the biggest tree they could find at Christmas. They were on everyone's guest list, and everyone wanted to be on theirs. And they died much too soon."

Detecting the sadness infecting her memories, he framed his next question in quiet sympathy. "How did it happen?"

"They were on their way home from a party, driving along a road infamous for its hairpin bends. It was raining heavily, the visibility was poor. They were involved in a head-on collision and killed instantly."

Again, his voice grazed her with compassion. "Ah, Emily, I'm sorry."

Aware her emotions swam dangerously close to the surface, she gave herself a mental shake, sat a little straighter in her seat and firmly changed the subject. "Thank you, but it all happened a long time ago, and we're here to talk about you, not me. So tell me, Niko, exactly what frightened you off after that impulsive kiss last week? And please don't say you were too busy checking the main fuse box to find the cause of the power failure, because Georgios already told me you left after receiving a phone call. Had you forgotten you had a previous date, or was I so inept compared to the other women you know that you couldn't wait to escape me?"

"Neither," he said. "I had to go to work."

"You *work*?"

"Well, yes, Emily," he said, laughing. "Don't most men my age?"

"Yes, but you don't seem the corporate type."

"I'm not."

"And it was the middle of the night."

"Right, again."

"So?"

"So I had to prepare to leave Athens at first light, the next day."

"To go where?"

"Overseas."

"How tactfully vague. You'll be telling me next you're involved in smuggling."

"Sometimes I am."

It was neither the answer she was expecting nor one she wanted to hear. Tired of his stonewalling, she threw down her napkin, pushed back her chair and stood up. "If this is your idea of explaining yourself, I've had enough."

"Okay," he said, grabbing her hand before she could bolt, "I delivered some urgently needed supplies to a medical outpost in Africa."

Abruptly she sat down again, her annoyance fading as the implication of his reply hit home. "Are you talking about Doctors Without Borders?"

"In this particular case, yes."

Their waiter came back just then to whisk away the remains of the mezedes and deliver their main course. A dozen questions crowding her mind, she waited impatiently as he made a big production of serving grilled calamari and prawns on a bed of rice. "How did you get there?" she asked, when they were alone again.

"I flew," Niko said.

"Well, I didn't think you walked!"

His mouth twitched with amusement at her acerbic response. "I happen to own a small fleet of aircraft. It comes in handy on occasion."

"Are you telling me you piloted your own plane?"

"In a word, yes."

"Going into places like that can be dangerous, Niko."

He shrugged. "Perhaps, but someone has to do it."

She stared at him, her every preconceived notion of what he was all about undergoing a drastic change. "Where did you learn to fly?"

"After finishing my National Service, I spent five years as a Career Officer with the HAF—Hellenic Air Force. That's when I first became involved in rescue missions. It irked my father no end, of course, that I chose the military over seconding myself to him and his empire."

"Is that why you did it?"

"Not entirely. I loved the freedom of flying. And providing humanitarian aid wherever it's needed struck me as a more worthwhile undertaking than amassing more wealth. How's your calamari, Emily?"

"Delicious," she said, though in truth she'd hardly tasted it. What she was learning about him was far more interesting. "You said a while ago that you own a fleet of aircraft, which I assume means you have more than one."

"Ten in total, and a staff of fifteen. We're a private outfit, on call twenty-four hours a day, seven days a week, and go wherever we're needed, providing whatever kind of help is required. Last month, we joined forces with the Red Cross after an earthquake in northern Turkey left hundreds homeless. The month before, Oxfam International called on us."

"Well, if you care so little for money, how are you able to afford all that? Does Pavlos support you?"

"You ought to know better than to ask such a question," he scoffed. "Even if he'd offered, I'd have starved before I took a single euro from him. And for the record, I never said I didn't care about money. It's a very useful commodity. I just don't care about his."

"Then I don't understand."

"I inherited a sizable fortune from my mother which, to give credit where it's due, Pavlos invested for me. By the time I had access to it at twenty-one, it had grown to the point that I could do pretty much anything I wanted, without having to rely on sponsors. And I chose to use it benefiting those most in need of help." He glanced up and caught her staring. Again. "Why do you keep looking so surprised?"

"Because you told me last week that you're not a nice man, and I believed you. Now I realize nothing could be further from the truth."

"Don't get carried away, Emily," he warned. "Just because I'm not immune to human suffering doesn't make me a saint."

"But you are, I begin to think, a very good man."

Irritably he pushed aside his plate, most of the food untouched. "The wine must have gone to your head. Let's dance, before you say something you live to regret."

She'd have refused if he'd been in any mood to take no for an answer—and if the prospect of finding herself once more in his arms hadn't been more temptation than she could withstand. "All right," she said, and followed him onto the dance floor.

Weaving a path through the others already swaying to the music, he waited for her to catch up with him and extended his hands in invitation. "Come here, sweet thing," he said, and she went.

Whatever resentment she'd harbored toward him had melted away, and left her completely vulnerable to him, all over again. Who could blame her, when the plain fact of the matter was that with a single touch, a glance from those dark green bedroom eyes, he could make a woman forget everything she'd ever learned about self-preservation? That he also turned out to be so thoroughly *decent* merely added to his appeal and made him that much more irresistible.

CHAPTER FOUR

IT FELT good to hold a woman whose curves hadn't been ravaged by malnutrition. Whose bones, though delicate and fine, were not so brittle that he was afraid they'd break at his touch. Whose breasts hadn't withered from bearing too many children she hadn't been able to nourish properly. Who didn't shrink in fear when a man touched her. Who smelled of flowers, not poverty.

"Stop it," he said, inhaling the sweet fragrance of her hair.

"Stop what?"

"Thinking. I can hear your brain working overtime."

"Well, I can't help wondering—"

He pulled her closer, enough for her warmth to melt the block of ice he carried inside, and make him whole again. Whenever he returned from a particularly harrowing assignment, a woman's soothing voice and generous, vital body always helped erase the hopeless misery he never got used to witnessing; the wasted lives, the terror, the shocking evidence of man's inhumanity to man. "Don't wonder, Emily," he said, glad she'd left her shawl at the table, and loving the ivory smoothness of her skin above the top of her strapless dress. "Don't ask any more questions. Forget everything and just be with me in the moment."

"Not easy to do, Niko. You're not who I thought you were."

Sliding his hand down her spine to cup her hip, he pressed her closer still. "I know," he said.

He was worse. Much worse. Not at all the high-minded hero she was painting him to be, but a man on a mission that was far from laudable where she was concerned. Blatantly deceiving her as to his true motives for dating her, at the same time that he used her to assuage his personal torment.

She stirred in his arms and lifted her face so that her cheek rested against his. The whisper of silk against those parts of her he couldn't see or feel inflamed him. "I'm sorry I jumped to all the wrong conclusions about you."

"You didn't," he muttered, fire racing through his belly. "I'm every bit as bad as you first assumed."

"I don't believe you."

They weren't dancing anymore. Hadn't been for some time. While other couples dipped and glided around them in a slow foxtrot, they stood in the middle of the floor, bodies welded so close together that even if she weren't a nurse well acquainted with male anatomy, she had to know the state he was in.

"What I don't understand," she continued, so intent on her thoughts that nothing he said or did seemed able to derail them, "is how you can show such compassion toward strangers, and spare so little for your father."

"I didn't bring you here to talk about my father."

Her hips nudged against him, a fleeting touch that

stoked his arousal to disastrous heights. "And I wouldn't be here at all, were it not for him."

"Thanks for the reminder," he ground out, dancing her back to their table sedately enough for his rampant flesh to subside. "With that in mind, I'd better get you home if you're to be on the job bright and early in the morning."

"Actually I usually don't start work until nine. Pavlos prefers to have Georgios help him bathe and dress, and I join him for breakfast after that."

He picked up her shawl and flung it around her shoulders. The less he could see of her, the better. "Even so, it's growing late."

She nodded sympathetically. "And you're tired."

"Among other things," he replied ambiguously, gesturing to the waiter for the bill.

Outside, the temperature still hovered around twenty degrees Celsius, warm enough for the top to remain down on the BMW. "Rather than having to drive all the way back to Athens after you drop me off, why don't you stay at your father's house tonight?" she suggested, pulling the shawl more snugly around her as he started along the shore road to the villa.

"No," he said, surprising himself because, at the start of the evening, he'd planned to do exactly that. Had had every intention of seducing her; of using her soft loveliness to erase the heart-rending images he'd brought back with him from Africa and, at the same time, prove his original theory that she would sell herself to the highest bidder. After all, she now knew he had money to burn.

But much though he still desired her, he'd lost his taste for using her. And if she was as duplicitous as he'd first suspected, he was no longer sure he wanted to know.

* * *

It was well after one o'clock in the morning. Within its walls, the villa lay smothered in the thick silence of a household at sleep. Except for Emily, who should have been exhausted, but was instead wide-awake and so disappointed she could have cried.

Pacing to the French windows in her suite, she stepped out on the balcony and promptly wished she hadn't. The classical marble statuary in the garden, gleaming white under the moon, was too reminiscent of Niko's stern profile as he'd driven her home; the cool whisper of night air on her skin, too much a reminder of his lips brushing her cheek as he kissed her good-night.

What had happened, that the evening was covered with stardust promise one moment, and over the next? They'd been so close, so attuned to one another when they were dancing. She'd known how aroused he was, had felt an answering tug of desire for him.

She'd thought, when he announced they should leave the restaurant, that after the way he'd held her, he'd at least end the evening on a high note with a kiss to rival the one from the week before. She'd wanted him to, quite desperately in fact, and why not? He'd redeemed himself so completely in her eyes, she was willing to fan the spark of attraction between them and let it take them to the next level. But rather than setting her on fire as she'd hoped, he'd brought her straight back to the villa and walked her to his father's front door.

"Thank you for a lovely evening," she'd said woodenly, hardly able to contain her disappointment.

"My pleasure," he'd replied. "I'm glad you enjoyed it."

Then he'd bestowed that pale imitation of a kiss on her cheek, muttered, "Good night," and raced back to his idling car as if he was afraid, if he lingered, she might drag him into the shrubbery and insist he ravish her.

What a contradiction in terms he was, she decided, turning back into her room. On the one hand, he was all cool suspicion laced with lethal charm and passion when it suited him, and on the other side of the personality coin, a reluctant hero and considerate escort more concerned about keeping her out past her bedtime than catering to his own base needs. Either that, or he took masochistic pleasure in keeping the women he dated off balance. And if that was the case, she was better off without him. One temperamental Leonidas at a time was enough.

"Out on the town till all hours of the night with that no-good son of mine, were you?" Pavlos inquired, glaring at her across the breakfast table when she joined him the next morning. "What if I'd needed you?"

"If you had, Georgios knew how to reach me."

"That's beside the point."

"And exactly what point are you making, Pavlos? That I'm under house arrest and not allowed to leave the premises without your permission?"

Ignoring her sarcasm, he said baldly, "You're asking for trouble, getting involved with Niko. Women are nothing but toys to him, created solely for his entertainment and pleasure. He'll play with you for as long as you amuse him, then drop you for the next one who catches his fancy. He'll break your heart without a second thought and leave you to pick up the pieces, just like all the others who came before you."

Not about to admit she'd pretty much reached the

same conclusion herself, she said, "I'm a grown woman. I know how to take care of myself."

He scowled. "Not with a man like him, you don't. He's bad news, no matter how you look at it. Take my advice, girl. Stay away from him."

A shadow fell across the floor. "Talking about me again, old man?" Niko stepped through the open French doors.

No custom-tailored Italian suit this morning, she noted, but blue jeans again, and a short-sleeved blue shirt revealing strong, tanned forearms. Not that the packaging counted for much. It was the man inside and his sexy, hypnotic voice that set her heart to palpitating.

Annoyed that he so easily snagged her in his spell, Emily averted her gaze, but his father continued to look him straight in the eye and said, "Know anyone else who fits the description?"

"Can't think of a soul," Niko replied evenly.

"There you have it then." Pavlos thumped his coffee cup down on the table. "Why are you here anyway?"

"To have a word with Emily, and to see how you're coming along."

"You needn't have bothered."

"Obviously not. You're as cantankerous as ever, which I take to be a very good sign that you're recovering nicely."

"And Emily doesn't want to see you."

"Why don't you let her tell me that for herself? Or does the fact that you're paying her to be your nurse entitle you to act as her mouthpiece, as well?"

"Just stop it, both of you!" Emily cut in. "Pavlos, finish your toast and stop behaving badly. Niko, the physiotherapist should be here soon, and I'll be free to talk to you then."

He shook his head. "Afraid I can't wait that long. I have a meeting in the city—"

"Then don't let us keep you," his father growled, snapping open the morning paper and feigning great interest in the headlines. "And whatever you do, don't hurry back."

Niko's face closed, and spinning on his heel, he strode off down the hall. But not before Emily caught the flicker of pain in his eyes that he couldn't quite disguise.

"That," she told Pavlos, "was both cruel and unnecessary."

"Then chase after him and kiss him better."

"An excellent suggestion," she said, pushing away from the table. "Thank you for thinking of it."

Niko had already reached his car when she yanked open the villa's front door. "Niko, wait," she called, running across the forecourt.

He turned at the sound of her voice, but made no move toward her. "If you're here to apologize for my father, save your breath," he informed her curtly. "I'm used to him."

"Well, I'm not," she said. "Look, I don't know why he's in such a foul mood this morning, but for what it's worth, I want you to know that I don't let other people dictate whom I should or should not associate with."

"In this case, you might be better off if you did," he said, once again turning to get into the car. "After all, he's known me all my life which makes him some sort of expert on what I'm all about."

Stepping closer, she stopped him with a hand on his

arm. Although his skin felt warm, the flesh beneath was unresponsive as stone to her touch. Undeterred, she said, "Perhaps I'd have believed that yesterday at this time, but I know better now and it'll take more than your father's say-so to convince me otherwise. So if you're using the scene back there in the house as an excuse to end our friendship, it's not going to happen. Now, what did you want to talk to me about?"

He regarded her broodingly a moment. "Your time off," he eventually admitted.

"Why do you want to know?"

"Why do you think, Emily? I want to see more of you."

Again, the tell-tale lurch of her heart warned her how susceptible to him she was. "Then why the mixed messages last night, Niko?" she asked, deciding to lay her misgivings to rest once and for all. "Do you blow hot and cold with all the women you date, or have you singled me out for special attention?"

He didn't bother to dissemble. Was, indeed, shockingly, hilariously blunt in his reply. "In case you didn't notice, my dear, last night when we were dancing, I was sporting an erection that would have done a stallion proud. That ought to have told you something."

Smothering a burst of laughter, she said with equal candor, "At the time, I thought it did. But after hustling me outside, you either decided I wasn't quite your type after all, or else you lost your nerve."

A flush of indignation stained his finely chiseled cheekbones. "I neither lost my nerve, nor anything else."

"Then why the hasty brush-off?"

"There's a time and a place for everything, Emily, especially seduction. I'm not the sex-in-the-backseat-of-the-car type of guy—which isn't to say I didn't want to take you to bed. But you'd given no indication you'd have welcomed such an overture. Just the opposite, in fact. You never stopped talking."

"If you'd bothered to ask," she said, "I could have told you we weren't as far apart in our thinking as you seem to suppose. I just did a better job of hiding it."

He blinked. "Are you sure you know what you're saying?"

"Very sure. I realized the moment I set eyes on you that the chemistry between us could easily become explosive."

"This isn't the first time you've left me at a loss for words," he said, almost stumbling over his reply, "and I have a sneaking suspicion it won't be the last."

"Well, don't misunderstand me. I'm not saying I'm ready to jump into bed with you, but…"

"But you won't turn me down if I ask you out again?"

"I'll be disappointed if you don't."

He slid his arm around her waist and pulled her to him. "When's the next time you have a few hours off?"

"Later this afternoon, from about three until seven."

"I'll pick you up at three-thirty. Wear something casual—slacks and a light sweater in case you get cold, and bring a camera if you have one. Today, we play at being tourists in the city."

Then he kissed her. Hard and sweet. On the mouth. And made it last long enough that when he finally released her, she had to clutch the top of the car door to keep herself upright.

She'd read the travel brochures and thought she knew what to expect of Athens. Traffic congestion and noise and smog. Ancient, crumbling ruins sitting cheek by jowl with towering new apartment buildings. And overshadowing them all, the Acropolis and the Parthenon. But brochures didn't come close to preparing her for the real thing.

Niko showed up not in the BMW but on a candy-apple-red motor scooter. Helping her onto the passenger seat, he plunked a bright red helmet on her head, fastened the strap, then climbed aboard himself and said, "Hang on tight."

On that note, they were off, zooming through the outskirts of the city, weaving in and out of traffic, zipping up steep hills, along narrow streets and through tiny squares, until suddenly the famous landmarks were everywhere she looked. She should have been terrified at the speed with which they traveled. With anyone else, she undoubtedly would have been. But seated behind him, her front sandwiched against his spine, her arms wrapped around his waist, she felt fearless, confident.

She loved the wind in her face, the aromas drifting from the tavernas, the energy buzzing in the air. Loved the feel of him, all sleek muscle beneath his short-sleeved shirt, and the scent of his sun-kissed skin.

Finally he parked and locked the scooter, then led her through a pedestrian avenue lined with restaurants and cafés, and along a marble path to the top of the Acropolis. Up close, the sheer size and majesty of the Parthenon overwhelmed her. "I can't believe I'm really here, and seeing it for myself," she breathed. "It's amazing, Niko. Magnificent! And the view…!"

She lapsed into silence, at a loss for words. Athens

lay at her feet, a sprawling mass of concrete occasionally interspersed with the green of pine-covered hills.

"Gives a pretty good idea of the layout of the city," Niko agreed, "but if ever my father decides he can get through an evening without you, we'll come back another time, at sunset. Enjoying a bottle of wine and watching the lights come on is equally impressive."

"What surprises me is that it's not nearly as crowded as I thought it would be."

"Because most tourists have gone home and left Athens to those of us who choose to live here. The smart ones, though, know that October is one of the best times to visit."

They spent an idyllic few hours wandering among the ruins, stopping on the way down the hill for iced coffee at a sidewalk café, and visiting a beautiful little church tucked in a quiet square. But although everything she saw left Emily awestruck, it was what Niko brought to the afternoon that left the most indelible impression.

His lazy smile caressed her, hinting at untold pleasures to come. His voice reciting the history of the temples held her mesmerized. The way he took every opportunity to touch her—holding her hand to guide her over the uneven ground as if she were the most delicate, precious thing in the world to him, or looping an intimate arm around her shoulders as he pointed out some distant landmark—filled her with shimmering happiness.

With a casual endearment, a glance, he inspired in her an unsuspected passion and yearning. The blood seethed in her veins. She had never felt more alive; never known such an uprush of emotion.

Too soon it was six o'clock and time to head back to Vouliagmeni. The setting sun slanted across the lawns and the front door stood open when they arrived at the villa. "Are you coming in?" she asked, as he propped the scooter on its kickstand and swung her to the ground.

He shook his head. "No, *karthula*. Why spoil a perfect afternoon?"

"I wish it didn't have to be like that," she said, removing her helmet.

He took it from her, slung it over the handlebars and cupped her face between his hands. "It is what it is, Emily, and what it's always been."

"Well, I find it very sad. It's not—"

He silenced her with a lingering kiss that emptied her mind of everything but the heady delight of his mouth on hers. "Oh," she breathed, when at last it ended.

He lifted his head and stared past her, then, "I think we should try that again," he murmured, and drawing her to him, kissed her a second time at even greater length.

An exclamation—most likely an expletive, judging by its irate tone—shattered the moment, and spinning around, Emily found Pavlos leaning on his walker, silhouetted in the open doorway.

"Wouldn't you know it?" Niko said cheerfully, releasing her. "Caught in the act by my disapproving *patera*. I'd better make myself scarce before he comes after me with a shotgun. I'll call you, Emily. Soon."

A moment later, he was gone, disappearing down the long driveway in a candy-apple-red blur of speed, and taking with him all the joy the afternoon had brought. Because she knew without a shadow of doubt that the reason he'd kissed her a second time had nothing to do with her. He'd done it for the pure pleasure of stirring his father to anger.

Unbidden, and decidedly unwelcome, Pavlos's earlier warning came back to haunt her. *Women are nothing but toys to him, created solely for his entertainment. He'll break your heart and leave you to pick up the pieces, just like all the others who came before you....*

CHAPTER FIVE

PAVLOS wore such an unmistakable told-you-so expression that Emily knew she looked as let down as she felt. Shuffling along beside her as she stalked into the house, he crowed, "Lived down to my expectations, didn't he?"

"You don't know what you're talking about, Pavlos," she informed him curtly, rallying her pride. "I had a fabulous afternoon."

"And I ran a marathon while you were gone!" He elbowed her in the ribs. "Admit it, Emily. He disappointed you."

"If you must know, you both disappoint me. Father and son—grown men at that—taking potshots at each other isn't my idea of adult entertainment. Have you had dinner?"

"No. I waited for you."

"I'm not hungry."

"Ah, girl! Don't let him do this to you. He's not worth it."

The edge of compassion softening his tone caused serious inroads on her composure, and that he happened also to be right didn't make the advice any easier to swallow. "He's not 'doing' anything," she insisted.

Except play fast and loose with her emotions, which she wasn't about to admit to his father.

That night when he was preparing for bed, Pavlos slipped on the marble tiles in his bathroom and split his forehead open on the edge of the sink. Striving to maintain calm in the face of chaos—Georgios panicked at the sight of blood, was sure his beloved master was dying and blamed himself for the accident—Emily directed him to call for an ambulance while she attended to Pavlos who lay sprawled on the floor. Although somewhat disoriented, he swore irritably and smacked her hand away when she tried to prevent him from struggling to his feet.

Leaning against the tub, he scoffed, "I'm not dead yet, woman! It'll take more than a cracked skull to finish me off."

"It's not your head I'm worried about, it's your hip," she said, applying a folded facecloth to the superficial cut on his brow. In fact, the sink had broken his fall and that he was able to sit on the floor without showing much evidence of pain was a good sign, but she wanted more scientific proof that he was as fine as he claimed.

The paramedics arrived shortly after and transferred him to the hospital for X-rays. Fortunately he'd incurred no further damage to his hip, required only a couple of sutures to his cut and vetoed any recommendation that he stay there overnight. "I didn't bring you all this way to look after me so you could turn the job over to someone else," he reminded Emily.

By the next morning, he sported a black eye but was otherwise his usual self. "No reason to," he snapped, when she suggested letting his son know what had happened.

But, "He has a right to be kept informed," she insisted, and left a brief message on Niko's voice mail.

He didn't acknowledge it until three days later when he again showed up unannounced as they were finishing lunch. "Very colorful," he remarked, inspecting Pavlos's black eye which by then had taken on a distinctly greenish hue. "Tell me, old man, do you plan to make a habit of abusing your body?"

"Accidents happen," his father shot back. "You're living proof of that."

Emily winced, appalled by the stunning cruelty of his reply, but realized that although he'd rather die than admit it, Pavlos was hurt that Niko hadn't bothered to stop by sooner.

"We all have our crosses to bear, *Patero*," Niko said scornfully. "Yours isn't any heavier than mine."

"Don't call me *patero*. You're no more a son to me than a dog on the street."

After their last confrontation, Emily had made up her mind she was never again getting caught in the middle when these two went at each other, but the insults flying back and forth were more than she could tolerate. "How do you the pair of you live with yourselves?" she asked sharply.

"By having as little to do with each other as possible," Niko said, addressing her directly for the first time since he'd entered the room. "*Yiasu*, Emily. How have you been?"

"Very well, thank you. The same can't be said of your father, but I guess that didn't much matter to you, seeing that you waited three days to visit him after his accident."

"Don't waste your breath appealing to his sense of decency," Pavlos advised her. "He doesn't have one."

Niko regarded him with weary disdain. "Unlike you in your prime, my career involves more than sitting behind a desk while my minions do all the work. I was away on assignment and didn't get back to Athens until this morning."

"Racing off on another mercy mission to save the world, were you?" Pavlos sneered.

"As to *thialo, yarro!*"

"You hear that, Emily?" Pavlos flung her an injured glare. "He told me to go to hell!"

Emily glanced from one to the other. At the father, his iron-gray hair still thick and his eyes piercingly alive, but his once-powerful body decaying, its bones so brittle it was a miracle they hadn't crumbled when he fell. At the son, a modern-day Adonis, tall, strong and indomitable. And both so proud, they'd have walked barefoot through fire rather than admit they cared about each other.

"I can't imagine why he bothered," she said witheringly. "The way I see it, he's already there, and so are you."

On that note, she left them. They might be determined to tear one another apart, but she'd be damned if she'd stay around to pick up the pieces.

Exiting through the French doors, she marched along the terrace and around the side of the villa to the lodge behind the garages. The widowed gardener, Theo, and his son, Mihalis, whom she'd met the day she arrived, lived there. Snoozing on the step outside the back door was their dog, Zephyr, a big friendly creature of indeterminate breed who, when she approached, wriggled over to make room for her to sit beside him and planted his head on her lap.

Niko found her there a few minutes later. "Is there space down there for me, too?"

"No," she said. "I prefer civilized company and you don't qualify."

"But the dog does?"

"Definitely. I'll take him over you any day of the week."

He shoved his hands in the back pockets of his jeans and regarded her moodily. "For what it's worth, Emily, I take no pleasure in constantly doing battle with my father."

"Then why don't you put an end to it?"

"What would you have me do? Stand by and let him use me as a verbal punching bag?"

"If that's what it takes…"

"Sorry, *karthula*, I'm not the subservient type. And I'm not here now to carry on with you where I left off with him."

"Why are you here, then?"

"To ask if you'll have dinner with me again."

"What for? So you can flaunt me in your father's face, the way you did the other day?"

Ignoring Zephyr's warning growl, he hunkered down on the few inches of sun-warmed step beside her. "Would you believe because I can't stay away from you, though heaven knows I wish I could?"

"Why? Because you blame me for your father's accident?"

"Don't be absurd," he said. "Of course I don't."

"Perhaps you should. I'm supposed to be nursing him back to health, not exposing him to further injury.

It's a miracle he didn't do more damage to himself when he fell."

"The point is, he didn't, and I knew it within hours of the accident."

"How is that possible if, as you claim, you arrived back in town only this morning?"

"This might come as a surprise, Emily, but I'm not completely heartless. I admit I'm away more often than I'm here, but I maintain regular contact with Georgios or Damaris, and know practically to the minute if a problem arises. Judging from their glowing reports, not only are you a dedicated and skilled professional who's taking excellent care of Pavlos, but you're earmarked for sainthood when you die—which, I hasten to add, I hope won't be anytime soon."

"If you care enough about him to phone them for an update on how he's doing, would it hurt you to tell him so?"

"Why would I bother when he makes it patently clear it's not something he wants to hear?"

"He might surprise you."

"You're the only one to surprise me, Emily, and I can't say I'm enjoying the experience. I've got enough on my mind, without that."

At his gloomy tone, she ventured a glance at him. Noticed the grim set of his mouth, the frown puckering his brow and felt an unwelcome stab of sympathy. "You ran into problems when you were away?"

"Nothing unusual about that," he said, shrugging. "My business is all about solving problems, as long as they're other people's. But I learned a long time ago that the only way to deal effectively with them is to draw a firm line between my work and my personal life, the latter of which I make a point of keeping complication free." He paused, sketched a groove in the dust with the toe of his shoe as if to illustrate his point and laced his fingers through hers. "But somehow, you've become just that, Emily. A complication. One I can't ignore."

"I don't see how."

"I know you don't. That's half the trouble."

"Try explaining it, then."

"I can't," he said morosely. "That's the other half."

She sighed, exasperated, and pulled her fingers free. "I'm not a big fan of riddles, Niko, and you don't appear exactly overjoyed to be involved with me, so let me put us both out of our misery. Thanks, but no thanks. I don't want to have dinner with you again."

Bathing her in a molten-green gaze, he inched closer. Slid his hand around her nape. "Liar," he murmured, the tip of his tongue dallying insolently with the outer curve of her ear.

The last time a man had tried that, she'd barely managed to suppress a revolted *Eeuw!* before she shoved him away. What was so different about Niko Leonidas, that his every touch, every glance, left her panting for more?

"Just because I refuse to let you play games with me doesn't make me a liar," she insisted weakly, almost paralyzed by the throb of tension unwinding inside her to affect body parts she was beginning to wish she didn't have.

"It doesn't make you any easier to resist, either."

"Then I guess we've reached an impasse."

For a long moment, he stared at her as if trying to fathom the solution to a dilemma only he could resolve.

Then with a shrug that plainly said, *Ah, to hell with it,* he rose to his feet with indolent grace. "I guess we have," he replied, and sauntered away.

"Good riddance!" she muttered, crushing the wave of disappointment threatening to engulf her. "Other women might trip over themselves in their eagerness to fall in with your every whim and wish, but I'm made of sterner stuff."

She repeated her little mantra several times during the rest of the afternoon, because it was all that stood between her and the urge to call him and say she'd changed her mind about spending the evening with him. To make quite sure she didn't weaken at the last minute, she went for a long walk on the beach, and ate dinner at a taverna. Upon her return to the villa, she played checkers with Pavlos for an hour, then pleading a headache, escaped to her suite.

Night had long since fallen, and closing the door behind her, she surveyed her sanctuary with a mixture of relief and pleasure. Damaris had turned back the bed-covers and made a fire against the chill of mid-October. Flames danced in the hearth and cast burnished-gold reflections over the polished antique furniture. The pleasant scent of burning olive wood filled the air.

Yes, she'd definitely made the right decision, Emily thought, tossing her sweater on the foot of the bed and kicking off her shoes. Although she couldn't deny the magnetic attraction between her and Niko, she couldn't ignore her feminine intuition, either. From the start, it had warned her that giving in to her attraction to him would invite nothing but trouble. If she didn't step back now, she'd find herself hopelessly, helplessly entangled with a man so far out of her league that she'd be guaranteed nothing but misery. After all, he'd made it graphically clear that his interest in her was purely sexual, and realistically, what else could she expect? He had no room in his life for a serious relationship, and even if he had, her future lay half a world away.

Warding off the unavoidable but depressing truth of the matter, she went into the bathroom and while the whirlpool tub filled, stripped off the rest of her clothes, pinned up her hair and lit a scented candle. Solitude was preferable to heartache any day of the week, she told herself bracingly, as she sank up to her chin in the hot water and let the air jets massage the day's tension into oblivion.

With the candle finally burned down to nothing, she dried herself with a towel from the heated rack, applied a generous dollop of body lotion to her water-wrinkled skin and pulled on a clean nightshirt. Then feeling limp as cooked spaghetti and so relaxed it was all she could do to stand upright, she tottered back to her bedroom.

Surprisingly the fire still burned brightly as if it had recently been replenished. And her shoes stood neatly aligned next to the armchair which, she noticed in appalled disbelief, was occupied. By Niko.

"I was beginning to think you'd drowned," he remarked conversationally.

Horribly aware that she wore nothing but a nightshirt whose hem came only midway down her thighs, she tried ineffectually to tug it lower. A huge mistake because, when she let it go, it sprang up with alarming vigor and revealed heaven only knew what of her anatomy. "Don't look!" she squeaked, shock rendering her incapable of a more quelling response.

"If you insist," he said, and very politely turned his head aside.

"How did you get in here?"

"Through the door, Emily. It seemed the most logical route to take."

If she had an ounce of backbone, she'd have matched his sarcasm and told him to leave the same way, but curiosity got the better of her. "Why?"

"I decided I owe you an explanation. Again!"

Wishing the sight of him didn't fill her with such desperate yearning that she was practically melting inside, she said, "You don't owe me anything, Niko. And you have no business being in my room."

"But I'm here regardless, and I'm staying until I've had my say."

"It seems to me we've been through this routine before and it got us precisely nowhere."

"Please, Emily."

She gave a long suffering sigh. "Then make it quick. I'm tired and I want to go to bed."

He slewed an audacious glance at her bare legs. "Could you put on something a little less revealing first? I'm only human, and staring at the fire doesn't quite cut it compared to looking at you."

Annoyed at the burst of pleasure his words aroused, she stomped back into the bathroom, grabbed the full length robe hanging on the door and dived into it.

"That's better," he said, vacating the armchair when she returned with only her hands, feet and head open to his inspection. "Why don't you sit here?"

"No, thanks," she informed him starchily. "I don't anticipate this taking very long."

He'd convinced himself this would be easy. All he had to do was reiterate his initial reservations, explain he'd put them to rest and no longer had ulterior motives for pursuing her. But the sight of her when she first came out of the bathroom had wiped his mind clean of anything but the raging desire to touch her all over. To lift that absurd scrap of a nightgown and bury his mouth at the cluster of soft, silver-blond curls she'd so briefly and tantalizingly revealed in her attempt at modesty.

"I'm waiting, Niko," she reminded him, sounding like his high school math teacher.

Would that she looked like her, too—moustache and all! "I want to start afresh with you," he said.

"I'm not sure I understand what that means."

He swallowed, grasping for the words that persisted in eluding him. "We got off on the wrong foot, Emily. You're my father's nurse, and I'm his son…."

"To the best of my knowledge, the status quo hasn't changed. I'm still his nurse. You're still his son."

How could he do it? How cut to the chase and say bluntly, *Despite pretending I no longer believed it, I remained convinced you were out to take him for all he's worth and decided my only choice was to seduce you, but have now decided I was wrong,* and expect her to understand? He wouldn't, if their situation were reversed.

"But something else *has* changed," he said instead.

"What?"

He took a deep breath and plunged in, laundering the

truth in a way that made him cringe inside. "Can we just say I'm tired of playing games and leave it at that? I'm not interested in using you to score points off my father, or for any other reason. I want to be close to you not because it'll annoy him to see us together, but because I like you for yourself. So I guess the only questions still to be answered are, do you want the same thing, or have I misread the signs and the attraction I thought existed between us is just a figment of my imagination?"

"It's not a figment of your imagination," she admitted, "but I don't understand why you'd pursue it when you said just this afternoon that I was a complication you didn't need."

"Overanalyzing is second nature to me. It's saved my skin more often than I care to count. But in this case, I took it too far."

She shifted from one foot to the other, clearly weighing his words. "Maybe not," she said judiciously. "Maybe you simply realized there was no future in a relationship with me."

"Never counting on the future is another by-product of my job. The only certainty is the here and now."

He took a step toward her, then another, until he was close enough to inhale the scent of her skin. She'd pinned up her hair, but tendrils had escaped to curl damply against her neck. The robe was at least two sizes too large and gaped at the front, drawing his gaze to the faint swell of her cleavage just visible above the top of her nightshirt.

The urge to kiss her, to hold her, nearly blinded him. "What do you say, Emily?" he asked hoarsely. "Will you take a chance on it with me?"

CHAPTER SIX

THE persistent voice of caution warned her not to fall for his line of reasoning. What was he offering her, after all, but the pleasure of the moment?

On the other hand, what had she gained in the past by pinning all her hopes on a better tomorrow? A degree in nursing, a crippling mortgage on her town house, a secondhand car and a short-lived, disappointing relationship with a medical student. Even her circle of friends had dwindled as more and more of them exchanged the single life for marriage and babies. Not that they completely abandoned her, but their interests no longer coincided as they once had. Her schedule revolved around shift work and case histories; theirs, around spouses and midnight feedings.

"Emily?" Niko's voice flowed over her, sliding inside the bathrobe supposedly shielding her from his potent appeal, to caress every hidden inch of skin, every minute pore.

Why was she holding out for a future that might never dawn, when the man who epitomized her every waking fantasy was offering her the chance to fulfill them? Giving in to her heart instead of her head, she lifted her gaze to meet his and whispered, "Why don't you stop talking and just kiss me?"

He groaned and reached for her. Cupped her face between his hands and swept his lips over her eyelids, her cheekbones, her jaw. And finally, when she was quivering all over with anticipation, he buried his mouth against hers. Not as he had before, with calculated finesse, but in scalding, desperate greed.

For the first time in her life, her natural caution deserted her, annihilated by a yearning so painful, she was filled with the consuming need to satisfy it at any price. Barely aware that she'd anchored her arms around his waist, she tilted her hips so that they nudged boldly against him exactly where he was most evidently aroused. His hard, unabashed virility inflamed her, scorching any remnant of doubt to ashes.

Somehow, her robe fell undone and he was touching her, his clever seeking fingers tracing a path from her collarbone and inside her sleeveless nightshirt to shape the curve of her breast. But she wanted more and tried to tell him so, angling herself so that her nipple surged against his palm, and pleading with him not to stop.

But stop he did. "Not here," he ground out, a sheen of sweat glistening on his brow. "Not in my father's house."

"But I can't leave," she whimpered. "What if he needs me and I'm not here?"

"Emily, *I* need you. I need you now."

Without a twinge of shame, she lifted the hem of her nightshirt and guided his hand between her legs. "You think I don't need you just as badly?"

Chest heaving, he molded his hand against her and pressed, flexing his fingers just so. The ensuing jolt of sensation ricocheted through her body and almost brought her to her knees. Gasping, she sank against him.

Steering her backward, he lowered her to the bed and touched her again, teasing the pivotal nub of flesh at her core that marked the dividing line between cool reason and clamoring ecstasy. And when she tipped over the edge in explosive release, he smothered her high-pitched cry with his mouth and stroked her until the spasms racking her body faded to an echo.

How many languid minutes ticked by before he pushed himself upright and, in a belated attempt to restore her modesty, covered her limbs with the bathrobe? Not nearly enough, and she clung to him. "Stay," she begged.

He shook his head. "I can't."

"Don't you want me, Niko?"

"So badly I can taste it. But not with my father's shadow hanging over us."

"Then how…when…?"

"Tell him you're taking the weekend off. We'll go away to someplace where we can be completely alone."

"What if he won't agree?"

"He doesn't own you, *karthula*," he said. Then, searching her face, asked, "Or does he?"

"Of course not, but he *is* my patient and he *is* paying me to look after him. And whether or not you accept it, he isn't as far along the road to recovery as he'd have you believe. To expect Georgios to assume respon-sibility for him would be unprofessional and negligent on my part."

"All it takes to solve that problem is a phone call to a private nursing agency for someone to replace you.

We're talking three days at the most. He can manage without you for that short a time."

"I suppose," she acknowledged dubiously, not because she wasn't sure she wanted to spend the weekend with him, but because she knew she'd have to fight Pavlos to get it.

A muscle twitched in Niko's jaw. "You know, Emily, if I'm asking too much—"

"You're not!"

"Are you sure?"

"Yes." She pressed her lips together and nodded. For pity's sake, when had she turned into such a wimp? She'd been in Greece over three weeks and more or less at Pavlos's beck and call the entire time. It wasn't unreasonable for her to ask for a break. "I'll work something out, I promise."

He brushed a last kiss over her mouth. "Let me know when it's arranged."

In the hectic two days that followed, she alternated between euphoria and bouts of horror at how shamelessly she'd offered herself to Niko. How would she ever face him again? But her yearning outweighed her chagrin and overriding Pavlos's objections, she booked the weekend off.

"A bikini and lots of sunscreen," Niko said, when she called to tell him she'd be ready to leave on Friday evening at six and asked what she should pack.

"What else?"

She could almost hear his shrug. "Something warm for the evenings, maybe, although the weather's supposed to be good. Shorts, a couple of tops. Not enough to fill a suitcase, by any means. Just throw a few things in a carryall."

"In other words, travel light and keep it casual."

"That about covers it, yes."

Much he knew, she thought, scurrying out to shop late Thursday afternoon while Pavlos napped. The clothes she'd brought with her to Greece were, for the most part, serviceable and basic. She hadn't come on vacation, she'd come to work, and in her profession that meant easily laundered cotton slacks and tunic tops, and comfortable, soft-soled shoes. She certainly didn't have anything designed for a romantic weekend with the sexiest man on the planet.

After dinner that night, she laid out her purchases, setting aside the dark red velour jogging suit and white socks and runners for traveling, but stuffing racy new lingerie, sheer nightgown, sandals and silk caftan, as well as shampoo, toothbrush, cosmetics and all the other items he'd specified, into a canvas tote designed to hold far less. He had said they'd be completely alone, but clearly didn't understand that it wasn't looking the part for strangers that she cared about, it was looking her best for him.

Although Pavlos had allowed a nurse from an agency to fill in for her while she was gone, he'd made it plain he was doing so under duress. To drive home the point, he sulked all Friday morning and ignored Emily all afternoon.

The one thing he hadn't done was inquire where she was going, or with whom, although from his dire mutterings, he'd obviously concluded it somehow involved Niko. So with her replacement up to speed on her duties, and rather than starting the weekend on a sour note with a confrontation, Emily collected her bag and slipped out of the villa a few minutes before six, to wait for Niko at the foot of the driveway.

Right on time, he drew up in the BMW. "You made it," he greeted her, slinging his arm around her shoulders in a brief hug.

"Did you think I wouldn't?"

"Let's just say I wouldn't have been surprised if my father had thrown himself on the floor and started foaming at the mouth when you tried to leave. And the fact that you're lurking here, hidden from view by anyone in the villa, tells me you pretty much feared the same."

"If I admit you're right, can we agree that the subject of your father is off-limits for the duration of the weekend?"

"Gladly." He tossed her bag in the trunk and held open the passenger door. "Hop in, Emily. I want to get underway while we still have some daylight left."

"Underway," she discovered was not aboard an aircraft as she'd half expected, but a fifty-two-foot sloop moored at a private yacht club in Glyfada, a twenty-five minute drive north of Vouliagmeni. Sleek and elegant, with a dark blue hull and the name *Alcyone* painted in gold across her transom, she was, Niko told Emily, built for speed. But without any wind to fill her sails and sunset no more than a crimson memory on the horizon, he was forced to steer her under diesel power to the tiny island of Fleves, just off the east coast of the Attic peninsula.

It was a short trip only, but what made it magical for Emily was the rising moon, which laid down a path of silver to mark their passage, and the luminescence sparkling in their wake like a handful of tiny diamonds.

Niko, in blue jeans and a lightweight cream sweater wasn't too hard to take, either.

After they'd dropped anchor, he set a lantern over the companionway in the center cockpit, told her to stay put and disappeared below, returning a few minutes later with a bottle of chilled white wine, crystal glasses and a small tray of appetizers. "I'd toast you in champagne," he said, taking a seat across from her and pouring the wine, "but it doesn't travel well in a sailboat."

"I don't need champagne," she assured him. "I'm happy just to be here with you."

He tipped the rim of his glass against hers. "Then here's to us, *karthula*."

The wine dancing over her tongue, crisp and cold, lent her courage. "You've called me that before. What does it mean?"

"Sweetheart." He raised one dark brow questioningly. "Do you mind?"

"No," she said, and shivered with pleasure inside her cozy velour jogging suit.

Noticing, he gestured below deck. "Dinner's in the oven and should be ready soon, but we can sit in the cabin where it's warmer, if you like."

"I'd rather not," she said, shying away from the closed intimacy it presented. Now that the rush and excitement of getting away was over and it was at last just the two of them, she was gripped with an almost paralyzing shyness. "It's so peaceful and quiet on deck."

"But you're on edge. Why is that, Emily? Are you wishing you hadn't agreed to spend the weekend with me?"

"Not exactly. I'm just a little…uncomfortable."

He scrutinized her in silence a moment, tracking the conflicting emotions flitting over her face. At last, he said, "About us being here now, or about the other night?"

She blushed so fiercely, it was a miracle her hair didn't catch fire. "Do we have to talk about the other night?"

"Apparently we do," he said.

She fiddled with her glass, twirling it so that the lantern light glimmered over its surface. From the safety of distance, she'd been able to put her conduct on Wednesday down to a temporary madness *he'd* inspired. But now, with no means of escaping his probing gaze, how she'd responded to him left her feeling only shamefully wanton and pitifully desperate.

What had possessed her to behave so completely out of character? Professionally she was ICU Nurse Tyler, capable, skilled and always in control. Socially, she was good friend Emily, affable, dependable—but again, always in control.

She did not rush headlong into affairs, she did not beg a man to make love to her and she most certainly did not brazenly invite him to explore her private parts. That she had done all three with Niko made her cringe. Yet, here she was, because embarrassed or not, she couldn't stay away from him. And that meant facing up to what had transpired between them.

"You must know how very difficult it was for me to leave you as I did," he said softly, divining so exactly the source of her discomfort that she wondered if she'd actually voiced her thoughts aloud. "I won't pretend I'm not eager to pick up where we left off, but only if you feel the same. We take this at your pace, Emily, or not at all."

She glanced around, at the velvet moonlit night; at the dark hulk of the island rising to her left. She listened to the silence, broken only by the gentle wash of the sea against the boat's hull. Finally she dared to look at the man staring at her so intently. "It's what I want, too," she admitted. "I'm just a little out of my element. This is all very new to me, Niko."

His posture changed from indolent relaxation to sudden vigilance. "Are you trying to tell me you're a virgin?"

She choked on her wine. "No."

"No, that's not what you're trying to tell me, or no, you're not a virgin?"

"That's not what I'm trying to tell you. I was referring to the setting—the boat, the glamour, the exotic location. As for whether or not I'm a virgin, does it really matter?"

"Yes, it does," he said soberly. "Not because I'll judge you one way or the other, but because if I'm your first lover, I want to know beforehand." He leaned across and touched her hand. "So?"

Another blush raced up her neck to stain her face, though she hoped it didn't show in the dim light. "I'm not."

Picking up on her discomfiture anyway, he burst out laughing. "Don't look so mortified," he said. "I'm not, either."

"But it was only once, and not exactly…a howling success. Contrary to the impression I might have given you the other night, I'm not very good at…well…*this*."

"I see," he said, making a visible effort to keep a straight face. "Well, now that you've got that off your chest, what do you say we have dinner and let the rest of the evening take care of itself?"

"I'd like to freshen up first." In reality, she'd like to put her head down the toilet and flush, or better yet, jump over the side of the boat and never resurface.

"Sure," he said easily. "I'll be a couple of minutes getting everything ready, so take your time. Our stuff's in the aft cabin, which has its own bathroom."

It had its own built-in king-size bed, too. Dressed in navy-blue linens, with a wide ledge and window at the head, and brass wall lamps on either side, it set the stage for seduction and sent a tremor of terrified anticipation fluttering in Emily's stomach.

Would she disappoint him? she wondered, unpacking her clothes and laying out her toiletries on the vanity in the bathroom. Make an even bigger fool of herself this time than she had before? Was she being too reckless, too naive, in straying so far out of her usual comfort zone? Or had she finally found the one man in the world who made all the risks of falling in love worthwhile?

Soft lights and music greeted her when she returned to the main cabin. The air was fragrant with the scent of oregano and rosemary. Navy-blue place mats and napkins, crystal, brushed stainless steel cutlery and white bone china graced the table. In the galley, on the counter above the refrigerator, were a basket of bread and a bowl containing olives, and chunks of tomato, cucumber and feta cheese drizzled with olive oil.

Long legs braced against the barely perceptible rise and fall of the boat, Niko stood beside the oven, arranging skewers of roasted lamb, eggplant and peppers over rice. "Not exactly a gourmet spread," he remarked, carrying the platter to the table. "Just plain, simple picnic fare."

"I'd hardly call it plain or simple," she said, thinking of the plastic forks and paper plates, which marked the picnics she usually attended. "How do you keep your dishes and glassware from breaking when you're under sail?"

"I had the boat custom built with cabinetry designed to keep everything safely in place. I'll show you later, if you're interested."

"Interested? Intrigued is more like it. At the risk of repeating myself, you're not at all the playboy I took you to be when I first met you."

Green eyes filled with amusement, he said, "You're an expert on playboys, are you?"

"No, but I'm willing to bet they don't put their lives on the line to help people in distress, and they don't cook."

"Don't let the meal fool you. I had it prepared at a local taverna. All I had to do was heat up the main course, which pretty much sums up my talents in the kitchen."

He brought the bread and salad to the table, poured more wine and clinked his glass against hers. "Here's to us again, *karthula*. Dig in before everything gets cold."

The food was delicious; conversation easy and uncomplicated as they discovered more about each other. They both enjoyed reading and agreed they could live without television as long as they had a supply of good books at hand, although he preferred nonfiction whereas she devoured novels. And neither could live without a daily newspaper.

Niko was an avid scuba diver and had explored a

number of wrecks off the Egyptian coast. The best Emily could manage was snorkeling in a protected lagoon and admitted to being nervous if she was too far away from the shore.

He'd seen parts of the world tourists never visited. She stayed on the safe and beaten track: other parts of Canada, Hawaii, the British Virgin Islands.

When they'd finished eating, she helped him clear the table. Dried the dishes he washed. Stacked the wineglasses in the cunning little rack designed to hold them. And loved the domesticity of it all. A man, a woman, a nest...

As ten o'clock inched toward eleven, he suggested they finish their wine on deck. The moon rode high by then, splashing the boat with cool light, but he took a blanket from a locker and wrapped them both in its fleecy warmth.

"I dream about places like this when I'm away," he said, pulling her into the curve of his arm. "It's what keeps me sane."

"What is it about your work that made you choose it? The thrill, the danger?"

"In part, yes. I'd never find satisfaction playing the corporate mogul sitting behind a mile-wide desk and counting my millions, despite my father's trying to buy my allegiance with more money than I could spend in a century of profligate living. To him, money's the ultimate weapon for bringing a man to heel, and it infuriated him that, in leaving me my own fortune, my mother stripped him of that power over me. It's the one thing she did that he resented."

"But there's another reason you decided on such an unconventional career?"

He shifted slightly, as if he suddenly found the luxuriously padded seat in the cockpit uncomfortable. "This isn't something I'd tell to just anyone, but yes, there's another reason. Using her money to help people in need eases my conscience at having killed her."

Aghast to think he'd carried such a heavy burden of guilt all his life, Emily burst out, "I know I've said this before, but her death was an unforeseen tragedy, Niko, and you're too intelligent a man to go on blaming yourself for something that wasn't your fault. That Pavlos let you grow up believing otherwise—"

"I thought we'd agreed not to talk about my father."

"We did, but you're the one who mentioned him first."

"Well, now I want to forget him, so let's talk about your parents instead, and satisfy my curiosity on a point that's puzzled me ever since you first mentioned it. You said they were killed in a car accident, so how is it that you were left with virtually no financial security? Usually in such cases, there's a substantial settlement, especially when a minor is left orphaned."

If she'd pressured him into confronting his own demons, his question very neatly forced her to address her own. "There was no settlement from the accident," she said. "At least, not in my favor."

"Why the devil not?"

She closed her eyes, as if that might make the facts more palatable. It didn't. It never had. "My father was at fault. He was speeding and he was drunk. Sadly he and my mother weren't the only victims. Four other people died as a result of his actions, and two more were left with crippling injuries. Because of the ensuing lawsuits, I was left with nothing but my mother's personal effects and a small insurance policy she'd taken out when I was born. And you already know how that was spent."

"They had nothing else of value? No stock portfolio or real estate?"

She shook her head. "We never owned a house, or even an apartment. Home was a top floor suite in a posh residential hotel overlooking English Bay in Vancouver. A place where they could entertain their socialite friends and host glamorous parties."

Niko muttered under his breath and she didn't have to understand Greek to know he swore. "So they could afford that, but never thought to provide for their only child's future?"

"They lived for the moment. Every day was an adventure, and money was meant to be spent. And why not? My father was hugely successful in the stock market."

"A pity he wasn't as committed to setting some aside for his daughter's future as he was to spending it on himself."

"He and my mother adored me," she flared. "They made me feel treasured and wanted. I led a charmed life, filled with warmth and laughter and love. You can't put a price on that."

"They were spoiled children playing at being adults," he countered harshly. "Even if they'd left you a fortune, it could never make up for what their fecklessness ended up costing you."

"Stop it!" she cried, not sure what angered her more: that he dared to criticize her family, or that he was right. "Just shut up!"

Throwing off the blanket, she climbed onto the side

deck and went to stand at the bow of the boat. It was the most distance she could put between them.

He came up behind her. Put his arms around her. "Hey," he said. "Listen to me."

"No. You've said enough."

"Not quite. Not until I tell you I'm sorry."

"What is it about 'shut up' that you don't understand? I'm not interested in your apology."

"And I'm not very good at taking orders. Also, I'm the last person qualified to comment on flawed relationships." He nuzzled the side of her neck, his jaw scraping lightly, erotically against her skin. "Forgive me?"

She wanted to refuse. To end things with him while she still could, and save herself more heartache down the road. Because that annoying voice of caution was whispering in her head again, warning her that this was just another in a long list of differences. They disagreed on too many critical issues ever to remain in harmony for very long. He didn't care about family. Didn't believe in love. Wasn't interested in marriage or commitment.

But the starch of her resistance was softening, leaving her body pliant to his touch, her heart susceptible to his seduction. A lot of men said the same things he had—until the right woman came along and changed their minds. Why couldn't she be the one to change his?

"Emily? Please say something. I know I've made you angry, hurt you, but please don't shut me out."

"Yes, I'm angry," she admitted miserably, "because you had no right trying to strip me of my illusions. And I'm hurt, because you succeeded." She spun around, dazzled by tears. "I've spent the last eighteen years wilfully ignoring the truth about the parents I so badly wanted to preserve as perfect in my memory. Thanks to you, I won't be able to do that anymore."

He swore again, so softly it turned into an endearment, and buried her face at his shoulder. She started to cry in earnest then, for lost dreams and fate's cruel indifference to human pain.

"Let me make it better, angel," Niko murmured, stringing kisses over her hair. "Let me love you as you deserve to be loved."

And because she wanted him more than she wanted to stay safe, she lifted her tearstained face to his and surrendered. "Yes," she said.

CHAPTER SEVEN

THE lover's grand romantic gesture—sweeping her into his arms and carrying her to bed—didn't work on a sailboat. Slender though she was, the companionway just wasn't big enough for them both at the same time. The best he could do was precede her into the main cabin and guide her as she backed down the four steps leading below deck.

Not exactly a hardship, he decided, steadying her with a hand on either side of her hips as she descended. She wasn't very tall, a little over one and a half meters, and weighed no more than about forty-six kilos, but as her slim, elegant legs crossed his line of vision, the prospect of laying them bare to his renewed inspection left him hard and aching.

Unfortunately, by the time he'd led her into the aft sleeping quarters, her eyes were enormous in her pale face, she was trembling and hyperventilating. Some men might have interpreted that as an eagerness that matched their own, but he'd seen too many refugees huddled in war zones with bombs exploding around them, to be so easily taken in.

Virgin or not, and for all that she'd seemed willing

enough when he'd asked her to let him make love to her, now that the moment lay at hand, she was afraid. And in his book, that meant ignoring the raging demands of his libido, because the day had yet to dawn that he satisfied his own needs at the expense of a woman's.

Instead he flicked on the wall lamps, and slipped a CD into the built-in sound system. With the soothing sound of a Chopin nocturne filling the silence, he drew her down to sit beside him on the edge of the bed and wiped away the remains of her tears. "You are so incredibly beautiful," he told her.

She managed a shaky laugh. "I doubt it. I never learned to cry daintily. But thank you for saying so. Most men hate it when a woman resorts to tears."

"I'm not most men," he said, running his fingers idly through her hair. It reminded him of cool satin. So did her skin when, grazing his knuckles along her jaw to her throat, he extended his slow exploration. "And you very definitely are not most women."

He touched her mouth next, teasing her lips with his thumb. Not until they parted of their own volition did he lean forward and kiss them softly.

Her eyes fell shut as if the weight of her lashes was too much to bear. She sighed. And when she did, all her pent-up tension escaped, leaving her flexible as a willow against him.

Still he did not try to rush her, but cupped his hand around her nape and touched his mouth to hers again. She tasted of wine and innocence, and only when the subtle flavor of desire entered the mix did he deepen the kiss.

Gradually she grew bolder. Her hands crept under his sweater and up his bare chest, deft and sure. She murmured, little inarticulate pleadings that said the fear was gone and she was ready. More than ready. Her hunger matched his.

Suppressing the urgency threatening his control, he undressed her at leisure, discarding her shoes and socks first, then her jogging suit. A practical outfit and attractive enough in its way, it did not merit lingering attention. But underneath, she wore peach-colored lace; a bra so delicate and fine, her nipples glowed pink through the fabric, and panties so minuscule they defied gravity.

Clinging provocatively to her body, they were so blatantly designed to stir a man to passion that he had to turn away from the sight before he embarrassed himself. Had to rip down the zippered fly of his jeans or suffer permanent injury from their confinement. Kicking them off, he yanked his sweater over his head, flung it across the cabin, and sent his briefs sailing after it.

Misunderstanding his abrupt change of pace, she stroked a tentative hand down his back and whispered, "Are you angry? Did I do something wrong?"

"You're the nurse here," he ground out roughly, spinning around so that there was no way she could miss the state he was in. "Does it look to you as if you did something wrong?"

She blinked. And blushed.

If he hadn't been such a seething mass of sexual hunger that the functioning part of his brain was concerned only with how soon he could satisfy it, he'd have told her how her shy modesty charmed him. But his stamina was nearing its limits and wanting his dwindling endurance to be focused on bringing her pleasure, he drew back the bedcovers and pulled her down to lie next to him.

Willing his obdurate flesh to patience, he undid the clasp of her bra. Slid the outrageous panties down her legs. And when at last she lay naked before him, feasted his eyes on her. Dazzled by her blond perfection, her delicate symmetry of form, and perhaps most of all by the sultry heat in her eyes, he shaped her every curve and hollow with his hands, and followed them with his mouth.

She undulated on the mattress, offering herself to him without reserve. Clutching his shoulders in swift bursts of tactile delight when he found her most sensitive spots. Arching, taut as a high-tension wire, as he brought her to the brink of orgasm. And collapsing in a puddle of heat as she surrendered to it.

That she was so responsive to his seduction gratified him, but it inflamed him, as well. He wasn't made of stone, and knew he couldn't go on indefinitely denying himself the same pleasure he afforded her.

She knew it, too, and reaching down, she closed her hand around him. With another of her engaging little sighs, she traced her fingers over his erection, glorying in its strength, cherishing its vulnerability. Did so with such reverence that she somehow managed to touch him elsewhere, in places he kept separate from other people. In his heart, in his soul.

The emotional onslaught, as singular as it was powerful, blinded him to the encroaching danger. Responsibility, finesse, all the vital prerequisites by which he defined his sexual liaisons, deserted him. He was consumed with the overwhelming need to possess and be possessed. Seeming to sense the latter, she angled her body closer and cradled him snugly between her smooth, beautiful thighs.

Her daring lured him past all caution. The blood pulsed through his loins. He could feel her damp warmth beckoning him, knew of his own near-capitulation, and with only nanoseconds to spare, he dragged himself back from the brink of insanity and sheathed himself in a condom. Then and only then did he bury himself fully within her.

Tilting her hips, she rose up to meet him, caught in his relentless rhythm, absorbing his every urgent thrust. She was sleek, hot, tight. Irresistible. She took his body hostage. Held him fast within her and rendered him mindless to everything but the rampant, inexorable surge of passion rising to a climax that threatened to destroy him.

It caught her in its fury, too. He felt her contract around him. Was dimly conscious of her muffled cries, her nails raking down his back, and then the tide crashed over him. Stripped him of power and tumbled him into helpless submission. With a groan dragged up from the depths of his soul, he flooded free.

Spent, but aware he must be crushing her with his weight, he fought to regain his breath, to regulate his racing heart. Finally, with a mighty effort, he rolled onto his side and took her with him. Glancing down, he found her watching him, her eyes soft, her lovely face flushed. A world removed from the trembling creature she'd been half an hour before.

Curious as to the reason, he said, "You were nervous when I first brought you down here, weren't you?"

"I still am."

It wasn't the answer he expected, but remembering her comment about her previous experience, he thought he knew what prompted it. "If you're thinking you disappointed me as a partner, *karthula*, be assured I could not ask for better."

"It's not that at all," she said. "Before we made love, I was afraid I'd end up liking you too much. Now I'm afraid because I know I was right."

Her admission splintered his heart a little, as if she'd driven a needle into it and caused a tiny wound. He was not accustomed to such quiet honesty from his partners. "Is that such a bad thing?" he asked her.

"Not necessarily bad. I knew making love with you meant taking a risk. I just didn't realize how big a risk."

Then don't think of it as making love, he wanted to tell her. Be like the other women I take to bed, and see it as enjoyable sex. But she was so aglow that he couldn't bring himself to disillusion her. Which, in itself, gave rise to another troubling stab to his hitherto impregnable heart. She brought out a protective tenderness in him that he found as frightening as it was unacceptable.

Reading his thoughts with daunting insight, she said, "Don't worry, Niko. I'm not so naive that I think this weekend is the prelude to a long-term relationship. I'm not expecting it to end with a proposal of marriage or a ring."

Why not?

The question so nearly escaped him that he had to bite his tongue to contain it. "I'm in no position to offer either, even if I wanted to," he said, when he recovered himself. "My career doesn't lend itself to that sort of commitment, and I doubt there are many women who'd put up with a husband who's away more often than he's at home."

"Exactly. Realistically, neither of us is in the market

for anything but a casual fling. I'm just not very good at 'casual.'"

"There's nothing wrong with liking the person you're in bed with, Emily, and if I haven't already made it clear, let me say now that I like you very much. I wouldn't have asked you to come away with me if I didn't."

Her smile turned into a thinly disguised yawn. "That's good," she said. "I'll sleep much better knowing that, but I need to brush my teeth first."

"Of course. I'll use the head—bathroom in nautical terms, in case you're wondering—in the forward cabin."

She slithered off the bed and disappeared, a too-fleeting vision of slender, lamplit femininity that stirred him to fresh arousal. But he had his own rituals to attend to, not the least of which was making sure the anchor was well set for the night. Nothing like having a sailboat run aground to ruin the romantic ambience.

When he rejoined her in the bed some fifteen minutes later, she lay on her side facing away from him and was sound asleep. Just as well, really. She made it too easy for him to forget the rules he'd long ago set for himself. To those he rescued—the orphans, the widows, the elderly—he gave everything of himself because they didn't trespass into his personal life. Those he associated with the rest of the time he'd learned to keep at a safe distance.

Even though he wasn't touching her, he lay close enough that the heat of his body coiled around her. She knew that if she turned, if she made the slightest overture, he'd take her in his arms and they'd make love again. And she couldn't do it. She was too terrified of his power over her. Terrified that as the pleasure he gave her built to an unbearable peak, she might utter the three words guaranteed to put an end to what she had rightly termed a fling.

He might like her very much, but that was light years removed from his wanting to hear her say "I love you." Not that she did love him. In fact, she knew very well that she did not. *Could* not. Because anyone with half a brain knew that blissful, incredible sex didn't equal love.

Men have a one-track mind, she once overheard an embittered nursing colleague say. *They want a woman between the sheets, and they achieve it by making you feel as if they don't want to be anywhere else but with you—until the next day or the next week, when they move on to someone else, and you're left feeling slightly shopworn and incredibly stupid. The only way to gain the upper hand is either to fool them into thinking you don't care if you never see them again, or else swear off sex altogether.*

Apart from her one dismal experience with the third-year medical resident whose ego had surpassed anything else he had to offer, Emily had subscribed to the latter. She would not risk her self-respect or her reputation for the sake of a tawdry one-night stand. What was best, she'd decided in what she now recognized as pathetic naiveté on her part, was to settle for nothing less than complete commitment before leaping into intimacy with a man. But that prudent argument was before Niko Leonidas swept into her life, and swept out all her pre-conceived notions of what was best.

Sharing the same bed with him now, and so graphi-cally conscious of him that her skin vibrated with awareness, she forced herself to remain completely still as she waited for his breathing to settle into the deep, even rhythm that signaled sleep.

Seconds passed. Spun into long, painful minutes. Nothing broke the silence but the whisper of the sea and the equally subdued sound of his breathing. He was a very quiet sleeper, unlike his father who snored lustily when he nodded off.

Cautiously she shifted her foot; tucked her hand beneath her pillow. And waited for a sign that he was as wide-awake as she was. He did not stir. Convinced it was now safe to do so, she stopped pretending, opened her eyes and admitted to the moon-splashed night the awful truth.

She *was* in love with him. She had been for days. She'd committed the ultimate folly and laid on the line everything she had to give, in exchange for what she'd always known could never be more than a passing affair. And now she was paying the price.

The painful enormity of what she'd allowed to happen overwhelmed her. Tears seeped onto her pillow and silent sobs shook her body. All at once she was a child again, left with a heart full of love and no one to give it to. She wanted Niko to look at her as her father used to look at her mother, as if she was the most beautiful, fascinating creature ever to grace the earth. She wanted the magic and passion and permanence they'd known. She wanted it all, and she wanted it with Niko.

In short, she wanted what he couldn't give her.

"Emily?" His voice swam softly out of the gloom. "Are you asleep?"

"No," she muttered thickly, "but I thought you were."

She heard the rustle of the bed linen, felt his hand glide over her silky nightgown and come to rest at her hip. "Anything but," he said, his voice sinking to a husky growl. "I'm lying here thinking about you…and wanting you again."

He inched the hem of her gown up past her knees. Past her waist. His hand ventured, warm and possessive, between her thighs. "Emily?" he said again.

Any woman with an ounce of self-preservation to her name would have slapped his hand away, but not Emily Anne Tyler. No, she melted at his touch. Rolled onto her back, let her legs fall slackly apart and advertised the fact that she was more than willing to accommodate him. Well, why not, some distant part of her brain rationalized. At this point, she had nothing left to lose and might as well hoard as many precious memories as possible of this brief enchanted interlude.

He kissed the side of her neck. Murmured in her ear all the words men were supposed to murmur to a woman they planned to seduce. Words calculated to break down her resistance, to make her compliant to his every wish. Eventually he lowered himself on top of her and, pulling her legs up around his waist, eased himself smoothly inside her. As if, she thought, struggling to retain a grip on reality, God had designed them specifically for each other.

He loved her slowly this time, transporting her in leisurely increments of sensual delight until she could hold back no longer, then supporting himself on his forearms to watch her as she climaxed. When he came, she watched him, too. Saw the grim line of his mouth as he fought a battle he hadn't a hope of winning. Saw how, at the last moment, he closed his eyes and groaned as his body shuddered in helpless surrender. The unguarded honesty of it all made her cry again.

"What is it?" he asked, clearly appalled. "Did I hurt you? Tell me, *mana mou.*"

"No," she said, because confessing the truth—that with every touch, every word, every glance, he made her love him all the more—wasn't an option. "Making love again was so beautiful, that's all."

A weak excuse, but thankfully he accepted it. Cradling her so that her head rested on his shoulder and his arm kept her close, he said, "It was magnificent. It will be the next time, too."

She was able to fall asleep on that promise, comforted by the steady beat of his heart beneath her hand and lulled by the gentle rise and fall of the sea beneath the boat.

They didn't wake up until almost nine o'clock. After a simple breakfast of yogurt and fruit, they took their coffee up on deck. Although summer's intense heat was long past, it was still a shorts-and-tank-top kind of day.

"By noon," he told Emily, pulling her into the curve of his arm, "you'll be lying on the foredeck, stripped down to your bikini."

"Mmm." She lifted her face to the sun. "Lolling in a bikini on a sailboat in October. Not too tough to take, I have to admit."

"Happy you decided to come away with me?"

"Who wouldn't be? It's lovely here."

Right answer, but it didn't quite ring true. Something was bothering her. "Are you sure?"

"Of course," she said, and promptly changed the

subject. "Will the water be too cold for swimming, do you think?"

"We can find out later, if you like, but it's a bit too early yet. Emily, is there something—?"

"Early! Heavens, Niko, it's after ten already. Do you always sleep in so late?"

"Only when I'm away on the boat. It's my one, sure outlet of escape from the everyday routine." He didn't add that the constant danger inherent in his work, the risks involved, took a toll. He left that part of his life behind the second he cast off from the yacht club and took to the sea.

"Burn-out, you mean? I know what that's like. It's one reason I agreed to come to Greece and nurse Pavlos back to health. I needed a change of scene."

"And the other reason?"

She chewed her lip thoughtfully. "I'd grown very fond of him during the time he was hospitalized. In a way, we'd become more like father and daughter than nurse and patient, and I didn't feel I could abandon him."

"More like grandfather and granddaughter, surely?"

"When you don't have any other family, you don't quibble about little things like that."

A month ago, he'd have taken that remark and found any number of hidden messages in it. Now, he took it at face value.

"Even after all these years, you still miss your parents, don't you?"

"Yes. Very much."

"And I made it worse with my comments last night," he muttered, cursing himself. "I tarnished your perfect memories of them."

"Not really, because nobody's perfect, not even my parents, for all that I tried so hard to idealize them. The truth is, I've sometimes thought it was as well they died young and together. They wouldn't have dealt well with old age or being alone. And I would never have filled the emptiness left behind if only one of them had been killed in the accident."

She captivated him with her honesty, which was pretty ironic considering his first impression of her had been that she wasn't to be trusted. "They might not have been perfect, Emily, but they came close to it when they made you. I'm sure they loved you very much."

"Oh, they loved me," she said, moving away from him and gazing mistily at the blue horizon, "but they never really needed me. If you must know, that's why I decided to become a nurse. I wanted to be needed. You don't, though, do you?"

Her question threw him. "Why else do you think I put my life on the line to help other people?"

"Because they're strangers who invade your professional life for just a little while. But your personal life...well, that's different. It's off-limits. A person only has to look at your relationship with your father, to see that."

She saw too much, and he wouldn't sink so low as to deny it. "Having him join the party isn't my idea of a good time, Emily."

She made a face. "My fault. I'm the one who mentioned him."

"Then I suggest we make a concerted effort to get rid of him. What do you say we take the dinghy ashore and go for a walk on the island?"

"I'd love to," she said with alacrity. "Let me get my camera."

Her relief was palpable. Because she didn't want his father hanging around, either, Niko wondered, or because she wanted to put distance between the two of them?

He shouldn't have cared, one way or the other. Annoyingly he did.

CHAPTER EIGHT

A GREAT suggestion, Emily concluded, watching as Niko tilted the outboard engine clear of the water and the bottom of the dinghy scraped onto the narrow strip of gravelly beach edging the island. Luxuriously comfortable though it might be, the yacht's big drawback was that it offered no means of escape when the conversation got out of hand. And it had, dangerously so, straying close to disastrous when she foolishly brought up the business of wanting to be needed. Another few minutes and her feelings for Niko, which she was so desperately trying to suppress, would have spilled out.

Hiding behind her camera gave her the chance to regroup. She took pictures of flowers enjoying a riotous last bloom before winter: wild geraniums and gaudy poppies; daisies and ice plant in shades of mauve and white. She snapped the yacht riding peacefully at anchor in the sheltered bay. And when he least expected it, she captured images of Niko; of his dazzling smile, his chiseled profile, his lashes lowered to half-mast as he squinted against the brightness of the sparkling sea.

The atmosphere on the island was different, she realized. Freer, less soberly intense. Here, she could breathe and not have to worry about keeping up her guard. If necessary, she could put distance between her and Niko. Contrarily, because she could, she felt no need to do so.

Sensing her change of mood, he matched it with a lighthearted teasing of his own. "If you didn't have a camera slung around your wrist, you'd be up to your neck in trouble," he growled with mock ferocity, grabbing her before she could escape after she'd caught him unaware at the water's edge and splashed him.

That kind of trouble she could handle. "I wish I could say I'm sorry, and mean it," she returned cheekily, and splashed him again.

Suddenly his laughter faded and twining her hands in his, he regarded her searchingly. "*I* wish I could take you away for a month, instead of a weekend," he said. "Being around you is good for me, Emily. You remind me that there's more to living than burying myself in work. I'm a happy man when I'm with you."

Her spirit soared at that. Could he possibly be falling for her, too?

Well, why not? Wasn't she forever telling her patients and their families that they should never give up hope? And hadn't she seen for herself, time and time again, that miracles did happen? Why couldn't one come her way for a change?

"Keep looking at me like that," he went on, his voice lowering to a thrilling purr, "and I won't be held liable for what I might do, which would be a mistake on two counts. This beach isn't designed for comfortable seduction, and even if it were, I didn't bring a contraceptive with me."

Flirting shamelessly, she glanced up at him in her

best imitation of a siren bent on luring him to destruction. "Then why don't we go back to the yacht?"

His eyes darkened, turned a deep forest-green. "Race you to the dinghy, angel."

Love in the afternoon was different, she discovered. Sunlight pouring through the window above the bed and casting dancing reflections of the sea on the cabin ceiling brought an openness to intimacy that, at first, dismayed her because it left her with no place to hide.

He soon put paid to that nonsense. He examined her all over, from the soles of her feet to the top of her head. He found the tiny scar on her bottom where she'd fallen on broken glass at the beach when she was little, and he kissed it as if it were new and still hurting.

He paid attention to every inch of her, sometimes with his hands, sometimes with his mouth and tongue, pausing every now and then to murmur, "Do you like it when I do this?"

Like? She'd never before felt such slow, rolling awareness of herself as a woman. He made her quiver with anticipation. He brought her body to electrifying life and made it yearn and ache and throb. He made her scream softly and beg for more.

Until him, she'd never climaxed. With him, she came so quickly and with such fury that she couldn't catch her breath.

His touch sent her flying so high, she could almost touch the heavens, and he knew it because he watched her the entire time. Knew to the second when she hovered on the brink, and tipped her over the edge into a glorious, sparkling free-fall she wished might never end.

Then, when she was dazed with exhausted pleasure and sure she didn't have the strength to lift a finger, let alone peak again, he buried himself in her hot, sleek folds and taught her otherwise. Caught in his urgent, driving rhythm, she swooped and soared with him again to a magnificent crashing finale.

At two in the afternoon or thereabouts, they put together a snack of fruit and cheese and ate it in the shade of the canvas bimini in the cockpit. They drank a little wine, and they talked, mostly about Niko as it turned out, which inevitably meant Pavlos crept back into the conversation, too.

"Was he cruel to you?" Emily asked, when Niko spoke briefly of his unhappy childhood.

"Not in the way you're thinking," he said. "Far from it. I never lacked for a thing. Clothes, toys, tutors, whatever I needed, he provided. When it came to my later education, there was no limit to how far he'd go to make sure I had the best. He sent me to the most prestigious boarding school in Europe—more than one in fact, since I managed to get myself kicked out of several."

"Then why the estrangement?"

"He didn't understand that there was more to being a father than spending money."

"Or else he didn't understand that you were crying out for his love."

"It was never about love with him. It was about power. And from his point of view, money and power are one and the same. Which is another bone of contention between us because to me, money's merely the means to an end. If I end up without any, I'll find a way to make more, but I'll never let it rule my life the way it rules his."

"Why do you think he sets such store by it?"

"Probably because he grew up without any. He was the by-product of an affair between a housemaid and the son of her millionaire employer who abandoned her when he learned she was pregnant. If you asked him what his most driving ambition had been when he was a boy, I guarantee he'd say it was to end up one of the wealthiest men in Greece, able to pick and choose his friends, his associates and, eventually, his wife."

"He appears to have succeeded."

Niko inclined his head in agreement. "Yes, but it took him years. He didn't marry my mother until he was thirty-one which, back then, was considered pretty old. She was just twenty, and the only daughter of one of his biggest business rivals."

"Is that why he married her—to score points over her father?"

"No," he said. "He really loved her. I have to give him credit for that much."

"What a shame he could never see you as her most lasting legacy to him."

"I was too much the rebel, refusing to toe the Leonidas line, determined to go my own way and to hell with anyone who tried to stop me."

He'd never been so open with her before. Was it the lazy afternoon heat or their lovemaking that made it easier for him to share his life story with her now? Whatever the reason, Emily was hungry to know everything about him and prepared to listen for as long as he was willing to talk. "Did he want you to go to university?"

"In the worst way, and was pretty convinced he could make it happen since I wouldn't have any money of my own until I turned twenty-one. He saw a business degree as the next logical step to my joining his empire. But I got out from under his control when I joined the air force, and there wasn't a damned thing he could do about it. After I left the service, I spent a year in England with a former UN pilot who taught me everything he knew about mercy missions, and introduced me to the finer points of the English language. After that, I came back to Greece, took over my inheritance and set up my own operation."

"And the rest, as they say, is history?"

He stood up and stretched. "*Ne*—and pretty dull at that, if you ask me, not to mention a criminal waste of a beautiful afternoon. What do you say to a swim?"

He was finished baring his soul and, for now at least, she realized she'd gain nothing by pressing for more. "Okay, if you're sure the water's warm enough."

"Only one way to find out, Emily," he said, dragging her to her feet. "You coming in of your own free will, or do I throw you in?"

"At least let me change into my bikini."

"What for?" He dropped his shorts and briefs, pulled off his T-shirt and climbed onto the swim grid in all his beautiful naked glory. "Nothing like going au naturel, as they say in polite society, especially as neither of us has anything to show that the other hasn't already seen."

"Once a rebel, always a rebel," she muttered self-consciously as she peeled off her clothes.

He favored her with a lascivious grin. "I hardly expected a nurse to be so modest, my dear. Even your bottom's blushing."

There was only one response to that remark and she

wasted no time delivering it. Bracing both hands against his chest, she shoved him into the water. He landed with a mighty splash and she followed suit before he had the chance to climb back on board and exact his revenge.

After the first chilling shock, the sea was deliciously refreshing. Heaven had never seemed so close, Emily decided, floating on her back with her hair streaming out behind her and the big blue bowl of the sky arcing overhead.

Niko, whom she'd last seen swimming in a powerful crawl toward the mouth of the bay, suddenly bobbed to the surface next to her. "You look like a mermaid," he said. "A particularly delectable mermaid."

And he looked like a sea god, she thought, her heart turning over at the sight of his broad, tanned shoulders, his brilliant smile and the thick lashes spiking in clumps around his remarkable green eyes. Small wonder she'd fallen in love with him. What woman in her right mind could resist him?

They climbed back on board and lay down on the foredeck to dry in the sun's benign warmth. He'd swum farther than he intended, a strenuous workout that left him pleasantly tired and happy just to lie next to her, his limbs touching hers, his fingers brushing lightly against her arm. Not moving, not speaking, just looking into her dark blue eyes and letting utter contentment sweep over him.

Was he falling in love?

He couldn't be. It was completely out of the question. A misguided romantic fantasy brought on by brain fatigue or some other disorder of the mind, because he absolutely refused to entertain the possibility that it might have something to do with his heart. Yet if it was so impossible, why did he suddenly hate the man who'd taken her virginity? She belonged to no one but him, and should have waited until he found her.

"What dark thoughts are chasing through your mind?" she murmured drowsily, peering at him from half-closed eyes.

The unpalatable truth rose in his throat, bitter as bile. Scowling, he said, "I have a confession to make. More than one, in fact."

"Oh?" A shadow flitted over her face. "Such as?"

"For a start, I'm jealous of my predecessor."

Clearly at a loss, she said, "What are you talking about?"

"I'm jealous of whoever it was that you slept with before you met me."

"I see." She pushed herself up on one elbow, propped her head on her hand and regarded him thoughtfully. "Should I be flattered?"

"I don't know. I've never found myself in this kind of situation before."

And that, he thought, was the whole problem in a nutshell.

Before he met her, sex had been all about mutual pleasure with no strings attached. He never lied to his willing partners, never made promises he couldn't keep, was never intentionally cruel. But sometimes he hurt them anyway because they wanted more than he could give.

Until now. Until Emily, when his initial plan had somehow gone terribly wrong and he found himself in danger of wanting to give much more than he could ever afford.

"That doesn't sit well with you, does it?" she said.

"No. I prefer to stick to the rules."

"What rules?"

"Those I've set for myself."

"And you're breaking them with me?"

"Yes," he said grimly, uncertain whether it was self-preservation or self-destruction that drove him to bare his soul so brutally. "When I first started seeing you, all I ever intended was to act as a decoy."

"A decoy?"

He heard the wariness in her voice edging closer to outright dismay, and wished he'd kept his mouth shut. But palming her off with half-truths left him feeling dirty and unworthy of her. And even if it didn't, he'd said too much to stop now. "Yes," he said. "To keep you away from my father. There being no fool like an old fool, I decided to step in and save him from himself— and you—by diverting your attention from an ailing old man to one who could better please you."

Dazed, she glanced away and focused her attention on the boat, appearing fascinated by its sleek lines, gleaming fiberglass deck and oiled teak. "So this weekend is all about proving a point?"

"No. That's the trouble. Now it's about you and me, and feelings I never bargained for. I tried to tell you this the other night, but I lost my nerve."

She wasn't listening. Instead she was scrambling to her feet and swinging her head wildly from side to side, a wounded creature desperate to escape her tormentor.

Springing to her side, he trapped her in his arms. She

lashed out at him, catching him a glancing blow on the jaw. "Let me go!" she spat. "Don't ever touch me again!"

"You're not hearing me, Emily," he told her urgently. "Everything's different now."

"Sure it is." She was sobbing. The sound drove splinters through his heart. "You've finally shown your true colors."

"No, Emily. I made a stupid mistake."

"So you decided to make it up to me by giving me a weekend to remember? How tedious you must have found it, pretending you wanted to have sex with me."

"I wasn't pretending! For God's sake, Emily, you of all people know a man can't pretend."

"So how did you manage? By closing your eyes and imagining I was someone else?"

He crushed her to him, shocked. "Never. It was always you. Only you, right from the start. I just didn't realize it at the time."

"And here I thought we'd put to rest that whole ludicrous notion that I was some sort of fortune hunter out to fleece your poor father." She wasn't crying now. She was encased in ice.

"We have," he protested. "You are what you've always been, as beautiful on the inside as you are on the surface."

"I don't feel beautiful," she said tonelessly. "I feel stupid and pathetic, because I let myself fall in love with you."

"Then I guess we're both stupid and pathetic, because that's what I'm trying to say. I'm falling in love with you, too, and the damnable thing is, I don't know what the hell to do about it."

"Then I'll tell you," she said. "You get over it. We both do."

* * *

The look on his face told her it wasn't the answer he wanted to hear. "Why should we?" he whispered against her mouth.

But the damage was done and nothing he said or did could put things right again. "Because there's no future in it for either of us." She pulled away just far enough to look him in the eye, then added pointedly, "Is there?"

"If you're asking me to predict what might happen tomorrow, I can't, Emily. All any of us ever has is today. Can't you let that be enough?"

Temporary bliss, in exchange for long-term misery? Not a chance! She was in enough pain already, and prolonging the inevitable would merely increase the agony. "No. I made up my mind long before I met you that relationships heading nowhere are a waste of time."

"I could change your mind, if you'd let me."

She was terribly afraid that he could, and knew she had to get away from him before he succeeded. He was kissing her eyes, her hair, her throat. Stroking his hands down her arms and up her bare back with killing tenderness. Sabotaging her with caresses when words failed to get him what he wanted, and already her resistance was dissolving under the attack.

"I don't want to be here with you anymore," she said, clinging to her vanishing resolve with the desperation of a drowning woman. "Take me back to the mainland."

"I will," he murmured. "Tomorrow."

"Tonight."

"*Ohi*...no." He lifted her off her feet and set her down in the cockpit. Traced his lips over her cheek and brought his mouth to hers and kissed her softly.

He made her legs shake, her insides quiver. He made her heart yearn. "Please," she whimpered helplessly.

"Give me one last night, my Emily."

"I can't."

He touched her fleetingly between the legs. "Tell me why not, when I know you want me as much as I want you."

She shuddered, caught in the clenching grip of rising passion. "Tell me why I'm inexplicably drawn to a man who isn't at all my kind of man," she countered.

"And what kind of man is that?"

"The kind who's not afraid of love. Who's happy with a nine-to-five job and a mortgage," she said, grasping at a truth she'd refused to acknowledge until now. "The safe kind who doesn't need to flirt with danger all the time in order to find fulfillment."

"Then you're right. I'm definitely not your kind of man."

But he pulled her closer, and the way her body tilted to meet his, welcoming the questing nudge of his erection, proclaimed otherwise. As if she'd finally found what she'd always been looking for. As if he was exactly her kind of man.

She was lost, and she knew it. The irrepressible pulse of his flesh against hers enthralled her. Lured her into forgetting how he had deceived and used her. Nothing mattered except to know again the pleasure only he could give. If, the next day or the next week, he reneged on his protestations of love, at least she'd have this weekend to remember him by.

The hunger, rapacious, insatiable, spiraled to unbearable heights. Casting aside all pretense at dignity, she sprawled on the cockpit cushions. At once, he was on top of her. Thrusting inside her, hot, heavy, demanding.

Perfectly attuned, they rose and sank together, pausing at just the right moment to drown in each other's gaze. There was no need for words to justify a decision that went against everything they'd just said to each other. They had come together because they could not stay apart. It was as simple as that.

CHAPTER NINE

WHEN they finally stirred and she mentioned that she'd like to freshen up, Niko ran a critical hand over his jaw, said he could use a shower and shave himself and told her not to rush. "We have all the time in the world," he said. "We'll have mezedes and wine and watch the moon rise, then eat dinner when the mood takes us."

So she indulged herself in a leisurely bath, and shampooed the saltwater out of her hair. After toweling herself dry, she massaged lotion into her sun-kissed skin, spritzed a little cologne at her elbows and behind her knees and put on the silk caftan, glad she'd had the good sense to smuggle it aboard. He'd said he was in love with her, but she sensed he'd made the admission reluctantly, and pinned little hope on his feeling the same way in the morning. If so, and if this turned out to be their last night together, she intended it to be one neither of them would soon forget.

Nor did they, but not for the reasons she'd supposed. The very second she joined him in the main cabin, she knew their plans had changed. He'd showered—his damp hair attested to that—but he hadn't shaved. There was no sign of the appetizers he'd mentioned, no tempting aromas drifting from the oven, no wine chilling. All that lay on the table was his cell phone, and one look at his face told her it had been the bearer of bad news. "Something's happened," she said, a sinking feeling in the pit of her stomach.

"Yes. I'm afraid we have to head back right away."

"Is it Pavlos?"

He shook his head. "I just got word from my director of operations that we've lost contact with one of our pilots in north Africa. He was scheduled to pick up an injured Red Cross worker from a refugee camp. He never showed up."

"What can you do about it?"

He stared at her as if she wasn't in command of all her faculties. "Go find him. What did you think—that I'd sit back and leave him stranded in the desert?"

"No, of course not." She swallowed, stung by his brusque tone. "Is there any way that I can help?"

"Change into something warmer, for a start. That thing you've got on won't do. Quite a stiff onshore breeze has sprung up. It'll be a chilly trip back to the mainland."

She must have looked as forlorn as she felt because when he spoke again, his voice softened. "I know you're disappointed, Emily. I am, too. This isn't how I'd foreseen the evening playing out. But when situations like this come up, I'm afraid everything else has to go on hold. A man's life could be at stake."

"I understand," she said. And she did. Completely. But what about *his* life? How safe would he be, rushing off to the rescue without knowing the danger he might be facing? "Will it be risky, your going looking for him?"

"It's possible, but so what? Risks come with the job. You get used to it."

You, maybe, but not me, she thought, the harsh reality of his vocation hitting home with a vengeance for the first time and filling her with apprehension. "How will you know where to start looking for him?"

"If he's turned on his epurb—electronic positioning beacon, that is—it'll lead me straight to him. If not, I'm familiar with the area, I know where he was headed and his coordinates before he lost contact."

"What if you still don't find him?"

"That's not an option," he said flatly. "He's just a kid of twenty-three, the eldest of four children and the only son of a widow. It's my job to locate him and bring him home to his family. They need him."

"But what if—?"

He silenced her with a swift, hard kiss. "No 'what ifs.' It's not the first time I've had to do this, and it won't be the last. I'll be back before you know it—by tomorrow night at the latest, but we really need to get going now if I'm to be ready to set out at first light in the morning."

Set out to where? Some vast arid region miles from civilization? Some rebel stronghold where human life didn't count for a thing? "Then I'd better get organized," she said, and turned away before he saw the desolation in her eyes.

"At least my father will be glad to have you back earlier than expected."

"I suppose."

He came up behind her and wound his arms around

her waist. "Did I mention how lovely you look, Emily?" he said softly against her hair.

On the outside, maybe. But inside, she was falling apart.

The nurse who'd replaced her was so happy to be relieved of her job, she practically flew out of the villa before Emily stepped in. "Is impossible!" she screeched, indignation fracturing her English almost past recognition. "He die, then *me niazi*! I do not care. One day more, I break his neck. *Adio*. Please not call me again. *Apokliete!*"

"Have a nice night," Emily said wearily, as the front door slammed shut in her face.

Pavlos didn't even pretend to hide his glee when she appeared at breakfast the next morning. "Didn't take you long to come to your senses, did it, girl?" he crowed.

"Try to behave yourself for a change, Pavlos," she snapped. "I'm in no mood for your shenanigans."

He smirked into his coffee cup. "That bad, was it? Could have told you it would be."

"For your information, I had a wonderful time. The only reason I came back early is that your son has gone searching for a young pilot lost somewhere over the Sahara."

His derision faded into something approaching concern, but he covered it quickly. "Damned fool! Serve him right if he got himself killed."

"I'll pretend I didn't hear you say that."

"Why not?" he retorted. "Ignoring the facts isn't going to change them. Wherever the latest hotbed of unrest shows up, you can bet he'll be there, and one of these days he'll push his luck too far."

Ill-timed though it might be, the truth of his answer could not be denied, and how she got through the rest of the day she didn't know. The minutes dragged, the hours lasted a small eternity. Morning became afternoon, then evening and, all too soon, night. Every time the phone rang, her heart plummeted. And sank lower still when the call brought no news of Niko.

"Better get used to this if you plan on sticking with him," Pavlos advised her, as the dinner hour came and went without any word.

"The same way you have?" she shot back. "You talk a good line, Pavlos, but you're as worried about him as I am."

"Not me," he huffed, but there was no real conviction in his tone and his gaze wandered to the clock on the wall every bit as often as hers did. "Where did you say he'd gone?"

"North Africa—the desert—I'm not sure exactly."

"Hmm." He drummed his arthritic old fingers on the edge of the table. "That's a lot of ground for one man to cover."

She closed her eyes. Fear beat a tattoo in her blood.

"Go to bed, Emily," Pavlos said with uncommon gentleness. "I'll wait up and let you know if we hear anything."

As if she could sleep! "I'm not tired. You should rest, though."

But neither made any move. Anxiety thick as molasses held them paralyzed.

Just after eleven o'clock, the phone shrieked into the silence one last time. Hands shaking, she grabbed it on the first ring. "Niko?"

She heard his smile. "Who else were you expecting at this hour?"

"No one…you…but it grew so late and you hadn't called—"

"You're going to have to learn to believe what I tell you, Emily," he said. "I promised I'd be back today, and I am."

"Yes." Giddy with relief, she reached for Pavlos's hand and squeezed it. "Where are you now?"

"At the office. I'll be heading home as soon as I've filed my report."

"And the man you went to find?"

"Had a fire in his control panel that knocked out his communications system. He made an emergency landing on a deserted Second World War airstrip. There are dozens of them, hundreds even, all over the Sahara. The one he chose lay nearly two hundred kilometers from where he was supposed to be, but his epurb was still working and led me straight to him."

"And he's okay?"

"He's fine, though I wish I could say the same for the aircraft. But the good news is, we picked up the man he was supposed to bring back and got him to a hospital, albeit twenty-four hours later than expected."

"You've put in a long day and must be exhausted."

"Nothing an early night won't fix. I'll see you tomorrow?"

"I can't wait," she said. "I missed you."

"Same here, *karthula*." His yawn echoed down the line. "I'd come over now, but—"

"Don't even think about it. Go home and catch up on your sleep."

"Will do. *Kali nikhta*, my sweet Emily."

"*Kali nikhta*," she replied. "Good night."

* * *

In the days following, she should have been completely happy. Although he vetoed any suggestion that he should terminate her employment, Pavlos was on the road to recovery and didn't need her as he once had. Accepting that she and his son were an item, he compromised by letting her take the weekends off.

She lived for the sheer heaven of those two days and nights. Niko's spacious penthouse in Kolonaki was their retreat. The living and dining rooms and en suite guest room opened onto a terrace. A small library and starkly modern kitchen comprised the rest of the main floor, with a gorgeous master suite upstairs. The decor was as spare and elegant as he himself, lacking any of the usual personal touches like photographs, but the huge collection of books and CDs told her much about his tastes and hinted at a man content with his own company.

He did his best to please her during their time together; to make it seem they were like any other couple in love. Working around his erratic schedule, they explored the countryside, going by scooter if the weather allowed but, with the cooler temperatures of November, more often by car.

They hiked in the pine-covered hills behind the town, took a picnic hamper and sailed down the coast of the Attic peninsula. Sometimes, they drove to out-of-the-way villages where they sampled wonderful local dishes in quaint, unpretentious tavernas whose walls were lined with wine barrels. Other times, they went into Athens and dined in fine style on the best the city had to offer. They danced cheek to cheek in the Grande Bretagne Hotel; made passionate love in his king-size bed.

If he had to break a date—and he did, often—he sent

her flowers, or texted messages to her in the night so that she found them on waking. In return, she tried to keep her anxiety under control when he was away, but never knew a moment's real peace until he returned. She couldn't sleep and walked the floor half the night. She couldn't eat because anxiety robbed her of her appetite. Noticing, Pavlos never missed the chance to tell her she was making the biggest mistake of her life.

She learned to live with all of it because the alternative—to put an end to it—was unthinkable.

Once, when Niko discovered he'd left his cell phone on his desk at work and had to go back to get it, he took her with him and showed her around the private airfield that served as his base of operations. The flat-roofed office building had only four rooms but was equipped with the latest in electronic equipment. Probably the aircraft sitting on the tarmac were, too, but when Emily first saw them, what struck her most forcibly was how flimsy they seemed.

"Are they what you use to fly overseas?" she asked, trying to mask her dismay.

Discerning it anyway, Niko laughed and said, "Were you expecting hot air balloons, my darling?"

"No, but these things are so small and...old-fashioned."

"Old-fashioned?" He regarded her in mock horror over the top of his aviator sunglasses.

"Well, yes. They've each got two sets of those spider-leg propellor things stuck on the front."

"I know," he said dryly. "They're what get them off the ground and keep them in the air."

"But why wouldn't you use jets? Surely they're faster?"

"Faster, but not nearly as versatile or fuel-efficient.

Twin-engine piston aircraft like these don't require nearly as long a runway as a jet, can land just about anywhere and fly at a much lower altitude." He eyed her mischievously. "Would you like me to take you up in one and show you what it can do?"

"No, thanks," she said hurriedly. "I'll take your word for it."

As they were leaving, they ran into Dinos Melettis, Niko's second-in-command. "Bring her to dinner," he insisted, after the introductions were made. "Come today. We have nothing on the board until later in the week, which makes it a good night to relax with friends, and Toula would love to meet the lady in your life. Toula," he added to Emily in an aside, "is my wife."

They accepted the invitation and had a delightful evening. "Never before has Niko brought a ladyfriend to our home," Toula confided to Emily in her careful English. "He is very enamored of you, I think."

The way he pressed his knee against hers under cover of the table and muttered between courses that he couldn't wait to get her alone again, Emily thought so, too. Yet for all that the passion between them burned brighter by the day, not once in all those weeks did they talk about the future. To do so would have shattered a present made forever uncertain by the demands of his job.

Although Emily did her best to live with that, what she couldn't get over, what terrified her, was the nature of the work that took him away from her, and the fact he always assigned himself to the most dangerous missions.

When she dared to ask him why, he said, "Because I have the most experience and the least to lose."

"But what about Vassili?" she pressed, referring to another colleague they'd bumped into one day at a kafenion in Athens. "You told me he's one of the most skilled pilots you've ever come across."

"He also has a wife and two-year-old son at home," Niko replied.

His answer and all it implied chilled her to the bone.

One Sunday evening in mid November, they stood on the terrace outside his penthouse, sipping cognac and admiring the night view of Athens spread out below. But even though Niko appeared perfectly relaxed and content, a shimmering tension emanated from him, one Emily now recognized all too well, and she braced herself for what she knew was coming.

He didn't leave her in suspense very long. "I'm off again tomorrow," he said, as deceptively casual as if he were planning to play golf, but then added guardedly, "I might be gone a bit longer than usual."

In other words, this undertaking was riskier than most. "How much longer?"

"Three days, possibly four, but you can count on my being home by the weekend."

"Where to this time?"

"Africa again."

A typically ambiguous reply. He never elaborated about his exact itinerary, was always deliberately vague about why he had to go. *Delivering food and clothing to an orphanage...survival kits to a village cut off by a landslide...a medivac rescue...supplies to a field hospital,* he'd say offhandedly when she questioned him, then quickly change the subject.

But she knew it was never as straightforward or simple as he made it sound. If it were, he wouldn't come back looking so drawn. He wouldn't wake up bathed in sweat from a nightmare he refused to talk about. He wouldn't reach for her in the night as if she was all that stood between him and an abyss of utter despair.

"Where in Africa?" she persisted now.

"Does it matter?"

"Yes, it matters."

He hesitated and she hung on tenterhooks, waiting for his answer. When he told her, it was so much worse than anything she'd let herself contemplate, was such a hellhole of violence, devastation and peril, that she felt sick to her stomach.

She knew how she was supposed to respond. Calmly. With acceptance. And she couldn't do it. Not this time. Instead she started to cry.

"Ah, Emily," he murmured and held her close. "Don't do this. We still have tonight."

But she'd broken the rules and commited the cardinal sin of wanting tomorrow, and tonight was no longer enough.

Her tears caught him off guard. Angry with himself for distressing her, and with her, too, because she'd known from the first the career he'd chosen for himself, he said, "This is why, until now, I've avoided serious involvement with a woman. When I take off on assignment, my attention has to focus on people whose lives, for one reason or another, are in jeopardy. Worrying about you is a distraction I neither need nor can afford."

"I know." She swiped at her tears and attempted a valiant smile. "I'm being selfish and unreasonable. Sorry. I don't know what came over me. I'm not usually so emotional."

She hadn't been during the early days of their affair, he had to admit. Lately, though, the smallest thing seemed to upset her. Just last week, he'd gone to pick her up at the villa and found her all teary-eyed over a bird that had flown into a window and broken its neck. He wasn't very happy about the poor thing's untimely end, either, but she knew every bit as well as he did that death was part of life and didn't differentiate between old and young, guilty or innocent.

"If this is harder than you thought it would be and want out," he said now, "just say so. I'll understand."

She closed her eyes against another bright gleam of tears and shook her head. "More than anything else, I want you."

"Even with all the baggage I bring with me?"

"Even then."

He wanted her, too. Enough that he'd willfully overstepped the limitations he'd imposed on his personal life prior to knowing her. And at that moment, with her body haloed in the nimbus of light from the city, and her beautiful face upturned to his in vulnerable despair, he had never wanted her more. "Then come with me now," he whispered, drawing her inside and up the spiral staircase to the bedroom. "Let's not waste the few hours remaining before I have to leave you."

That night, unlike some when his desire for her overrode any attempt at finesse, he loved her at leisure. Caring only about pleasing her and driving the demons of fear from her mind, he kissed her all over. He seduced her with his hands, with his tongue. He hoarded the scent and texture of her skin. He watched the slow, hot flush of passion steal over her, tasted the honeyed warmth between her thighs. He commited to memory the tight rosy buds of her nipples and the little cry she made when she came.

When at last he entered her, he did so slowly. Wished he could remain forever locked within her tight, silken warmth. And when his body betrayed him, as it always did, he surrendered all that he was or ever wanted to be. *"S'agapo, chrisi mou kardhia,"* he groaned. "I love you, Emily."

He awoke just after dawn, left the bed quietly and in order not to disturb her, took his clothes and went to the guest bathroom to shower and prepare for the day ahead. When he was done, he returned to the master suite and stood a moment, watching her sleep.

Early sunlight caught the sweep of her eyelashes. Cast a pearly shadow along the line of her collarbone. Her hair fell in captivating disorder over the pillow. Her arm reached across to his side of the bed as if seeking him.

He wanted to touch her. Put his mouth on hers and whisper her name. And knew he could not, because doing so would make it impossible for him to leave her.

Turning away, he picked up his bag and quietly let himself out of the penthouse.

CHAPTER TEN

COMPULSIVE worry took over her life and gnawed at it until it was full of holes. Holes that tormented her every waking hour and haunted her dreams.

Niko had willingly flown into an area where none of the rules of the civilized world applied. Every day, news reports of unspeakable atrocities made the headlines. Murder, banditry and torture were commonplace; starvation and disease had reached epic proportions.

Intellectually Emily recognized that helpless men, women and children desperately needed the kind of humanitarian relief people like Niko dedicated themselves to providing. But the Geneva Convention had no meaning for the perpetrators of the crimes being committed, and those trying to help were finding themselves subjected to increasing violence, some of it so extreme they were being evacuated for their own safety. Others had lost their lives for the principles they believed in.

What if he became one of them?

Self-fulfilling prophecies were dangerous in themselves, she realized, and in an effort to divert her mind into other channels, she turned to anger. Why had he left without saying goodbye? To spare them both the pain of a farewell, or because he cared more about strangers than he did about her?

But that line of reasoning merely shamed her. How could any thinking person, let alone a woman who'd made caring for those unable to care for themselves her vocation, be so blindly selfish? His compassion for others was one of the main reasons she loved him so desperately.

She then turned to optimism, telling herself that he was the best at what he did. He'd never lost a pilot and to make sure he never did, insisted every man involved in his operation, himself included, constantly hone his skills to remain at the top of his game. "Emergencies aren't the exception," he'd once told her, "they're the rule, and we're always prepared."

How could she not support such heroic measures? How could she resent his taking a few days away from her to make a difference in the lives of those so much less fortunate? By Saturday, she'd be in his arms again and the nightmare would have passed.

But the weekend came and went with no word from him. By Monday morning she couldn't hold herself together any longer and broke down in front of Pavlos. "I'm worried sick about him," she sobbed.

"That's what happens when you get involved with a man like him."

"You make it sound as if I had a choice about falling in love with him, but that's not how it works. It happened despite my better judgment."

"What can I say? I tried to warn you, girl, but you wouldn't listen and now you're caught in a trap with no way out."

"You're not helping," she wailed, swabbing at her tears.

He looked at her sadly. "Because I can't help. I learned a long time ago that where my son is concerned, worrying's a waste of time. He's going to do what he wants to do, and to hell with anyone or anything that stands in his way."

"How do you sleep at night, Pavlos?" she cried bitterly. "How do you turn your back on your only child and not give a damn whether he lives or dies?"

"Years of practice at being unpleasant, girl. The way I see it, if I make him dislike me enough, he'll survive just to annoy me. My advice to you is the same as it's always been: forget you ever met him. You're better off not knowing what he's up to."

But she'd passed that point of no return weeks ago, and the uncertainty of not knowing was killing her. Another endless night of pacing the floor, and she'd lose her mind, so that afternoon while Pavlos napped, she took a taxi to the airfield. Better to learn the worst than be held hostage to the horrors her imagination so willingly conjured up.

The big hangar stood empty and only five aircraft waited on the tarmac, but several cars were parked outside the flat-roofed office. Not bothering to knock, she opened the door and stepped inside.

Huddled around a chart spread out on the desk in the reception area, three men and a woman talked quietly. She recognized Dinos and Toula; the other two were strangers. On hearing the door open, all four looked up and at the sight of her, their conversation subsided into a ghastly silence that fairly screamed of disaster.

"Emily." Dinos came forward with a smile. But it was a poor, pitiful effort that soon faded.

"You know something," she said, every fear she'd entertained over the last week crystalizing into certainty. "Tell me."

He didn't pretend not to understand what she was talking about. "We know nothing," he told her quietly. "We are waiting—"

"Waiting for what? To learn he's been taken captive? That he's dead?"

"There is no reason to assume either. He is a little overdue, that is all."

"Overdue?" She heard the shrill edge of hysteria climbing in her voice and could do nothing to control it. "He's *missing*, Dinos!"

At that, Toula came forward and grasped her hands. "*Ohi*. Do not distress yourself, Emily. He will return. He always does."

"How do you know that? When was the last time anyone heard from him?"

Again that awful silence descended, so thick it caused a tightness in her chest. She'd experienced the same suffocating sensation once before, the day she learned her parents had been killed.

"Thursday," Dinos finally said. "But in itself, that is not necessarily significant. Sometimes it is safer to remain incommunicado in hostile territory than risk giving away one's whereabouts."

He was lying and doing it badly. "You don't have the foggiest idea where he is or what's happened to him, do you?"

His gaze faltered and he shrugged miserably. "No."

She felt the tears pressing hot behind her eyes and fought to control them. "When were you planning to tell me? Or aren't I entitled to be kept informed?"

"Today I come to you," Toula interrupted. "That is why I am here first. To learn what is latest news and hope it will be good."

Hollow with despair, Emily said, "How do you do it, Toula? If Dinos doesn't show up when he's supposed to, how do hold on to your sanity?"

"I believe," she said, her dark eyes filled with pity. "I pray to God, and I wait. It is all I can do. It is what you must do also. You must not lose faith."

"Toula's right, Emily." Dinos touched her shoulder gently. "You must believe that whatever has happened, Niko will find his way back to you."

"*Neh*...yes." The other two men nodded vigorously.

"There is nothing you can do here," Dinos continued, guiding her to the door. "Go back to the villa and wait for him there. I will call you the very second I have anything to report. Where did you leave your car?"

"I came by taxi."

"Then Toula will drive you home."

Dinos didn't call. No one did. Instead as she was passing through the foyer late on Tuesday afternoon, she heard the sound of a vehicle departing down the driveway. A moment later, the doorbell rang. Fearing the worst, she rushed to answer and came face-to-face with Niko.

Bathed in the orange glow cast by the setting sun, he leaned against the wall, his left arm held close to his chest. "I hear you've been inquiring about me," he said.

She'd prayed for just such a miracle so often in the

last few days. Had rehearsed exactly what she'd say, what she'd do. But now that it had come to pass, she was at a loss for words and simply stared at him.

In one respect, he looked much as he had that long-ago day they'd met at the airport. Same blue jeans, open-necked shirt and black leather bomber jacket. Same rangy height, black hair and mesmerizing green eyes. But that man had been the picture of health. So strong and invincible, he could have taken on the world single-handed and emerged victorious. Had picked up his father as if Pavlos weighed no more than an infant.

This one looked ill. Gaunt, hollow-eyed and barely able to support his own weight, let alone anyone else's. The sight paralyzed Emily. Left her speechless with dismay.

"Well, Emily?"

Collecting herself with a mighty effort, she said, "You haven't shaved in days."

The ghost of a smile touched his mouth. "Somehow, I'd expected a warmer welcome. Perhaps I should have stayed away longer."

"Perhaps you should have," she said, shock giving way to irrational anger. "Perhaps you shouldn't have come back at all."

His gaze drifted over her and came to rest on her face that she knew was ravaged with pent-up misery. "Emily, *karthula*," he murmured, a wealth of regret in his tone.

Her insides sagged. Melted into tears that flooded her eyes and washed her aching heart clean of everything but the burning need to touch him. To feel the tensile strength of muscle and bone beneath his clothing, the steady beat of the pulse at the corner of his jaw. To prove once and for all that she wasn't dreaming and he wasn't a ghost, he was real. "I didn't mean that," she cried, launching herself at him.

He grimaced and fended her off with an involuntary grunt of pain, reinforcing her initial impression that something was terribly wrong. His eyes, she noticed belatedly, held a feverish glint and a film of sweat beaded his upper lip.

"What happened to you?" she whispered.

His careless shrug turned into a flinch. "Just a minor scratch to my shoulder. Nothing to get excited about."

"I'll be the judge of that," she said, drawing him over the threshold.

He stepped inside, but staggered against a table just inside the door, sending it and the vase of flowers it held crashing to the marble floor. The noise brought Damaris and Giorgios running from the kitchen.

"I need a hand here," Emily panted, buckling under Niko's weight as she struggled to hold him upright. "Help me get him upstairs to a bed."

From the rear of the house, Pavlos spoke. "My room is closer. Bring him this way."

Between the three of them, they half-led, half-dragged Niko the length of the central hall and into the suite. As they eased him onto the bed, the front of his jacket fell open to reveal a spreading bloodstain on the upper left corner of his shirt.

The housekeeper gasped faintly but Emily immediately went into professional mode. "Pass me my scissors, Damaris," she ordered calmly, peeling off his jacket. "I'll have to cut away his shirt. Giorgios, I need clean towels, disinfectant and hot water."

Under the shirt she found a blood-soaked dressing covering a ragged puncture wound slightly to the right of his shoulder joint and just below his collarbone. "I'd say being shot amounts to a bit more than a minor scratch, Niko," she said, hoping nothing of her inner panic showed in her voice.

"What makes you think I've been shot?"

"I'm a nurse. I know a bullet injury when I see it, and this one's infected. A doctor needs to look at it."

"A doctor already has. Who do you think patched me up?"

"Someone in too much of a hurry from the looks of it. I'm taking you to the hospital."

He closed his eyes, weariness etched in every line of his face. "You'll do nothing of the sort. If I wanted to spend another night in a hospital, I wouldn't have had Dinos bring me here."

"I'm not Dinos, and I'm not taking any chances with your health."

"And I'm not a child."

"Then stop behaving like one and do as I ask."

"Forget it. I didn't just escape one hell to be thrown into another."

She looked for support from Pavlos who stood impassively at the foot of the bed, his gnarled old fingers gripping its rail. "For heaven's sake, will you talk some sense into your son, Pavlos?"

He shook his head. "No point trying, girl. His mind's made up."

Frustrated, she swung her attention back to Niko. "Fine. Have it your way. But don't blame me if you end up dead."

He opened his eyes a slit. "As if you'd let that happen, *karthula*. You're my angel of mercy."

"Let's see if you still think so after I'm finished with you."

She put on a pair of surgical gloves and began her task. As far as she could tell, he'd sustained no permanent damage. She found no sign of an exit point when she rolled him over on his side, which meant the bullet had lodged in his flesh and hopefully been removed by the doctor who'd treated him.

"Yeah," he mumbled, when she asked. "I told him he could hang it on his key chain."

He'd been lucky. As gunshot injuries went, she'd seen much worse, with major organs and bones damaged beyond repair. Nonetheless, the point where the bullet had entered his shoulder was ugly, with swelling around the sutures and angry red lines radiating from the wound site. And therein lay the reason for her alarm. "When did this happen, Niko?"

"A few days ago."

Typical vague answer, she thought, exasperated. "Were you hospitalized?"

"Overnight."

"Did you receive a tetanus shot?"

"*Neh*. In my other arm."

"Are you sure?"

"I was shot in the shoulder, Emily, not the brain. Yes, I'm sure. I can still feel where they shoved the needle in."

One piece of good news at least. "You'll be feeling this, as well," she warned, knowing she was going to hurt him. But he'd left her no choice. Bits of debris from the dressing and heaven only knew what else were adhered to his sutures and had to be removed. "It isn't going to be pleasant."

"Do what you have to do and get it over with," he ground out.

Brave words and nothing less than she'd expect from a man who refused to admit to any sort of weakness, but as she probed at the raw edges of his wound with surgical tweezers, then irrigated the area with warm water, the tendons on his neck stood out like cords.

Finally, with a clean dressing in place, she said, "That's about it for now."

"Good. Hand me my jacket and I'll be on my way."

He struggled to sit up, turned gray in the face and toppled back against the pillows.

Her patience snapped at that. "Try not to be a bigger fool than you already are, Niko Leonidas! The only place you're going is to bed, and you won't need your jacket for that."

He eyed her malevolently. "*Ade apo tho re,* Emily. You're beginning to annoy me."

"Not half as much as you're annoying me. Giorgios, grab his good arm and help me get him upstairs. We'll put him in the room adjoining mine—and I suggest," she added sweetly, addressing Niko again, "that you don't fight me on this. You've suffered enough pain for one night."

Although his glower was black as thunder, he offered no further resistance except to mutter, "Your bedside manner could use improvement, woman. Escaping rebel forces was a walk in the park compared to this."

But by the time they got him upstairs and into the bed Damaris had rushed to prepare, he had no fight left in him. "Clean sheets," he murmured on a ragged sigh. "Never thought they'd feel so good."

A moment later, he was asleep.

Emily left the connecting door between their rooms open and checked on him frequently during the remainder of the night, concerned as much about his rising temperature as the injury causing it. At one point, he opened his eyes and stared at her in the dim light as if he didn't know who she was. Another time, she heard him muttering her name deliriously and, placing the back of her hand against his cheek, realized he was burning up. Without knowing the extent of any vessel damage, she daren't give him aspirin and had to settle for sponging him down with tepid water. It helped temporarily, but never managed to subdue the fever completely.

From the outset, she'd known that what she could do for him would be, at best, a stopgap measure, and had hoped the new day would make him more amenable to accepting the kind of treatment only a physician could provide. But when, despite her efforts, his temperature spiked dangerously just before dawn, she knew she couldn't afford to wait for his permission, and phoned Pavlos's family physician.

She and the doctor had developed a strong mutual respect in the months since she'd come to Greece, and he brushed aside her apologies for disturbing him at such an ungodly hour. "I'll come at once," he said, after listening without interruption as she related the situation.

He arrived just as the sun was rising, subjected Niko

to a thorough examination, treated the infected gunshot wound and wrote out a prescription for topical and oral antibiotics. "Be glad you have a first-class nurse in residence, young man," he told Niko, when he was done. "You'd be hospitalized otherwise, whether or not you like it."

Then turning to Emily before he left, he added quietly, "Change his dressing regularly, and make sure he takes. in plenty of fluids to replace what he's lost. If you're at all concerned that he's not getting enough, don't hesitate to call and we'll rehydrate him intravenously. Other than that, bed rest and medication should do the trick. Unless I hear from you sooner, I'll stop by again in the morning."

For two days, Emily was unconditionally happy. She had her man safe, close by and on the road to recovery. Although he slept a good part of the time, he always sensed when she was near. "Hey, angel," he'd murmur drowsily, fumbling for her hand, and her heart would swell with love.

The reprieve was short-lived. By the Thursday, he was chafing at being confined to bed and insisted that moving around was the best way to regain his strength. On Friday, he made it downstairs for breakfast, which was all it took for hostilities to resume between him and his father. And as usual, she found herself caught in the middle.

"What are you doing down here?" Pavlos demanded testily when he saw him.

"I have better things to do than lie around in bed all day, old man."

"Such as what?" Emily put in, horribly afraid she knew the answer.

"Unfinished business," he replied cryptically.

"If by that you mean going back to Africa and getting shot again, forget it."

"Don't tell me what to do, Emily. You're not my keeper."

"No, I'm the woman who loves you."

"More fool you," Pavlos chipped in, "because you have a jealous rival, my dear, and it's called death. He flirts with it constantly and has done for years."

"*Pre sto diavolo*—go to the devil, old man!" Niko retorted irascibly. "You know nothing about what motivates me, and even less about my relationship with Emily."

"I know she deserves a man willing to give her more than you ever will."

"Someone like you, I suppose?"

"At least she wouldn't be pacing the floor wondering where I am half the time."

"Because you can barely make it as far as the front door under your own steam."

They were like two lions fighting over the day's kill, the older one battling for dominance over a younger, more powerful adversary, and it sickened her.

"I could strangle the pair of you!" she exploded. "You're both so full of Greek pride, you can't see past it to what you're doing to one another. Or maybe you can, and you don't care."

"Stay out of it, Emily," Niko warned her. "This is between him and me."

"I won't!" she said, so angry she almost stamped her foot. "Pavlos is your father, for pity's sake, and you're his only child. You're all the family either of you has left and it's past time you put this senseless feud aside and made peace with one another. I know I would, were I in your place."

"But you're not," Niko said, so coldly that she shivered, "so can we agree to disagree and leave it at that? What you and I do in the bedroom is one thing, but you don't hear me interfering in your life the rest of the time. I'd appreciate it if you'd afford me the same sort of courtesy."

If he'd slapped her, she couldn't have been more shocked. "I thought we were about more than what happened in the bedroom."

He looked almost as shattered as she felt. "We are," he muttered, raking a furious hand through his hair. "I love you, you know that."

She'd once believed those three words were all it took for a man and a woman to make their relationship work, but she'd been wrong. They meant nothing if they came wrapped in resentment and soured what was once beautiful.

"Maybe you do," she said dully, "but not nearly enough."

CHAPTER ELEVEN

BEFORE he could respond to her accusation, let alone refute it, she was gone from the room. Seconds later, the front door slammed, drowning out the sound of her racing footsteps.

"That went well." Pavlos sneered. "Have anything planned for an encore?"

"Butt out," he growled, and turned to go after her.

"Do her a favor." The old man's voice followed him down the hall. "Let her alone. She's better off without you."

Maybe she was, but it wasn't in Niko's nature to give up without a fight. He'd be dead by now, if it were. And they'd invested too much of themselves in each other for it to end like this, over careless words spoken in the heat of the moment.

Wrenching open the door with his good hand, he stood on the step and shaded his eyes against the late morning sun. She'd already cleared the circular parking area and was swerving past an outraged peacock, which happened to be obstructing her path as she fled across the south lawn.

Intent on stopping her, Niko gave chase. Another dumb

move, he soon realized. Every bone in his body crunched as he hit the ground running. He covered no more than about forty meters before he was gasping for breath, and his shoulder was throbbing almost as badly as it had when he'd first been shot. He hadn't a hope of catching anything that moved, let alone a woman bent on putting as much distance between him and her as she was. And if that wasn't indignity enough, his father was now standing in the open doorway, watching the whole debacle.

"Emily!" The effort of raising his voice almost brought Niko to his knees.

She swung back to face him. *"What?"*

He couldn't answer. His lungs were bursting and black dots danced before his eyes. Humiliated by his weakness, not to mention his audience, he bent over, his chest heaving.

Seeing the shape he was in, she made her slow way back to him. "I already know how cruel you can be," she said, "but I had no idea you were stupid, too. You've probably made your wound bleed again and undone all the progress you made. Keep it up and you'll wind up in hospital, whether or not it's where you want to be."

"I want to be with you," he wheezed.

"Whatever for? We have nothing in common outside the bedroom, remember?"

"We both know that's not true."

"Then why did you say it?"

"Because I was—*am* frustrated as hell. I can no more tolerate not being in charge of my life than I can abide being on the receiving end of my father's grudging hospitality. The sooner I move back to the penthouse, the better for everyone."

"You're in no condition to go back to the penthouse," she informed him flatly.

"Too bad. I'm going anyway. Pavlos and I bring out the worst in each other. We always have." He grabbed at her hand. "Come with me, angel. It's Friday and we have the whole weekend ahead. Let's spend it together, making up for lost time."

"I don't know about that. Given your recent history, I doubt you're going to be feeling very…energetic."

"My upper torso might not be quite up to par, but below the waist everything's working just fine," he assured her. "Fully recovered or not, I want you so badly it hurts. More than that, I need you."

"You're only saying that to get your own way."

Annoyed, he snapped, "I thought you knew me better than that, Emily, but since you apparently don't, let me make one thing clear. I've yet to resort to lying in order to get a woman to sleep with me, and if you think that's what I'm doing now, then perhaps you should just keep running in the other direction and not look back." He released her hand and took a step away. "There, you're free. Off you go."

She bit her lip. A lone tear drizzled down her cheek. "I can't. I love you."

"Then why are we standing here arguing?"

"I don't know," she said and, closing the distance between them, buried her face against his neck.

"Go with him," Pavlos said, when she told him Niko was set on returning to the penthouse after lunch, then surprised her by adding, "and don't worry about being back here on Monday. Stay a week, or however long it takes to get him back on his feet. Judging from what I just saw, he's not quite the iron man he'd like to think he is."

"But you hired me to look after you," she protested, although they both knew he hadn't needed a resident nurse in days.

"Right now, he needs you a lot more than I do."

"I'm afraid you're right."

"Then pack a bag and be on your way. How are you getting into the city?"

"By taxi."

"No need. Giorgios will take you in the Mercedes. It'll be more comfortable for superhero."

She dropped a kiss on his cheek. "Thank you, Pavlos. You're an old softie under all that grump."

He swatted her away with rough affection. "Watch your mouth, girl, and don't be so quick with the gratitude. My son's about as cussed an individual as you could ask to meet, and I don't expect you'll have an easy time with him."

But she didn't care if she didn't have easy, as long as she had time.

They'd no sooner arrived at the penthouse than it started to pour with rain. Huge drops danced wildly on the terrace. Veils of cloud swirled outside the floor-to-ceiling windows, bringing an early dusk to the afternoon and obscuring the outside world. They didn't care. Wrapped in splendid isolation and with days of being together stretching before them, they didn't need sunshine. All they needed was each other.

That night, they sent out for dinner, ate it by candlelight and retired early. Knowing the day had wearied him, Emily didn't anticipate they'd make love, nor did she mind. She was happy simply to lie beside Niko in his big bed and feel the steady beat of his heart beneath her hand because, a week ago, she'd been afraid she'd never do so again. But he was alive, they were together, and that was all that mattered.

Proximity, though, was a powerful aphrodisiac and desire stole over them in quiet waves, with none of the tempestuous urgency they were used to. He turned on his side and his leg brushed hers, hair-roughened skin against smooth, warm thigh. His hand whispered over her hips to the hem of her short nightie and drew it up past her bottom. His mouth searched out hers and he uttered her name in muted invitation when she reached down and found him already hard.

All silken, pulsing heat, he positioned himself between her legs and slid inside her. They moved together in a slow, sweet symphony, adoring one another with soft murmurs of love. They climaxed in unison, the passion unspooling between them, lazy as waves rolling ashore. They fell asleep locked in each other's arms, sated with pleasure, and awoke to a morning washed clean and sparkling with sunshine.

So began a week she knew she would remember for the rest of her life. Sometimes they slept late. Other times, they went grocery shopping, arriving early at the markets to choose from a bewildering selection of food, and coming home loaded with goodies. Succulent lamb for souvlaki, or ground beef for moussaka. Fresh prawns and squid, cheese and olives for mezedes.

Ignoring Niko, who laughed and reminded her they were buying for two, not an army, she lingered at the

fruit and vegetable stands, choosing jewel-toned eggplant, vivid green peppers and bright red tomatoes, as
well as lemons, tangerines and melons. She went to the
bakery for bread still warm from the oven, and a quaint
little shop at the entrance to the Plaka that sold honey,
coffee, yogurt and nuts.

She learned to make tzaziki and saganaki. Even tried
her hand at baklava. Although he had a housekeeper
who usually came in every couple of days when he was
in residence, Emily sent her away, preferring to change
the bed linens and take care of the laundry herself, while
Niko caught up by phone with what was happening at
the airfield.

They took walks around the city. Visited museums
and ancient churches. Explored art galleries and antique
shops. Sometimes they'd go out for a meal. Mostly they
stayed home, preferring to be alone.

They made love whenever and wherever the mood
took them. Suddenly, urgently, in the late afternoon,
on the rug in front of the fire in the living room, with
the scent of burning apple wood filling the air.
Sleepily, in the middle of the night, spurred by heaven
only knew what dreams might have woken them.
Wildly, hilariously, on the desk in his study, while he
tried to conduct a serious phone conversation with
Dinos at the office.

They lazed on the big overstuffed couch in the living
room and read or listened to music, taking unhurried
pleasure in simply being in the same room together.

It was like being married, except marriage was one
subject they never discussed. To do so would have meant
talking about the future which, in turn, would have

brought that other world into focus. The one that took him away from her. Better to live in a fool's paradise.

But that dreaded other world intruded anyway, evidenced by a restlessness in him that increased as he regained his strength. Phone calls to the office weren't enough to satisfy him. He started spending time at the airfield again, an hour or two at first until, by the middle of the second week, he was back at work pretty much full-time. Domesticity had palled, even if his desire for her hadn't. He was raring for something more challenging than building fires or checking the firmness of tomatoes in the marketplace.

"I'm the boss," he said when she remonstrated with him. "Bosses are supposed to lead, not sit at home and let others do the job for them."

Matters came to a head on the third Sunday. All day, he'd been on edge. Finally, with evening closing in and Christmas carols playing on the stereo, he poured them each a glass of wine and came to sit next to her on the couch. "I have something to tell you, *karthula*," he began.

She knew what it was, without his having to elaborate. "You're leaving again."

"Yes."

"When?"

"Tomorrow."

"With so little advance notice?"

"Not exactly. I've known for a couple of days now that I'd be going."

"Where to this time?"

He looked at the fire, at the red roses she'd arranged in a vase on a side table, at the book lying facedown on the arm of the couch. He looked anywhere but at her, and her stomach turned over in a sickening lurch of prescience. "Oh, no," she whispered on a trembling breath. "Please tell me you're not going back to that horrendous place."

"I must," he said.

"Why? To get shot again, fatally this time?"

"People there are in terrible straits and they need help. And I need you to understand that I can't turn my back on them."

Anger welled up in her and she struck out at him, slamming her fist against his right arm. "What about what *I* need, Niko, or doesn't that matter to you?"

"I have given you all of myself."

"No. You give me what's left over after you take care of other people."

"Not so. You're what keeps me sane when the world around me erupts into madness. Before we met, I didn't care if I never came home. Now, I live for the time that we can be together again."

"Sure you do," she said, tears clogging her voice. "I'm the warm body that makes you forget the horrors you left behind, but it doesn't change the fact that you care more about strangers than you'll ever care about me."

"I don't deserve that, Emily."

"I don't deserve to be left waiting and wondering if you'll come back to me in one piece or a body bag."

"No, you don't," he said, setting down his wine and going to stand at the glass doors leading to the terrace, "which is why I never promised you forever. I've always known I couldn't give it to you."

So there it was, the end of the affair, delivered with the

uncompromising honesty that was his trademark. They'd
finally run out of borrowed time and the tomorrow she'd
tried so hard to postpone stood on the doorstep.

Hollow with pain, she said, "We were never a good
fit, were we?"

"Never," he admitted, after a horrible, tension-
filled pause.

"Always a ships-passing-in-the-night sort of thing."

"That about covers it."

But his voice was all rusty, as if he'd choked on a
peanut. And she…she was perilously close to sobbing.
She had followed in her parents' footsteps and gambled
everything for the pleasure of living in the moment.
And in doing so had lost everything. Their biggest mistake had become hers, too.

"So…o…o." She drew out the word on a long, quivering sigh. "I guess this is goodbye."

"I guess it is."

"It's for the best."

"Probably."

She dug her fingernails into her palms; bit the inside
of her lip until she tasted blood. "I'll collect my stuff
and get out of here. You must have a lot to do and don't
need me underfoot."

He didn't argue, just straightened his shoulders and
turned back to confront her, his face unreadable. "Fine.
I'll drive you back to the villa."

And subject them both to more suffering? "No," she
said. "There's a taxi stand right outside your building.
I'll take a cab."

She left her untouched wineglass next to his and
went upstairs to the bedroom to throw clothes, shoes and

toiletries haphazardly into her suitcases. She had to get away quickly, before she fell down on her knees and begged him not to leave her.

At last she was ready. All that remained to be done was walking away from him. If there'd been a back entrance to the penthouse, she'd have taken it and spared them both the agony of a last goodbye, but he remained in the living room which opened off the long hall leading to the foyer.

"I think I've got everything," she said, staring straight ahead because, if she looked into his jade-green eyes one more time, she'd lose it completely.

"Anything you've forgotten, I'll send to the villa."

"Thanks." She swallowed painfully. "Take care of yourself."

"You, too."

She tried to open the door. Fumbled with a latch, which refused to budge. Was dimly aware of movement in the room behind her and renewed her efforts, not wanting him to come and help.

She could not look at him, or speak to him, or let him come near her again. She could not.

Eyes streaming, she made one last effort. The blasted latch clicked, but still the door refused to budge because, she realized, staring blurrily through her tears, he was holding it shut. Over the tormented thud of her heart she heard his voice so close behind her that his breath wafted warm and damp over her nape. "Emily, don't go," he begged. "It doesn't have to end like this."

She wilted, empty of pride and so full of hurt that she had no fight left in her. Dropping her luggage, she turned in his arms and clung to him, accepting that she was as helpless to refuse him as she was to change the course he'd set himself long before he met her. "I'm so afraid for you," she sobbed.

"I know, sweetheart," he said, kissing her eyes, her tears. "I know."

Hounded by the remorseless hunger, which had held them in thrall from the first, they sought the only comfort left to them and went at each other like mad things, giving the lie to any notion that being apart was better than being together. She clawed at him, desperate in her need, raking her hands down his shirt-front to tear open the buttons. He pinned her against the door, yanked up her skirt and ripped off her panties. Freeing himself from his jeans, he hoisted her off her feet, pulled her legs around his waist, and drove into her as if she was all that stood between him and damnation.

After that, there was no question of her leaving. Instead they tried to do what they'd done so successfully for over two weeks. They tried to play house.

He sorted the clothes he'd take with him in the morning. She folded them, the way a good wife would, and put them neatly in the canvas carryall that held enough to see him through as many days as he'd be gone. Too many, she noticed, counting three pairs of jeans, eight shirts and as many changes of undershorts and socks.

They tried to talk about anything except where he'd be tomorrow night at that time, but the conversation stalled at every turn and they'd subside into stricken silence before making another valiant attempt at normality.

They sat down to dinner, but abandoned the table when neither of them could eat. Their gazes met and held, and broke apart again when the emotion in their depths threatened to overwhelm them.

"Let's stop this," he finally said. "Come to bed, *khriso mou*. Let me hold you in my arms and love you one last time before I go."

She tried, fusing her body with his in a desperate, hopeless attempt to stop time. Amassing his every word, his every touch, and hoarding them against an empty future. She wished she could shut down her mind and simply listen to her body. But the specter of his flying off into the teeth of danger, of death, haunted her. It left her drained, deprived of everything that gave her life meaning. "Please don't go," she finally beseeched him. "If you love me at all, please stay and keep me with you."

"I can't," he said.

And she couldn't, either. He was an adventurer, at heart as much a rebel as those he fought against, albeit for different reasons. Risking life and limb gave him a rush she'd never understand. She needed stability—a real home, a husband, children—and she couldn't live suspended indefinitely on the fine edge of sanity, wanting what he couldn't give her.

Light from the en suite bathroom filtered into the room, crowding the corners with shadows but providing enough illumination for her to watch him sleeping. With the hours racing by much too fast, she committed to memory the curve of his mouth, the clean line of his jaw and cheekbones, his lashes, so long and thick he could sweep a street with them.

Beyond the windows, the sky grew imperceptibly lighter, precursor of a new and hellish dawn shouting that today was their last day. She did not want to hear or see it, and closing her eyes, she pressed her body close to his, inhaling through every pore the very essence of all that he was.

6:30 a.m.

Time to make a move.

Deactivating the alarm clock before it disturbed the silence, Niko took a moment to savor the warmth of her body next to his. Feigning sleep himself, he'd listened to her crying softly throughout the night. It had taken every last milligram of self-control for him not to reach for her and tell her what he knew she wanted to hear.

I'll send someone else in my place, and stay with you. We'll get married, make a home together, raise a family.

Exhaustion had claimed her before temptation got the better of him. Now she slept, with strands of her pale blond hair spread over his shoulder as if to bind him to her. She looked young, beautiful. Defenseless as a child, and unutterably sad.

He had done that to her. What had started out to be no more than a harmless flirtation designed to show Pavlos that his trust in her was misplaced, had blossomed out of control. Niko had seen it coming, but had done nothing to put an end to it. She had captivated him like no other woman he'd ever met, and he'd made the fatal mistake of falling in love with her.

Worse, selfish bastard that he was, he'd let her fall in love with him. And now he had to leave her because he knew that happy-ever-after wasn't in the cards. Of his fifteen employees, ten were pilots. The youngest was single and still living at home. Five of the remaining nine were divorced, victims of a career that demanded too much of the women who'd once loved them enough to take their names and bear their children.

He did not want that for her, for them. He'd rather lose her now, with the good memories still intact, than wait until all the joy and passion had turned bitter with resentment.

6:31 a.m.

Stealthily he eased himself off the bed, collected his clothes and, as he'd done before, went downstairs to shower and dress in the guest suite. As a rule, he stood under the jets an indecently long time because there was no telling when he'd next have access to hot water or clean towels. But that morning he made quick work of preparing for the day ahead.

6:49 a.m.

Ready to go. A better man than he'd ever be would have picked up his bag and left. He couldn't go without a last farewell, and went to the library to find pen and paper.

I love you enough to set you free to live the kind of life you're looking for, he wrote. *The man who can give it to you will be lucky indeed. Be happy, Emily.*

Then stopping by the living room, he plucked a rose from the bouquet she'd arranged, and stole back upstairs.

She lay exactly as he'd left her. He ached to kiss her. To whisper her name. To taste her mouth one more time.

For once, he did the right thing. He placed the note and the rose on his pillow and left her.

CHAPTER TWELVE

"HE'S gone again," Pavlos said, his wise old eyes absorbing everything in a single glance. "He's left you."

Too awash in misery to put a brave face on things, Emily collapsed into the chair next to his. "Yes."

"So what now?"

"I think I must go, too, Pavlos. There's nothing more for me here." Except a rose already wilting, a note that put a final end to hope and a heart in shreds.

"There's me."

She shook her head sadly. "I've taken advantage of your generosity too long already."

"Rubbish! You nursed me back to health, put up with my bad temper and—"

"And now you're well again." Or as well as he'd ever be. His hip had healed to a degree, but his eighty-six-year-old body was worn-out, and there wasn't a thing she or anyone else could do about it.

"You gave me a reason to get out of the bed in the morning," he insisted. "I've grown fond of you. You're like a daughter to me and will always have a place in my home."

For a moment, she was tempted. To be needed,

wanted; to be part of a family, however small…hadn't she longed for just such peace of mind and heart ever since she was nine? But common sense told her she'd find neither in this house. She'd never hear the doorbell without hoping it was Niko come to tell her he'd changed his mind, that he wanted forever after all, and he wanted it with her.

If Pavlos had been truly alone, it might have been different, but he had the devoted Giorgios and Damaris to take care of his daily needs, and a family doctor who visited three times a week. She'd be leaving him in good hands.

"I'm fond of you, too, and I'll never forget your kindness," she told him gently, "but my life is in Vancouver. I have a house there. Friends, a career, financial and professional obligations to honor."

"And I'm not enough to make you turn your back on them." He sighed and nodded acceptance. "Will you keep in touch?"

"Of course."

"I don't suppose I have to tell you that my son is a fool."

"No more than I was, Pavlos."

"I tried to warn you, girl."

"I know you did."

The trouble was, his warning had come too late. It had been too late from the moment she and Niko had set eyes on each other. The attraction between them had blazed out of control, instantaneous combustion bent on destroying anything that stood in its path. The fear that she might live to regret giving in to it had dissolved in the lilting excitement, the sheer *aliveness* of being in love. Nothing compared to it.

What she hadn't known was that when it ended, it

took more than it had ever bestowed. Without Niko she was empty, incomplete. She had known him less than three months and in that time he had turned her life upside down, stolen everything she had to give, and left her with nothing.

Or so she believed when she said goodbye to Pavlos. And perhaps, if she'd chosen a different career, she might have ascribed the mood swings and exhaustion she brought home with her to the unavoidable emotional fall-out of a love affair gone wrong. But nursing school had taught her well. She was attuned to her body and as the old year came to an end, she hardly needed a home pregnancy test to confirm the cause of the fatigue and faint but undeniable nausea that hounded her every waking hour.

The future Niko had insisted no one could predict was staring her in the face with a certainty that eliminated any possibility that she might one day come to forget him. He would be with her always in the shape of his child.

The realization shattered the blessed numbness, which had cushioned her since the day he'd left. She was a twenty-seven-year-old, highly trained medical professional, for pity's sake! Of all people, she should have known how to protect herself from an unplanned pregnancy. How could she have been so careless?

Except she hadn't been, nor had Niko. Even at their most spontaneous they'd taken precautions, to the point that he'd joked about buying condoms in bulk, to cut down on the number of trips to the drugstore! But there'd been a few times during their last two weeks together that they'd almost left it too late to be safe. Idiot that she was to have exposed herself to such risks, she must have conceived then.

Her doctor, whom she went to see in late January, soon put paid to that theory. "You're well into your second trimester, Emily. About sixteen weeks along, I'd say."

"I can't be." Unless…had they cut things too fine on the boat? Been too carried away by the newness of their affair to be as responsible as they should have been?

"Are you sure you last menstruated at the end of October?"

"Pretty sure," she said, vaguely recalling her period had been lighter than usual. Nothing more than spotting, but she hadn't paid much attention at the time. She'd been too busy falling in love.

"What about the father?"

"What about him?"

"Are you going to tell him?"

"No."

"Why not?"

"Because we're not together anymore. He's not into parenthood, at least with me."

That night, she lay in bed, surrounded by all the comforting things that spelled home. The blue and white toile de jouy wallpaper she'd hung herself. The handmade wedding ring quilt she'd bought at auction, three years ago. Her reproduction four-poster bed and matching rosewood bombe chest of drawers. The silver-framed photograph of her parents and two small oil paintings she'd found at an estate sale, the summer she'd graduated from nursing school.

They were proof she didn't need a man around, she

told herself. Closer to her due date she'd put a rocking chair in the alcove near the window, where she'd nurse her baby, and a white bassinet next to her bed. When he grew too big for that, she'd turn the second bedroom into a nursery. Paint clouds on the ceiling. Stencil unicorns and pixies on the walls—oh, and a guardian angel, because every child had to have a guardian angel, even if he couldn't have a father.

A father…Niko…

Memories of him rushed to the forefront of her mind. Of his warm breath tickling her neck when he leaned over to kiss her good morning. His mouth against hers, his voice in her ear.

Of his long, strong body and olive skin. The planes of his chest, the swell of muscle over his shoulder, the lean, taut curve of his buttocks.

Of his beautiful face, and his mesmerizing eyes and the way they turned dark when the passion he tried so hard to contain rode roughshod over him.

Of his laughter, his wicked sense of humor… *You've left me with an erection that would do a stallion proud, Emily….*

Oh, to hear him laugh again! To see him, to hold him!

As winter turned to spring, she struggled to put the past behind her, but it wasn't easy with his baby growing inside her. Wouldn't have been even if she wasn't pregnant.

Any mention of humanitarian aid brought him vividly alive in her mind. A melody they'd listened to together, the scent of aftershave on another man, a stranger, when it belonged only to him, were enough to turn a good day bad. He was in her heart, in her soul.

But in every other respect, she was alone. Alone and

pregnant, because although he'd paid lip service to loving her, when put to the test, the father of her unborn child chose to risk life and limb in some benighted corner of the world, rather than risk his heart to her.

Well, let him, she'd tell herself, furious at her own weakness. She'd had her fill of reluctant charity, growing up as she had in her aunt's house where she'd never been welcome. If Niko couldn't commit to her without reservation, she didn't want him at all.

Anger was so much easier to bear than grief, even if they did both boil down to the same thing in the end.

"Will you be able to manage financially?" her friends asked when they heard she was about to become a single parent.

"Yes," she said, the irony not escaping her that her baby's grandfather was responsible for the substantial savings she'd amassed. "I have it all planned out. I can work for another five months, then after the birth, take a year's maternity leave, and when that ends, hire a live-in nanny to look after the baby."

But her calculations misfired. On the twelfth of May when she was only thirty-three weeks into her pregnancy, and contrary to anything she or her doctors had reason to expect, she gave birth to a three pound, eleven ounce daughter.

As a nurse, she knew that a mildly preterm baby's chances of surviving without lasting complications were excellent. As a mother, she wore herself to a shadow fretting over the tiny, delicate creature who had taken her heart by storm from the second she entered the world.

She named her Helen and brought her home when

she weighed five pounds. "At least she looks all there," the well-meaning woman next door remarked, stopping by the next day to inspect the new arrival. "For a preemie, that is."

Emily's friends were somewhat more encouraging. "She's adorable, so petite and feminine," they agreed, flocking around the bassinet.

To Emily, she was the most beautiful baby ever born. She brought light to a life which, since the day Niko left, had been too often filled with darkness. Sitting in the rocking chair, with her baby at her breast and the dogwood trees blooming outside the window, Emily found a measure of peace that had eluded her for much too long.

Spring melded into summer. If it wasn't too hot, Emily would tuck Helen into her stroller and take her for walks in the park or along the seawall. She'd nurse her in the shade of a sun umbrella on the patio.

She'd kept her promise to stay in touch with Pavlos, and at first they'd exchanged frequent e-mails but, as the months came and went, they'd written to each other less often. He never mentioned Niko, had little to say about anything really, and she decided against telling him about her pregnancy. What was the point in upsetting him?

After Helen was born, she wasn't so sure she'd made the right decision. Would learning he was a grandfather bring a little joy into Pavlos's life, or merely create an even deeper rift between father and son? More to the point, could he keep it a secret from Niko?

She had no doubt that, should he find out she'd had his baby, Niko would feel obligated to do the honorable thing and marry her. And that, she knew, would merely invite long-term misery for everyone. He would never settle happily for domesticity, and she wouldn't—*couldn't* live with his career choice. No child needed a daredevil for a father. Better to have no father at all than one who, as Pavlos had once pointed out, flirted with death every time he went to work.

As summer advanced, Helen continued to thrive. Although still small for her age, she gained weight steadily, clocking in at over six and a half pounds when she was three months old.

One morning, Emily had put her down for her morning nap and was folding laundry at the kitchen counter when she received a distraught phone call from Giorgios. Pavlos had taken a turn for the worse and was not expected to recover. He had refused to be admitted to hospital and was asking for her.

"What about his son?" she said. "Has he been contacted?"

"We have tried, but he is far away."

Typical! she thought. Why stick close to home and your ailing father, when you could be somewhere else giving your all to strangers?

"Will you come, Emily?"

How could she refuse? Pavlos needed her. "Yes, but it'll take me a little time to make the arrangements."

"I am afraid he does not have much time left." Giorgios's voice broke. "He is tired of fighting to live, Emily. Many times, he asks me, 'What for do I wake up each morning to an empty house?'"

"You tell him he has to hold on," she said fiercely. "Don't you dare let him die before I get there."

* * *

She and Helen arrived at the villa by taxi two days later. Obtaining a passport for her baby at such short notice had taken some doing, but Emily had appealed to a sympathetic government official who, when he'd heard her situation, had cut through the bureaucratic red tape in record time.

As the cab rounded the last curve in the driveway and the villa came into view, nothing seemed to have changed. The palm trees rose tall against the deep blue sky. The flower beds blazed with color under the sun. Proud as ever, the peacocks strutted over the immaculate lawns.

Inside, the house told a different story. The atmosphere was somber, oppressive, although her showing up with a baby caused something of a stir.

"Yes, she's mine," Emily said to a stunned Damaris. Then, to Giorgios, "Am I in time?"

"*Neh.* When he heard you were coming, he found new strength. He is awake and just a few minutes ago asked how soon you would be here."

Lifting Helen from her infant seat, she said, "Then let's not keep him waiting any longer."

She had witnessed death in all its guises many times in her career, but even though she thought herself prepared, she was shocked when she saw Pavlos. He lay against his pillows, so frail and shrunken that a stiff breeze could have blown him away. His face was the color of parchment, his eyes closed, and had it not been for the shallow rise and fall of his chest, he might have already been dead.

"Hold her for me for a second, will you?" she whispered, passing Helen to Damaris, and approached his bed. "Hello, darling," she said softly.

He opened his eyes. "You came," he said, his voice a pale imitation of what it once had been.

"Of course."

"You're a good girl."

Stifling a rush of grief, she took Helen from Damaris and laid her in his arms. "I've brought someone with me," she said. "Say hello to your granddaughter, Pavlos."

He gazed at Helen who stared up at him from big blue eyes. Almost inaudibly, he whispered, "She is Niko's child?"

"Yes."

Tears trickled down his face. "I never thought to see the day. *Yiasu, kali egoni.* Hello, my little one."

"Her name's Helen."

"A good Greek name." The breath rattled in his beleaguered lungs. "A beautiful name for a beautiful child."

"I thought you'd approve."

He tore his eyes away from Helen. "How could I not? She is of my blood and has you for her mother. Tell me all about her."

"Tomorrow," she said, seeing that he was tiring fast. "For now, Pavlos, try to get some sleep."

He groped for her hand. "Sleep will come soon enough, girl, and we both know it is not one from which I will awake. Talk to me while there is still time. I want to know everything."

"Stay with him," Damaris murmured, scooping Helen into her arms again. "I will look after the little one."

"Take Giorgios with you when you go," Pavlos

wheezed. "His mournful face and death bed vigil weary me."

"Poor man," Emily said, when they were alone. "He loves you so much, Pavlos, and all this…" She indicated the oxygen tank and other hospital paraphernalia in the room. "It probably scares him."

"I know, and it hurts me that he is so overwrought. I would spare him seeing me like this, if I could. He has been more of a son to me than Niko ever was."

"Niko loves you, too."

"Save me the platitudes, girl! I am dying. If he cares about me at all, why is he the only one not here now?"

Footsteps crossing the adjoining sitting room came to a halt in the open doorway. "But I *am* here," Niko said. "I came as soon as I heard."

CHAPTER THIRTEEN

HORRIFIED, Emily froze, battered by panic and such a welter of conflicting emotions that her instinct was to run as far and as fast as she could to escape him. Anything to suppress the surge of longing aroused by the sound of his voice, the craving to touch him again. Anything to prevent his finding out about Helen. But what if he'd already seen her and recognized her as his? And even if he hadn't, how could she justify leaving Pavlos when he was clutching her hand so desperately?

Reining in her emotions, she drew on the control which had served her so well as a critical care nurse. With deceptive calm, she swiveled in the chair and in one sweeping glace took in everything about him from the top of his head to his dusty flight boots.

He looked like hell. Fatigue smudged his eyes, he hadn't shaved in days and he needed a haircut. Judging by their appearance, he must have slept in his jeans and shirt longer than was good for them or him, and the crystal was cracked on his flight computer watch. But more than all else, he looked unutterably sad.

"I'll leave the pair of you alone together," she muttered, rising to her feet.

"No," Pavlos wheezed, his eyes beseeching her.

Niko crossed the room and pressed her down on the chair again. "Please stay, angel," he said. "What I have to say is as much for you as for my father."

"Don't you dare upset him."

"I won't."

He pulled a chair close on the far side of the bed and took his father's other hand. The contrast between them, the one so big and strong and deeply tanned, the other so weak, with every vein showing through the paper-thin skin, was painfully moving to behold.

"If you're here to dance on my grave," Pavlos said, the faintest spark of the old hostility charging his words, "you needn't have rushed. I'm not dead yet."

"And I thank God for that, *Patera*, because I want to tell you I'm sorry I've made such a poor job of being your son."

"An *epiphaneia* at this late date?" Pavlos let out a croak of feeble laughter. "What brought that on?"

"I have just come back from a hell where political corruption and genocide rule the day. I've witnessed mothers ripped away from their newborn infants, fathers murdered before their children's eyes and been powerless to prevent either. I've met thousands of orphans infected by diseases, which will kill them before they grow to be adults. I have buried a dead baby and wept over his grave because there was no one else to mourn him."

Momentarily overcome, he cleared his throat and rubbed his thumb lightly over the back of his father's hand. "In the end, the devastation and ruin defeated me. What was I doing, trying to mend broken families in a foreign country when my own was falling apart at home? By what right had I held you at a distance, *Patera*, when your greatest sin was wanting to give me a better life than you had when you were young?"

"You're my son," Pavlos said. "Stubborn and proud and hell set on making your own way in the world, just as I was at your age. And you wanted to make that world a better place."

"Yes, I did. But I neglected you in the process. Have I left it too late to ask your forgiveness?"

With great effort, Pavlos lifted his other hand and laid it alongside Niko's stubble-covered jaw. "Ah, my foolish boy," he said hoarsely. "Don't you know it's never too late for a father to welcome his son home again?"

Niko started to cry then, harsh, horrible, rasping sobs that tore through his body. Emily couldn't bear it. Springing up from her chair, she stumbled to the French doors in the sitting room and ran out to the terrace.

At the far end, a path led away from the villa and wound through the gardens to a marble bench set in a shady arbor screened from the house by a grove of lemon trees. Reaching it, she sank down on the seat's cool, hard surface and wrestled with the demons plaguing her.

She had fought so hard to get over Niko. To shut herself off from dreams of him vivid enough that she awoke with the scent of his skin, the silken touch of his intimate flesh, taunting her. She'd struggled to find a foothold in a world without him. To build a safe, secure, contented life around her baby.

And for what? To fall for him all over again in less time than it took to blink, swayed by tears she'd never thought to see him shed, and words she'd never believed she'd hear him utter? Casting aside his indomitable pride, he'd revealed his innermost heart and in so doing, had walked right back into hers.

She could not allow it. Could not risk being dragged back into the morass of misery where loving him had landed her before. She had a child to protect now. Helen needed a mother who was whole, not half a woman pining for what she couldn't have. If she acted quickly and discreetly, she could leave the villa without anyone being the wiser. It was the best thing, the only thing to do.

Mind made up, she went around the side of the house to let herself in the front door, and came face-to-face with a harassed Georgios. "I've been looking for you, Emily. Your little one is screaming with hunger and Damaris cannot comfort her."

Right on cue, Emily's breasts started to leak and a quick glance at the clock on the wall showed her it had been over two hours since she'd last nursed her baby. Leaving would have to be postponed a little longer. "Please ask Damaris to bring her to me in the drawing room. It's cooler in there."

"If you'd rather be upstairs, everything's ready in your suite."

"Thanks, Giorgios," she said, "but now that Niko's arrived, I won't be staying here after all."

"Pavlos will be disappointed."

"I don't think so. We had our time together. Now it's his son's turn."

Niko sat with his father until he drifted off to sleep, then quietly left the bedroom and went in search of Emily. He and Pavlos had made peace at last. Now it was time to mend things with her. He'd hurt her badly. Hurt them both, for reasons which, in retrospect, struck him as unforgivably egotistical on his part. Well, no more. Things would be different from now on.

The house was silent as a tomb. An unfortunate comparison, he thought with a pang. Already the scent of death, indefinable but all too familiar, pervaded the atmosphere. But as he drew level with the pillared entrance to the formal day salon, a place so seldom used that he couldn't remember the last time he'd set foot in it, a soft, dovelike murmur caught his attention.

Thinking a bird might have flown in from the garden, he stepped quietly into the room and instead discovered Emily sitting by the open window, a lightweight shawl of some sort draped over her shoulder, her head bent attentively over the infant at her partially exposed breast.

The shock almost felled him. Yes, he'd urged her to find a man who could give her what he'd thought he never could, but not once in all the months they'd been apart had it occurred to him that she'd take his advice to heart so quickly or so thoroughly.

As though sensing she was being observed, she looked up and caught him staring. Her eyes widened and quickly, almost defiantly, she drew the shawl over the baby—a newborn, from what he'd been able to observe, probably no more than a few weeks old.

"Well," he said, affecting amusement when what he most wanted to do was howl with disappointed outrage, "I hardly expected this."

She tilted one shoulder in a dismissive little shrug. "What can I say? The day's been full of surprises."

He angled a glance at the baby, although all he could

see were its tiny legs and the little red soles of its feet poking out beneath the shawl. "Boy or girl?"

"Girl."

"Does she look like you?"

"Some people think so."

"Lucky her. And you're happy?"

"Deliriously. I have everything I ever wanted."

"Really?" He'd never have guessed. She was fidgety, tense, the picture of uneasiness. Rearranging the shawl needlessly. Looking anywhere but at him.

There was something else not right about the picture of contentment she was trying to present, and watching the nervous fluttering of her fingers, he all at once realized what it was. "In that case," he said, "why aren't you wearing a wedding ring?"

Of all the questions she'd feared he might ask, this one had never crossed her mind, and she briefly considered trying to come up with an inspired lie to throw him off the scent. Since she'd done such a good job of fooling him into thinking she'd found some other man to take his place, why not continue with the charade? But suddenly she'd had enough of the deceit and the subterfuge. She'd tell him the truth, or at least an edited version of it, and if he persisted in leaping to all the wrong conclusions, that was hardly her problem. "Because I'm not married," she said.

"Why not?"

"I rushed into a relationship with the wrong man, we went our separate ways and I'm bringing up my baby alone. Don't look so disapproving. It was my choice, and hardly unique in today's world. Hundreds of women make the same decision every day."

"You're not one of those women, Emily," he said. "You should have held out for the husband you always wanted."

"Well, I didn't. I had a baby instead."

His unforgettable green eyes scoured her face, undermining her resolve to remain coolly disinterested. "It's not too late for you to have both."

"I'm afraid it is. There aren't too many men out there willing to take on another man's child."

"There's me," he said. "If you'll have me, I'll marry you."

She was so unprepared for his answer that she almost dropped Helen. "Don't be ridiculous! The Niko Leonidas I know doesn't invest in marriage."

"That man doesn't exist anymore. He grew up and learned what was important in life."

"He used to believe helping those in need was important."

"He still does."

Bristling, she said, "I'm not in need, Niko. I can manage very well on my own."

"You misunderstand. What I'm saying is that I haven't abandoned the causes I've supported all these years. I still believe in doing my part and I always will. I just don't need to keep proving it by playing Russian roulette with my own life. There are other, more effective ways to make a difference."

"Marrying me isn't one of them," she said. But oh, how she wished it were!

He crossed the room in swift strides and came to where she sat. "Listen to me," he implored. "I love you. Give me a chance to show you how much. Let me make a home for you and your baby. Let me be a father to her. I don't care who else's blood runs in her veins. That she's yours is reason enough for me to love her as if she were my own."

"Oh…!" She pressed her trembling lips together and fought to hold back the tears. "This is so not what I expected when I woke up this morning."

"Me, neither. If you need time to think about it—"

"We both do, Niko. Right now your father needs you more than I do, and you're too emotionally fragile to be making any other major decisions."

"Not to the point that I don't know my own mind. In deference to my father, I won't pressure you to accept my proposal now, but I won't be put off indefinitely."

"There's more at issue here than just you and me, Niko. My situation…well, it's not exactly what you think."

"Do you love me?"

"Yes."

"Are you married?"

"I've already told that I'm not."

"Then there are no issues that can't be worked out."

He ran his hands down his crumpled shirt and dusty jeans. "Look, I'm a mess, inside and out. I'm going home to get cleaned up and pull myself together, but in the event that you're worried my proposal is some spur-of-the-moment impulse on my part—"

"Is it? You are a man who likes to rush to the rescue, after all."

"The person I'm rescuing this time is myself, Emily. It's taken me a long time, but I've finally set my priorities straight. Only a fool discards the treasures that bless his life. I was on my way home to tell my father that even before I heard he was dying. To my lasting regret, I've left it too late to make it up to him for all the wasted years. I won't make the same mistake with you."

He left her then, but not as he had before. Not empty of everything but despair. She'd once read that when it rains in the desert, all the cacti burst into glorious flower. For such a long time her spirit had been arid as a desert, but his words made hope bloom in every corner of her heart and fill it to overflowing.

While he was gone, Giorgios came to tell her Pavlos was awake again. She went to him immediately.

His tired eyes brightened when he saw she'd brought Helen with her and he tried to reach out to hold her, but the effort was too much for him and he sank back against the pillows. His pulse was weak and erratic, his breathing labored as his poor old heart struggled to keep working, and he soon drifted asleep again.

Niko joined her not long after and took up his post on the other side of the bed.

Sensing his presence, Pavlos muttered haltingly, "You here, son?"

"I'm here, *Babas*."

"You'll be a rich man when I go."

"Not as rich as I'd be if you stayed."

"Not enough time left for that, boy. It's up to you and Emily now."

"I know."

"You take good care of her."

"I will."

"And my granddaughter. Be a better father to her than I ever was to you."

Startled, Niko shot Emily a quick glance, but he said only, "I won't let you down, *Babas*."

"Never have, boy," Pavlos said, his voice barely above a whisper. "Always made me proud...should have told you before now."

He never spoke. He subsided into sleep again, deeper this time, his respirations so shallow they barely moved the sheet covering him. Emily busied herself checking the IV solution and oxygen, hoping to avoid the inevitable question about his father's comment, but Niko's attention remained fixed on Pavlos.

An hour passed, and then another. Helen squirmed and scrunched up her face, the prelude, Emily knew, to a very vocal demand for food. "I'll nurse her in the other room so she doesn't disturb him," she told Niko.

"Don't take too long," he said.

Afternoon slipped toward dusk. Giorgios brought tea and sandwiches. Damaris took Helen and put her to bed in a drawer she'd taken from a dresser, which was lined with soft blankets. The doctor paid a call, met Emily's gaze, shook his head regretfully and said he'd be by again in the morning.

Throughout the night, Emily and Niko kept vigil. Lost in their own thoughts of the man who'd made such an indelible impression on them both, they spoke little. At six o'clock the next morning, Pavlos died.

"He's gone, Niko," she said. "It's over."

He nodded, bent his head and gathered his father's frail body in his arms.

Leaving him to make his private farewell, she slipped from the room and went out to the terrace. In the half-light of dawn, the flower beds shone like pale clumps of stars. It was going to be another beautiful late August day. The first of many without Pavlos.

She didn't hear Niko join her until he spoke. "He was rambling, wasn't he, when he said the baby's mine?"

"No," she said, too sad and exhausted to prevaricate. The truth had to come out sooner or later, it might as well be now. "You're her biological father."

"That's impossible. We always used protection."

"We couldn't have been as careful as we thought,"she said.

"How old is she? She looks practically newborn."

"She's three months old."

"How much does she weigh?"

"Nearly seven pounds now, but she was less than four at birth. She looks small because she was born seven weeks early."

He almost staggered. "Why didn't you tell me?"

"I tried to when you found me with her yesterday. You wouldn't let me."

"I'm not talking about yesterday afternoon, Emily. I'm talking about the last nine or ten months. I would have married you at once, if I'd known."

"I know you would. I didn't want you on those terms. I still don't."

"I was afraid that might be the reason," he said. "I seem to have a real talent for screwing up the relationship that means the most to me."

And he walked back into the house, a man so bowed down with sorrow that she couldn't bear to watch him.

CHAPTER FOURTEEN

SHE saw little of him in the week that followed. Arranging the funeral and the myriad tasks associated with it kept him occupied. Pavlos had many business associates and the stream of callers coming to the villa to pay their respects was endless.

Emily helped poor Damaris, who was run off her feet providing refreshments, and spent many quiet hours in the gardens with Helen, wondering what the future held. Although he'd made time to get to know his daughter, Niko treated Emily more like a sister than a lover. Had she ruined their chances by keeping their baby a secret? she wondered.

She received her answer when he sought her out as she sat in the shade of an olive tree, on the lawn overlooking the Saronic Gulf. For the last two days, they'd had the villa to themselves again, but it was too lovely an afternoon to spend indoors.

"We've pretty much laid the past to rest, Emily," he announced, dropping down beside her on the blanket she'd spread on the grass. "Now we have to take care of the future. I said I wouldn't rush you for an answer to my proposal, and I've tried to keep my distance, but I'm afraid I've run out of patience."

Her mouth dropped open. "Are you saying you still want to marry me?"

"More than I've ever wanted anything in my life. The question is, do you trust me enough to want to marry me?"

"Why wouldn't I trust you?"

"Well, let's see. I showed myself to be devious and un-scrupulous by trying to expose you as a fraud. I seduced you, then agreed that we weren't a good match and might as well end our relationship. I left you, and you had a baby you didn't dare tell me about because you quite rightly thought I'd make a lousy father. Shall I go on?"

"No. We've laid the past to rest, remember, so let's do as you suggest and talk about the future."

"Okay. Here's what I've decided. Although I'll continue to support the causes I hold dear, I'm retiring as a pilot and sharing management of the company with Dinos. I intend to take an active role in overseeing my father's investments as he always wished me to do. Giorgios and Damaris have been very loyal to my family, so if you and I get married and you're agreeable, I'd like to live here and keep them and the rest of staff on. How am I doing so far?"

"Very well. I couldn't ask for better."

"Is that a yes to my proposal?"

"I'm not sure," she said coyly. "You moved into the villa a week ago and have been sleeping in a room down the hall from mine and your daughter's ever since. Do you plan to keep on doing that?"

"Not if you'll let me sleep in yours."

"Then it's a yes."

He closed his eyes and let out a long, slow breath. "Thank you for that, angel," he said. "I've been a very sad and lonely man since my father died, disappointed in myself on many levels and so afraid I'd blown any chance I might have had with you."

"I've been sad, too, Niko," she said, "but it hasn't changed the way I feel about you. I love you. I always will."

"I love you, too, so much more than you'll ever know. I love our daughter and will protect you both for the rest of my life."

That night, they lay together in bed with Helen between them. After fussing all evening, she'd finally fallen asleep.

"How beautiful she is," Niko whispered, his gaze tracking her face feature by feature. "Her ears are like little shells and look how tiny her nose is."

"She has your dark hair," Emily told him.

"She has your mouth.'

She smiled. "She is *our* baby."

"Yes," he said. "And I think you should put her in the drawer so that we can practice making another just like her, *mana mou*."

They made love, taking slow delight in rediscovering each other. He traced his tongue over the pale blue veins in her swollen breasts. She kissed the scar on his shoulder where he'd been shot. With hands and mouths and whispered words of love, they found the magic they once thought they'd lost and made it new and wonderful again. And when, at last, he entered her, they clung together and let the passion roll over them in sweet, endless waves and carry them to the far shores of ecstasy.

Afterward, Emily curled up in his arms and, hearing Helen whimper in her sleep, murmured drowsily, "We really must buy her a proper crib, don't you think?"

"Tomorrow, my darling," he said, bringing his mouth to hers in a lingering good-night kiss.

He tasted of lemons and sunshine and all things Greek. Of the fabulous turquoise sea, the dazzling mango-tinted sunsets, the ethereal dawns.

He tasted of forever.

HARLEQUIN *Presents*
EXTRA

THE MARRIAGE BARGAIN
Bid for, bargained for, bound forever!

A merciless Spaniard, a British billionaire,
an arrogant businessman and a ruthless tycoon:
these men have one thing in common—they're all
in the bidding for a bride!

There's only one answer to their proposals they'll
accept—and they will do whatever it takes to
claim a willing wife....

**Look for all the exciting stories,
available in June:**

The Millionaire's Chosen Bride #57
by SUSANNE JAMES

His Bid for a Bride #58
by CAROLE MORTIMER

The Spaniard's Marriage Bargain #59
by ABBY GREEN

Ruthless Husband, Convenient Wife #60
by MADELEINE KER

HARLEQUIN *Presents*

International Billionaires

*Life is a game of power and pleasure.
And these men play to win!*

THE ITALIAN COUNT'S DEFIANT BRIDE
by Catherine George

Alicia Cross's estranged husband has
reappeared—and is demanding his wedding
night! Francesco da Luca wants his feisty
runaway bride back, especially when
he discovers she's still a virgin....

Book #2830

Available June 2009

Eight volumes in all to collect!

REQUEST YOUR FREE BOOKS!

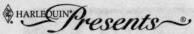

2 FREE NOVELS PLUS 2 FREE GIFTS!

YES! Please send me 2 FREE Harlequin Presents® novels and my 2 FREE gifts (gifts are worth about $10). After receiving them, if I don't wish to receive any more books, I can return the shipping statement marked "cancel." If I don't cancel, I will receive 6 brand-new novels every month and be billed just $4.05 per book in the U.S. or $4.74 per book in Canada, plus 25¢ shipping and handling per book and applicable taxes, if any*. That's a savings of close to 15% off the cover price! I understand that accepting the 2 free books and gifts places me under no obligation to buy anything. I can always return a shipment and cancel at any time. Even if I never buy another book, the two free books and gifts are mine to keep forever.

106 HDN ERRW 306 HDN ERRL

Name _____ (PLEASE PRINT) _____

Address _____ Apt. #

City _____ State/Prov. _____ Zip/Postal Code

Signature (if under 18, a parent or guardian must sign)

Mail to the **Harlequin Reader Service:**
IN U.S.A.: P.O. Box 1867, Buffalo, NY 14240-1867
IN CANADA: P.O. Box 609, Fort Erie, Ontario L2A 5X3

Not valid to current subscribers of Harlequin Presents books.

**Want to try two free books from another line?
Call 1-800-873-8635 or visit www.morefreebooks.com.**

HP08R

------------------- ★ -------------------

With automatic good manners he nodded toward them all, but did not speak. He looked at the body lying on the floor, the terribly damaged face staring upward. He saw the handbag lying on the floor.

He walked forward, forcing himself to study well what he saw. He stared for some minutes before turning away. "No, that is not my wife. Yes, she wore jeans like that. Yes, she had such a handbag, but the body is not hers."

Inspector Lodge met Coffin's eyes with a meaningful stare: I hope you know what you are doing.

Archie Young muttered something about the material in the handbag.

"I don't care what is inside the handbag. That is not my wife," said Coffin in a quiet voice. "It is not Stella."

------------------- ★ -------------------

"Butler has built her considerable reputation on superbly crafted psychological thrillers that examine the bleaker aspects of human nature."
—*Booklist*

"This is a provocative and intense story with two very strong characters at its heart."
—*Mystery News*

GWENDOLINE BUTLER

COFFIN'S GAME

WORLDWIDE.

TORONTO • NEW YORK • LONDON
AMSTERDAM • PARIS • SYDNEY • HAMBURG
STOCKHOLM • ATHENS • TOKYO • MILAN
MADRID • WARSAW • BUDAPEST • AUCKLAND

COFFIN'S GAME

A Worldwide Mystery/July 2000

First published by St. Martin's Press, Incorporated.

ISBN 0-373-26353-8

My thanks to Professor Geoffrey Lee Williams for help about terrorism and terrorists, and to Inspector Euan Forbes and John Kennedy Melling for details of technical procedures.

Author's Note

One evening in April 1988, I sat in Toynbee Hall in the East End of London, near to Docklands, listening to Dr. David Owen (now Lord Owen) give that year's Barnett Memorial Lecture. In it, he suggested the creation of a Second City of London, to be spun off from the first, to aid the economic and social regeneration of the Docklands.

The idea fascinated me and I have made use of it to create a world for detective John Coffin, to whom I gave the tricky task of keeping there the Queen's Peace.

*A brief Calendar of the life and career of John Coffin,
Chief Commander of the Second City of London Police.*

John Coffin is a Londoner by birth, his father is unknown and his mother was a difficult lady of many careers and different lives who abandoned him in infancy to be looked after by a woman who may have been a relative of his father and who seems to have acted as his mother's dresser when she was on the stage. He kept in touch with this lady, whom he called Mother, lodged with her in his early career and looked after her until she died.

After serving briefly in the army, he joined the Metropolitan Police, soon transferring to the plainclothes branch as a detective.

He became a sergeant and was very quickly promoted to inspector a year later. Ten years later, he was a superintendent and then chief superintendent.

There was a bad patch in his career about which he is reluctant to talk. His difficult family background has complicated his life and possibly accounts for an unhappy period when, as he admits, his career went down a black hole. His first marriage split apart at this time and his only child died.

From this dark period he was resurrected by a spell in a secret, dangerous undercover operation about which even now not much is known. But the esteem he won then was recognized when the Second City of London was being formed and he became Chief Commander of its Police Force. He has married again, an old love, Stella Pinero, who is herself a very successful actress. He has also discovered two siblings, a much younger sister and brother.

For the urban terrorist, logistics are expressed by the formula MDAME.

> M mechanisation
> D money *(dinheiro)*
> A arms
> M ammunition *(municos)*
> E explosives

> —*Minimanual of the Urban Guerrilla*
> Carlos Marighella

Despite the popular image, there is no reliable archetype of terrorist personality. While they are undeniably cruel, virtually none has been found to be clinically mad. But there are always exceptions.

A recurring syndrome is what psychiatrists call externalisation, coping with failure by blaming an outside source.

> —*Terrorism*
> Professor Geoffrey Lee Williams
> Alan Lee Williams
> Institute for European Defence and Strategic Studies

PROLOGUE

'THE CHEMIN DES DAMES, that's the name,' said Charles. 'Do you know that in 1917 the whole French Army was in revolt because of the terrible deaths of the Chemin des Dames. That wonderful army that Napoleon built, reduced to chaos and despair…that's the mood I want to create with our bombs. Then we can rebuild society.'

Not me, thought Jerry. I'm a soldier, I get instructions from above, I do the job, and walk away. Also, I get paid.

There were three of them in the rented room above an empty shop in Mordecai Street; the neighbours, such as took any interest, thought they were charity workers helping Africa or Tibet.

Present were Jerry, the supreme professional, the leader and the technician on the bomb, Andrew, an old colleague on the bomb run, and Charles, the college graduate, the sort to go out on a crusade. Jerry found him useful, but did not trust him.

Nor did he trust the fourth member of the team, known as the Secret Card, brought in by Pip for local knowledge and inside information on the Second City Police.

None of them used their own names, not even Jerry and Andrew. Only Jerry knew and had contact with the man next in the chain of command, and he knew him only as Pip. Jerry knew that they were only the second team, not entrusted with the bigger bomb, but they were operators.

The local knowledge of the Card had told them which street was strategically placed for a bomb, near a big supermarket for maximum damage, yet neutral; a thoroughfare where people took not much notice of each other and where cars and vans could park unnoticed. Arch Road, with Percy Street, in which many houses were empty, just round the corner. Arch Road—put the bomb there.

'Cameras, videos?' Jerry had queried, having observed the police cameras going up on street corners in the Second City.

'None in Arch Road, nor Percy Street yet. The city has to persuade local businesses to come up with the cash.'

That was where the Card's knowledge of the police had come in useful.

The Card was not present at this last meeting before the bomb. Might be due for a quick exit. Jerry would decide.

In any case, the group (and there were others of whom this little coterie knew nothing) would soon split up and disappear.

Job done.

But Jerry had not quite taken in the tricky character Pip had enlisted in the Card.

Pip could have enlightened him, but saw no reason to do so.

ONE

THERE WERE TWO great explosions on the same day in the Second City that autumn. One bomb went off, near the entrance to the new tunnel under the Thames which the Queen had opened but two years before. The tunnel was not damaged. The other bomb went off later in a shooting street. Most of the damage was in the ancient riverside borough of Spinnergate, but it had been heard as far away as East Hythe, and even Swinehouse, further east, had felt the blast. The new rich areas of Evelyn Fields and Tower Hill with their loft conversions in old warehouses and their smart flats in former factories had been spared—to the fury of Spinnergate, which was not smart or converted in any way. There had been deaths and more injuries in the second bomb, houses and offices nearby were blasted, but the tunnel itself was already open, with traffic running through it. Still, the Second City was used to surviving onslaughts, having come through the ravages of Romans, Vikings, and Normans, not to mention later enemies, amongst whom they numbered all governments, whether home-based or across the Channel. The habit of the population was to pick itself up and get on with living while cursing its rulers.

They did regret that the complex system of video cameras placed high on many buildings around the Second City had yet to be extended to lesser streets, where it might have provided better clues. Instead they had to wait for the bombers to claim their work. Which they did, only when they thought they were safely away.

It was war, after all.

The other explosion, more personally aimed, was about to happen.

SIX DAYS AFTER the explosions, a row of houses which had been damaged in the blast was being tidied up. There was no major structural damage and the repairs, which were in the hands of a local firm, were expected to be finished quickly. The firm, William Archer Ltd, a small outfit which knew Percy Street well, glad of the work, was not going to rush, tacitly admitting that if the bomb brought work it was not altogether a bad bomb.

Bill Archer, the boss and owner of the firm which his father had started, was in a bad mood, irritable because of the absence of his office manager who had taken some days off. Peter Corner had gone sick, sending a brief message that he had migraine.

'Didn't think men got migraine,' grumbled his employer, 'that's for women. Why can't he just take an aspirin and come in?'

'You can be quite ill with migraine,' said his wife, who had taken the message on the telephone. She was in the office doing the work herself so that if anyone had a grievance it was her. 'You pay him women's wages anyway.'

'I pay him what he deserves, and I won't pay that if he doesn't turn up. Nancy boy. I bet it was a man on the phone to you.' Mrs Archer admitted silently that it was. 'Gone off together somewhere, I bet.' Bill was sharp. He often had labour problems. He employed casual labour, taking them on for a job and then sacking them. It was the way of his work, he would say; there had always been casual workers in the building trade. There were always men to be had. For instance, at this moment, he had a former bank clerk, a university graduate doing a thesis on economic history, and a seaman without a ship. His son and a nephew—his sister's son—he employed all the time.

'I'll be round the corner in Percy Street.' He picked up his jacket as he departed.

Bill Archer's son, George (they went in for royal names), was in charge and his cousin, Phil, was doing most of the work.

Number five Percy Street was the third house in the row and had been empty and up for sale for six months or so. This was known by both George and Phil who had been given the key by the house agent and told to get on with the roof and the windows and ceiling in the top floor front room.

PHIL RAN UP the stairs cheerfully, his first job of the day and a light one. It was very early in the morning; he liked to get a good start. He was a thin and eager man. Behind him came Tom McAndrew, taller, heavier and older, he it was who was working on a thesis and looking for a university job. Any job. But he was a good brickie and could turn his hand to anything electrical. Woodwork and plumbing, no.

Phil pushed open the door. The wind blew through the shattered windows and shivered up to the rafters through the torn ceiling. If it had not been for the wind, he reckoned, there would have been more of a smell.

On the floor, face in profile, was a body.

'Don't touch,' said Tom, putting out a restraining hand, 'better not.'

Bill, who had been talking to his son in the street outside the house, could be heard coming up the stairs. He was not going to be pleased.

A CALL FROM George Archer in his capacity as works foreman on the job brought a police patrol car to inspect 5 Percy Street and then two more senior officers to take another look.

Sergeant Mitchell and Detective Ellis Rice arrived before the police surgeon and before the Scene of Crime team. They stared down at the body lying on the floor of a room where the ceiling was half down and the windows out. They made a quiet, delicate, gloved inspection of the corpse and her possessions. She had a short fall of fair hair, she wore jeans, a white shirt, tucked in and belted, and on the hands were bloodstained white cotton gloves. There was a handbag on the floor. Mitchell carefully put on plastic gloves, then opened the bag and looked inside. He raised an eyebrow. Silently, he let Rice see what he had been seeing.

'That bag hers?' asked Archer, who had come up the stairs with them. They had told him to stay behind, but he had ignored this advice.

'Could be.'

'It's a good bag.'

It was; soft leather with an initial in gold.

'That is no bomb injury,' said George Archer, staring at the corpse. 'Not the face.' He said this sadly; he was a former soldier who had served in the Falklands, he knew what wounds were and how they were made. Hands had done this work. Brutal, determined hands.

'No,' said Mitchell. 'Not disputing that.' He crouched down to replace the woman's handbag on the floor beside her. He turned in query to his colleague. A meaning look passed between them: a question wanting an answer.

'It can't be,' said the other. 'Can't be her.'

'There's the handbag,' said Mitchell. 'That means

something. Could have been stolen, I suppose.' He walked away. 'This is too much for us.'

'SOCO will be here soon.'

Mitchell had made up his mind. 'That's not enough,' he called over his shoulder. 'I am going to telephone.'

Within the hour, two very senior detectives had arrived. The first to march up the stairs, quickly and lightly, was Chief Superintendent Archie Young. Behind him, climbing with that soft creeping movement that had won him the nickname of the Todger, was Inspector Thomas Lodge, a man of specialized knowledge and many tongues. He was an outsider who ran his own game.

The two men walked into the room together, one tall and burly although quick moving, and the other several inches shorter, while the recently arrived SOCO team stood back.

Archie Young surveyed the body, then knelt down for a closer look. 'I can't say; I ought to be able...I knew her—know her,' he amended. 'I simply can't say, the face has gone.' He looked at Inspector Lodge. 'Any views?'

'That can probably be reconstructed. To some extent. In the long run it will be of use. Fingerprints also.'

'You are looking at this from your point of view,' said Archie Young with some irritation. As you usually do, he muttered to himself. 'I can't go round collecting fingerprints to check if this is the body of the woman we think it is. Not this woman.'

'The circumstances are unusual,' said Inspector Lodge calmly.

'They bloody are.'

Lodge drew his lips together. He rarely swore, but when he did he had a wide-ranging vocabulary in which to do it, from Russian to a couple of Chinese dialects, picked up in Soho.

'There's nothing for it: we have to get the Chief Commander himself.'

'He's away, isn't he?'

'Back today, here now.' Archie Young looked at his watch. Still early, but he reckoned the Chief Commander would be in his office.

'In situ?'

'Yes, here and now.'

Lodge nodded gravely, watching as Archie Young drew his mobile phone from his pocket. 'I hope that phone is protected,' he said.

'It is, as you know very well. All mobiles are in this Force, no one can eavesdrop.' And to himself, Archie Young said: No wonder they call you the Todger. I wouldn't have you with me now if I didn't have to; you are the king of this particular territory. 'Sir,' he began, when John Coffin, Chief Commander of the Second City Police, answered on his private reserved line, and found himself stumbling, wondering how to go on.

FOUR DAYS AFTER the explosions, Stella Pinero had gone away.

Before her going, there had been a moment of confusion and despair. And in the theatre, too.

Stella Pinero was lost. She had stood centre stage and realized she had lost her words, lost where she was in Act One (that bit she could remember), and very nearly forgotten what play it was.

Tension, that was the cause. Fear, yes, she could say that too.

A voice prompted her: 'What letter?'

Stella came to herself. 'You thought the letter had

been destroyed. How foolish of you. It is in my possession, it was a swindle, Sir Robert.'

An Ideal Husband, she said to herself, that's the play. Why on earth did I choose to produce that play here in my own theatre, when I had a free choice? Because it is popular with my audience, and I serve that audience.

And because I have husbands on my mind; I am terribly, terribly worried about my own husband.

At last a voice got through to her: 'Your carriage is here, Mrs Cheveley.'

Stella once more came in and obliged with the speech: 'Thanks. Good evening, Lady Chiltern.'

Then she realized what she had said and what it meant. It was a painful moment. Oh God, I must have gone through almost an act on autopilot. This could happen, all actors knew the phenomenon, but it would not do. She gathered herself together and carried on.

Stella Pinero as Mrs Cheveley—she had naturally given herself the female lead—went backstage and sought comfort. Alice Yeoman was standing in the wings, watching.

Stella had been persuaded to employ Alice by her husband, John Coffin. 'She's the child of a chap I served with,' he explained. 'We did a job together, he saved my life, got hurt himself. When he died last year, he asked me to look after the girl…he'd been too old a father and her mother was gone. I don't see myself as a father-figure, but I promised I would see the girl through.' There had been a bit more to it, but this was not something to talk about. Alice was like Bill Yeoman and yet different.

'That was the time I was out of touch with you,' said Stella.

'I wasn't in touch with anyone much, I was fighting

my way back.' After a bad time in his life and career, but he did not say this aloud. 'I owe her, give her a chance.'

'Sure. She will have to be a good worker.' But Alice was quiet, alert and industrious. There was a private side to her: the easy, all-knowing, uncensorious common-wealth of the theatre observed that Alice trawled the town a bit. Stella wondered whether Coffin knew—but did it matter?

Alice was a tall, well-built young woman, not a very good actress but not one to be underrated. Stella grabbed her, physically took her by the arm and stared in her face. Alice opened her eyes wide with surprise. 'Tell me, quickly, was I terrible?'

'No, just the same as usual. Good, I mean. Stella, you're always good,' said Alice quickly. Alice was a minor member of the company with a few lines that prevented her being a mere walking understudy, but she was also deputy stage manager and helped with props; in short, a humble member of the theatre, while Stella Pinero was a famous actress with a long career behind her and this very theatre named after her. But this was a democratic company in which leading lady and minor actress could talk to each other on friendly terms. Alice admired Stella and also feared her. Not only was Stella famous and practically the owner of the Pinero Theatre in the old church, together with the Theatre Workshop and the small Experimental Theatre—all great things in themselves—but her husband was Commander John Coffin, Head of the Police Force of the Second City.

Stella went into her dressing room, sat down in front of her looking glass where she stared at her reflection. She was still a beauty, would be till she died; she had grown into beauty, a rare benefaction of nature but one given to her.

Her make-up needed touching up, and mechanically she redid her lips and puffed on some powder. Her mind was not on it, but her hand was so used to the job that it smoothed her eyebrows and checked the line of her lips with its usual skill.

She was not on for some time in the next act so she could sit back, breathe deeply and give herself good advice. Such as:

Stop going into a panic.

Pretend it's all a joke.

Tell your husband.

Oh, no, not John, not yet.

Her call came, the first call, to remind her she should soon be in the wings awaiting her cue. Stella remembered the days when a boy came round to bang on your door with the news: you're on, Miss Pinero. Now, the word came over the intercom.

She moved towards the wings, not waiting to be prompted.

She could hear the dialogue. Here was Lady Chiltern (acted by Jane Gillam, a beautiful girl, very nearly straight out of RADA where she had won an important prize). Lady Chiltern was a difficult part because she was so humourless and stupid, but Jane was doing what she could with it.

'Mrs Cheveley! Coming to see me? Impossible!'

And here was Fanny Burt as Mabel Chiltern—she had better lines and even a few jokes, but Wilde reserved the best dialogue for the men: 'She is coming up the stairs, as large as life and not nearly so naturally.'

Not brilliant dialogue, Stella thought as she moved forward, but it got you on stage.

Here she went: 'Isn't that Miss Chiltern? I should so much like to know her.'

Stella stayed alert through the rest of the play. She had come to a decision. Speed seemed necessary, so she was off the stage as soon as the applause finished—to her pleasure there was a good show of enthusiasm—and slipped away to her dressing room without a word to the rest of the performers.

There were thirteen members of the cast; in the original production there had been fifteen, but money was easier then, and Stella had been obliged to cut out the two footmen. Of the remainder, ten were what she thought of as her 'repertory company' inasmuch as they performed for her whenever she produced a play herself and did not buy one in. Most of these actors were young, and local, from the drama department in one of the nearby universities. Stella had early realized the importance of cultivating your neighbourhood to win affection and bring in the audiences. She had a lot of support always from the friends and families of her young performers.

But you also needed an outsider to provide some extra excitement and here Jane Gillam, a star in the making, and Fanny Burt came in. The two men, Michael Guardian and Tom Jenks were attractive performers. Stella Pinero herself provided glitter.

In her dressing room, Stella let her dresser remove her hat and garments as Mrs. Cheveley. She did not appear in the last act, but had duly turned up for the last curtain. 'You pop off, Maisie,' she said to her elderly dresser. 'I know you want to get home. I will finish myself off.'

'I'll be dressing Miss Bow next week?'

'That's right.' Stella was creaming her face, removing

the last of her make-up—she never used much, the days of heavy slap were over.

Stella had introduced a fortnightly change of programme to entertain her limited audience in the Second City, which made a frequent change of programme an economic necessity.

'A bit of an unknown quantity,' said Maisie, hanging up a green silk mantle. As an old hand, she was allowed a certain freedom of speech. 'But she's done well; starring roles straight from college.'

'Yes.'

Irene Bow was a graduate of the University drama department; she had been lucky with parts and had performed well in the Theatre Workshop production of *Barefoot in the Park*, and her crisp, rapid style of delivery would go down well in Michael Frayn's *Noises Off*. Stella now had two weeks to herself.

'You have a nice rest then, Miss Pinero,' said Maisie. 'You've earned it.'

If only, thought Stella.

Maisie turned round at the door. 'Are you all right, Miss Pinero?'

'I'm fine.'

'You look a bit white.'

'Don't you worry, Maisie.' Stella was rapidly doing her face, repairing what ravages she could and concealing any paleness with a thin foundation cream from Guerlain. 'You get off.' What she meant in her silent heart was: Please go away and leave me to think.

Stella went to a locked drawer on the make-up table and withdrew a thickish envelope. She looked at it for a moment before opening it.

Three old letters, two very recent ones, and a photograph. How wrong she had been to let that photograph be taken.

Not drunk, not mad, just silly, she told herself. I cannot even claim that I was so young, she added. He was, I wasn't. Stupid, I was, carried away by emotion. Even now, when she knew what he was, what he had become, she remembered his physical beauty.

She looked away from the letters, and inside herself let the dialogue go on: I did not know then that I would meet John Coffin again, that I would marry him and become the wife of a top policeman. When I married John, I tried to tell him of a few past affairs, but he laughed and said he did not want a General Confession, and he had not been without lovers himself.

It was, she admitted to herself, one of her treasured moments, because it showed what a nice man John Coffin was, with a knack for good behaviour. He was also tough-minded, resolute and quick-tempered. Oh dear, she could hardly bear to think of all that being turned against her.

He was fair, she told herself, very fair.

For some reason, she found this no comfort as she stared at her face in the looking glass, for fairness could be a very sharp weapon. She touched her cheek with a careful finger. 'I must look after my skin, stress is bad for it. Maisie was right, I am a wreck.'

She leaned, resting her chin on her right hand, and, ever the actress, mimed tragic despair.

Possibly not a wreck, she allowed herself, withdrawing her hand, she had been a beauty and still was. Like many actresses she could make herself beautiful. She turned way from the looking glass to get dressed.

Her hasty movement knocked the letters and the photograph to the ground. Three old letters from her, and two new ones from him. Unwelcome, unwanted letters, threatening letters, demanding letters.

Pip Eaton, student, actor, stared up at her from the photograph on the floor. How he had changed from what he had once been, to a treacherous beast. Once her lover, now... What could she call him but a blackmailer, a criminal, a traitor?

No, be fair, she told herself bitterly, it is you, Stella Pinero, whom he invites to be the traitor. And to betray whom? Your own husband, not sexually as a lover, but professionally as a policeman.

A reviewer had once called Stella the 'modern comic muse'. Stella had valued that comment, she knew that she was a very good, possibly great comic actress, but now she felt a sting. Life had offered her a comedy, she reflected bitterly, and now she was being asked to play it as tragedy.

She put the letters and the photograph into her big black crocodile handbag which she had bought when she had won the Golden Apple Award on Broadway, and forced herself to calm down.

She could always kill someone. Preferably, Pip; if not, then very likely herself.

Her husband was away from home tonight, she would have the place to herself. There were times when it was better to be on your own.

DRESSED IN HER street clothes, Stella sped through the back corridors of the Pinero Theatre, ignoring a wave from Jane Gillam and a cheerful shout from Adam Fisk, who had played Lord Chiltern, to join them for a drink—they were going on to Max's for a meal afterwards. 'Can't manage tonight,' she called over her shoulder. 'Have a lovely time.'

'What's the matter with her?' said Adam to Fanny and Jane. 'She always comes at the end of the run. Tradition.'

'Her husband, I expect,' said Jane.

'Why do you say that?'

Jane shrugged. 'Just think so.'

Stella stepped out into the open air, took three deep and calming breaths, then walked briskly to where she lived with the chief commander in the tower of the old church now converted into the theatre. There was one good thing about living on the job: you did not have far to walk home.

She let herself in, switched on the light that illuminated the winding stair and listened, in case Coffin had come back, then walked up the stairs into silence.

There was no cat or dog to greet her, both animals of the earlier generation had died within a few months of each other as if, rivals and enemies as they were, they could not endure life without each other. And although Stella had often cursed the old cat, a battered old street cat, for waking her in the morning with its paw on her face, and grumbled at the dog for demanding that late-night walk, she missed them, too. They had been replaced by a sturdy white peke called Augustus, but he had declared himself Coffin's dog who must go where the boss went, so he was off now with Coffin on his travels.

She made herself a pot of coffee, prepared a sandwich with cheese and, defiantly, a crisp spiced onion, something no performer would normally do, which she sat at the table in the kitchen eating. The strong hot drink, together with food helped her to clear her mind.

'I don't see the way forward yet, but I know I need to think it over and I will do that best on my own.'

She could not talk it over with her husband because it was his career that could be ruined.

'I am not a fool,' she said aloud. 'I know it is not the sexual element that would do him in—society is not so unsophisticated—nor the fact that I look as though… No, I won't utter what it looks as if I am doing. And it's not that, even, it's the security side that would destroy him.'

She drank some coffee. The darkness outside seemed to creep in behind her eyes so that she could not see. 'Emotional mist,' she said in a loud voice, shaking her head.

She went down the stairs to the large sitting room one floor below and poured herself a large glass of whisky which she then carried upstairs. She had seen tired detectives come back to life after a slug of it, so she guessed it would do the same for her.

As she sipped it, she heard a rustle at floor level. She turned slowly to see what was there. A small grey mouse sat staring back at her. In the old days the cat had brought them in as an unwanted present for her mistress. This one must have made its way there under its own steam, or be a survivor. She found that thought comforting.

'Hello, friend,' she said. 'Don't worry, you are safe with me tonight. I know how you feel: trapped in a hostile world.' She drank some more whisky. 'Fear not. Appearances to the contrary,' she added, 'I won't eat you.'

The mouse slid quietly away on his own business. He was a resident, knew the ways of the house, would not be seen again for some time.

Stella finished her whisky, then took herself upstairs to her bedroom. Off the bedroom was a small dressing room contrived out of a corner of the room.

She looked at her clothes hanging in a neat row behind a glass door. She changed into a comfortable trouser suit, packed a small bag.

One more task and the most painful: a lying letter. She hated deceiving her husband, partly because she was a naturally truthful person—which all actresses must be, since nothing shows up more on the stage than falseness—but also because the chief commander had a sharp eye for an untruth.

Dearest,
    A late call from Silverline Films for the part of Annie Burnett, the prosecutor, in their new detective drama series. My agent says I simply must try for it... I am flying out to New York overnight.
    Give me time. I will get in touch. I have to think

Truth will out, she told herself, as she wrote the last words.

Then she scrawled: 'I really want this chance'. Again the truth; she did want such a chance, if offered. Her career had been on hold lately, and Coffin knew she fancied this part. Heaven knows, she had talked about it enough. He would believe her, accept the letter.

'All my love,' she ended.

Then she went across to the fax machine which lived on a shelf from which the messages popped out and slid to the ground. None there at the moment.

She wrote a note for her assistant in the theatre—away for a few days—and the same to her co-producer, both of which she then faxed out to them.

Hardly had she moved a step away when the fax rang and a message spilled itself out in front of her. Slowly, feeling heavy with premonition, she bent down to pick it up.

IN THE NEXT MINUTE THE TELEPHONE WILL RING.
ANSWER IT.

Stella picked up her bag and turned away. That was one bell she would not answer.

SHE WAS AT THE DOOR when the telephone rang. It became hard to breathe. She hesitated, knowing that she wanted to ignore it, but she was like a rabbit before a stoat. Stuck, frozen.

But you never knew with telephone calls. Perhaps it really was a summons from her agent. She knew it would not be John Coffin. He was driving down the M40—probably, she didn't really know where he was. He had a professional knack of disappearing. The thought went through her mind as she picked up the telephone; if he can disappear, so can I.

She held the receiver in her hand without speaking.

'I know you're there, Stella. I can hear you breathing.'

'How did you get this number?' Silly question, it was supposed to be secret, but it was this man's life's work to get at secrets.

A laugh came back as a reply. 'I want to meet you, Stella. I think you need to see me to take me seriously. This *is* serious.'

Stella did not answer.

'Come on, Stelly, I won't eat you.' He laughed, and Stella felt sick. 'Meet me at Waterloo, under the clock. Remember, that, Stelly? It was always the same place, wasn't it? Be there.'

Stella stood there, still clutching her bag. 'No, no, I can't, I can't.'

She picked up her bag, went down the staircase and out of the door.

Outside, in the night air, she looked around in case anyone was there.

Silence, quiet. Not a mouse stirring.

A WHOLE DAY AFTER Stella had gone away, John Coffin, Chief Commander of the Police Force of the Second City of London, let himself into his home. He was back some twenty-four hours before he was expected, and meant to have a quiet time working. He was accompanied by the white peke Augustus who had appointed himself dog-companion to Coffin and insisted on going everywhere he could with him. Coffin had gone away after the bombs had exploded; his departure had not been unconnected with that happening. His assistant, Paul Masters, kept him in touch.

Coffin was glad to be back; he had observed that the play running at the Pinero Theatre was no longer *An Ideal Husband* which meant, he hoped, that he would find Stella at home.

He put down his bags and ran up the stairs, calling out: 'Stella, I'm back.'

He was a big man, but spare of frame and light on his feet. His hair, which had been reddish in his youth, had darkened with the years and was now greying neatly about his temples. He was neat in everything he did. Thin as a young man he had never put on weight, although he took no exercise, other than running up and down the stairs of his home in the tower; he took part in no sports and never had. 'We didn't in my day in working-class London,' he said once, 'except a bit of street football and pavement boxing. Pugilism, more like,' he had added thoughtfully. But there was muscle beneath the suits, which, under Stella's control, were well and expensively tailored. Still done in the East End of London, but now he knew where to go. And how to pay.

'How come you have such muscles here and there?' Stella had said once.

'Inherited,' Coffin had answered. 'Runs in the family.' Though he had hardly had family. Orphaned, he had only discovered in later life that he had a disappearing, much married mother, who had provided him with two siblings, one half-brother, a stiff Edinburgh lawyer, and the other, from another alliance, his darling half-sister. Mother herself remained an absentee, except for leaving some extraordinary memoirs.

Silence.

From behind a curtain on the window where the stair curved, he saw a tail, then a cautious beady gaze.

'Oh, hello, boy,' Coffin said. 'You still here? Better not let Stella see you. You and I are going to have to stop meeting like this.' Augustus bustled up the stairs behind him, ready to take part in the game, but the mouse was gone.

The quiet of the tower was telling its own story; it spoke of emptiness. Stella was not here.

The place did not feel like home without Stella in it. He knew why; marriage with Stella had given him the stable home life which a first disastrous marriage had failed to do.

Coffin had been in Edinburgh where, amongst other things, he had visited his half-brother in the large, handsome, frigid house he inhabited. William matched the house; so much so that Coffin found it difficult to relate

to him as a brother, even half a brother. Their meeting
had been stiff and formal as they talked over the research
Coffin was trying to do on the life of their eccentric
parent. Sometimes, he thought his mother might still be
alive and building up yet another family; though she
would be near her century now, he did not put it past
her. He wished he had known her, but disappearing was
her game.

He was back home now and miserable. In Scotland
he had been at a conference of top policemen held in a
remote house. It had been one of those conferences
which had appeared to be on one subject but which had
had a covert purpose.

Coffin had learnt a few things at Melly House that
would concern him and his district, and had been, tactfully, informed of certain others. He, in his turn, had
passed on certain information.

Knowledge, he reflected, as he read Stella's note, is a
painful thing. She will ring, probably from New York. I
will know from the tone of her voice if I ought to raise
what I learnt at Melly House. He was desperately anxious but he kept calm; he knew he must.

The time passed quietly, with no call from Stella. He
had ahead of him several busy days, a meeting in central
London, two committees, one about finance. The bombs
in his district, the need for increased security all round,
had meant extra spending.

He knew that Stella usually stayed at the Algonquin,
so he rang there first. Miss Pinero was not a guest, he
was told politely. She was well known there and a welcome visitor, but, regretfully, she was not staying at the
hotel just now.

If she could afford it, or if someone else, like the film
company, was paying, Stella liked the St Regis.

But Stella was not there, either.

Finally, he did what he should have done at first, but disliked doing: he telephoned her London agent. He knew that Doria Jones thought he was bad for Stella's career, that he kept her cooped up in the Second City when she ought to be adorning the London or New York stage. In short, she thought Coffin was a chauvinistic, oppressive spouse.

Doria's secretary answered his call, saying in her polite but chirpy voice that Doria was out of town and would not be back until the late evening.

In the evening, he worked on papers and prepared a speech he had to give at an official dinner. That done he had a meal, then a drink, and fell asleep. Then, late as it was, he telephoned Doria at home.

She replied in person, sounding surprised to hear him. She had a soft, sweet voice and always said that Stella was her favourite client—which may have been true.

'No, darling, I don't know where Stella is. I did not send her an urgent message. Definitely not.'

She was willing to go on talking about this, but Coffin was not. 'Thanks, Doria, I got it wrong. My fault. Sorry I bothered you.'

He put the telephone down. 'Stella, damn you, where are you?' Coffin's life had ruled out trusting people. Stella was an exception. He still loved and trusted her, but he wanted to know where she was.

Coffin did not sleep much that night. 'If I have lost Stella, either physically or emotionally, because she wasn't what I thought she was, I would not die. I would go on, because I have learnt how to survive, but I would be shrunken.'

In the dawn he went down to the kitchen and made some coffee, which he sat at the table drinking. The sky outside was pink with light. He couldn't see the mouse but he heard a rustle by the window.

'Could she be dead?' he asked himself. 'If what I heard in Melly House was true, then the company she is mixing with might easily kill her if they scented danger.' He felt a groan rising inside him. 'I am part of the danger, although God knows I don't want to be.'

It was not all his fault though, and he knew that, too. Stella had to bear her share.

'When she gets in touch, comes back, we will work this through somehow,' he told himself. He finished the coffee, made toast, put some cheese down for the mouse, then ate the toast standing by the window watching the sun slowly rise into view.

He felt better. At intervals he told himself that he would certainly know if anything had happened to Stella. He would sense it. Would he, though? Wasn't that precisely the sort of fallacy he would discourage in other people?

On the other hand, he would be told, someone would tell him, he was the person who was told things, he was in a position to know what was happening.

Anyway, Stella would telephone soon. Or walk in the door, then they could talk things over. 'I don't blame you for anything, Stella,' he would say, 'but I must know.'

Didn't that sound pompous, precisely the sort of comment that would make Stella stamp out of the room in a rage? Phrase it better, Coffin. You will when you see her, it will happen.

'You may never see her again,' a voice whispered in his ear.

The information appertaining to Stella—lovely professional phrase that, if a little pompous—was nothing much, merely her name on a list, but it had been fed to him so discreetly, almost anonymously and without comment. He had been observed, though; notice taken, as you might say.

He was surprised to find that during all this inner conversation he had driven himself to work and had arrived, safely, too, in his office.

He sped through the outer office where two uniformed officers manned the defences, then with a brisk good morning to them he entered the inner office where three people worked—his assistant Paul Masters, and the two secretaries: Gillian, and the new girl, Sheila, who had replaced the elegant Sylvia—before hurrying into his own room which was empty and quiet, and smelt of furniture polish with a touch of disinfectant. Pine, he thought.

'Got back early,' he announced, as he passed through to his work-laden desk. The usual files to read and initial, a larger than customary folder of letters to sign (and there would be more when his secretary came in, but she was tactfully leaving him for a few minutes), and the notes of telephone calls received and to be returned.

A call from Archie Young, but no message. Coffin frowned. This was unlike Archie who was always businesslike and not mysterious. He rang his secretaries; Sheila answered.

'Do you know anything about these calls from Chief Superintendent Young?'

Sheila Heslop had been with him for six months now, more or less taking charge of the outer office and organizing Gillian, who was about to take study leave. In a quiet way, she organized the Chief Commander, too.

'He rang me first to see if you were in, sir,' she said carefully. 'I suggested that he speak to Inspector Mas-

ters, but he said he wanted you. I think he had something
he wanted to talk to you about.'

'Oh, well, I expect I will be here.'

'I rather think he might be ringing again,' she said,
with what might have been a touch of nervousness. This
made Coffin answer her sharply.

'What makes you say that?'

'Just a feeling, sir.'

Coffin looked at his watch. Still early, still time for
Stella to ring.

He took up the report on the bombings in the Second
City, which came with photographs and a video of the
bombers.

In two seconds the phone went. Coffin picked it up
eagerly to hear Archie Young's hesitant voice. 'Something you ought to see, sir. A body…Percy Street.'

'I'LL DRIVE YOU round, sir,' Archie Young had said.
'Unless you would rather use your own driver?' He
could see someone had better drive the Chief Commander. Coffin had a new driver—not a member of the
force; police officers cost too much to train to be used
as chauffeurs.

'He's away,' said Coffin. 'Thank you, Archie, you
drive.'

So tense he felt sick, Coffin let Archie Young lead
him into the house in Percy Street. There was a ring of
fellow officers there, the SOCO team, the police surgeon, and Inspector Lodge.

With automatic good manners he nodded towards
them all, but did not speak. He looked at the body lying
on the floor, the terribly damaged face staring upwards.
He saw the handbag lying on the floor.

He walked forward, forcing himself to study well

what he saw. He stared for some minutes before turning away. 'No, that is not my wife. Yes, she wore jeans like that; yes, she had such a handbag, but the body is not hers.'

Inspector Lodge met Coffin's eyes with a meaningful stare: I hope you know what you are doing.

Archie Young muttered something about the material in the handbag.

'I don't care what is inside the handbag. That is not my wife,' said Coffin in a quiet voice. 'It is not Stella.'

TWO

ARCHIE YOUNG and Coffin were back in the Chief Commander's office. Coffin had watched with an expressionless face as the body, which he refused to own, was packed into a black bag to be transported to the mortuary. The police used the one in the University Hospital where a special room had been allocated to them.

Archie picked up the blue leather handbag, now packaged in a piece of plastic. 'I think you should look at what was found in this bag.'

Coffin gave it a bleak look. He was not sure, but he thought he was angry with Archie. For certain, anger from somewhere, caused by someone, was welling up inside him. Perhaps it was from the pain, for there was pain all right. He said nothing but continued to stare at the bag.

'You thought you recognized the bag.'

The bag was dark leather, very soft and quilted with a gold chain and gold emblem on the front. Even Archie Young had seen similar ones around, swinging from the shoulders of the fashionable. Some were genuine, others imitation. This one looked the real thing.

'Stella has one like it. I gave it to her. Chanel, she chose it herself. But there must be many others, they are so fashionable.' Which was why he had given one to Stella, who had a taste for what was fashionable and expensive.

He studied the soft blue leather object, reluctant to open it, even to touch it.

'Better open it, sir. Or shall I do it for you?' A thin pair of transparent plastic gloves was held out, ready. Still reluctant, Coffin smoothed on the gloves; he knew the rules.

'No.' Coffin stretched out his hand, now masked, and lifted the tiny gold fastening. The bag yawned open in front of him. 'It's been damaged, the bag should open more slowly.'

'Yes, I reckon it's been wrenched apart. Not malice, I don't think. Whoever did it wanted to be sure that it fell wide apart. So you could see what was inside. At a glance.'

Coffin looked at Archie Young sharply. 'You meant something by that.'

'Take a look, sir.'

Coffin frowned as he drew out a photograph. He laid it on the desktop in front of him. Archie, watching the Chief Commander closely, saw the colour melt from his face to be replaced by a pallor and then a flush that spread to his throat and touched his temple. Coffin put out his hand and covered the picture. He looked up at Archie Young: 'That photo is a fake. Stella is not mad, bad and dangerous.'

'No,' said Archie. 'Of course not.' But he said it awkwardly, half defensively.

'Stella does not eat human flesh. God, no. That woman—' he tapped the picture— 'is eating an arm, I can see the wrist. A bleeding human arm.'

'Bit of,' said Archie even more awkwardly. And it wasn't actually dripping with blood. The blood, if that was what it was, looked dry.

The picture, of course, was a fake, but why? And the face, and the body, what you could see of it, was certainly Stella Pinero's.

Archie felt miserable: it was a bloody awful thing to have happened. No, he mustn't keep using that word, there was too much blood around as it was. He looked with sympathy at the Chief Commander, who seemed suddenly older.

'The dead woman is not Stella,' said Coffin. 'And this photograph is not of Stella.'

He's a good man, Archie said to himself, whatever she's done to him, he doesn't deserve this.

The devil got a hold of his tongue because he heard himself say: 'Some anthropologists think that kissing developed from biting.'

'Thank you.'

There was a pause during which Archie Young tried to think of something sensible and wise to say, before he decided that silence might be best.

Coffin shook himself, like a dog coming in from the rain. 'Let's get down to this. We are policemen, investigators. Who is the dead woman, and how did she die?'

'We don't know the answers yet to the first question. As to the second, it looks as though she was strangled. The face was beaten after death.'

'And the next thing, after establishing identity…' Coffin started the sentence.

If we can, said Archie Young silently to himself. He had dread feelings about this dead woman.

'Is to find out how and why she was carrying my wife's handbag. If indeed it is Stella's and not a replica,' Coffin pushed on. 'And that in itself is a strange thing. Why?'

It's all strange, Archie thought, mighty strange. 'Of course we will find out who she is,' he said, with more confidence than he felt. He grappled with another problem: how to refer to the Chief Commander's wife in the embarrassing present circumstance.

He compromised. 'Miss Pinero might be able to throw some light on it when questioned.' Coffin looked at him gloomily, even apprehensively. Archie floundered on. 'The bag might have been lost or stolen.'

'With the photograph in it?'

Wonder if he'll have a breakdown, Archie thought. He looks as though he could. On the edge. But no, he's a strong fellow, mentally and physically. Except he loves that woman, that's always dangerous. 'It's a joke that photograph,' he said.

'The dead body is not a joke,' said Coffin savagely.

Archie Young was silenced. From the outer room, Coffin could hear Paul Masters chatting away cheerfully. Too cheerfully, he thought sourly, and there was a woman laughing. For a moment, he thought it might be Stella, but it was one of the secretaries. He knew the voice, there was a brassy ring to it which today he found irritating. She laughed again, damn her. He wondered if he could institute a no laughing rule like a no smoking rule.

'I don't know where she is,' Coffin heard himself saying. 'I have not the least idea in the world where Stella has gone.'

That, thought Archie, is one of the comments you are better off not hearing. He liked and admired the Chief Commander, he liked and admired Stella Pinero, too, but he wanted to keep out of their relationship. Let them sort it out. She would turn up. You had to allow actresses their freedom. 'She'll get in touch,' he heard himself saying.

Coffin looked at his old friend and colleague and suddenly realized he was being offered sympathy. He laughed and pulled himself together.

'I am sure she will, Archie, and it had better be soon.' There was a note in his voice which suggested that Stella, when she returned, would have some questions to answer. He stood up. 'I'd better get back to work.'

The Chief Superintendent rose too. 'Anything new on the bombers?'

Coffin shook his head. What he had learnt on his trip north was confidential even from Archie Young. 'Nothing much,' he said in a noncommittal voice. 'Inspector Lodge was first in to inspect the body in Percy Street, I suppose?'

'Pretty smartish,' agreed Archie Young. 'Asked to come with me as soon as he heard about it. He was told, of course.' Anything to do with the bombed area was for him to know about, he was their expert, the local, middle-range one. All the foremost terrorist watchers had probably been in Edinburgh or wherever it was the Chief Commander had really gone. On this point, Archie had his reservations. Edinburgh first, and then on to— where?

'I suppose he hoped he'd got a dead terrorist.'

'I don't know what he hoped. He doesn't show his mind, that one.'

The two looked at each other. They would be glad to be rid of the Todger, but life was not so simple.

'He's very good at what he does,' Coffin allowed. Not a loveable man, but who would be in that job. He could not regard himself as a totally loveable person. He heard Stella's voice: 'No, darling, not a cuddly person. Many good qualities and I love you madly, but not cosy.'

Was that why she had gone away? Was she running away from him?

Did Stella love him? He had never felt totally sure. You had to remember that she was an actress.

And where was she, damn her.

'I'll take the bag with me,' said Archie Young, reaching out a hand for the bag in its plastic container. 'Forensics, and all that.'

Coffin nodded.

'If I could suggest, sir, you might have a look round at home to see if Miss Pinero's bag is there or not.'

'I will, I will.' He would get round to it when he felt less sore.

'Or she might say herself…' Archie left the rest of the sentence delicately unsaid.

'When we speak again, I will certainly be asking,' said Coffin. He watched the Chief Superintendent depart with careful, depressing tact, closing the door quietly and not smiling.

Feeling unloved and out of sorts, Coffin slumped back in his chair and went to work on the mound of papers in front of him. Word processors, far from reducing this load, added to it daily. A truism, of course, but he was not in the mood to be original.

He wondered where Stella was and why she had said nothing which was true; but he shrank from the painful thought that perhaps it was better he did not know more. A lie had to hide something, didn't it?

'I would not have this feeling if it were not for that terrible photograph. Which was not a joke. A fake, but not a joke.' And also because of the information gently passed over to him in Scotland. At the time he had tried to reject it, shrug it off as a case of mistaken identity, or a computer error, or someone's genuine mistake, which did happen even with the men he was being briefed by. Now he did not know.

He unlocked the bottom drawer of his desk. From inside, he withdrew a bundle of letters. Underneath was yet another, smaller bundle, older and grubby, as if much opened and read. All the letters were from Stella, he had kept every letter she had written to him: the older packet dated from when they first met, before they quarrelled and parted. The more recent letters were since they met again, and were written by Stella when away filming or on tour. He had asked her to write as well as telephone and he had written back.

'My secret hoard,' he said aloud. He never asked if Stella kept his letters.

There were no photographs. 'I hate being photographed except in the way of publicity business,' Stella had said, adding with a giggle: 'Besides, photographs are dangerous.'

Yes, Stella, they certainly are.

He packed the letters in his briefcase to take home where he could study them to see if they could tell him who took that photograph of Stella and, more importantly, who doctored it.

Who did you know, Stella, who could treat you in that way? Who wanted to make you look half-woman, half-beast?

HE PICKED UP THE telephone. Paul Masters answered promptly, as if he had been awaiting the call.

'You know what's been going on?'

'Just a bit, sir. If I may say so, sir, don't worry.'

He's sorry for me. Coffin accepted the gift with resignation. No doubt there was sorrow and pity all around him at Headquarters, seeping out into the whole police division which he commanded. Many a laugh and a joke too.

But the photograph was not to be laughed at. Some strange fish had swum into his pool and must be accounted for, and, if necessary, caught.

'Get me Chief Inspector Astley, Paul, please.'

'She's here actually, sir. Outside. Shall I send her in?'

'Yes, do.' So had it been Phoebe laughing?

She swung into the room a second later, her face grave. She had not been laughing. But she smiled when she saw him. 'I was on my way to you. I knew I had to see you to tell you what the latest was.'

'You know about the body in Percy Street? Of course you do.'

Phoebe advanced into the room with the confidence of an old friend and ally; she perched herself on the windowsill. She invariably dressed soberly for work; today she wore black trousers with a cream silk shirt, but there was always the impression with Phoebe that underneath was lace and silk, probably in red. It was a tribute to her impact on her colleagues because, as she confided to her friend Eden when she heard the rumour going around about her red knickers, in fact they were white cotton, 'from my favourite high street store, and made in Israel'.

'Mind if I smoke?'

'Yes. I thought you'd given that up.' In an early brush with what might have been but was not something malignant, Phoebe had given up all sins of the flesh from food to sex. Rumour had it that those days were over. Rampantly, cheerfully over.

'I've started again.' She lit up. 'When under stress.'

'And you are under stress?'

'I'm catching it from you.'

'Right,' said Coffin. For a moment he said no more. He trusted Phoebe, to whom he would probably speak more openly than to anyone else. Except Stella. The Stella he had lived with and loved, but it looked as though there was a Stella he had never known. I won't allow this thought to enter my mind, he told himself. I have to trust Stella, to believe in Stella.

'I was coming to see you because the Todger called me in.' She looked at him gravely.

'He would do,' said Coffin. Phoebe's area of responsibility touched upon that of Inspector Lodge. They did not like each other, but there was respect.

'I went round to Percy Street, the body had gone by then. I was told why they had thought it was Stella and got you round there, although I am bound to say I would not have thought it was her for a minute.'

'There was another factor...' he could hardly bring himself to call it a reason.

'The handbag? I was told about it and what it contained.'

'That was why I was brought round at speed,' Coffin said gloomily. 'I understand it, the bag has gone for forensic testing, and I am supposed to be going through Stella's things to see if the one she owned, her bag, is still there. But I am not doing it because I am perfectly certain the blue Chanel bag is the one and original.'

'Could be,' said Phoebe, 'but I shouldn't let it worry you, it's just a dirty trick. We'll sort that one out, don't worry. Her bag was used to create the illusion, someone wanted to distress you.'

'Someone succeeded.'

'But it wasn't Stella, and I am surprised that the illusion held for as long as it did. Once the body was moved and taken round to Dennis Garden for examination.' Phoebe picked a loose piece of tobacco from her lips, and smiled slightly. Professor Garden, an academic from the local university, was a pleasure to cross swords with. 'Once Dennis got it on the table—even before, I should guess—he knew not only was it not Stella Pinero but that it was not a woman. Too flat, no breasts.' She went on talking, giving him time to start breathing again; he seemed to have stopped. How long can the brain go without oxygen. 'The pelvic structure, of course. Quite different, you can always tell.'

'I suppose that, unconsciously, I saw that too. I knew it wasn't Stella.' Coffin went to the window to stare out. He could see across the road to the big car park where his own car had its privileged place; looking beyond was a large modern school where he had once given away the prizes, and further away the roof of the University Hospital where Dennis Garden taught and operated on the living and gazed upon interesting corpses with whom he was able to set up a relationship at once intimate yet impersonal. He fancied he could see one of those discreet, black-windowed ambulances turning in now to deliver another customer for Dennis's attentions. Coffin turned back to Phoebe. 'I suppose as Lodge called you in he thinks there is some terrorist connection.'

'His antennae are twitching,' said Phoebe.

Coffin came back to sit at his desk. 'That needs thinking about.' He tried to wave away Phoebe's cigarette smoke. 'I wish you'd put that out.'

'Fag finished.' Phoebe crushed the cigarette out on the sole of her shoe, then threw the stub away. The need for the counter irritant was over: Coffin was back on the job.

'PITY ABOUT THE FACE,' said Professor Dennis Garden. He sounded genuinely moved. 'The hair was a hairpiece on a band. Very good quality.'

'It does make identification difficult,' agreed John Coffin.

'Not only that, but from what I can make of the bone structure, he had a graceful, pleasing face. Small-boned altogether, or he would never have got into the jeans,' Garden said in a regretful tone.

'Strange there wasn't blood,' observed Coffin. 'Not much on the hair or hairpiece. What do you make of that?'

'Not much at the moment.' Garden was giving nothing away. 'I have not examined the body properly yet.'

'There was not too much blood in the room where he was found, but he was probably killed there. Interesting in itself. I wonder why?'

Professor Garden smiled happily. 'Your problem, my dear, not mine. I deal with only this end of the affair. It's for you to fiddle out the rest. If you can.' He waved a hand to an attendant. 'Seen all you want? Right, let's put this poor fellow away to rest.' The attendant wheeled the trolley to the refrigerated cage. 'I shall have to be at work on him later, but I promise you I'll do it delicately.' His pale blue eyes glinted with amusement at Coffin. 'Bit below you, isn't it, to be taking an interest in a simple case like this?'

'I always knew it wasn't my wife,' said Coffin bleakly. He knows all about it, every last detail, probably seen a copy of the photograph, or a drawing, or heard it with every elaboration and joke that his colleagues' humour could devise…

'Of course, of course. Very nasty moment it must have been. But soon over, you knew at once it was not Stella.' He crossed himself carefully. Amid a myriad of other interests in Dennis Garden's life was a feeling for a god. He was not always sure which god but he knew it was one to keep on good terms with. Besides, he liked Stella (inasmuch as he could admire any woman, his tastes not going that way), and wished her well. He would not have enjoyed doing a postmortem on her. He had an idea already that he was not about to enjoy this one.

'What about the hands?' Coffin asked.

'Ah, you saw the significance of the gloves?'

'One of the ways I knew it was not my wife,' said Coffin. 'I knew that Stella would not wear white gloves with jeans. So, what about the hands?'

'You were right to be worried; the fingers were cut off at the knuckles.'

Coffin nodded. 'No fingerprints then? What about the thumb?'

'Even the thumb has gone... Whoever did it was taking precautions about identification... But don't worry too much, science is wonderful, something might emerge that helps.'

But he was glad it was not Stella's body they were discussing. He was skilled in morbid anatomy; he taught it, even enjoyed doing so, but one does not want to cut up one's friends. Although there is always pleasure in a job well done. Already he had it in mind that he would identify this body for the police. No one got the better of Dennis Garden. Anyway, damn it, the face—he knew how to reconstruct the face. He had a sense of knowing that face.

He saw the Chief Commander to the door. What was she doing though, the beautiful and talented Stella, wandering away without warning to her husband when their marriage was supposed to be a notable success?

Not a man you could play around with, he considered, watching the Chief Commander's retreating back. There was something to the set of Coffin's shoulders that suggested he might not be easy.

COFFIN SUMMONED Inspector Lodge to see him. Lodge arrived with speed, suggesting to Coffin's anxious mind that he had been expecting a call.

'You went round to Percy Street very fast. Was there any special reason?'

The Todger took it quietly. 'I wondered if we might have a terrorist there.'

'Any other reason?'

The Inspector became even quieter. 'Always interested when something like this turns up…it's my job.'

Coffin waited.

'In confidence, we have had an insider working here, I thought it might be my plant.'

'And is it?'

Lodge shrugged. 'No identification yet.'

'Is your insider a man or a woman?'

'A man,' he said with reluctance. How he hated to part with information, Coffin thought.

'So it could be the dead man?'

'I am waiting to find out more, see who's missing, run checks, but yes, I think, yes.'

'And why was he dressed up like my wife? With a handbag containing a photograph of Stella? Any views?'

Lodge looked away, then back so that his eyes met Coffin's bleak gaze.

'Ah,' said Coffin, understanding what he saw. No need to make mysteries here, he told himself, least of all to yourself. This man has been told what was shown to me with relative delicacy…yes, I have to say they tried to be humane.

No more was said on that secret subject. Lodge departed murmuring that he would keep the Chief Commander in touch, but it looked at the moment that this was a terrorist killing. How his man had been flushed out, he did not yet know, but it was vital to find out.

'He was a good man,' he said. 'I don't know who got on to him or how, but by God I am going to find out.'

'A traitor in our midst,' said Coffin sadly.

'I hope not, but we may have to face it.'

'Let's meet for a drink sometime soon,' said Coffin. There was a hole here that needed mending, patching up, and it was his job to do it.

AFTER LODGE HAD GONE, Paul Masters came in with a tray of coffee and a file of papers.

'Hot and strong. And this is today's list: a CC and Accounts meeting at midday. A delegation from Swinehouse…ethnic problems. And Anthony Hermeside from the Home Office is inviting himself to lunch…'

Coffin groaned.

'Yes, good luck, sir. I have all the notes you will need to brief you on him in the folder. Oh, and Hermeside doesn't drink.'

He departed in polite good order. He had arranged what he could, smoothed Coffin's path and now it was up to the Chief Commander.

Coffin drank his coffee, which was, as Paul had said, hot and strong, there was cream to go with it and a new sort of chocolate biscuit, all confirming once again that everyone knew everything and quite possibly more than could be known—rumour always magnified a story—and he was being offered comfort.

He drank some more coffee, gazing at a corner of the room where it seemed to him a part of his own mind was circling.

'Ever been betrayed?' he asked this self.

'Many times and oft,' Old Sobersides up in the corner, who seemed to know more about his life than he did himself, came back with. 'And you just have to get on with it.'

He had asked for a report on the body in Percy Street to be delivered quickly, and it was now on his desk.

The report, put together with speed by Sergeant Mitchell said:

The body is that a white male, probably aged between thirty-five and forty. He was not dirty, he had not been living rough, nor was he undernourished. His hair, beneath the wig, was dyed.

Cause of death was a neat stab wound which had not bled profusely. We will know more about this when the pathologist reports.

It appears that he had been killed in the room where he was found. Blood traces, cleaned up but still to be seen, indicated this. Forensics are working it now.

Also, it is clear that he had walked there, wearing the clothes in which he was found. A video of him rounding the corner out of Jamaica Street shows him on the afternoon of the day within twenty-four hours of which he died. He was alone.

A first search of the rest of the house has turned up nothing except bomb-damaged furniture. Bed linen and towels in a cupboard in the upper bedroom, along with some old clothes.

A copy of the relevant part of the video is attached.

It was a blurred dark picture but one in which a figure, wearing jeans, swinging the Chanel bag over a shoulder, could be clearly seen turning the corner.

Good work, Mitchell.

He studied the picture again. Yes, there he was, centre

picture, clearly shown. The end of the street was more blurred.

Well, that was it, for the moment.

TAKING ADVICE FROM his darker, grimmer self, Coffin did as he was told and got on with the job, following the appointments laid out in his diary and pointed to by Paul Masters.

Used as Coffin was to the dead times in an investigation when nothing seems to move forward, he found it hard. In a way, it was Inspector Lodge's case if the dead man was indeed his man. Equally, because of the involvement of Stella, Coffin ought to keep out. He did not intend to do so.

He worked through the day, keeping his head down to avoid the interested eyes and hints of sympathy, but his temper was not improved by either.

Paul Masters had accompanied him into one committee meeting to keep the notes.

As they entered this last meeting together, Paul Masters passed on one more message to the Chief Commander. He was sensitive to his chief's moods and knew at once that he would not be pleased at what he was about to learn.

The message was in a sealed envelope, but nevertheless, through his own channels, Paul knew what was in it.

'From Chief Superintendent Young, sir. He wanted you to have it soonest.' You might need a strong drink when you've read it, instead of this committee of ways and means.

Coffin went into the room, already full of committee members, took his place at the head of the table, surveyed them bleakly, muttered an acknowledgement, then opened his letter. Why is it, he was saying to himself, that even colleagues you liked and respected (not always the same thing by any means) turn into trouble when they become committee members?

He read the letter quickly. 'Thought you would wish to know that the dead man has been identified as Peter Corner, who was working undercover for Lodge. He had taken a job as office assistant and manager of the firm of builders repairing the house in Percy Street where he was found. He was identified by his underclothes, which had not been changed when he was dressed up as a woman. He had an invisible coded number, as is the rule, inside his pants.'

Coffin looked up from the letter. He could already tell that the bad news had been saved until last. 'Lodge has sealed off the room which Corner rented in Pompey Land, Spinnergate. He found some notes there in which Miss Pinero's name was mentioned.'

Damn, damn and damn, thought Coffin, even as he opened the meeting in a polite, calm voice.

Archie Young had scribbled an additional line or two himself which Paul Masters was not privy to since it had not been typed and thus was out of the chain of communication.

'Series of photographs of Stella, taken in a bar, in company with an unknown man.'

Damn again, so the dead man had been watching Stella. Of course, she knew a lot of men, met them in the way of business.

Old Killjoy, his other self, who had come along with him and was nesting in the corner of this room, said sceptically: So?

Still, if there was anything bloody to come out, he

would rather Archie Young knew than anyone. Not sure about Lodge, though.

He became aware at this point that the committee was waiting for him to speak. He forced his two selves to fuse, and took up the duties of a chairman of a difficult committee which must get down to business.

IT WAS THE LAST committee of the day. He considered telephoning Archie Young, but knew, suddenly, he wanted to be at home. He collected the dog, who had spent the day with the two secretaries who were his devoted slaves, put him in the car with his briefcase and overcoat to make the short journey back to the old church tower which still dominated the Pinero Theatre complex.

He parked the car, dragged out the dog, who wished to stay comfortably where he was, and unlocked the heavy front door to his home. Because of security this was something of a complicated business.

'Stella?' He stood at the bottom of the staircase, looking up. 'Stella?'

There was no answer. Instead a kind of deadness as if no one really lived here any more.

Coffin sat on the bottom step, Augustus leaned against him, and they communed with each other on the misery of those left behind.

But life had to go on, as Augustus presently reminded Coffin by letting out a low, hungry growl. It was his asking growl, and said, 'Food.'

'All right, boy.' Coffin got up. 'Don't know what I've got for you, but if all else fails we will go to eat at Max's.' Max had started with a small simple eating place not far from the old St Luke's church, but skill and hard work from him and his family of pretty daughters had given it great success, to which he added a restaurant and bar in the Stella Pinero theatre.

Max had, however, helped Stella to fill a deep freeze with meat and fish dishes so Augustus and Coffin shared a warmed-up chicken casserole. Then Coffin made coffee while Augustus retired to bed.

In the silence of the living room, Coffin took out the packets of Stella's letters. He opened first the collection which dated back to their earliest days together. Stella was a good, gossipy letter writer.

Will I find someone here, Stella, who is your dangerous friend?—Friend? I should not use that word.

He read quickly, seeking likely names: here were Ferdy Chase, Sidney Mells, Petra Land. These names came up frequently, not surprising really, he reflected, because in those days Stella had been a member of the Greenwich Repertory Company as had those performers.

One or two names, not to be associated with that group, but of whom Stella had gossipy stories to tell, came in: a man called Alex Barnet…a journalist, Coffin decided, and a woman referred to simply as Sallie, someone with the surname Eton, probably adopted. Actors always invented good names.

The letters were full of theatrical stories and jokes. The story of Marcia Meldrum at the height of her powers, screaming in fury when the bit of moveable scenery (Norman Arden was famous for his moveable scenery) rose up and took her wig with it. All right, she was famous for her thin hair, and her scalp had shone through, but her furious speech had gone down in theatrical history. And the tale of Edith Evans, her youngish lover and the staircase, yes that had a wicked twist to it.

Was this why I kept them? he asked himself. No, it was because when I had them, I hung on to a bit of

Stella, and I always had this feeling that she meant more to me than I ever did to her.

Where was I when Stella wrote to me? The letters had various London addresses, so from that he knew they came during the restless period when he was moving around from lodgings to lodgings. All in various parts of South London, he noticed. Not the best part of his life.

Then a long gap when the two did not meet—let's not go into that now, I am depressed enough—but it had been marriage, death and disaster for him. Stella had swum on the top of the water much better, making a success of her career, a short marriage but bearing a daughter, now a success in her own right, living far away and not much seen but in loving communication with Stella. Stella was better at human relations than he was, he reflected.

Another batch of letters. They were married now, but she still wrote when in New York or Edinburgh or on an Australian tour.

New names, but that was understandable because in the theatre you were friendly with the people in the play with you and then you all moved on.

Josie Evans, Bipper Stoney (what a name to choose, but a well-known singer), Heloise Divan. Marilyn and Henry Calan…yes, he remembered those, nice people.

One or two names hung around with Stella saying, And do you remember? Ferdy Chase, was one. Also Sallie…sex of the latter not clear. Coffin had assumed a woman, but now wondered if Sallie was not a man.

Stella just briefly mentioned names and meetings. Coffin knew he could run a check on these names.

Sylvia Soonest, Arthur Cornelian. Some of the names he remembered and could put a face to. Eton again.

Then he folded all these letters away and turned his mind to the photograph.

He knew he dreaded picking up anything of these latter letters but it had to be admitted that the doctored photograph did not show a very young Stella.

He forced himself to think about the photograph again: you could not see her face except in profile, and the curve of her back.

Fake, fake, fake, he said to himself. Come back home and tell me so, Stella.

The door bell rang, loudly, twice. It was Phoebe on the doorstep with a bottle under her arm.

'Came to see how you are. Had anything to eat?'

'I think so.' He tried to remember. 'Yes, the dog and I found something in the freezer.'

'Have a drink then. Not a bad wine, not the best claret in the world, but that would be hard to find round here. And this is, so my worldly friends tell me, drinkable.' She rolled the word round on her tongue as if she found it a bit of a joke. She looked towards him to see if he found it a joke, too. No, no laugh. 'We will drink this together and get really sozzled.' At least you will, if I can manage it.

They sat down together at the kitchen table in front of the big window which looked across the road to the old burying place now secularized into a little park. It was seldom used, too many ghosts for most people. The cats of the neighbourhood found it a good hunting ground.

The bottle of wine was opened and, after the first glass, Phoebe decided her old friend looked better.

'Now what would you do,' she said, 'if this was not Stella but another woman who was missing?'

'Oh, send people like you to find her.'

'And how would they know where to look?' She filled his glass again. They drank in silence for a moment or two.

'I suppose I'd search for an address book, or a diary. Take a note of bills, anything that might give a hint.'

She just looked at him.

'But it's Stella,' he protested. Stella's privacy, how could he invade it?

'If Stella is in danger—and I think that photograph on the dead man suggests she is—you have to find her.' She filled both glasses again, almost emptying the bottle. 'Can I help? Want me to do it?'

'No. Thanks, Phoebe, but no.' He stood up. 'I am probably going to hate myself for what I am going to do.' He held out a hand. 'Thanks for coming.'

In the bedroom, Stella had a pretty white painted desk, very small, where she kept her private letters, as opposed to the professional ones which her secretary at the theatre kept on file. Very few letters, but he put them aside to be studied. A postcard with a view of the Tower of London, a scrawl on the back which said: 'See you, love and remembrance, A.'

There was a blue leather diary with notes and reminders of engagements, mere initials which he could make nothing much of at the moment.

A big white card with letters in gold, advertising the Golden Grove Health Hydro, was tucked under the blotter but near to the telephone. The telephone numbers in neat gold print had been copied in large pencilled letters in the margin.

Coffin was aware of this trick of Stella's: she was shortsighted so that she sometimes wrote the telephone number she wanted out in bold letters to be seen while she dialled.

Worth a shot, he thought. It was late evening but they would probably answer. Wouldn't want to miss a booking.

'Good evening,' said a soft girlish voice, 'the Golden Grove Hydro. Can I help you?'

He introduced himself. 'I think my wife, Stella Pinero, is staying with you. Can I talk to her?'

There was a pause. 'But Mr Coffin,' the soft voice was plaintive, reproachful, 'she cancelled. You yourself rang to say she could not come.'

Coffin put the receiver down, only too aware that whoever had rung, it had not been him.

He dialled Phoebe Astley's number. He had to talk to someone.

Profile of the Average Terrorist

THERE IS NOT an average terrorist. Remember that fact.

They come in all shapes, sizes, ages and sexes. Do not think you will know one by the look in their eyes. You may live next door to one, or have sat next to one in the tube. One may be a friendly neighbour, or drive your local taxi. You could even have married one.

Do not believe that you will be able to read that face, whether it is one you love or hate. The face is a mask, the mask will not be dropped; love will not do it, nor hate, nor amusement; the wearer has been trained not to drop it. A terrorist who drops the mask is a dead terrorist.

As a genius they are not long-lived, owing to the hazards of the craft (Carlos Marighella, author of the guerrillas' *Mini-manual* died young, shot dead). You will not find many old terrorists, although there must be some, probably sleepers, the hardest to spot. Occasionally a survivor, an ageing member, will be put into cold storage to be defrosted and brought up to room temperature if needed for use.

The terrorist may be a college graduate or relatively uneducated. But he or she will almost certainly be a person of some intensity. This might become apparent in conversation. Certain keywords like 'state' or 'nation' or 'police' might provoke reaction in the untutored terrorist. The trained one will know how to join in the majority view. On the surface. Any relationship will be on the surface. Truth need not come into it.

You will not know them by their table manners: if you ask them to dinner, they will not eat you. As far as possible they will have been trained to sink into the background. But this in itself is interesting to watch and may be a sign to make you alert.

Some terrorists are groomed to be front men. Shouters, these are called, and are probably the least dangerous of all, although this can never be certain. It may be that one of the chief functions of the shouter is to flush out your own sleepers.

Remember, there are no safe defenders of the faith, whatever the faith, yours or theirs. Conviction, whether inherited or taught, is always dangerous.

Alan Arden

THREE

COFFIN AND PHOEBE Astley met over a drink in Max's. It was late, but Max never closed when there was custom; he stayed behind the bar, serving their late meal and drinks himself and listening to the gossip. Except for Mimsie Marker, who sold newspapers outside Spinnergate tube station, he was the best informed man in the Second City.

'I didn't ring, so who the hell did? But the girl stuck at it, apparently keen to remind me of what I had not done.'

'So what will you do about it?'

'Don't know yet. Doesn't seem much point in banging on about it to the health place, any more than grumbling at the Algonquin. What she meant by booking in, I don't know.' Coffin was eating a ham omelette. He had found to his surprise that he was hungry. Phoebe had a large sandwich in front of her.

Max was watching them with interest from behind his long counter which was covered with a white linen cloth. He had been dealing with an exuberant wedding party, and was presently working out his profit margins while he kept an eye on Phoebe Astley and the Chief Commander, an old friend.

Phoebe put her hand on Coffin's. 'Look, don't worry too much... Stella is good at looking after herself. And she's a fighter.' Phoebe was one herself, and she recognized another. 'She'd fight for you, too. Perhaps she is doing that.'

'Think so?' Coffin finished his mouthful of omelette. 'What exactly do you mean by that?'

Phoebe took a long, thoughtful drink of coffee, then said: 'That photograph, however contrived, means trouble for Stella and, by transference, for you. And if she thought that, then she'd be out there doing something about it.' She took another drink of coffee and nodded towards Max, who came hurrying over with the pot, showing no sign that he wanted to close up for the night. Probably been reading my lips, Phoebe thought, and wants to know what is going on. She had long suspected Max of supplying news to the media. In the nicest possible way, of course—he was a nice man—but for money. Money and Max had a close and old relationship. 'That's all, just an idea, something or nothing.' Then she lit a cigarette.

'Thanks, Phoebe.' Coffin knew support when he heard it. And it was true enough, a happening like the dead body with Stella's bag containing that photograph would do no man's career any good. He hoped a lid could be put on the news, but while his close colleagues would probably keep their mouths shut, there was no hope the story would not get around. With embellishments. 'In a way, I hope you're right. But I wish she had not just cleared off. She could have told me where she was going.'

'She did.'

'But it wasn't true.'

'Give her a break. It's not much of a lie. May even be what she intended to do, until something happened. Came in the way. So maybe she tried the health place, perhaps to hide, and it didn't work out.'

Coffin gave her a measured look. Things must really be bad if Phoebe was being so kind. He thought about it for a moment. 'So what else have you got for me?' he asked.

'You could tell, could you? I must have a more revealing face than I ever knew.' She frowned. 'Something I picked up in the car park back at Headquarters…it's about the body found in Percy Street. It looks as if there is some doubt about the identity.'

'But I thought the identification as one of Lodge's young men was positive.' God knows that had been bad enough, but in a way, out of his hands.

'The clothes were identified,' said Phoebe. 'Not the man.'

Coffin said, slowly and heavily, 'There are, of course, many ways of identifying a man other than through his underclothes.'

'You've got it. Once Garden got down to work on the body, he could see that it didn't fit any of the details provided by Lodge: age, body weight, length of bones, even hair colour…all wrong.'

'What is Lodge doing about it?'

'Archie Young has taken over, it no longer being entirely within Lodge's sphere.'

'It never was entirely,' said Coffin.

'No, well, you know how he is; he does rather grab, and he grabbed first time round, on grounds of security. Still is, of course, if you think about the mark on the pants. He's got a problem there.'

'Oh, yes. I was thinking of those pants,' said Coffin grimly. 'What about asking his chap?'

'That's what Archie Young said: "Ask him, perhaps he's given up wearing them." Bit flip. The Todger went total. Not easy to do apparently—ask, I mean…Peter Corner isn't around. Of course, they are a secretive lot in that outfit, not straightforward.' Like us, she meant.

'They take off, it seems, on their own little games. Still, those were his pants.'

'They came from somewhere and were put on the dead man. Alive or dead. Why was he wearing them? Where is the owner?'

'Odd, isn't it?'

'It's more than odd, it's bloody odd.' He stood up.

Phoebe drank the coffee which Max had poured for her. 'Don't go rushing off. Dennis Garden has closed up for the night, and the Todger has gone home in a huff. He likes to feel his feet on solid ground and he can't at the moment.'

'Then he shouldn't be in the job he's in.' Coffin sat down again. 'Has he gone to bed too?'

'I am not in a position to know that,' said Phoebe, 'but it's reported he said: "I am seriously disturbed".'

'And Archie Young?'

'Ah, well, he was more violent. A bit scatological, in fact.'

'Not like him.'

'Relieving his mind. He saw straightaway that it opened the field up: What has happened to the chap who owned the pants? Did he part with them willingly and, if he did, then why?'

'And who is the dead man and why did he die? Yes, that's another set of questions. But Lodge knows the identity of the original owner.'

'Oh, he does. And when he thought he was dead, that was one thing, but now he is missing and may be alive.'

Coffin considered. He could see that they were plunging into very murky waters, and although not unwilling to plunge in, for indeed it might become necessary, he did not wish to do so now and with Phoebe.

'But lowly workers in the field are not admitted to the

knowledge of what that chap was,' said Phoebe sardonically. She, like many of her colleagues, had a sceptical attitude to officers like Inspector Lodge; it was thought that they were a dodgy lot. 'Of course, Lodge is only a kind of minder, keeps in touch with the boys in the field. I bet they don't tell him much.'

Coffin was silent, being privy to more secrets than Phoebe. He, too, had a side to his work which had touched a hidden world.

'But, of course, we have our own ways of finding out what we want to know,' said Phoebe, who had clearly got into her counter-irritant phase and meant to take him out of himself. 'And so the word is that his sleeper was working in the office of the building firm as dogsbody and office manager, and is now missing.'

'Better than being dead, I suppose.'

'Yes, but you see that's struck terror into Lodge's heart, because perhaps his man was not his man after all, or not totally, and has gone missing because he has been dealing the cards twice, if you see what I mean.'

'That's just guessing, though.'

'But intelligent guessing, which we are good at. To be verified tomorrow morning by a call to the office. Fingerprints, that sort of thing. And where the chap lives. Going over everything with that toothcomb I never seemed to see around.'

She wasn't drunk, Coffin thought, but tired and letting words go to her head. Or rather her mouth.

'It's no joking matter.'

'Who's joking? I'm not joking. In fact, I am quite melancholy about it all. I knew the chap. Not for what he was, of course, simply just as a good-looking chap who came my way.'

So he was good-looking, Coffin noted. 'How did you

get to know him?' Not a question to ask Phoebe, who followed where her wind of fancy took her.

'He came round to talk about my bomb damage and we went out to have a drink. We planned to…well, never mind what we planned, that's off.'

'He might come back.'

Phoebe pursed her lips. 'No good. If he comes back and works for T. Lodge and co, why is he cosying up to me, I ask myself. To find out what we know that he or his masters might like to know? Then again, if he is really working for the other team, the prospect of what he wanted from me is even worse. No, a straight up-and-down builder was all I was looking for.'

A faint, very faint, set of ideas were beginning to take shape in Coffin's mind. Let it settle, he told himself. See what happens. Sleep on it.

He realized with surprise that he might, after all, sleep. He paid Max, gave him a healthy tip, and saw Phoebe home. Or did she see him home? He could feel her resolute, sensible presence beside him as he drove home.

At the bottom of the stairs, he took a deep breath. The telephone was ringing; he moved fast up the stairs. It might be Stella.

But no. 'Inspector Lodge here, sir. Could we talk?'

He was unsurprised. 'Yes, I thought you might want to.'

'I knew you would guess, sir. I put up the act of being willing to hand over the case to Archie Young, but, of course, I can't do that. Not entirely. He knows it, too. Pete Corner is my man, I must be interested. Those were his clothes… I have to find out how and when and why he parted from them. Also where he is. We have a system for keeping in touch.'

'I know.'

'He hasn't used it. He may have reasons—I hope he
has—but if he doesn't turn up soon, then he has to be
found. It's a bit of a problem. We have his clothes, but
not his body... And that's apart from other complications.'

Who but the Todger would refer to Stella as a complication?

'Do you want to come round here and talk further?'

'I suppose I have said it all, sir. I shall be digging, of
course...'

Digging was the word, and whatever he dug up, even
if about Stella Pinero, would be in his hands, and those
who controlled him.

'I understand,' said Coffin.

'Knew you would, sir. I can't help myself.'

Of course not, the Todger was only part of a network.
As he was himself, for that matter. 'Better to have everything out...whatever.'

'There is something else: I have been a little concerned about Corner myself lately.'

He put the telephone down.

No STELLA. But Augustus was asleep on the bed. He
raised his head, muttered something, then went back to
sleep.

Coffin sat on the edge of the bed while he thought
about life. There was a smell of Stella's scent on the bed
linen which even the furry smell of peke could not over-
lay. Coffin closed his eyes.

He was beginning to see Stella more and more as
victim. He leaned back against the big square pillow,
and closed his eyes.

The darkness stayed with him as he slept, but now
writhed and twisted in strange shapes. Every man's horror

was upon him: he had lost his wife. Worse than losing a cat or a dog, a shade worse than losing a child? Nothing between them: he had lost a wife, had lost a child, he knew how it felt, but Stella was something more, she was part of his whole life, woven into the fabric.

When he woke into daylight, with the dog sprawled by his side, practically eyeball to eyeball, the presence of Stella had faded somewhat. She was still there, but more comfortably, as if she did not want to cause him too much misery.

It had turned warmer by the time he got to his office. He could see through the windows of this modern building where men in shirtsleeves were moving around, answering telephones, or watching flickering screens.

He hurried past, nodding a brief good morning to the outer office so he could get to work. Work would be his salvation, as it had been once before. It would not bring Stella back from wherever she was and for whatever reason, but it would make it easier to bear. A sense of her did not exist in this office.

There was plenty of work, not all of it connected with the bomb in the Second City. The day-to-day routine, which he had initially resented and performed badly, he had now come to enjoy. He was good at it too—or quick and neat, anyway, which counted as virtue. On a day like this, it was as good as aspirin and better than whisky.

The Second City was getting steadily more crime-ridden. In front of him he had a letter suggesting that something should be put in the water piped to families with a record. No recipe given. The front office ought to have filtered this letter out, not sent it in for his consideration. But perhaps they wanted to give him a laugh.

Then he read the signature: the writer was a distinguished member of the House of Lords. A tactful reply would have to go out to a man who was on one of Coffin's important committees, a man he might meet socially tomorrow or the next day, and who clearly had become exceedingly eccentric.

The thought depressed him but, hell, what did it matter? Senility was nature's way of easing you off the scene, maybe allowing you a little amusement on the way while giving plenty of annoyance to your friends and relations.

He worked away quietly, dictating letters, handling telephone calls as put through to him, ignoring the voices from the outer room. Paul Masters seemed to be in good tongue.

It was still mid morning.

Then Phoebe rang: 'Archie Young and the Todger combined forces and made Dennis Garden begin work really early. He hated it, but did the job. He's just about ready to announce what he has found, cause of death and so on. The Todger and Archie are there now and I think they would like you to be there too… In the circumstances.'

'I'm busy.'

'Won't take ten minutes.'

'Are you sure you don't already know and can't tell me?'

'I am absolutely sure. I will come round and drive you.'

Dennis Garden received them all in his office in the University Hospital. It was a big new hospital and he had a big new office.

He looked pale, being up too early in the morning did not suit him, but he was freshly scrubbed and smelt of a mixture of disinfectant and verbena.

'Nice to see you, Chief Commander.'

No one shook hands. 'So what is it?' asked Coffin.

In a few short sentences Garden told them what would

be in his report. He said the man died from a stab wound, but he had had a weak heart, so nature had helped, then he was beaten about the face, fingers cut off, and laid out afterwards. Dead about four days.

'Did he struggle?'

'Possibly,' said Dennis Garden. 'But he was not a healthy man, and he had been out on a cold night.'

'Are you suggesting exposure, then?'

Garden shook his head. 'He might have suffered from chilling, but he had taken a mixture of drugs beforehand. It all weakened him, though I agree, the absence of a struggle is puzzling.'

Coffin began thinking it out. 'So why was he got up like that? For a bet? For money? Someone picked him up? I wonder where that was.'

Archie Young cleared his throat. 'Near the Armadillo in Power Street probably, that's a likely spot.'

'A good guess,' agreed Dennis. He was subdued and quiet, not his usual manner of brisk confidence that God was in Dennis's heaven and all was right in his world. 'Not that I have any personal knowledge of the place,' he added stiffly.

Coffin wondered about that; he could imagine Dennis at a table there, quietly leading the band. 'But we are no nearer establishing identity,' he said.

'Not quite. He was known to me. We met occasionally. He'd been on the stage; nothing great, period drama, panto, that sort of thing. He liked dressing up.' As you live, so you die, Coffin thought.

'He went up for parts even now every so often—didn't get many. He had a tiny private income so he survived. As I say, I knew him socially. Di Rimini, he called himself. Not his real name; he liked play acting. If someone offered him money to dress up, he'd take it.'

Garden was offering an interesting suggestion: di Rimini had been paid to put on the clothes. Coffin could believe it.

Coffin looked at Archie Young. They knew Garden's ways socially. It depended what society you moved in.

'Would you call him a friend?' he asked bluntly.

'In passing. In passing only. A young friend.'

'But you knew him. So there was really no point in cutting off the fingers and rubbishing the face.'

'Of course, I can't say about that,' said Dennis stiffly. 'That's for your teams to decide. But whoever killed him could not have known that I had met him and that I would be doing the postmortem.'

Nor known that you could recognize his body even if his face was gone, thought Coffin cynically.

Dennis Garden met no one's eyes but twisted his lips wryly. There was not much more to be said. Promising a speedy official report plus photographs, he opened the door for them. Relieved, Coffin thought, to see them go. 'This is all off the cuff,' he said, as Coffin passed.

Coffin nodded. 'Of course.'

'Pity him being one of Dennis's boys,' said Phoebe, as they made their way out. 'Muddies the waters a bit. You could see Dennis feeling it.' She did not hide the satisfaction in her voice. 'He shouldn't mix it so much; one sex or the other, not both at once.'

'Really?' asked the Todger, something of a puritan. 'Difficult operation, I should think.'

'It can be done,' said Phoebe, smiling. 'No personal knowledge, of course.' She reined in the smile as she spoke to the Chief Commander. 'May I drive you back to the office, sir?'

'I AM SORRY ABOUT Dennis Garden,' said Coffin, once they were alone in the car.

'I'm not, I enjoyed it.'

'I could see you enjoying it.'

'He was rude to a friend of mine once.' The car was moving swiftly through the streets. 'Pity about the dead man, but he was going to die anyway. This way someone picked him and found a use for him. First time in years, I should think. Except for Dennis, of course.'

'You knew what Dennis was going to say, didn't you?'

'Let's just say that with the help of a friend who works in the mortuary, and a little intelligent guessing, I knew something.' She smiled. 'Might as well come clean; Francesco di Rimini under his real name of Edward Bates, did a little work as a snout, as did my friend. I gather Bates did it more for the pleasure of nosing round and picking up scraps of info—which might or might not have been true—than for the money.'

'Might have been why he was killed.'

'Doubt it, don't you, sir? He wasn't big time.'

'Thanks for telling me.'

'Oh, you would have been informed. I just got there first.'

They had arrived and Phoebe parked the car neatly where he had but a few paces to walk to the main door.

Coffin was still thinking it all over. The puzzle remained: 'But why kill him at all? Why use the body, dress him up, make him look like my wife?'

'Ah, why indeed. To get at Stella?'

'Again, why?'

Phoebe transferred her car keys from one hand to the other then put them in her handbag. None so blind as those...she murmured to herself. 'To get at her is to get at you.'

Coffin digested this, which he knew already, so Phoebe was not being as clever as she thought she was. 'Well, it hasn't hit the news desks yet.'

'Not yet. But it will. The press and the TV will know

soon, but Archie and the Todger will be sitting on them. Won't last. Be in the *Evening Standard* lunch-time editions, I expect. Mimsie Marker will be selling in the hundreds.'

'Especially if—' he stopped.

'There won't be a mention of Stella. Not at first.'

'No, I can't make up my mind what to do.' He smiled wryly. 'Can't send out a general search message, she'd kill me.'

Then he heard himself say loudly: 'I think she's dead. I think Stella is dead.'

'If there had been an accident, you would have heard by now.'

'I wasn't thinking of an accident.'

'Stella wouldn't do anything silly,' said Phoebe. 'She wouldn't kill herself.' She had a sudden picture of the vibrant, lovely Stella, of whom she had nursed some jealousy but nevertheless liked for all that. Besides, Stella valued her own appearance and even in death she would not damage it. A woman knew the strength of that feeling, thought Phoebe.

'Not suicide,' said Coffin. 'Murder.'

The loved ones of those who go missing fall into two groups: those who are convinced the dear one will come back even as the police are trying to get them to identify a dead body, and those who know from the beginning that the loved one is gone for ever. He could hear his own voice now, trying to bring reason to both parties, rational, quiet, useless words.

Coffin was surprised to find he belonged with the second group.

FOUR

ON THE RIVER near to Petty Pier stood a large house which the proprietor, Emmeline Jessimon, ran as a set of small service flats. The only service she gave was to change the linen and towels and tidy up once a week. Linton House had been run as a small hotel, but Mrs Jessimon had decided that one-room flats—self-catering, of course (she provided a minute kitchen unit with a tiny cooker and refrigerator)—would bring in a greater profit with less work. Money in advance, naturally. Two of the flats were occupied by leaseholders. One, an elderly widow called Mrs Flowers, was no trouble; the other was a tenant who came and went, as well as sometimes lending the flat, or so it seemed, to friends. This flat worried Mrs Jessimon. But on the whole it was easy work, she said to herself.

Usually this was true, and she had the help of the caretaker from the school round the corner, who helped with the boiler and the rubbish. True, he was on holiday at the moment (Bermuda, of all places), but she had his stand-in, a young chap called Vince. What a name for a man who cleaned out the drains in an emergency—if that was his real name; on occasion he seemed to forget, which made her wonder. Still he was nice, if silent, and she liked his help. But tenants had their own ways of making a nuisance of themselves, from falling asleep while smoking and setting fire to the sheets, to breaking such china as she provided. There was a notice in each apartment proclaiming CATERING ON REQUEST, but as

one tenant, a theatrical on tour, had said: It would be a
brave soul who faced Ma Jessimon's cooking. In fact,
she just went round the corner to a Chinese takeaway.

On the same day that Coffin decided that Stella was
dead, Mrs Jessimon (the Mrs was honorary) was checking up on the tenants in one of her apartments. First the
quick let.

An interior monologue went on: Gone then. Luggage
gone, clothes gone. Not that they had much. Fly-by-
nighters, knew that the minute I set eyes on them. Can't
fool me. Still, they paid for the week. Money in it for
me. I might let it again. Change the linen, tidy up, check
the fridge—don't want anything going bad in it. Remember the time that man left an uncooked rabbit in it?
Thought it was a dead baby, I did. Perhaps, it was, for
all I know. Into the dustbin with it. Nothing there this
time, not even a bottle of milk. Now milk, when not too
stale, comes in handy.

Then she moved on to the next tenant, the permanent
one, if you could call her that. She had been in. Paid for
everything: milk, bread... She came with a man, but it
was her that paid. You don't see that so often, even these
days. I think men should always pay, it's what they are
for. Lovely looking, she is. So was he. In a way.
Younger than her. I suppose that's what she paid for.

No, I mustn't be unkind. He must have fancied her—
kept his arm around her all the time. Must have been
hot. It was a warm day.

Never heard them go. Not that it matters.

Could that be blood? Drops of it, on the floor. I'll
never get that out of the carpet. Now I must be sensible,
he probably cut himself shaving. Or she did...stupid to
think otherwise. Don't want the police prowling around.
It's her place. Not my responsibility. Tidy up, close the

door behind you. Lock it. Quietly now. The tenant in number four likes to listen.

That's it, quietly down the stairs. You could fall and break a leg, you're so strung up. Never mind. A glass of sherry will do the trick. No, gin. It's a gin day. A gin and tonic, and a nice cup of tea and a rest. Then you can tidy up the room. A pity she couldn't do it before she left. It's a woman's job. All that blood. A man should pay and a woman leave things neat and tidy.

Nor should a woman notice things better left unnoticed. I didn't notice the kitchen knife on the floor.

She came with a man, and she's gone with a man.

ACROSS THE SECOND CITY in the casualty department of a big, anonymous hospital, De Allegra, junior registrar, was so tired that he was talking to himself. Most of it was aloud and listened to by his patient; some, however, was a silent conversation in his head.

Lost a fair bit of blood, muttered Dr Allegra to himself. Bit more and there would have been real trouble. Don't think a transfusion is needed here. Just as well, since the hospital is short of blood. Funny thing to be short of: there it is pumping away inside everyone in the city, millions of pints, but you had to get it out, keep it sterile and spend money on it, then shove it into people. And money was short. Of course, if you were dying you would probably get blood. Better not to count on it, though. Three months as a junior reg had made a natural optimist into a cynic. He did not believe the patient's version of what had caused this wound.

Aloud, he said: 'This may hurt a bit, I shall give you a local, but you will probably still feel it... Yes, sorry about that... About a dozen stitches, I think.'

He whistled as he worked and went back to his own

thoughts: wish I wasn't so tired. I did make a bit of a night of it, but a chap needs something to look forward to at the end of the day with the blood and the needle... I don't think I'm cut out for surgery. Perhaps I might switch to psychiatry. Not doing a bad job here, nasty wounds.

Aloud, he said: 'Nearly done. I'll give you some pain-killers... How did you say it happened? Accident?' Going silent again, he said to himself: Some accident.

'You'll have a scar there, I'm afraid.' You don't work in anything where looks count, I hope. He had the sense to keep that last comment to himself. 'Fade with time, you know.' He didn't know, but you had to give hope: this was the most positive thing he had learnt as a doctor.

He stood back to study his handiwork; it looked good. He observed also some scratches on the hands, which made him even more sceptical of the 'accident'. Looks almost as if someone had taken a bite, he thought, more than one bite, but he said nothing. Not then. Have to see the police later on, though...

THE YOUNG DOCTOR was not the only one interested in strange behaviour in odd men. Inspector Lodge got a telephone call from his vanishing 'sleeper'.

'Wondered where you were and what you were up to,' Lodge said.

'I've been taking an interest in Stella Pinero. I followed her; she went off in a car with a man—not willingly, I thought.'

'Well? Is she of interest to us?'

'Probably not. I tailed the car and traced them to a set of service flats. I couldn't get any information from the owner, an old biddy called Jessimon, although I have good access to her. After a day or two there, Stella Pinero left. I had to decide whether to follow her or the man. I followed her. She went first to a house of a woman who works in the theatre, and then home.'

'Go on,' said Lodge urgently. 'I want more.'

But the caller was gone.

Damn him, thought Lodge. Is he being straight with me? He would like to see me out and himself in, I know that much.

FIVE

THE STELLA PINERO Theatre missed Stella. The performers in the playhouse missed her, the Theatre Workshop (always more notional than real since the area was used for many other projects) and the tiny Experimental Theatre in the old church hall missed her even more. Without Stella the whole complex felt a void. She gave it life.

'Not to mention money,' said Letty, Coffin's half-sister and a major contributor to the theatre's funds. She had flown in, talked to Coffin on the telephone, heard a more or less uncensored version of events, told him to toughen up and be a man (which he had taken badly), and come round to the theatre.

Now she was standing in Stella's office where unanswered letters were piled on the desk. 'Where the hell is Stella? Without her, I'm hurting.' Financially, she meant. Coffin had long ago decided this was the only way Letty could be hurt, since three marriages and possibly many other alliances had left her undented. Even financially she seemed to have many ways of replenishing the coffers: a successful lawyer, a banker and player with big money targets, this was the love of her life.

'We are very near the overdraft limit; it's one of the reasons I flew back from New York.'

New York this time, but it might have been Zürich or Johannesburg or Hamburg, wherever the money was moving.

Coffin's wandering, disappearing mother had deposited her children round the world like misplaced luggage. She had left Coffin in London, Laetitia in New York, and William in Scotland, where he, too, had gone into law. One way and another the law had claimed all three. It said something about their mother, Coffin thought: she had been beyond the law, so all her children had run for cover in it. Unconsciously, of course, not aware of their motivation, since their mother had never allowed them to know her. Disappearance was her theme. She had left her memoirs with Letty, perhaps trusting her business sense most. They were now with John Coffin, who struggled at intervals to make them into something that could be published. Such a life deserved fame, he had said to Letty, even if posthumous. Assuming his mother was in fact dead—nothing seemed certain about that lady.

'Stella will be back,' said Alice. Letty had seized on Alice, whom she did not know, as she arrived at the door of the theatre where a dress rehearsal of *Aylmer's End,* the next play in line in the Experimental Theatre, was just beginning. Alice looked a commanding and somewhat enigmatic figure. Not one to appeal to Letty. On Alice's side, Letty looked like a natural enemy.

'Who is in charge here?' Letty knew that since Alfreda Boxer, the theatre manager, had departed—to die quietly it was rumoured—there had been much shifting of management personnel.

'Stella interviewed another manager before she went away,' said Alice artlessly. 'But I don't know what decision she came to.'

'So there's no one?'

'We all help out. And Debby Anglin has been coming in as a temp…she's doing a degree at the university in business studies. And I've been helping as secretary, because since Jacky's boyfriend won a prize in the lottery we haven't seen her any more.'

Letty rolled her eyes. 'As I said: no one. Good job I'm here.' Why did Alice give her the impression she might as well have been talking in a foreign language?

Alice looked at her with envy: this year Letty's hair was a soft blonde with a hint, just a hint, of silver here and there; she was wearing a brightly checked dress cut by a master's hands; and she was thinner than anyone had a right to be. Alice almost hated her.

Letty took from the desk all the papers she judged important, saying she would deal with them. There was a lot of her money in the theatre and she intended to save it. She gave Alice a questioning look. The plays? she was asking.

'There's always one on the stage and one in rehearsal and one on the go in the background—casting and that sort of thing,' said Alice, in her usual neutral yet edgy manner.

Letty patted her arm. 'Cheer up. Don't be nervous. Know what my first husband taught me? Never trust a man who is nervous. What has he got to hide? Applies to women, too. Act confident.'

'I feel nervous.'

'Stella will be back,' said Letty. Maybe without an arm or a leg—why did that thought flash through her mind?—damaged in some way, but back.

In the theatre bar, run by Max as she remembered, she saw a group sitting at a table drinking coffee. They looked up as she walked over.

'Letty Bingham.' She held out her hand. 'Stella's business partner.' She did not recognize any of them from past performances, but she knew that Stella's casts came and went. One of the girls had a face she had seen before, probably on television. They introduced themselves: Jane Gillam, Fanny Burt and a slightly older girl, Irene Bow. It was she whose face seemed familiar, and yes, Letty knew the name now, and she had been on television. Would be somehow, Irene had a televisual face if ever there was one. The two young men stood up politely.

'Michael Guardian, and this is Tom Jenks… We are both in *Noises Off.*'

'I am glad you've come,' volunteered Jane. 'We've felt a bit lost without Stella.'

'You're all doing fine.' Irene Bow patted her arm.

'It's all right for you,' Fanny said. 'You're only here for a few weeks or so of rehearsal time and then going off on tour, but we are going to be here for the next three months.'

There was a murmur of agreement from the two young men. Letty felt they were all watching her to see what she would say. 'I will keep an eye on things,' she promised. It was about all she could say, and perhaps not too convincing, but they looked relieved. 'I'll keep the money side in order, that I can promise. There hasn't been any special trouble?'

'Oh, no,' said Jane.

'Except for my dresser buggering off,' said Irene Bow.

'Old Maisie? She really only works for Stella. She wanted to do you, Irene, because she admires you so much,' said Jane, who had obviously appointed herself peacemaker-in-chief.

'Only she hasn't.'

'She sent a message saying she couldn't come in. She probably felt ill.'

Irene Bow laughed. 'Oh, well, I'm used to roughing

it. Good job it isn't a costume drama, although some of the changes are quick.'

'I'll see what I can do,' said Letty, as she moved away.

On the way out, she stood for a moment watching the rehearsal of *Aylmer's End*, the work of a local author, and seriously doubted if this particular play would do. But who could tell?

The set was a sitting room with a fireplace, dead with no fire. A table with four chairs round it and three people mid stage. All wore blue jeans and identical checked shirts. One wore an apron, thus denoting sex.

'This place is a cesspit,' proclaimed the young actress who was centre stage; it was she who wore the apron. 'A sexist cesspit.' She took off the apron, and threw it towards one of the men. 'Here, you wear this.'

'Shit,' said the actor. He left the apron on the floor where it had fallen, moved towards the fireplace and began warming his hands, 'I am not playing that game.'

Lesser Albee, thought Letty, would-be Wesker, a touch of the Osbornes. Perhaps Alice was right to be nervous.

She turned away. It was interesting, she thought, how quickly Stella and her company of players had been able to bring about that dusty, musty theatre smell of scenery and painted furniture in what had been not so long ago a church.

As Letty walked across the courtyard to her brother's dwelling in the church tower, she admitted that, absent though she might be, Stella was a professional and probably knew that everyone of the author's friends, enemies and relations (who might be the same thing) would come to *Aylmer's End*. She also noted with some respect for Stella's acumen that the play ran for only three days, and no matinees—the afternoons being reserved for readings from Shakespeare: *Hamlet, A Midsummer Night's Dream,* and *Twelfth Night.* 'Set texts for end-of-term exams,' she told herself. Yes, Stella would get her money back, and probably pay for the next generation of young performers whom she would employ in later productions. She was not adventurous, but, as her business partner, Letty could not be critical. Indeed, she was grateful that Stella was not the sort of producer to have those mad, original four-o'clock-in-the-morning ideas that lose money.

All the same, she would have liked Stella to show up. Had she gone off on some sexual fling? No support from her brother for that theory; he would have none of it. With some irritation, Letty thought he would rather his wife were dead than unfaithful. Yet there was a lot he was not telling her. She did not count herself psychic, but she had much experience in lies and evasions—it was her job, after all. And Letty was convinced a man came in somewhere.

She paused at the bottom of the tower where her brother lived, wondering if he was there. Then she heard the dog bark, so she pulled on the bell till it rang loud and long. She was aware that many security cameras and spyholes protected the tower, thus Coffin certainly knew who was ringing the bell. No doubt he was looking at her.

She waited patiently till she heard Augustus bark again, from nearer this time, which heralded the approach of her brother.

'Ah, so you *are* here. In hiding?'

'Working at home.' He looked tired and drawn, but was as neatly dressed as ever in well-cut trousers with a grey silk shirt.

'Same thing,' she said, pushing past him, patting Augustus on the head. 'I preferred the old dog, really. I like a dog who looks as though he has lived and Gussy here is a bit bland, aren't you, old boy? Right, right, you didn't ask me, and the old dog died. This one will do.' Augustus showed his teeth at her, not entirely amiably, as if he understood a judgement was being passed on him. 'I have been to the theatre, had a look round. We certainly need Stella there. I can do the money, but she has the flair. There's a play being rehearsed at the moment which will fall on its face if she isn't there to pull it together. I didn't get any clues as to why she had gone.'

'Her dresser, Maisie, might be helpful,' said Coffin, closing the door. 'But she seems to have gone to ground, too.'

'Not with Stella?'

Coffin shook his head. 'I don't think so. It seems she's taken herself off for a little holiday. She prefers to work exclusively for Stella, you see, so if Stella is not playing, she's free if she chooses—that's the usual rule. I've put Phoebe Astley on to finding her... Come on up and have a drink.'

Letty looked at him, raising an eyebrow.

'No, I'm not on to the whisky. I will have tea, the Englishman's ruin. You can drink what you like.'

She followed him up the stairs to the kitchen, where there was a teapot; she touched it to check: hot. 'I talked to a girl called Alice. She may have been keeping something back, I couldn't be sure. I suppose they have all been questioned?' She sat down opposite Coffin.

'They don't know where Stella is, or why she went off—I am sure of that. But Maisie may,' said Coffin, adjusting his feet so that Augustus could settle there with comfort to them both. 'Yes, she was close to Maisie.' There was pain in his voice. He had thought that Stella was close to him. Would she tell things to Maisie that she would not tell him? The answer seemed to be: Yes.

'I could go to see where Maisie lives, if you like?'

'No, leave it to Phoebe Astley,' he said, his voice heavy. 'It may need the official touch.'

In other words, thought Letty, you want it all kept under the official cover.

She poured milk in her tea and drank it down, then got to her feet. 'If I hear anything, in any way, of course I will let you know. Meanwhile, I must be off, usual address.' Letty maintained a smart Docklands maisonette, part of an old factory. It was one of her many addresses around the world.

'I know where to find you.'

'Shake yourself up and get out into the world again, that's my advice to you.'

'Thanks, Letty.' Coffin managed a smile. Letty always knew best.

'I will keep an eye on the business side of things at the theatre. You can rely on me there.'

He saw her down the stairs, with Augustus trotting behind. 'Like me to take the dog for a run?' she offered.

'No, thanks, Letty. I will take him, he's company.' Coffin leant forward and kissed her on the cheek. It was a rare embrace between them.

Letty walked round to where she had parked her car. She sat there for a minute, considering the Chief Commander's state. He's wretched. Damn Stella, what does she think she is about? She drove away angrily. Wait till I see her. If she ever did.

BY THE TIME Coffin and his little acolyte got to the top of the stairs, the telephone was ringing. He picked it up in a mixture of hope and fear.

'Phoebe Astley here. You on your own?'

'Go ahead, Phoebe. I'm on my own. What is it?'

'I thought you might have someone with you.'

She must be sitting round the corner in her car, using the mobile.

'My sister has just left.'

'Saw her car. Didn't know how things were between you two.'

Yes, you do, Phoebe, Coffin said silently. What you mean is that you don't like Letty, another female powerhouse like you are. How could you like each other?

'I haven't managed to see Maisie, and the neighbours weren't much help, although one of them said they had seen a man sitting in a car watching the house. May mean nothing. Others say they haven't seen her for some days, but they say she's like that: pops off to see friends, doesn't care about the garden, it can run wild for all she cares. They like her, though, a good sort if you're in trouble.'

'Is that all?'

'No,' Phoebe sounded trouble. 'She's worth digging out... Eden says that Maisie has been worried about Stella for some days.' Eden Brown worked in the theatre's costume room (among other tasks; she filled in where necessary and was happy to do it). She had once managed a dress shop in Calcutta Street in Spinnergate, and had fallen into trouble and been investigated by Phoebe Astley. Events had moved on and Eden had taken herself happily to work for Stella, whom she adored, and now shared a flat with Phoebe, both parties enjoying a cautious friendship. 'I'd like to have another look round Maisie's place. I might want to go in…check over the house.'

'Have you any solid reason?'

'No, just a feeling about Maisie. She might even know where Stella is.' And why, she said to herself; a question from which she knew the Chief Commander flinched, and from the answer even more.

'Before you do this, come up—I want a word.'

'Right now? OK. If you lend me the dog, I can pretend I am taking him for a walk while I have a prowl round Gosterwood Street.' She took a breath. 'Just got to make another call on my mobile. I'll be up in a minute.' She did not wish Coffin to hear her call.

She made a call to Chief Superintendent Young: 'We're in action.'

The Chief Superintendent, who had also had a call to something of the same effect from Letty Bingham, nodded to himself. 'It's always the women who work the trick with him,' said Archie Young. He did not say it unkindly, for he liked the Chief Commander, but rather as one who states a fact.

WHEN PHOEBE BANGED on his door, the Chief Commander was ready for her. 'I'm coming with you, Augustus can stay here. I'll drive.' Don't want you doing anything illegal, he thought. But he did not say so aloud.

'OK, sir, if that suits you. You know where Gosterwood Street is?'

'Of course I do: parallel with Calcutta Street where Eden had her shop.'

Phoebe nodded.

'Let's go, then. Does she live there alone?'

'I believe so. It was her mother's house which she inherited.'

'They are small, those houses,' said Coffin thought-fully. 'Pity the neighbours weren't more help.'

'They're a clannish lot round there. They dislike peo-ple prying. Can't say I blame them, really, but it can make investigation tough.'

'You had a look at the house?'

'Twice. First time I just stood there looking. Second time I rang the door bell and got no answer. Thought I might go back, third time lucky. I didn't know what to make of the house last time, to tell the truth. The neigh-bours said she might be away, but they could have been saying that to get rid of me.'

'They knew you were a police officer?'

'Knew me a mile away,' said Phoebe cheerfully. 'I had the feeling that Maisie might have been there watch-ing from behind a curtain.'

Gosterwood Street, like Chislewood Street which ran behind it, nearer to the river, was a row of small, flat-faded houses, some brightly painted and well kept up, and others down at heel. Maisie lived in a house painted red and white, these being her favourite colours in which she had felt free to indulge when her mother died, leav-ing her a sum of money in an insurance policy. Maisie had painted the house and bought a new bed, thus far her ambitions reached.

'Maisie's popular,' Phoebe said. 'They had an epi-demic of scarlet fever down the street last year—wouldn't think it, these days, would you? But it hap-pened, and Maisie went everywhere nursing the sick and helping them.'

'Didn't they go to hospital? There's one close, isn't there?'

'Not far. Some did, but others stayed at home and kept quiet about it.'

Coffin did not answer, he was already thinking about Maisie and what she might know about Stella. Their relationship was close, but exactly how much Stella would tell Maisie was a mystery. She had known Maisie a long time, they had worked together for years, and theatre people had strong bonds. But Stella could be reserved, she might not have said much, possibly not much at all. They might get nothing from this call, even if Maisie was there.

He parked the car in the only space available in Gosterwood Street, which was lined with battered old cars, few of which looked roadworthy. 'We will have to walk from here.'

'It's just down the road, the fifth house.' Phoebe had it clearly marked in her mind.

'Looks closed up,' said Coffin, as they approached.

'Can't tell, she could be in the back.'

'Do you really think so?'

'It's worth a try. Let's see what happens when I ring the bell. Loudly.'

Coffin watched her walk up the narrow path and ring the door bell. There was no answer. But Phoebe would not give up. She walked round the side of the house. 'I am going to look round the back,' she called over her shoulder.

'You think she's dead, don't you? Stella, I mean.'

'Fiddle. Of course I don't.' But although Phoebe did not say so aloud, she did think that Stella Pinero, the lovely, successful actress was dead. She only hoped that her husband had not killed her. 'I couldn't think that,' she said to herself. But alas, she could.

'Why do you think she's dead?' she asked herself as she rounded the corner of the house. 'I don't know. Just one of those terrible feelings one gets. Also, I don't believe Stella would go missing. Not her style.' She shivered. 'I feel as if a helicopter was hovering low over me.' But there was nothing in the sky.

There was a big black dustbin waiting to be emptied by the side of the house. Phoebe lifted the lid automatically. You never knew with dustbins. There was room for a body inside, but she did not expect to find one.

Coffin came up behind her. 'Empty?'

Phoebe held the lid back so he could see. 'More or less. There is a streak of something on the lid...could be blood.'

'Yes,' coffin observed, 'but it may not be human blood. Nor is it new blood, it's dried and dark. Several days old. Forensics won't be able to do much with that.' The thought was not pleasing him. 'Let's have another go at rousing Maisie.'

He walked back to the front door and rang the bell. The noise could be heard echoing through the house, but no one came. Coffin pointed: 'Streak of blood by the bell. Someone with blood on them rang the bell...'

Phoebe opened her mouth to say something but thought better of it.

'And don't say the butcher,' said Coffin.

'I wasn't going to. Butchers don't deliver these days.'

Coffin turned away. 'There ought to be more blood or less.'

'That's a terrible thing to say.' She caught up with Coffin. When she got a look at his face she thought: You have become a terrible person.

'If Stella is dead, there would be more blood. If the blood is hers, then Maisie knows where she is and I do not. But get the blood checked all the same.'

Bitter, too, thought Phoebe. 'I don't think there is enough blood, and it's too dry.'

'Bang on the door. Maisie may be inside.'

'I don't think so.'

He was already walking away. He drove back in silence, but not to his home. He took them both to his office at police headquarters. Phoebe thought this was a marginally good sign; better to go there than sit alone in his tower.

He strode through the outer office where Paul Masters was working quietly, head down, in the little hutch he called his private office. He saw Coffin come in but said nothing.

Gillian was occupied with filing, and also kept her head down. The efficient Sheila was not to be seen.

Phoebe hesitated for a moment, met Paul Masters' eye, gave him something between a nod and shrug, then turned to go back to her own office where, as always, there was plenty of work waiting for her. He needs leaving alone, she said to herself.

He did not notice she had gone.

Coffin worked quietly on the sort of routine matters that bored him but went with the position; they occupied only the surface of his mind.

Paul Masters tapped on the door and came in quickly. 'Chief Superintendent Young would like to speak to you, sir.'

Archie Young was right behind him and in the room before Coffin could answer.

'Forensics have been over where the dead man lived. He had a one-room flat down by the harbour, Jamaica Place. Dennis Garden obliged with the address, he had visited him there. We would have got there anyway, of course.'

'I know Jamaica Place, it's an old warehouse.'

'That's right. Turned into dwelling places about ten

years ago. Anyway, the dead man had lived there for three years or so. Francis di Rimini, he called himself. Edward Bates he was born. Did a bit of acting. Worked as a model. Drank a lot, lived a bit rough... Didn't mind who he picked up.'

'I get the picture,' said Coffin.

'Dennis Garden says he had been dead for several days when he was discovered. Signs of a struggle in the flat, so there was a possibility that he had been killed there, but the video set us right there. All the same, he was meant to be found.'

Coffin stood up. 'I want to see the flat.'

Archie Young nodded. 'Thought you might say that. I'll drive.'

No one stood on guard outside the flat in Jamaica Place, but a young policewoman was inside. She recognized the Chief Commander, saluting nervously.

Coffin smiled at her but said nothing. An open door led to the main room from which opened the small kitchen on one side and the bathroom on the other. Two white-uniformed forensic workers who were on their knees by the window rose politely as he came in.

He walked into the middle of the room where he stood looking around.

The room was plainly furnished and none too tidy, with the remains of a meal on the table where an almost empty wine bottle stood. The air was stuffy. A chair was overturned in one corner.

'A splash of blood on the back of the chair,' said Archie Young. 'More in the bathroom. Someone did some bleeding. Probably the dead man himself, shaving possibly. Garden says he was dead when his face was bashed in. He wasn't killed here, we have him on the video, walking down Jamaica Street. Pity we didn't have a camera on Percy Street, but that's economy for you, can't have them everywhere.'

'Yes, I know. So Garden thought he might have been picked in the street, and made use of.' Coffin was walking round the room. 'I'm not so sure, life is not usually so obliging. I wonder whether Garden might rethink the drugs side of it... Someone might have seen to it that he needed a fix and got at him through that.' Or just wanted him in the mood.

'I'll get him to check again. He won't like it, though.'

Dennis Garden was well known for claiming omniscience. Archie Young knew him of old, a hard man to convince of an idea he had not thought of himself.

'Even Garden can make a mistake.'

Coffin stood in the middle of the room. 'So the picture is that Francis or Frank or Ed Bates, or whatever he called himself, left under his own steam, less conspicuous, then his face was smashed when he was moribund...some blood. The fingers were then cut away— that must have taken some doing.'

'Chop, chop.' Archie allowed himself a moment of flippancy which he at once regretted. It was all right for Garden to make jokes about dead bodies but not for Archie Young. Although, as he remembered, Dennis Garden had been quiet about this dead man, whom he had clearly liked.

'I wonder where the bits are, by the way.' Coffin was not smiling.

'A search is being made,' said Archie. Probably inside some pig by now.

'He was dressed in pants and jeans, clothes that must have been brought in on purpose. Oh, and a wig popped on his head and a handbag belonging to my wife tucked beside him.'

'That's the picture.'

'So he was ready to be found in the bombed building, all dressed up in the clothes that did not belong to him. Was it meant to be a joke on us?' Coffin gritted his teeth. 'If so, I'm not laughing.'

He went into the kitchen, where there was a mess of dirty dishes in the sink and the smell of generations of curry takeaways.

In the bathroom, one more forensic worker was standing by the lavatory. Even beneath the tight cap and buttoned whites it was clear that this one was a woman, young and attractive.

She looked at him gravely, then indicated a plastic envelope, the contents of which she had been studying.

'You were talking about the fingers, sir—I couldn't help overhearing…' she paused.

'So?'

'There is the tip of a finger in this bag; a little finger, I would say. It was tucked away behind the lavatory.'

Archie Young had come up behind the Chief Commander. 'What's it wrapped up in?'

'It seems to be a handkerchief, a woman's handkerchief. There's an embroidered initial S.'

COFFIN HAD A habit of summarizing events in a case at a certain point, sometimes in a notebook, sometimes in his head. When in his head, he saw it like a blackboard with his own writing in large letters, headings underlined. He realized that it derived from the easel in his schoolroom of long ago. Did schools still use boards? He bet they still used underlining and listed points: one, two, three.

He was running over his mental headlines now as he and Archie Young drove away.

Maisie, that was his first headline. Maisie knew things about Stella that he did not. They had been friends, those two, for a long while. She trusted Maisie.

Why not me? was the painful question he could not help asking. The answer came quickly: because it concerns me.

Better find out what there was to find out about the blood on Maisie's door. By asking Maisie, if she could be located, how it got there. If she knew. People did not always know what was in their bins.

Then there was the finger in a handkerchief with the initial S on it. But not Stella's—never Stella. Put there on purpose to drag Stella in, he told himself savagely.

The underpants on the body aping Stella.

Stella, always Stella.

It was something more deliberate than a connective coincidence.

'IT'S LIKE A Victorian melodrama,' said Coffin. 'The heroine's handkerchief turns up to incriminate her.' Archie Young made a sympathetic noise, but kept his eye on the road where the traffic was heavy. It was hard to know what to say. 'Plenty of people with the initial S,' he managed.

'I never see Stella with a handkerchief,' went on Coffin, his voice irritable. 'She's always leaving little bits of tissue about the place.'

Then Coffin started to laugh, not loudly but with genuine mirth. 'What a fool I am! Good sense is coming back. Stella has been my wife for a long while now. She has learnt the rules. Whatever crime she committed, she knew not to leave so many clues around.'

'We'll find out who is behind it all, but it looks personal, sir. Either aimed at you or Miss Pinero.' Archie

always had difficulty in knowing how to address Stella.
He never felt happy with whatever he managed: Stella
was Mrs Coffin and no doubt would be Lady Coffin
quite soon, but she felt more like Miss Pinero. She would
never, as Congreve had it, dwindle into a wife. Archie
Young's wife was attending to his education and recently she had taken him to a production of Congreve's
The Way of the World.

He watched the Chief Commander walk towards his
front door. The tower was dark, but there were lights on
in the theatre. Coffin looked tall and too thin; Archie
wished the man had someone to come home to. Where
was the dog? Distantly, he heard the sound of Augustus
barking. Not as good as a wife, he thought, as he drove
away, but better than nothing.

COFFIN LET HIMSELF into his tower and stood at the bottom of the staircase. There was a faint smell of scent on
the air. He took a step forward.

Stella came running down the stairs. She was carefully
made up, her hair looked newly washed and set, she was
wearing jeans and a soft cashmere sweater which looked
new.

'There you are, darling. Here I am back. How are
you?'

He felt both relief, a powerful happiness, and a wave
of anger. 'Where have you been?'

'At a health farm, darling. I told you.'

That's a lie for a start, Coffin told himself. She came
right up to him and threw her arms round him. He held
her tight. He thought she winced as he gripped her arms.

SIX

YOUNG AND LODGE, who had a tactful, remote relationship as men who handled tricky jobs, were drinking together in the bar favoured by the Second City's topranking CID officers. Without being friends they had a quiet respect for each other, although Archie Young would have preferred not to have the Todger on his patch. But in the present situation, the way things were with bombs and terrorists around, he recognized the necessity of someone like Lodge and that perhaps they were lucky to have him and not one of the rougher boys. There was a look about their eyes that he did not like: seen too much, heard too much, done too much, trust no one, it said. And, in consequence, I don't trust you, Archie said to himself. Liking did not come into it. There was certainly this side to Inspector Lodge, but he kept it hidden better. (As also to the Chief Superintendent himself, but deep, deep down.)

The chosen pub, the Sevastopol Arms had earned its name because of its position. There, in a straight line across the river, but not visible because of the buildings that were in the way, stood the Woolwich Arsenal in whose sheds had been forged the guns and armament that went to the Crimea. The Sevastopol was an old dark brick building, deceptively small from the outside and larger within. It had defied being modernized and brightened, remaining sombre but comfortable, which pleased its own peculiar clientele who did not want dancing, music or karaoke, but did want excellent beer and good whisky.

'What do you make of Miss Pinero?' Lodge kept his voice down. He had been introduced to Stella, he had seen her act, but he knew that there were reservations about her in the Second City Force. She was treated with a certain formality since it was felt it distanced the Chief Commander from what was viewed in some quarters as an awkward relationship. She brought trouble, didn't she, from her different world?

'Lovely lady,' said Young, loyally.

'To look at, yes.'

'She's generous and kind,' Archie persevered.

'And?'

'I didn't know too much about her life and interests till recently. My wife's a pal of hers.'

'We know a touch more now,' said Lodge grimly.

'That photograph was a fake.'

'Oh, yes, we're agreed upon that. But she is there, in the picture. It does suggest she has some strange friends. Or has had in the past; the picture of her looked a mite younger than she is now, so, an old friend.'

'They don't have to be friends,' said Young stoutly. 'Or even known to her. Actresses have a lot of photographs taken, matter of business, and hand them out. Publicity and all that.'

'If she wasn't away, we could ask her.' Lodge stopped short of using the word question. You did not talk about the Chief Commander's wife except with care.

'Sure,' said Archie. 'Like your chap. Not nice for him having his pants used that way. Not nice at all.'

They looked at each other in silence.

'Point taken,' said Lodge. He got up to go to the bar. 'My turn, I think. Same again?'

Archie nodded. He was breathing heavily, as if he had been running. He was aware that Inspector Lodge had access to information that he did not have, and he suspected that John Coffin also knew more than he had talked about. Sat on all the right security committees, didn't he? Damn the woman. If she ruined the boss, he, Archie, would want to kill her.

The Todger came back with two glasses, together with a sandwich for each of them. He put them down carefully, then sat down himself. 'I'll come clean with you. I am worried about my man's probity. Checks in when it suits him, tells me something, mentions seeing Miss Pinero...then he's off again. Silence.'

Telling me this, because he knows it's what I want to know, thought Archie Young. Of course, he knows we are worried sick about the Chief Commander's wife. I don't want her to be dead, but, by God, if it would make things easier, I might be up to doing it myself. Then he laughed. Probably not, though; there are things you will do for a mate, but not kill their wife for them.

'Does that mean you think your chap is a doubtful security risk? Working double?'

'We don't know. Have to consider it, though.'

'Don't you always?'

Lodge allowed himself one of his rare smiles. 'Yes. In fact, there is probably a check running on me now.'

'Oh, you are a lovely lot,' said Archie Young, drinking deep. 'Let me know if I'm included, won't you?'

'Couldn't say if you were, but always count on it, that's my advice.'

Archie looked at him over the top of his glass and saw that he was not joking. 'What a word. I've been told that the most useful terrorist is the one in the humblest position. Not noticed, you see, but noticing everything.

I suppose sex comes into it, too: men are probably more useful than women.'

'Not always,' said Lodge. 'Drink up, I've got to get home. My wife expects to see me some time.'

'Mine is away,' said Archie Young. So Lodge did have a wife; he felt faintly surprised. 'On a course. Got her own career. Mind you, I respect her for it.'

'Good for you.'

'Wouldn't matter if I didn't, she'd still go ahead. She'll end up in the House of Lords, I daresay, with a life peerage—if they haven't all been abolished by then.'

'Would that make you Lord Young?'

'I shall have to think about that.'

Lodge stood up. 'I'd better get off.' He was not enjoying working life at the moment and it showed.

'Funny business for both of us,' said Archie Young, trying to be helpful. 'Miss Pinero being dragged in, whether it's her fault or not, is a bugger. And for you...' he paused, wondering uneasily what it was that he and the Todger both knew.

Lodge shrugged. 'Delicately put.'

'It's a delicate matter.'

'Certainly is.'

'Seems almost a manufactured performance, putting on an act,' went on Young, 'using Miss Pinero, using your chap's underwear, cutting off the fingers of the dead man, and yet choosing someone who is identified without trouble.'

'A queer sort of show,' said Lodge.

'Show?' said Archie Young, raising his eyebrows. 'Yes, good word, show it is.'

They had placed their mobile phones on the table in front of them like twins. Now one began to ring.

'Yours or mine?' said Lodge.

'Mine,' Archie Young sighed. 'Hello?' He listened, all the amusement leaving his face. 'Right, I'll be there.' He pocketed his telephone, then turned to Lodge. 'That show we've got on the road, another character had joined it: a body's been found.'

SEVEN

'LET'S GO UPSTAIRS.' Coffin released Stella from his embrace and gave her a little push towards the winding staircase. 'Up, and we can talk.' And you'd better make sense, because I am in no mood to be played with.

Mixed with the sheer physical relief at having her back, the joy of seeing her, mixed with these was anger. He didn't want it there, was half ashamed of it, but there it was: a black streak winding through the joy.

'I ought to get round to the theatre,' Stella said. 'Business talk, you know.'

'We'll talk first.' He put his hand firmly under her elbow and propelled her upstairs.

She spoke over her shoulder breathlessly as they went up the stairs, not resisting their progress, but a touch reluctant. 'I really should go to the theatre first, you know. There must be all sorts of problems and so on that need sorting out, even if I wasn't away very long.'

'Long enough,' said Coffin.

Stella smiled. 'Not that long, darling. But piles of stuff on my desk, you must have seen it, messages from Alice—she's being very helpful, you gave me a friend there.'

'Did I?' He did not want to talk about Alice.

'I ought to be checking the accounts. Naturally I can't leave the money side to Alice.'

'Letty is doing that.' They had nearly reached the level of the kitchen.

'Oh.' Stella did not sound quite pleased.

Oh, yes, thought Coffin. Come on, my lady, I want to know where you have been and why.

One more turn of the staircase brought them to the large, light sitting room. No one had been thinking about Augustus, but he had his own methods with Coffin and was now first into the sitting room. When he got there he turned round to face them, his tail wagging.

'Hello, Gussie,' said Stella, bending down to pat him. 'How's he been?'

'Fine. With me all the time.'

'He always is.'

Coffin pulled up a chair. 'Sit down, Stella.'

'Don't order me about.'

'I'm not, Stella, but you look tired. In pain, too, I think, from your arm. Yes, I noticed.'

Without a word Stella sank back into the armchair. 'Aren't you going to sit?'

'Presently.' He walked about the room for a minute, pacing up and down, then he drew another chair towards her, leaned forward and took both her hands in his. 'What's up, Stella? Where have you been? Why did you lie about where you were going?'

'Not exactly a lie. Just a change of plans.' Her voice was nervous.

'Oh, come on, Stella, you can do better than that.'

She put her hand to her head. 'I can't think.' Her sleeve fell back, revealing a white bandage, badly applied.

Coffin looked at it, took in its appearance, but said nothing.

'I really think I should go across to the theatre, even if Letty is there. Very decent of her, I know how busy she is.' She looked at her watch. 'The curtain will have gone down if I don't hurry and they will all have melted away. You know what they are like.'

'I know,' said Coffin, somewhat grimly.

'Letty will have gone, surely, but Alice Yeoman will be there.' Stella stood up.

'How's she doing?' He wanted to know.

'Not too bad. Bit of time off here and there.'

'Not ill, is she?'

'No, just a spell of menstrual trouble,' said Stella, with the insouciance of one who had never let that sort of thing trouble her. Actresses couldn't, could they? You went on regardless.

'Let's talk about something else. I don't think you are ready to tell me where you have been.' Stella gave him a wide-eyed, shocked look. 'Do you remember that blue Chanel handbag I gave you?'

'Of course.'

'Where is it?'

Stella frowned. 'I don't know what this is about... I suppose the bag is in the dressing chest where I keep my good bags. You gave me this one, and I treasure it,' she said, defensively.

'Go and get it, please.'

'What is all this?'

'Just get it, please.'

He went to the window to look out while she went to the bedroom on the next floor of the tower. From the window on this side he could see across the road to the lights in the old churchyard, now a park, not so long ago the scene of a murder. Augustus came to lean heavily and lovingly on his left leg.

The wait was long enough to make Coffin wonder whether he ought to go upstairs to join Stella. She hadn't looked well. He was angry with her, but he loved her, the two strands came together strongly in his mind, the one fuelling a fire in the other. Damn you, Stella, he thought.

Presently he heard the door open behind him. 'You were quiet.'

'No quieter than you.'

'I wouldn't be singing at the window.' Augustus stood up, scenting disharmony; it did not distress him, as his proprietors may have thought; he found it interesting, even exciting, but a dog had to know where to position himself. 'Did you find it?'

'No. It's not there. I must have left it somewhere or put it away somewhere else. But...'

Coffin interrupted her: 'Any idea where?'

Stella stopped short with what she had been about to say. She was visibly angry. 'What is this? Why does it matter? I am just back, I'm tired, I want a bath and a drink... It could be in the theatre, I might have left it there. Alice Yeoman will know, or Maisie. If I left it there, then one of them will know.'

'Go and look. Please.'

'Why the hell should I?'

'I will tell you when you come back.'

'I'll go later. I need to wash, have a drink—'

All the anxiety and anger inside Coffin rose within him: his hand went up, he was as near as nothing to hitting Stella in the face. He had never hit her or any woman. All the violence inside him, and there was plenty, was repressed, controlled.

He took a deep breath.

'All right, I will tell you now: while you were away, missing, out of touch, so that I did not know if you were alive or dead, the body of what appeared to be a woman with hair your colour, about your size, wearing jeans and a shirt such as you wear was discovered in a bombed house in Percy Street. The corpse's face was bashed in and the tops of the fingers cut off. By the side of the body was a Chanel handbag with a photograph of you inside it. Not a nice photograph, Stella: you appeared to be eating human flesh.'

He stopped talking, out of words, out of breath. Augustus sidled away.

Stella said nothing, but she threw out her right hand as if to steady herself.

'I almost hit you, Stella.'

'I know.'

There was a silence. Augustus shifted himself uneasily round the room.

'I'll go,' she said. She did not look back. Augustus began to trot towards the door, looked at Coffin and thought better of it. Stay here, dog, time to be prudent.

Coffin watched her go.

He was troubled. Why, oh why, this insistence that she had not been gone long? More than a day, Stella, more than you want to admit. She would have to answer questions soon.

THE THEATRE WAS quietening into silence. The curtain had come down both in the Stella Pinero Theatre and the smaller Experimental Theatre, but the bar and the restaurant were open and would be until midnight; it was a private club when the performance ended, Max knew his customers. In addition, there were always a few people hanging about backstage to talk to friends.

No one recognized Stella as she made her way quietly backstage; she was wearing jeans and dark spectacles with her hair drawn back. She was a beautiful woman and always would be, but everything about her—hair, eyes and make-up—was deliberately soft tonight as if she had turned off an inner light.

It was quieter here in the recesses of the theatre than in the bar, probably because those of the cast of *Noises Off* who had not fled home were in the bar themselves. The Theatre Workshop was dark this week, and the Experimental Theatre, as she remembered was doing *Aylmer's End* together with Shakespeare to music with help from a local school. That would be long since over.

Irene Bow, Jane Gillam, Fanny Burt, Michael Guardian and Tom Jenks, all of whom had been in *An Ideal Husband*, were also in the current production.

Irene Bow was probably not far away because there was a trace of her scent on the air; her passage through the theatre front and backstage was usually armed by a whiff of her current favourite fragrance. They changed but were always strong and expensive, a bit like Irene herself, as Tom Jenks had said ruefully, having been one of her short-term lovers. Probably all the time he could afford, his friends had said.

Yes, there was Irene at the door of her dressing room talking to Alice Yeoman. Nothing scented and expensive about Alice, who wore tan trousers and a soft linen shirt. No make-up, and no scent.

'Who is that shouting...?' Alice was looking around her.

'Oh, you're always hearing shouting,' said Irene impatiently. 'Here's Stella.'

They greeted Stella with pleasure and surprise. Since little gossip or speculation about her had reached the theatre, all was normal as far as they were concerned. In Irene's case, this meant she was thinking and talking about herself and her part.

'Oh, Stella, you can help here.' Irene fixed her large

eloquent eyes (hadn't one disgruntled lover called them 'pop eyes'?) on Stella, who, having had a painful few days and facing the prospect of further unpleasant hours ahead, reflected that if she had been captured by a remote Indian tribe, kept hidden in a deep cave and now just released, Irene would still have come forward with a complaint about her dressing room.

'Irene's not happy about her dress,' said Alice, her voice calm.

A frown flickered across Irene's face which both the other women could read: she did not like a junior member of the cast to call her Irene, though she was forced to admit that it was done now. But she could let them see how she felt, delicately, quietly; she could get the message across.

'There's a good deal of running around in the first act, indeed all the time, and that dress, besides making me look like a sweet pea, is too tight. I have nearly split the seams as it is,' she said, in her lovely, rich voice. Ophelia lamenting Hamlet could not have grieved with more eloquence.

'Irene's so slight, too,' said Alice in a level voice.

'Who made the dress? Was it made here?'

'Yes,' said Irene. 'Here.'

Ah, there's the rub, thought Stella. Irene wanted one made by her own designer, if she has one, and if she hasn't then I bet she is in the process of getting one as a prestige symbol. Just for a moment, Stella managed to forget her own anxiety. 'Get them to let it out,' she said promptly. All right, I've annoyed you, Irene, but so what? This is my theatre. She turned to Alice. 'I may have left a blue Chanel handbag over here. Have you seen it around?'

Irene bounced away down the corridor, knocking into Mick Guardian.

'Came back for my car keys... If they aren't here, then they're lost. Any chance of a lift?'

Irene ignored this. 'Stella is hopeless, getting worse. Losing her looks too, getting quite skeletal.'

Not your trouble, old love, thought Mick. You're going the other way, putting on weight. Could you be pregnant? But no, no embryo could nest happily inside Irene.

He passed on, found his car keys in his pocket, and made his way back to the exit.

Stella and Alice Yeoman were looking for her blue handbag. It was not in her dressing room, all neat, tidy and empty, not in her office, not even in the wardrobe room where no one was around and which was not so neat and tidy. Never was.

'Wouldn't be here,' Stella said.

'You never know. Maybe someone saw it around, thought it belonged in here, tidied it away. Is it important?'

'Yes.'

Alice frowned. 'I think I did see it, but I can't remember where. What about asking Maisie?'

Stella said, in a low voice, 'She's having a few days off.'

'Oh yes. So she is.' Alice looked thoughtful. 'I'm sorry, Stella, I'd like to help.'

'If you can't, you can't. If it turns up, let me know.'

'Yes, sure. You know, we had a lot of people backstage lately. Guided theatre tours, several of them in.'

'Brings in money.' Money for the theatre complex was always on Stella's mind. Letty's too.

'If someone saw the bag and said, ''Oh that's Stella

Pinero's,'' and it happened to be a fan of yours, they might nick it.'

'Or even if they just liked the look of a Chanel bag.'

Alice nodded silently.

'Right. Well thank you, Alice. I will be in tomorrow. Plenty to do, I guess.'

'Miss Bingham has been in.'

It was a probe, and recognized by Stella as such: Alice could tell there was something going on and wanted to know what it was. For her part, Stella could tell the girl was studying her face, taking in the tension, trying to read it. She had probably noticed the bandage wrapped round her forearm, even though her sleeve was drawn over it, and wondered about that too.

'I expect the Chief Commander is pretty busy, what with the bomb—or was it bombs? And the murder. If you've been away, you might not have heard.'

'I had heard.'

'What a thing. I think there's a lot in it we haven't been told about, keeping it quiet. One of Professor Garden's boyfriends, so the word is.'

Stella shook her head. No answer was the best answer.

WHEN SHE GOT BACK, Coffin was drinking coffee and watching television. Pretending to, more likely.

'Not there,' she said. 'But Alice Yeoman thinks it was once around. May have been stolen, may still be there. She will let me know.'

'She's reliable,' said Coffin, absently. He was her patron and must put in a good word.

'Letty seems to have been around.'

He didn't answer but got up and walked towards her.

'What would you have done if I had hit you, Stella?'

'Hit you back.'

Coffin looked at her and laughed. 'Good girl. I do love you, Stella.'

He put his hand on her arm, and stroked the bandage. 'Now, tell me how you got that, and what you have been up to.'

'It goes back a bit.' She turned her head away.

He moved her chin, gently. 'Look at me.'

'You know how it is with some actresses—a fresh lover with each play; it's almost expected. I've never been quite like that…but all the same…'

'It happened?' he prompted, still gently.

'Yes, quite a few years ago, before you came back into my life. He was—is—a lot younger than me. I suppose that was part of the attraction, I was flattered.' She stopped, speech was difficult. 'Pip Eton, that's his name.'

Coffin looked at her with love and sympathy. 'Go on.'

'It really didn't outlast that season at Chichester. Shortly after that you and I started seeing each other again. Well, we had already started to meet—you came down to Chichester.'

'I remember.'

With some pain, Stella said: 'I think now that may have been a factor in Pip's attraction to me. He may have been told to take me up.' She stopped. He could see she was having difficulty in coming out with it.

He decided to help, even if brutally. 'You mean he had his eye on you because of me?'

She smiled at him, and he saw that he had given her what she most wanted: a moment of relief. 'I didn't see it then, but yes, looking back, yes, it probably was… He liked me, though,' she added quickly. 'I could tell, he was a good actor, but not that good.'

She stopped again, so he gave her another prod. 'Go on. I suppose it was hot and strong while it lasted?'

Stella sighed. 'It was; short, though, I went to London and then on tour and forgot him. Well, more or less. Our paths didn't cross, and though I thought he might seek me out, he didn't. I went on to Australia.'

'What did he do?'

'He dropped out. Did a bit of telly, nothing much, and then nothing at all... I think now he was under orders.' Another pause which, this time, Coffin did not interrupt. 'Then he telephoned me.'

'When?'

'About a month ago...can't be sure of the exact day. He left a message on my answerphone. Then he telephoned me at the theatre, spoke to me there.' She plunged on. 'Not loving, nothing like that. Quiet, but...I don't know what to say: threatening, but quietly, so quietly that I didn't grasp at first what was happening. No, that's not true, I did, but I couldn't believe it.'

'Threatening what?'

'Threatening that if I did not do what he wanted, he would sell photographs of me to the media.' She looked at him piteously. 'I want you to believe that these photographs were doctored... I was in them, yes. Pip did take some photographs of me, he was good, but these—' she shook her head.

'And what did he want you to do?'

Instead of answering directly, Stella said: 'I always knew he had a political side.'

She looked at her husband and read his expression. 'You're not surprised.'

'Your name had come up.'

She covered her face with her hands. 'Oh, God. So you knew.'

'Not all of it. Not as much as I hope you are going to tell me.'

'He intended that I should be a channel to you, that through me he could both feed you information and gather it.

'I wanted to get away and hide, just for a little while. That's why I told those stories about where I was going. Confusing my trail. But I didn't get that far: Pip was outside when I left, he got me in his grip.'

'What do you mean by that?'

'I mean, he pulled me to his car and drove to where he lived, a rather nasty flat in a road off the main road leading through Spinnergate towards the City. I could see where we were going, he didn't attempt to stop me seeing. I was a prisoner, or at least I felt like one and I certainly couldn't get away easily. He said he would not let me go until I had agreed to do what he wanted.'

'Which was?'

Stella shrugged. 'To spy on you, to let him spy on you and all your dealings with any terrorists. Stupid of him really, since I could say yes and then go away and renege on it. I didn't say yes.'

'How long were you there?'

'I don't know. I got a bit confused about time, as if I'd been drugged... I was given food and drink. I think there was someone else there...man or woman, I don't know, but I am sure I heard low voices. Then he started to threaten me. I thought he was going to hit me, so I hit him first.'

'You mean, you had a fight?'

'A sort of scuffle. No, it was more than that. He was wearing a shortsleeved shirt and I bit his arm.' She sounded puzzled, as if she wasn't sure what had really happened. 'I suppose my teeth were the only weapons I had. He had a knife and my arm got hurt, and I think he got stabbed too in the scuffle…' She sounded puzzled again. What had happened? 'There was blood…'

Coffin said, 'You aren't talking like yourself, Stella. More like a badly written play.'

'If I am, then it's because it is the only way I can talk about an experience that seemed unreal to me. It was real, I suppose. I knew that when I hit him.' She was frowning. 'I think I got hold of a knife; I seem to remember it was a bread knife—you know, the sort with a jagged edge…' She saw Coffin looking at her with a frown. 'I was a fool to let him get me into his car, but the truth is I can be gullible sometimes, act without thinking. I did so then.'

He saw she was trembling, and he put his arms round her. 'It's over, Stella. So what happened then?'

'He shouted and went out of the room. I daresay it was painful, I meant it to be. He was gone a long while. I may have gone to sleep. I have wondered if there was some dope in the tea he gave me. Then I realized I was on my own, the flat was empty, so I left in a hurry in case he came back. I walked down the road, and soon I had an idea of where I was.'

'But you didn't come straight back here?'

'No, I was near where Maisie lived. I went there and she tidied me up and gave me a cup of tea… I came home then.'

'I shall have to get hold of Pip Eton. He's not your friend, Stella. I don't know if he knew the man whose body we have, but he certainly provided the photograph found with him.'

The telephone rang at this point, and Augustus leapt away in alarm.

'He doesn't like sudden noises,' murmured Stella.

'He's going to have to get used to it,' said Coffin, as he picked up the telephone. He listened for a moment, not saying much. 'Right, thank you. Let me know if and when you have an identification. Cause of death, too. If you don't know it already.'

He turned to Stella. 'There's another body.'

Stella made a surprised noise. 'They don't alert the Chief Commander for every body found, surely?'

Coffin was silent for a moment. 'This one is different. I think I shall have to go and look at it.'

It was late evening, but a fine, bright one with a moon, and the body was not far away.

Stella watched her husband depart with foreboding. All those things I am going to have to talk about that I would rather keep quiet, she thought. She could see her face in a looking glass on the wall and knew that it needed rebuilding.

Actresses could disappear and come back as someone else, and now was the time for her to do this. If she could manage it.

She knew she was going to have to answer questions, even if so far she was being handled with kid gloves, but the time would come when the gloves would be off. She thought of Archie Young and knew he would be getting ready for her.

EIGHT

THIS ONE WAS DIFFERENT.

It was a fresh body, not long dead, that much was clear even to the first person who found it that evening where it was nestling in an alcove outside the old St Luke's church, presently a theatre.

That first viewer was the theatre security man, Luke Locker by name, who was taking his usual end-of-performance look around. He did it in a relaxed way, since except for the odd drunk and the occasional pair locked in lovemaking in the shadows (which he tactfully ignored), there had been no trouble. His wife was away and, not being able to afford Max's prices, although Max could be generous with the odd sandwich, he had been living on fish and chips. He was just meditating whether, if you kept eating fish and chips, you ended up smelling like a fish. Fried at that. Was that sexy or not? His wife had been away some weeks, so his mind ran along those lines.

What he saw ahead of him, lit up by his torch, awoke him from his comfortable fantasies.

A guy?

But no, it was not November, nowhere near Guy Fawkes' night, nor did this figure have that jolly, jokey look of a good Guy. Sinister, this one.

At first he had thought the figure was leaning against the wall of the alcove between two buttresses of the former church. After a closer look, he decided the right word was propped up.

He drew nearer and saw flesh. It might be one of those acting kids putting on a performance. They did such things, but this time...he shook his head. Although he did not like actors, he had observed that they did not fool about with their craft.

He made himself take another look. He put out a hand to touch the face under the paper hat... Then he jerked back.

'Bloody hell, a deader!'

He could just make out the writing on a card pinned to the chest, and what he read there made him even more uneasy.

THE THEATRE manager and the big girl, Alice, took over the telephoning, and he waited by the figure until the police arrived, being careful not to touch.

First a patrol car, soon followed by a detective sergeant with a woman detective.

Then the SOCO team.

Then the police surgeon to certify death but not to move the body till the pathologist and the forensics had done their bit.

There was quite a crowd now, sidelining Luke, who was obliged to hang around because they were going to question him later. He knew one of the uniformed police. He had been at school with her. A nice fat girl she had been then. Now she had thinned down into being big and muscular. Elspeth Butt.

He sidled up to her. 'Funny business.'

The body was by now lying on the ground being examined by the police pathologist attended by the police surgeon. The pathologist was a man Luke did not know, but did not think he would like if he did. He noticed the man was treated with great politeness. Did someone call him Dennis? Or was it Sir Dennis?

'Funnier than you know.' She hardly looked at him, too intent on watching the pathologist, who was making a delicate first examination.

'Yeah?'

'Not the first body we've got.'

'I heard.'

A burst of laughter from a trio of her peers interrupted anything she might be going to say.

'And *whose* body are you?' one of them sang out, while the others roared with laughter.

Then fell silent.

'It's the big man himself,' said the singer, falling silent as the Chief Commander came into the light.

COFFIN LOOKED down at the figure. It was dressed in a jacket and kilt, but both were made of newspapers, cut and pinned. Coffin studied them, observing the dates to be various. A paper hat sat on the dead man's head, looking indescribably jaunty. The man's face was partly obscured by the newspaper, but enough was visible to see he was not old. A thinnish face with dark hair.

A big label with printed letters was fixed to the dead man's chest; A PRESENT FOR STELLA, it read.

'I see why you called me in,' said Coffin. A photographer had stood aside politely as he arrived. The SOCO officer was dusting the wall of the alcove for fingerprints, muttering to himself that there was nothing to be got from rough stone.

'Thought you'd want to see.' Archie Young stepped back so Coffin could get a closer look. 'The MO said he's been stabbed, as far as can be observed. Whether he died from this wound is not clear yet, but he will do

a proper examination when the photographer and the
SOCO are through. We don't want the newspapers removed yet and there may be other injuries.'

'Any identity?'

'None at the moment. I expect we will get something
soon. There was a crowd from the theatre buzzing round
him when he was found. They had been eating in Max's
restaurant. None of them identified him. Max doesn't
know him either. Wouldn't expect it, really.'

Coffin met Archie Young's eyes and did what was
required of him. 'I have to tell you that Stella is back. I
can get her down to have a look: she may know him.'
He nodded at Young. 'Do you mind if we don't go into
this in detail now?'

Young nodded, thinking: You might be surprised how
much we all know about you and your wife's move-
ments. 'I don't like the way her name is cropping up
lately,' he said. 'Seems all wrong, somehow.'

'You can imagine how I feel.'

'We'll get it sorted out, sir. You know how it is: when
you're as well known as she is, your name gets dragged
into all sorts of dramas.' He was trying to choose his
words carefully; he was more moved than he wanted to
show.

Coffin looked down at the body. 'Why the skirt?
Mean anything, do you think? See any symbolism?'

'I think a kilt—let's call it a kilt—is simply easier to
make out of paper than trousers. It's all mad, I don't
think we can describe this killer as sane.'

'But why the paper at all?'

Young shook his head. 'Your guess is as good as
mine. It might mean something or nothing, according to
how mad the maker of the clothes—if you can call them
that—is.' To himself he thought it was just another way

of getting at Stella Pinero. Like the message. He looked at Coffin: 'I hate to ask, but…'

'Yes, well, as I just said, Stella must be asked whether she can identify the body.'

'I don't suppose she'll be able to, but you never know,' said Young. 'Anything she might come up with will help.'

'She may have something to tell us.' She is going to have to talk, he told himself, regardless of whether either of us likes it.

Archie Young looked at Coffin expectantly.

'She will tell you herself,' said Coffin. He looked at the body again. A thin, tanned face under the paper hat. 'Is there a wound on the arm?'

'Yes, professionally dressed from the look of it. Possibly in a hospital. But the MO has only had a peep so as not to disturb the wrapping.'

'It hasn't been examined then?'

'No, not yet. For now, the cause of the wound or whatever is unknown.'

'I wouldn't be surprised if it was a bite,' said Coffin. Or several bites, he added gloomily to himself. Young looked at him in surprise. 'In that case, the identity of the man can be established quite soon. Stella had better come down straightaway; she hasn't got far to come.'

STELLA HAD showered, got into jeans and a silk shirt, and restored her appearance. One thing about being an actress, she thought, it does teach you how to create a face. With lipstick, cream rouge and eyeliner, she had made herself look like a lady ready to face the world. Perhaps a lady who'd had a shock recently but had come through and was prepared for the next one. Not exactly a tough lady, but a lady on guard.

She took the summons to view the corpse with apparent calm. 'Right, I'll come now. If you think I can help.' She walked down the staircase, out of the door, and swung left into the quadrangle that fronted the theatre.

The area had been screened off while the dead body itself, after being carefully photographed in situ, had been lowered to the ground for examination before being carried away. Otherwise it had not been disturbed.

A policewoman ushered Stella through. 'This way, if you please, Miss Pinero.'

Coffin stepped forward. 'Sorry to drag you here, Stella, but I think you can help us.' He spoke without looking anyone in the face. 'Stella will, of course, tell you anything you want to know.'

Stella nodded without speaking. She looked down at the dead face. She read the notice saying that this was a present for Stella and shuddered. 'Yes, I know who it is. I know him as Pip Eton.'

'Was that his real name?' asked Archie Young.

'I don't know. He was an actor. Actors have many names.'

Somehow, Inspector Lodge had sidled past the screens to be among those present. Late as it was, there are always people around in the theatre so that an audience was half-formed, although kept back by the police. Stella could see the tall figure of Alice, with Max and one of his daughters edging forward. Max caught her eye, moving his head in something between a bow and a nod. Alice stared straight ahead as if she couldn't believe what she saw. The girl who stood next to her, one of the wardrobe staff—a dogsbody called Frankie as Stella remembered—was laughing. Theatre people were not like the rest of the world.

Stella knew she had to say something to Archie Young.

'I know his name, I can tell you a little about him, I wish it were otherwise.' She paused, and took a deep breath. 'But how did he get killed and why is he dressed like that?'

No one answered.

Coffin said: 'You'll have to tell him the lot, Stella. And we had better do it in our own sitting room. Come up, you two.'

Stella looked at him. 'I'll go first and make some coffee. Can I have your key? I didn't bring mine.'

She was thinking as she climbed the stairs ahead of the others. Tell a straight story, she told herself. Archie Young will believe you, but Lodge may be difficult.

She made the coffee carefully, taking her time. She heard feet pass on the stairs, then she carried the tray up. Voices were talking quietly in the room ahead.

She listened for a moment. He's already told them everything; all I need do is answer any questions.

They were sitting waiting for her, with Augustus sprawled across Coffin's feet.

Good for you, boy, she thought. 'Good dog,' she said aloud. Augustus looked at her steadily with his round black eyes. He liked Stella, who was kind to him, but he preferred Coffin. There was something about his smell that suited Augustus, whereas Stella's smell was lighter and sweeter. Augustus knew a few words if not many, and one of the words he knew was 'dog' which applied to himself.

Stella hesitated at the door, then Coffin stood and came over to take the tray. 'Thank you, love.'

'You're ready for me?'

He nodded. 'I've run through what you told me.'

'Thank you.'

'I thought you would prefer it.'

Stella poured the coffee and handed it round. 'Well, you know all now, all I can tell you. It's hard for you to believe, but I don't know who killed Pip or when it happened, except that I didn't do it.'

'Never thought it for a minute,' said Archie Young. 'You did well to hold out the way you did.'

'He was stupid to think I would help.'

'He didn't know you as well as he thought he did,' said Coffin.

'He wanted me to be a channel through which he got information... Unluckily, I was wild in the days when he knew me.' She looked at her husband. 'You wouldn't have been proud of me then. Not the wife for a leading police officer.'

'You're a different person now.'

'It had been a long while,' said Stella. 'I daresay I have changed.' She smiled at her husband.

Inspector Lodge had received his coffee in silence. Now he spoke: 'He's not known to me, not under that name,' he said. 'But he must be in the records somewhere. Fingerprints, photograph, and so on. We'll find him, and then we can move on to who killed him and why. You say you did him some injury?'

'Yes, but not enough to kill him.'

'Nasty business.' Lodge drank some coffee. 'Hard to understand the reasoning behind propping the chap up like that, dressed that way.'

'And leaving the message for me,' said Stella. 'It frightens me.'

'As it was meant to do,' said Lodge. 'Nice coffee.' He finished his cup, replacing it on the tray. 'He's a frightener, this chap, that's what he is.' He thought about it. 'Or was.'

Stella said: 'He had changed…that's how it felt to me.'

'As it happens,' said Coffin tersely, 'he is dead.'

'Not long dead, so the police surgeon thought at the first look,' Archie Young put in. 'Matter of hours. Not killed on the spot, though. Probably killed by the stab wound, but he couldn't be sure at that point. He had other wounds, made earlier so it seems. That would be when you had your struggle… And you don't know where you were taken and detained?'

Stella shook her head. 'No, I was bundled in the car, I saw the way at first, down towards the Spinnergate tube station, but then we shot into a maze of side streets… I suppose I should have tried to remember more.'

'And when you escaped?'

'I found the main road, and got on a bus…'

She knows more than she is saying, he decided. 'You would have been confused,' he said in a soothing voice.

He was talking for the sake of talking and he knew it. To see the pain on the face of the wife of your boss and find it mirrored in the eyes of the Chief Commander himself made it a very embarrassing occasion, but questions would have to be asked; he had put off talking to Stella long enough.

He lowered his eyes: they had to work through this on their own and come out the other side. If they could.

To his relief, his mobile phone rang. He looked at Coffin, who nodded. 'Take it.'

Archie listened. 'From the office,' he said, then handed the telephone over to Coffin. 'Here, see what you make of this.'

Coffin nodded. 'Phoebe? Yes, go on, I'm listening…

Where did you get this?' He kept his eyes on Stella's face as he talked. Other people do have miseries as well as me, he thought, I must get over this on my own. I am in love with her, but I don't believe she is in love with me. Not any longer.

He put the receiver down, still looking at her. I remember happiness, he told himself. Well, let her hear this, see how she reacts.

'Phoebe Astley had had a call from a friend who works in Summers Street substation. A doctor from Paget Road Hospital walked in with a report. A patient came in…said he had been attacked by a strange woman whom he did not know. She had bitten him, then knifed him. No, he had not attacked her back. No, he could not understand it, thought she must be mad. After he'd finished treating the man, the doctor asked him to wait, wondering if he should report it, but the man cleared off before he could stop him… After a bit the doctor thought he ought to refer the incident to the police. Which he did.'

'And it got back to us?' said Lodge thoughtfully.

'Phoebe's young friend is bright. And I'm sure that Phoebe has been making discreet soundings here and there. I'm not surprised she should come back with information, she does.' Perhaps he wished she had not come back with this particular titbit.

There was silence in the room. Then Archie spoke.

'Our dead body. He had a recently stitched wound.'

'Looks like it,' said Coffin.

'Pip Eton.' Stella bowed her head. 'I suppose he would go to a hospital… It's not true what he said, you know, the way he describes what happened. I was hurt by him… I suppose I did hurt him back. Did the doctor believe him?'

Coffin's face relaxed into a smile. 'As a matter of fact, no. Thought he was a liar.'

Stella said, 'Thanks. I feel like crying.'

'I think the doctor was puzzled by the wounds, and by the man, although he kept a professional silence.' Coffin looked at his wife.

This is a private conversation, thought Archie Young. I shouldn't be listening.

'You should have gone to hospital yourself, Stella,' said Coffin.

'I was bleeding, I'm a good bleeder,' Stella said, with melancholy pride. 'I went to Maisie, she tidied me up. She did a first aid course once.'

Inspector Lodge was studying the Chief Commander's face. 'Is that all?'

Coffin withdrew his attention from his wife. 'No,' he said slowly. 'Something else the doctor had to say: he thought that the patient had someone waiting for him… Apparently he went to the window to look out and saw him again…walking with someone, he thought, towards a car, but he was called away at that point so could not be sure.'

'Could he see who?' asked Lodge.

'Not from what Phoebe's heard,' said Coffin, a trace of reluctance in his voice.

'Sex? Man or a woman?'

'Seen from the back: tall, wearing jeans, probably a woman, could have been a man.'

Lodge looked at Stella. No one could call her tall, nor manly.

'Astley did well,' said Archie Young, rising to his feet. 'Got contacts all over the place and they work for her, I've noticed that before.'

'She's going round to the hospital to see the doctor herself.'

'I shall go too, although I don't suppose the doctor will have much to add,' said Lodge. 'But this man Eton seems to come into my territory.' He turned to Stella. 'I should like to talk to you again, if that is all right?'

Stella nodded. 'Of course.'

'I shall be present,' said Coffin quickly.

'Welcome it, sir,' said Lodge.

He was punctilious, but his very politeness set a division between them.

Both Young and Lodge refused Stella's offer of more coffee as they left.

'WHAT DO YOU make of that?' asked Archie Young, as they walked across the courtyard to where the police activity continued; SOCO were still taking photographs.

'God knows.'

Lodge walked on in silence, then he said: 'You realize that the killer must have come from the theatre?'

Archie nodded. 'I had worked that out.'

'I suppose it would be quiet enough to do a bit of killing there?'

'In certain places, if you knew your way. I think so, yes.'

'Of course, he might not have been killed there.'

'No.'

They walked on, nearly up to where the police unit was working.

'Terrorism doesn't just come from outside,' said Lodge heavily. 'It's inside, too. Do you understand what I'm saying?'

'I think so.'

'Has to be so in this case if the Eton chap—if that

was his name, probably not his only one—was involved.'

Archie Young did not answer.

'If you learn anything I ought to know, you will tell me?' Lodge went on.

'Of course.'

Lodge nodded. 'We aren't much liked, my sort. I can understand it.'

They had come up to the brightly lit enclosure now.

'What's the woman Astley like? I haven't had much chance to get to know her. We will never be buddies. My sort and her sort don't understand each other easily.' He smiled wryly.

'Good at her job.'

'I got that. I don't find it easy to work with women, but I can see I shall have to.'

'Phoebe is easy.' In some ways, while in other ways she was not, being immensely protective of her own territory, but the Todger could find that out for himself. 'She's done some good work. Very good work.'

As it happened, Phoebe was ahead of them, talking to one of the workers. She nodded as they approached. 'Hi.'

'You came through with some interesting news,' said Archie Young. 'How did you get it?'

She shrugged. 'Luck. My friend had passed the word, and then I was in Summers Street station talking to one of the CID sergeants; he was there when the doctor came in, the hospital where he has a clinic is a street or two away: Paget Street. The flat in Jamaica Place where the first dead man lived comes in the same precinct, so I've been in and out checking on this and that.' She was carefully vague. One did not give too much away. 'It was just a guess that this body had anything to do with the doctor's story.'

'We don't know for sure that it has,' said Archie, 'but it makes a good guess. Miss Pinero was able to add something.'

Phoebe stared at him alertly, and then turned towards Inspector Lodge, who was looking down at the paper-clad corpse.

'Not my man, anyway,' he said. 'That's a relief, I can tell you.'

'Did you think it would be him?' Archie Young was surprised.

'Always expect anything in this job. It's a theatrical business.'

'Yes, well, the theatre comes into it somewhere. He may even have been killed here. He was almost certainly undressed here and dressed again... On the other hand, perhaps not. Mustn't take anything for granted. I can see you've noticed what the newspaper is.'

'Yes,' said Lodge. 'We can all read, can't we?'
The Stage.

STELLA SAID: 'Did you notice that he almost asked for your permission to cross-examine me?'

'He'll be correct.' Coffin was quiet. 'But it will have to be done.'

'I'm sure of it. You'll be there, anyway.'

'I will.' He patted the sofa. 'Come and sit down, Stella. I want to say something.' Yet he found it hard to get started. 'Two men, killed for reasons we don't know. One was a friend of Dennis Garden, and the other...'

'I knew him, and I thought I'd be the one that was killed, not him.'

'Why was he left like that? That's a question to ask.'

Stella shook her head. 'I didn't kill him. I wouldn't leave a message naming me. You do believe me?'

'I believe you, Stella, but there is a link with the theatre...you saw what he was covered up in—I won't say "dressed"?'

Stella looked at her hands. She was quiet for a minute, then she said: 'Yes, with pages of *The Stage*. You would need more than one copy to dress a man.' She raised her eyes to her husband. 'We had quite a pile of back numbers in my office. I think they may have been used.'

'And you can't remember where you were imprisoned?'

Stella shook her head.

She knew that this denial would not hold for ever. In time she would talk, and answer questions.

Coffin would start probing, then Archie Young, then the man Lodge.

She began to think of what she would say. She usually had her best lines written for her, but this time she must write them herself.

NINE

THOSE TWO GREAT and dissimilar institutions the Police Force and the Theatre have one thing in common: loyalty. Whatever criticisms are spread within their ranks (and there is as much of that as anywhere else) are contained within it. Some may seep out and be picked up by outsiders, and the press is always on the lookout for something, but sticking together is more admired than gossiping beyond the walls.

Thus when Stella Pinero went into work the next morning no one reminded her, although they were all thinking about it, that she was under suspicion for two murders. There was plenty of police activity, but no one mentioned either killing to Stella. All were pleased to see her, possibly the more so because it meant that Letty Bingham would not be omnipresent. Letty's commanding ways were not popular in the St Luke's theatre community, which preferred Stella's more relaxed rule.

Alice, not as tidy as usual, greeted her with what was almost a smile from a young woman usually solemn of face. She was there as a protégée of John Coffin, which sometimes seemed to weigh on her, so although always polite to Stella, she was reserved, cautious. Stella herself wondered if the young woman disliked her, but that seemed too harsh a judgement on someone who worked so hard and whom she herself had tried to claim as a friend. 'She's unknowable,' Stella once said to her husband. 'Just shy really,' he had answered. 'Her father was a good copper, her mother was a bit of a wild one, so

I've heard. Both dead, of course.' Stella had said: 'She's not wild.' Which was true, for Alice was solemn and quiet, so much so that her fellow thespians, although liking her, wondered whether the theatre world was the right life for her. She didn't mix; when she did go out for a drink with the others or joined them for a snack in Max's she was almost wordless, although showing herself to have a sharp sense of humour when she did speak. The current speculation among the company was that she was a bastard sprig of the Chief Commander's and found her position embarrassing.

Stella did not know of this speculation, of course. 'I'm glad to be back at work,' she said simply to Alice.

Likewise John Coffin, who had walked into his office to be greeted politely by Paul Masters and handed a folder of papers. Several of these contained reports on the two murders. But there were other events in the Second City calling for the attention of the Chief Commander: an armed raid on a big bank in Spinnergate with one guard badly wounded; a fire raging in a railway tunnel, and the study of the two bombs.

Coffin had risen early, leaving a note for Stella and taking Augustus with him. After giving the dog a quick walk in the park across the road, he had put him in the car to wait while he talked to the police on duty outside the theatre complex.

The body had been taken away, but the forensic squad were still at work and looked like being there for some time.

'Apparently happy, with a base of sadness,' was Paul Masters' judgement that day on his chief. He liked Stella Pinero—you couldn't help it, she had such charm—but if there was to be a division of loyalties, then he was John Coffin's man. Had to be.

There had always been what Paul thought of as a 'streak of silence' in Coffin, when he put on his official face and you got no further. He thought that this face was set firmly in position now.

'Can't blame the man,' he muttered to himself as he went back to his own desk. The two secretaries looked at him curiously, waiting to see if he would say anything, pass any comment, and when he did not they went back quietly to their own work. Silence was the only thing just now.

But nothing could stop their thoughts. Sheila had a friend in St Luke's. They're all talking about the body in the theatre, wondering how anybody could have put it there with the place milling with people, let alone strip the man's clothes off and get him dressed the way he was.

Coffin, too, was worrying away at this puzzle, although he knew miracles, even black ones, could be performed in the theatre.

Coffin worked through his papers, dictated a couple of letters, and answered several telephone calls. He did not want to talk to anyone and was glad not to have to. He and Stella had shared a bed but otherwise had not communicated; he hoped it was a loving silence, though he had his doubts. Love on his side, if mingled with a touch of anger, but what on Stella's?

Slowly, he had to admit that there was a part of Stella's story that he did not believe. She was not telling the truth.

So events were fizzing away inside him. Eventually he telephoned Archie Young, who was not available, and then Phoebe Astley, followed by Inspector Lodge. All of whom were denied him, and for whom he left terse messages.

'Probably together, deliberately keeping out of my way while they work. I suppose it's called tact,' he decided morosely.

He waited, working on quietly, seeing those people who had appointments with him, later taking a polite lunch with a visitor from abroad who might have been from outer space as far as Coffin was concerned.

Paul Masters witnessing the tight control the man was keeping over himself, became increasingly concerned about him. Paul was anxious on all levels, but he did not know what to do about it.

So far, neither Young nor Lodge nor Astley had rung back. Paul had made discreet enquiries himself to discover that all three were out of touch.

He did not accept this as natural, nor did he think the Chief Commander accepted it. For some reason they were keeping their distance.

Stella Pinero telephoned, but Paul had to say that the Chief was out giving lunch to a distinguished visitor from abroad but would be back soon. Did she wish to leave a message?

No message.

Stella picked up a note in his voice and bit her lip. She could imagine what was being said about her. She knew how much Coffin was admired, and respected, so if she was thought to have harmed him, she would be pushed out into the cold. Nothing would be said, of course, but she would shiver. 'I was only going to tell him about the *The Stage* newspapers, but he probably knows already.'

Her mind went back to that morning. She had awoken to find her husband gone, having left her a pot of coffee and a note on the table telling her not to worry. Fat chance, she thought, I am all worry.

Then she picked her way through the police lines, being checked at intervals, and explaining who she was and that she was on the way to work. She was far from sure the identification helped, but it certainly aroused interest.

She turned away from the telephone, and stared down at her desk while admitting to herself that she felt frightened. No new feeling, of course; she was frightened before every first night, sometimes before every performance, all actors knew the feeling, but this was different. Much more sharply personal.

Alice put a cup of coffee down in front of her. 'Brought you this.'

'Thanks.'

'You look as though you need it.'

She took a sip. 'You've put sugar in.'

'You want the energy.'

Stella sighed. 'You aren't wrong there.' I never had you down for a sympathetic soul, she thought, but you are offering it. 'I see the returns are holding up. Last week, anyway.'

'Been nearly a full house most nights.'

'That's good.' She stared down at the papers in front of her. 'I'm worried about the coming week.'

'It's the same show.'

'I know.' What she did not say—though both knew what she was thinking—was: But what about the murder? Murders really, and my name involved.

Alice said: 'Bring more people in, I bet.' She started to move away.

'If they can get in. It's like a fortress, or haven't you noticed?'

Stella drained her coffee cup, then stood up. 'Hang on.' She went over to the set of shelves which was usually loaded with scripts, books, folders of this and that, and dusty collections of old newspapers. *The Stage* had a space to itself. 'What became of all the old copies? Where are they?'

'I thought you'd know.'

'Tell me.' Stella was short with her.

'The police came in, had a look round, and took them away. All that were left... A lot had gone already.'

'Why wasn't I asked for permission?'

'No one said anything to me, Miss Pinero. They just came in, one in uniform and one in plainclothes—CID, I suppose—swept through and took them.'

'I suppose everyone is being questioned?'

'I haven't been done yet. I think they started with Max's staff. Of course, Jane and the others don't come in until later, so they will catch them then. As far as I can see, the police are just working their way through.'

Stella nodded. 'My turn will come.'

'Shall I take your cup?'

'Bring me another one, please, Alice, so I can get my strength up. I think I can hear police feet outside, and it makes me feel weak.'

Alice laughed; she did not believe Miss Pinero was weak.

'I hope we can open tonight. I will have to be firm about that.'

'I think Miss Bingham has fixed that.'

'Oh, has she? Is she in?'

'I think she was. She may have left; she said something about Geneva and then New York on the phone.'

Leaving me in it, Stella thought.

'How could someone have got the body to the alcove without being seen?' said Alice.

'Oh, Alice, when you have worked in the theatre

longer you will realize anything can be done. People either don't see or don't take it in. They expect things to be moving round…there are plenty of trollies and such like that are in use all the time. The killer used one, I expect. Daresay the police will find out which. And not that difficult…' she shrugged.

Alice shook her head. 'I don't know. I still think it's strange that no one noticed. I mean, someone killed, people around and not noticing. Of course, the corridors were quiet.'

'A year or so ago a schoolgirl was raped and murdered in a roomful of her friends and they slept on.'

Alice absorbed this, her eyes darkening, and nodded sadly. 'Does point to someone in the theatre, though.'

'That I do not dispute.'

Kind of her not to name me, thought Stella. Perhaps she is shouting my name inside herself. Or perhaps not. She's being loyal to the Chief Commander, who got her this job, and behind him she is being loyal to her father who got killed while working for that same Chief Commander.

Their eyes met: dark brown and deep blue.

'Your mascara has run a bit on the right eye, Miss Pinero,' observed Alice. 'You don't mind me mentioning it?'

Stella took out a tissue and went to the big looking glass on the wall. 'No. Thank you for telling me.'

'I know you like to look immaculate.'

Stella smiled but said nothing as she dabbed at her eyes. You know I have been crying, she thought. You know I'm in pain, mental and physical. She touched her arm, I ought to have gone to see a doctor. Maisie did her best, but I don't think it was enough. I hope an infection doesn't set in. I don't suppose he had AIDS.

Supposing he did?

Oh well, the postmortem would show all.

Alice said awkwardly, as if she did not believe what she was saying, 'You know we're all your supporters here.'

'Thank you for saying that.' Even if it is not true. She finished repairing the damage to her face; it was amazing what a bit of make-up would do, for your morale as well as your looks. She began to feel more cheerful as she retouched her lipstick and gave her lashes a fresh brush of mascara. She was an actress, after all. 'I am playing to my face,' she said, staring at her image. 'That looks better, so that's how I am.'

'Oh good.'

'Let's hope it lasts longer than the lipstick.'

'You can always put more on,' said Alice, in a serious voice.

Stella gave her a quick look to see if she was being laughed at, but no, it did not appear so. Unless Alice was a better actress than she suspected. You always had to take that into account. Life in the theatre made you a cynic.

She shuffled the papers on her desk. 'Back to work.'

'There's a fax from Miss Bingham there, I put it on your desk just before you came in,' said Alice, 'saying she has got to go to Geneva but will be back this evening.'

Stella found it, and read it. Miss Moneybags herself in operation; Geneva would be a natural landing ground. 'Darling Stella, just to say I have to attend a business meeting in Geneva, flying out and back this evening, late. Don't worry and look after yourself. Love from Letty.'

I suppose she does like me, thought Stella. I have

never really been sure. But then, do I like Letty? Admire her, yes, respect her, yes, and fear her a little, too.

Let's face it: I'm jealous of her influence on my husband. Oh, well, if he gives me the elbow, she will have him to herself.

But I won't think about that. 'Thanks, Alice.'

Alice took her dismissal with a slight smile, disappearing down the corridor along which she saw Jane and Fanny advancing. 'She's there, free and in need of cheer,' she said to them as they passed.

Jane waved her hand in reply without saying anything. She was friendly to Alice in a distant kind of way but did not regard her as a real inhabitant of theatreland.

'She's so broadshouldered and hefty, I always wonder if she's a lezzie.'

'Doesn't necessarily go with body size,' observed Fanny mildly.

'Well, there's something. Don't like her, you know. Don't trust her.'

Fanny smiled. 'You don't trust many, Jane, love, not even yourself.'

'Not even myself,' agreed Jane seriously. 'I question every move I make when I'm on stage, it's valuable. So when I do anything, I know it is *right*.'

'You take yourself too seriously, love. Lighten up. Anyway, you've got this wrong: Alice is not a lezzie, she has a man; I've seen them together. Roughish, I thought he looked, if that interests you. You always say you are interested in human nature.'

Jane bowed her head, as if she knew it, but knew it was the burden of great talent. Within ten years, Fanny was to win an Oscar and be lauded as a spontaneous and natural actress. And where was Jane? No one knew. Acting in repertory in the Channel Islands, someone at din-

ner at the Garrick said. Or was it in the Byre Theatre in
St Andrews?

Stella was pleased to see them. 'Things to talk about,'
she said briskly. 'As you know, the university drama
society is mounting the next production but one in the
small theatre.' She looked down at her notes. '*King Lear,*
ambitious of them but there you are.'

The big theatre would be blank for a week, then the
next production for Jane and Fanny and Tim would be
J. B. Priestley's *An Inspector Calls,* this being both fashionable now with the intellectual element from the two
local universities of the Second City as well as drawing
in the cheerful medium-brows who simply wanted to be
amused.

The three women were talking it over when Tim came
in. 'Hi, there, Stella, nice to see you. I say, this is a
business: a dead body of our own. By golly, I'm glad I
was already in my digs with my landlord to testify.' He
grinned. Tim made no bones about where his sexual
tastes lay. Dennis Garden himself was giving him a
room. And more—as Tim constantly let all his friends
and enemies (he had some of those too) know.

'No one could ever call you reticent, Tim,' said Stella.
'Come on, to work.'

'Let's hope we are all around to perform,' he said,
sitting down.

'Someone will shoot you one day.' Fanny gave him
a push.

'Can I smoke?'

'No,' cried Jane, whose vocal cords were sacrosanct.

'OK, OK,' laughed Tim, who had no intention of
smoking anyway. 'Only asked to annoy.' He looked at
Stella and got a smile in return; she knew very well that

he was deliberately, and kindly, offering himself as a person she could laugh at.

Dennis must be doing the postmortem at this very moment, he thought, so I might be the first to know exactly how the chap died. But no, Dennis is too professional.

IT SO HAPPENED that the University Hospital in Paget Street where Dennis was indeed at work, was also being visited by Phoebe Astley and Inspector Lodge.

The main building of the hospital was a depressing grey stone block which had started life as a Municipal Public Health Hospital, then been absorbed by the National Health Service and raised to the status of a university teaching hospital. Many smart new buildings had been added. The interesting thing was that it had always been a good hospital and much loved by the people of the district who had been born there and sometimes died there.

Now it was modern and up to date; only the smell which floated out of the walls of the oldest part of the building and which no disinfectant could mask spoke of its ninety-odd years of history. And it lived on the usual knife edge.

Astley and Lodge walked in through the entrance hall side by side. They had agreed to come together to track down and then interview the young doctor who had treated Pip Eton. Phoebe was out of temper with Lodge, who had kept her waiting.

Before seeing him park his car and going out to meet him, she had occupied herself first in discovering the name of the doctor she was interested in and had then passed the time reading the memorials to past members of the hospital killed in all wars since the turn of the

century. At least one war had taken place in a faraway
country of which she hardly recognized the name, part
of an empire long since passed away, but a tribute, certainly, to the pugnacity of the medical staff of old London. 'Suppose I ought to have known that,' she thought,
as she strolled past the marble and brass memorials.
'They haven't changed: show them a fight and they're
in it.'

She toured the lobby again, avoiding hurrying nurses
and speeding doctors with coats flying. No memorials to
the Falklands Campaign or the Gulf War....too soon,
perhaps. They were political souls, here in the Second
City, and might not have approved of either enterprise.
In the old days it was King and Country and that was
it. The last two campaigns had been professional affairs,
of course, volunteers not needed.

She was still thinking about it as she went to meet
Inspector Lodge. He was all apologies. 'Sorry to keep
you waiting. I was held up by a telephone call, you know
how it is.'

'I used the time to find out the name of the doctor
who was on duty in the outpatient clinic that evening:
Dr Allegra. He's over here from South Africa, finishing
his training. He's here now, which is lucky for us.'

'Busy, I suppose?'

'Sure to be, but we can break in.'

'Does he know we're coming?'

Phoebe nodded. 'He will be expecting us. Follow me,
I know where to go.'

Lodge followed her in silence down a corridor to a
long room filled with people, emergencies of one sort or
another—a broken arm, a possible poisoning, a sick
baby: there were two of those, one crying, one deadly
silent—waiting their turn to see a doctor. A polite young

woman at the desk said she would ring through to Dr Allegra, if they wouldn't mind waiting.

Since there were no seats left, they leant against a side wall.

Lodge seemed gloomy. 'Ever had an investment go wrong?' he asked.

'Never had an investment.'

'In a person.'

Phoebe looked at him in surprise. 'Ah, that… Well, the usual number. Happens to us all.'

'My man—the one I had planted in the building firm, remember?'

'The missing one?'

'I've heard from him now. Once… Don't know now if I can trust him.'

'What are you saying?'

'I don't choose these chaps that work with me, I'm just a channel. They do the dirty work, but you have to trust them. I don't know now. He says he is working on someone important, the real thing.'

'The murderer? Or the bombers?'

'I suppose so—both, the claims, connected,' said Lodge doubtfully. 'If I can believe him.'

'Did he name anyone?'

'No, that's part of my worry. He wasn't explicit. I could have done with a bit more detail. More concrete, if you get me.' He sounded regretful. He likes that man, Phoebe thought.

Phoebe had her eyes on the young man who was coming towards them with a professionally harried look. He held out his hand.

'Inspector Astley? I'm Dr. Allegra…' He had a slight South African accent, rather attractive to Phoebe's ears, as indeed he was himself, being tall and fair and nicely muscular. All assets appreciated by Phoebe.

She shook his hand and let Lodge introduce himself which he did promptly.

'Not easy to talk here,' said Allegra, surveying the noisy, crowded room. 'And I don't have a room of my own—too junior—but there's a kind of common room.'

The room to which he took them was long and empty with a few soft armchairs and a table with a coffee machine on it.

'Like a coffee?'

Phoebe accepted it, while Lodge shook his head.

'So he's dead, this chap?' said Allegra. He shook his head. 'I knew there was something wrong there.'

'How do you know he's dead?' asked Lodge gruffly.

Allegra was surprised. 'Is it a secret?'

'We haven't released his name.'

'Word gets around. It's that sort of place. A gossip mill, that's what it is. Everyone was talking about the corpse in the theatre…pretty weird, it sounded, and I thought: ''That's my guy.'' I'd been worried about him, there was something not quite right.'

'Go on,' said Phoebe.

Dr Allegra looked hopefully at Phoebe. 'I don't suppose you smoke?'

'No.' A lie but what else to say to a doctor?

He sighed. 'You are wise; my case exactly, but if you had wanted a cig, then I could have had one with you.'

Judging by the smell in the room, his colleagues were not above lighting up as the need took them. He saw her looking at a half filled ashtray and smiled ruefully.

'Yes, walking wounded we are here.'

Lodge found this interplay tiresome. 'So, what is it

you have to tell us, Doctor?' He made the word 'doctor' sound like a threat.

Dr Allegra looked down at his hand, stretched his fingers, then retracted them, causing Inspector Lodge to draw in his breath irritably.

'I'm really trying to be straight about this, say what I observed. I thought he was a thorough liar, and although he had a nasty wound I did not think he was telling the truth about how he came about it. He seemed unclear about whether he had been bitten or stabbed. I thought he liked the drama of a bite. There were certainly two serrated, macerated wounds. But I thought they were knife wounds which had been...' Here he hesitated, '...touched up, but not by teeth, another knife or scissors. Yes, scissors might have done it, and they could have been self-inflicted. Whether this was so or not... I thought he had been wounded but done the rest himself. Self-wounding, a known thing. After thinking it over, I decided to report it.'

'By that time, you knew of the murdered man found in the St Luke's theatre?'

'I did. Word gets around, like I said.'

'The postmortem will give us some idea on the wounds. It wasn't the wound that brought him to hospital that killed him, of course.'

'No, what I saw was not life-threatening. It might have got infected, but I stitched and swabbed it. I think it hurt.' There was a touch of satisfaction in Dr Allegra's voice, clearly his patient had got across him. 'There was something else: he didn't say he was going, and while I went to get some dressings for him to use at home, he made off.'

'Not polite,' said Phoebe.

'No, and then, a few minutes later, I saw him getting into a car. He was laughing. To himself, I suppose,' Allegra added thoughtfully. 'Although I think he had someone with him...a man... Couldn't see... I didn't care for him. Capable of putting on an act.'

'Well, he was an actor,' said Phoebe.

To himself Lodge added: And also, if we are to believe another performer, a man capable of violence, threats and of having terrorist connections. Did he believe that 'other performer', as he called her? His inner jury was still out on that one.

PAUL MASTERS took several calls both before lunch and after, explaining to all callers that Coffin was out entertaining an important visitor but would be back later. Yes, he assured both Lodge and Phoebe Astley, their messages would certainly be passed on. And, no, he did not know why the Chief Commander was not answering calls on his personal mobile. As far as he knew, it was working.

'Doesn't want to,' was what he said to himself. He knew from past experience that Coffin was capable of ignoring calls when he chose. 'Wants to think.'

And plenty to think about, he mused, as he sat back to his own work. Himself the survivor of several unhappy relationships, he reckoned he could have given the Chief Commander a tip or two on how to handle Stella Pinero. Tougher, rougher, would have been his advice.

'I wonder where he is, though,' he said aloud. 'Nothing in his diary.' Not that Coffin always followed the rules and let you know where he was, but Paul Masters usually had a better idea than most.

Sheila Heslop looked up from her word processor. 'I know where he is. I saw him as I came back from lunch.' Sheila had taken a late lunch because her mother was visiting her. 'Speeding along the road towards St Luke's Theatre. I live that way myself. He was going so fast he nearly knocked an old chap off his bike. I think he slowed down after.'

'Sure it was him?' It did not sound like the way the Chief Commander usually drove. 'I bet you were driving pretty fast yourself.'

'Recognized the car,' said Sheila, returning to her work. 'And I was going quite slowly, as it happens. I had Mum on board and I was dropping her off at her favourite shop. You don't drive fast when you've got my mother on board. It was the boss all right. Reckon he's in a mood?'

Paul did not answer.

COFFIN HAD DONE more than slow down, he had pulled over and switched off the engine. 'I could have killed that man,' he told himself. He knew he was capable of violent moods, but he thought he had disciplined himself out of them after the disasters of his middle years. Apparently not; anger was still there inside him, like a stream running deep and only waiting any opportunity to burst out.

His mobile phone had rung several times as he had driven from the smart restaurant where he had given lunch to the eminent French policeman where their talk had been quiet and secretive. Each time the phone sounded, Coffin had ignored it. Now, parked by the kerb with the traffic roaring past, he made an outgoing call.

For a time, he thought he might not get an answer. Try the theatre then, perhaps she was there.

But then a hoarse voice shouted back at him. Nothing had ever succeeded in convincing Maisie that you did not need to shout over the telephone.

'Hello. Who's that?'

'Maisie, you know who it is: John Coffin.'

'Oh, didn't recognize your voice.' She was not unfriendly, merely surprised. 'You sound different.'

He did not believe her, but ignored it. 'Anyone there with you, Maisie?'

'No, only me and the old cat.'

'I want to ask your a few questions.'

There was a hoarse murmur.

'How long have you known Miss Pinero?'

'Oh, ever such a long while.'

'Since when? When did you first meet her?'

Maisie said hoarsely, 'I don't like to talk about Miss Pinero when she's not here.'

'I haven't got time to muck about, Maisie. Just tell me when you first met her.'

He could hear heavy breathing across the line; whether it was the cat or Maisie he could not be sure. 'Come on, Maisie.'

Maisie sighed. 'I don't like talking about Miss Pinero on the telephone. I'd rather do it face to face.'

'No time. When did you first meet?'

'I don't know why it matters, sir, but she did a season in repertory at the old Spinnergate Theatre. I was working there. We got on, and it was just about when her career took off...' Coffin could hear a kind of shrug. 'We stayed together.'

'And she lived in Spinnergate then?'

Maisie thought about it. 'I believe so,' she said at length. 'As far as I know.'

'It would have been a long way home each night to the flat she had in Blackheath,' Coffin pointed out. 'And she had been earning well. A film and TV work.' Unconsciously he was revealing the eye he had kept on Stella all those years they were apart.

'I don't know about that, sir,' said Maisie. 'Not my business. I think I ought to go now, the cat wants to be let out.'

Coffin took pity on her. 'Yes, it's all right, Maisie. I have asked and you have answered. You've told me what I want to know.'

'I have?' said a disturbed voice.

Coffin heard a scuffling noise as he finished the call: it might be the cat, if Maisie really had one, or Maisie herself.

COFFIN DROVE ON to St Luke's. He did not go to his own apartment in the tower; he knew he had a better chance of finding Stella in the theatre itself. He parked the car, got out, and felt as if he had Gus tumbling out after him. One day he would have to train Augustus to stay at home alone, but he never seemed to have the time. There was one good thing about Augustus, he never got lost, he was always right behind you. Coffin could almost hear his snuffling breath now. He was not a barker, and only rarely a fighter, but he was a heavy breather.

He walked in, looking for Stella. In mid afternoon a lull had descended upon the place; he was aware of a rehearsal taking place in the small theatre, and of distant voices here and there, but otherwise the place was quiet.

Stella was not in her office, nor in the manager's office, neither was anyone else. Eventually, he was alerted by Augustus, who had run on ahead and was now barking joyfully in the wardrobe room. This was a suite of three rooms and Stella was in the first. On her own, pensively studying a long dress.

'Pity Donna Karan doesn't do stage clothes,' she said, with a sigh. 'Or does she? Not that we could afford her.'

'Stella…'

She swung round. 'Oh darling, I didn't realize it was you, I've been trying to get hold of you.'

'Oh, good. Any special reason?'

'Just to talk to you. Touch you.' She came up and kissed him; he did not return her kiss.

She drew back. 'You aren't very responsive.'

'You'll find me responsive enough at the right time.'

'It's known as empathy,' she said coldly, taking a step away. 'I think you've lost it.'

He ignored the remark. 'What have you got on your feet? Flat shoes, good. You can walk in those.' He took in what she was wearing. 'Jeans and a cashmere sweater. That'll be warm enough, I think. It's not that cold, and we shall be walking fast.'

'I am not going out, I'm busy here, there's a lot to do.'

'I'm taking you for a walk.'

Stella was silent. Then: 'You're serious.'

'It's very serious for me.'

'Where are we going?'

'Let's go outside and start walking.'

Stella picked up her big shoulder bag and dropped it over one shoulder. It was heavy, her bags were always heavy. Then she said nothing until they had gone through the corridors and out of the building. 'Can't we drive?'

'No, it's a walk—a walk of discovery—and you are going to find the way.'

'Is this a game?'

'Call it that if you like. My game.' Coffin's game.

TEN

STELLA WITHDREW her arm from his grasp, which had been firm, almost hard. 'Where are we going?'

'Just walk on, my love.'

'Am I your love?' Was it a question?

'You will always be that, Stella.' But his tone was quiet, more determined than passionate, as if she had fallen into a part in a play which she could now walk out of. I signed that contract, she told herself, mustn't forget it.

She walked on in silence, along the busy Spinnergate main road with buses, lorries and the battered old motor cars which the district specialized in passing them at speed.

They came to a crossroads where they stopped. 'Which way?' she asked. She looked at her husband's face: expression not promising.

'I want to get to where you were taken that night.'

'But I don't know.'

'Memory is a strange affair: I think as we walk along you might find you do know the way. Or can remember bits. Will you try?'

'I suppose so. But I think it's a waste of time.'

'You came along this road when you escaped from your captivity, you must have done, because Maisie lives down there—' he pointed to a side road. 'So which of these four roads did you come down?'

Stella thought about it, then she pointed. 'It must have been the left turn. Yes, I seem to remember looking across the road and seeing that oak tree.' She pointed to the large oak, now shedding its leaves, on their side of the road. 'I think I got on a bus.'

'Right, let's go down that road. Heaverside Road.'

'I don't want to. If you are playing a game, then I am not.'

He took her arm firmly in his. 'Onward, Stella. You do remember this bit of your journey? Of course, you could lie to me, but somehow I don't think you will.'

'Why not?' She was walking briskly if reluctantly, half dragged along.

'Because you know I will know, I will read your face. I am the professional here, Stella. So you may decide to keep silent. That won't work either: I shall see your eyes. You will look where you do not want to go.'

'All right. Yes, I do recall this bit. Damn you.'

He ignored this. 'Let's walk on. You might enjoy it if you give yourself to it.' There was a certain irony in his tone.

Stella let herself be taken along. 'I used to feel safe with you, it was one of your attractions.'

'I always wondered what was.'

'I don't feel safe now.'

'Oh, you're safe enough,' he said cheerfully. 'Safer than you've ever been.'

'I hate you in this mood.'

'It's not a mood, Stella, more a state of mind.' His tone was polite, formal.

They had passed two turnings on their side of the road, ignored a pedestrian crossing leading to a row of shops down Pedders Street, a narrow street at right-angles to Heaverside Road, and were heading towards Spinnergate tube station. Coffin drew Stella's attention to this.

'We've gone beyond Eliot Street and Pattern Lane…you didn't want to turn down either of those?'

Stella stopped dead. 'I wasn't thinking, just walking.'

'Ahead is Arrow Street. Does that ring a bell?'

She shook her head. 'I don't know what you mean.'

A bus came down Arrow Street stopped a little beyond Eliot Street.

'You must have got off that bus you spoke of somewhere around here, then walked to Maisie's. You remember that?'

'Yes, of course I do. I recognize where we are, naturally.'

'So let's go down Arrow Street.'

Arrow Street was a long, narrow thoroughfare, heavy with traffic. On one side there was a terrace of new houses, and on the other were two megalithic blocks of flats. It was a respectable but dull street. Another red bus was already appearing at the end of it with a lorry of frozen food passing on the other side.

'Not a street I like,' said Coffin. 'Had a couple of nasty murders down here a few years ago. Shouldn't let it influence one's feelings about a place, but somehow it does. I can see the blood on one of the victims still: a small child. Beaten then burnt. Only half-burnt, though, so there was blood and charring on the body. I remember hoping that the kid had been dead when the burning started. You wouldn't remember the case.'

'I don't.'

'The other case was even nastier. In that flat over there—' He pointed towards the top floor of the first block. 'Some poor sod is still living in it. Wonder if he knows what went on there. I daresay. I doubt if the neighbours would have spared him the lovely knowledge.'

He put his arm round her. 'Let's get on... If we go down Arrow Street...it is straight as an arrow's flight isn't it?...you are bound to remember where you got on the bus and that will give us a clue to where you must have walked.'

'I do remember...it was at the end of Arrow Street.'

'Coming back, is it? Memory is like that....patchy. You think you have forgotten, and then suddenly, there it is in your mind, all fresh and clear. Let's go on down Arrow Street; not worth getting on a bus. Getting tired?'

Stella shook her head. 'No, I am not tired.' Many things: disturbed, even angry, but not tired. Some emotions drive away fatigue.

'We can take it slowly.' As he walked, he went on talking. 'You know this part used to be all part of the Shambles...where the cattle came in off the boats and were slaughtered. In the days before refrigeration, of course.'

'I didn't know that.'

'No, why should you. I never like to think of all that death handed out...mass killing. Must give a feeling to a neighbourhood.'

'You're not talking like a policeman.'

'I'm not all policeman.'

'Or perhaps it's just part of your technique... I haven't seen this side of you before. Well, I wouldn't would I?'

'Technique?'

'Yes, to unsettle a suspect. And, as a matter of fact, it's working,' she said angrily. 'I can't bear to think of all those sheep and cows.'

Coffin laughed, his mood lightening. He took her hand.

'And don't say you love me for it, I'm not in the mood.' But she did not take her hand away.

Suddenly their feelings towards each other seemed to have changed. 'She's going to do it,' Coffin told himself. 'She's going to show me, tell me.'

But they were both wary as they walked the length of Arrow Street.

Coffin wondered if he had been right to tell her about the Shambles. Not true, he had made it up on the spur of the moment, but it seemed to have worked.

'You didn't bring Augustus, after all,' she said.

'No, he's not a good walker over a distance. Prefers the car.'

'So do I.'

'I thought it was better this way. You sweep past things in a car; on foot, noises and smells bring back a memory which you might otherwise not have picked up.'

Smooth, Stella thought, very smooth. Perhaps he really believed what he was saying. Things were going to come out, she could tell. Impossible to keep quiet any longer. Stupid of her to have tried.

'For instance,' he went on, 'see that man over there?'

She looked; the man was well dressed in a dark suit, carrying a briefcase and what appeared to be a copy of *The Times*. 'Businessman of some sort. Lawyer, accountant? He looks prosperous.'

'Oh, he is: he runs the local outfit of prostitutes.'

'He's looking at you as if he knew you.'

'He knows me, all right. As I know him. He may acknowledge me or he may not. Depends on business.' Coffin was watching the man with some interest. He was going across to a man sitting in a car, he addressed him briefly, then moved away. 'I didn't know there was a contact there, but there is, although I don't think my friend was glad for me to see it. I guess they would have talked longer if he hadn't seen me watching.'

'Who is the other man, then?'

'He is a banker. I shall have to think about it, he may be putting money in. Better than Lloyds or the Stock Exchange, much safer. Provided you know the right people.'

'I suppose he does.'

'That's what I will be thinking about. My friend thought I might be one of the right people once, if the correct amount of currency changed hands. Well, he learnt otherwise.' Coffin sounded amused. 'Now, see that woman across the road?'

'The one who has just come out of that rather nice house?'

'Yes, and you're right, it is a nice house.'

The woman was beautifully dressed in a pale suit, with a flow of blonde hair. A crocodile bag swung from her shoulder.

'What do you think she is?'

Stella gave her a knowledgeable look over. 'She's not an actress, but…I don't know, she's a performer of some sort.'

'I'll say she is. She belongs to the stable of our friend now disappearing down the road.'

Stella was surprised. 'Upmarket for Spinnergate.'

'Fifteen years ago you would have been right. Now…' he shrugged. 'Since the City moved in not so far away, prices have risen. Of course, the girls come and go, it's an ageing profession.'

'So is the stage,' said Stella, with feeling. Without meaning to, she quickened her step and marched on down Arrow Street.

'A walk down Arrow Street is never wasted.' Coffin caught up with her. 'Here we go.'

Arrow Street ended in a small open space with a traf-

fic roundabout in the centre; China Street forked off to
the right and Kettle Street to the left. Both were lined
with small pleasant houses and shops. It was one of the
nicer residential areas in Spinnergate.

Coffin looked at his wife. 'Which way appeals,
Stella?'

'I think I remember the pedestrian crossing,' she said
nervously. 'Into China Street.' She looked along the road
and then at Coffin. 'We may be getting close.'

The Pelican crossing changed from red to green and
they crossed the road in silence.

'Let's take it slowly now, so you can look about you,
see what clues you get. It was dark when you were taken
there?'

'Yes.'

'But daylight when you escaped?'

Stella thought about it. Then she nodded.

'But you were in a state of shock, so not noticing as
well as you might be. Still, let's see what happens. Even
in the dark there are smells. There may be a smell in
China Street that reminds you of where you were.' His
voice was grave and serious.

He's playing this game better than I am, Stella
thought. It's nearly over, anyway. I know that. I can tell
that he knows it, too. Why are we both playing it to the
end? Her answer came at once: because I am frightened.
I will have killed something. Trust, I guess, or worse.
What could be worse, but love, of course.

They were passing a baker's shop which proclaimed
that tea and coffee with pastries were to be had all day
and every day.

'Could we stop here for a cup of tea?' Stella pleaded.

'I was going to suggest it.'

'Were you?' Was that good or bad for her? She found

herself all the time now trying to formulate an assessment.

'Well, perhaps that is an exaggeration, but it did cross my mind. You look tired and we don't yet know how far we have to go, do we?'

'No,' said Stella, in a hollow voice.

The baker's shop smelt pleasantly of fresh bread. Perhaps they permeated the air with some special scent, thought Stella cynically. Nothing was baked on the premises.

But the little room at the back where the tables were laid with fresh clothes and real flowers was welcoming. She sank down on a straight-backed chair while Coffin went to order the tea.

'Can we not talk?' she said when he came back. 'Or simply be quiet?'

'Two Indians, milk and some lemon for you, is that all right? Silence? Why not? Although the woman who took the order seemed to want to talk; she knows you, I think. Saw you in the theatre, I suppose.'

The tea, when it arrived with a plate of shortbread biscuits, was served in blue-and-white china; it was strong and hot. Stella drank thirstily.

She noticed that Coffin, never as fond of tea as she was, drank slowly. Too many cups of canteen tea as a young copper climbing the ladder...and occasionally falling off, he had added with a wry smile; he could always laugh at himself.

The wall behind Coffin was covered with a large looking-glass in which she could see herself. She could also see the woman who ran the shop. She was a large, plump redhead with a friendly face but sharp eyes. Those eyes were now looking at Stella.

Stella realized that the woman was trying to catch her

eye. She looked down at her tea to avoid the contact. How hard it was not to look up and see.

She sipped some tea. Come on, woman, she told herself. If this is a game, you can play it too. You make the rules, too. Damn it, you're an actress.

She lifted her head to give the woman a radiant smile. She saw Coffin looking at her.

'Never discourage a fan,' she said, still with a smile. '"No talking" is over, is it?'

'Yes,' Stella stood up. 'Just give me a minute while I go to the cloakroom.' She passed through the shop, had a quick word, still smiling, with the woman behind the desk, and disappeared. She was not gone long.

Coffin was waiting for her outside when she came through the shop.

'Are you sure you're up to this? You want to go on?' he asked her gravely.

She nodded, walking forward. 'Come on, it's this way, I think.' She turned to look him straight in the face: 'As I remember.'

There was a cul-de-sac off China Street called Fish Alley. An unpromising name for a group of pretty apartments overlooking the river.

At the entrance to Fish Alley, Stella halted. 'Down here, I think.'

'Sure?'

She nodded towards a dark shop on the corner. 'That shop is a coffin-maker's...not many of them left now, most coffins are mass-produced. I couldn't forget that shop, could I?'

Coffin considered that it was the first time he had ever considered his name—a good Kentish name—an embarrassment.

There was an aged, worn inscription on the glass

which read; COFFIN MAKER TO HIS MAJESTY KING
GEORGE III.

'Can that be true?'

'Shouldn't think so,' said Stella, 'but it's very imaginative. They are imaginative round here.'

A wizened little old man's face peered at them through the dusty glass. He smiled and waved.

'George III,' said Coffin, waving back. 'Or does he think I am?'

'I don't think he's sure.' Stella could see the old man's intent, cheerful, battered, old face. 'He seems to know you.'

'Very likely he does, my face gets known for what I am. Let's admit it: we are both well known in our different ways. Hard to hide.'

Stella nodded. 'I know where I am now. I remember.' She pointed. 'On the right. That small block. It's the middle flat. I remember running down one flight of stairs.'

'I am pleased. It's very helpful to know where you were held and where Pip Eton was living.' Coffin sounded positive, as if he had got what he wanted. He smiled at his wife encouragingly. 'Clever Stella, I knew you would come through for me. We must let Archie Young and Inspector Lodge know.'

So we must, thought Stella dismally, all of them must know and come tramping around. She felt suddenly weary, as if she was being walked over herself. 'Is that it? Can we leave it there? Walk back. Or ring for a cab, I am a bit tired.'

Coffin would have none of it. 'No, Stella. Now we have got this far, we must look over the place, check it out. Not touch things—forensics will want to do that— but verify it really is where you were held.'

Fish Alley, near to the Petty Pier, was quiet with a few cars parked along the kerbs; a woman was pushing a pram along the road, and a mongrel dog, tail up, trotted cheerfully behind her.

'Lead the way, will you, Stella?'

She hesitated, then walked forward slowly. It was coming, it had to be, she saw the truth was arriving.

'It's called Linton House, I see.' Coffin was following her. 'A grand name for a modest establishment.' He was studying the numbers listed on the wall in the entrance lobby. 'Must be number 2A. No name given. Understandable, I suppose. Incognito is the name of the game.'

For the first time, Stella understood that he was as nervous as she was. 'A flight up,' she said.

As they mounted the stairs, a woman put her head out of a ground-floor flat. 'Thought I heard voices. Nice to see you, Miss Pinero.'

Stella smiled and nodded. 'Mrs Flowers, here I am.'

'I heard you here yesterday.'

'No,' Stella shook her head. 'No, not yesterday.'

'Oh.' Mrs Flowers sounded surprised. 'Thought I heard someone up there above.' She started to withdraw backwards through the door. 'Oh, well, you know how it is. It's an old house, the floorboards creak all the time.' She gave a jovial laugh, a wave of the hand, and closed the door.

'Old gossip,' said Stella. 'Used to watch what went on.'

'She sounds useful.'

'Oh, yes, send your police questioners in. Make her day.'

They had arrived outside the door of 2A. Coffin surveyed the neat grey door with its shining brass bell. 'I suppose we shall have to break in. No problem, I've done it often enough in the way of duty. I remember once I had to break into a house where there were five people dead around a dinner table.'

'It won't be necessary to break in,' said Stella, lips stiff and her throat tight. 'I have a key.'

'You took it with you when you left? Cool of you, Stella.'

She did not answer, but put the key in the lock, turned it twice, then pushed the door open.

Beyond the door was a small hall, carpeted in soft grey, the walls painted white. Light streamed in through the open doors of the sitting room on the right and a bedroom on the left.

'Smells empty,' said Coffin. 'No one dead here, anyway. You can always tell by the smell.' He closed the front door behind him, then stood looking at Stella.

'Honesty time,' he said. 'You knew this place before. If you were taken here, it was not by chance.'

Stella did not answer. She put her hand to her throat. She looked into her husband's eyes and saw something there that she did not wish to see. In their long and difficult relationship, sometimes on, sometimes off, he had shown her anger, but behind it she had always seen love. Now she saw a kind of opacity. For the first time, she could not read him.

'Honesty time,' she repeated. 'That's a good line.'

'Stop acting, Stella.'

'Sorry, can't help it. You're frightening me.'

'Even that is acting.'

And he was right.

Stella shook herself as if she were trying to throw out one persona, the actress, and get back into another, her own proper self. She led the way into the sitting room. 'Let's go and sit down.'

The sitting room was a long narrow room with windows at both ends, it was a room which looked as though it was basically tidy and in good order, but over which disorder had marched. A cup and saucer on the floor, an overturned chair, empty beer cans all around.

Stella righted the chair before sinking down on the chintz-covered sofa.

The action was, as she saw herself, a dead giveaway, if one were needed.

'You own this place, don't you, Stella?'

'Yes.'

'I would have known anyway. It smells of you, Stella. You didn't know that, did you? How could you? But I can tell.'

'I hope it's a nice smell,' she said, playing for lightness.

'Now I want to know all about it—and the truth, mind.'

'I don't know where to start.'

'Not at the beginning, not why you own this place or since when or what you do with it—that can come later.' He saw her wince. 'Tell me exactly what happened that day you packed your bags and announced you were going to several places where you never went and probably never intended to go.'

That is how he talks to a suspect, Stella thought. But then, I am a suspect. 'I did intend to go to the health farm. But Pip Eton was waiting outside. He grabbed me and made me drive to here.'

'And why here?'

Stella licked her lips. 'I didn't know it, but he was living here; had been for a few days, I think, maybe longer.'

'And how did he get in?'

'He had a key… I had given him one, years ago.'

Coffin nodded. 'So, years ago, you gave a key to Pip Eton—I won't ask why—and he kept it. Right? And, without you knowing it, he let himself in and began living here. Is that right?'

'Yes, but I don't think "living" is the way to describe it… He was just here. Using the place.'

'For what?' And, when she did not answer: 'I must know, Stella.'

Reluctantly, she said: 'I think he must have used it as a kind of base, a meeting place for people like himself…'

'Terrorists.'

She bowed her head. 'I didn't know. I only learnt what he was, what he had become, when he entrapped me, trying to make me turn informer on you. I refused then and I always would have refused.'

Coffin nodded without saying anything.

'But you have a secret life of your own which you did not tell me of. I didn't know that you had a part on a hush-hush committee which he called ATA1. He told me that, not you.'

'Secret information. It's just work, Stella, part of my job.'

'I would never have let him use me. He had been trying for ages, much longer than I let you know. I just laughed him off at first, I didn't think you knew anything secret. I was wrong about that, you had your own secret life. In the end, he tried force, he attacked me. I just defended myself.'

'I believe you. But you owned this place, you knew where you had been taken, even if by force, and you knew Pip Eton—rather well, I suspect, Stella.'

'In the past,' she said quickly. 'All in the past.'

'Lodge isn't going to like it. I can't say I do myself, but I'm glad you have told me everything.'

He walked to the window and looked out. A quiet street scene. 'You didn't keep much of a watch on this place.'

In a much louder voice, Stella said: 'Since my marriage to you it has played no part in my life. I have lent it to various friends, not many, and that was all. It was an investment now, a place I might sell when it suited me.'

'It wasn't that all the time.'

'No. Performers have their own stresses, a quiet place, where I could take...yes, a lover, helped me to unwind. But not since you and I met again, never.'

'You never took me there.'

'No. Can't you see why? You were serious.'

Coffin smiled. 'All this took some getting out of you.'

There was a pause.

'You knew...you knew all the time, everything.'

'I admit it. That secret side of my life informed me as a matter of course. You can imagine how I enjoyed it. Naturally it was done in a very tactful way; they didn't come out and say, ''Your wife is in contact with a very bad character indeed, a chap on our wanted list'', but I got the message. I wanted you to tell me. I needed you to tell me yourself.'

She covered her face with her hands. 'I feel terrible.'

He came back from the window where he had been standing to sit beside her on the sofa. 'I've had my own ups and downs, you know: nearly chucked out of the Force once. I was in limbo for a bit, and then on a kind of approval.'

'Will you have to resign now?'

He didn't answer, but stood up. 'Let's have a look

over the flat. Forensics will have to come and check it out.'

'There's only the bedroom and the kitchen, besides the bathroom,' Stella explained.

'Kitchen first.'

The kitchen was small, with a compact white refrigerator and shining sink. The whole room looked unused. Coffin swung open the refrigerator door and a waft of cold air came out, but except for a carton of stale milk, it was empty. There were crumbs of bread and a wrapped loaf by the side of the electric cooker and two teabags in the sink in company with a dirty mug.

He looked in the rubbish bin which held a few beer cans and a bottle that had contained whisky.

'Someone was here, but not doing much eating,' he said. 'Let's see the bathroom.'

A quick look showed a bloodstained towel slung over the handbasin. Coffin looked but did not touch.

'Bedroom now.'

This room was dominated by a large double bed. It was tidy, but when he pulled back the duvet the undersheet was tousled, as if someone had been sleeping there.

'Your lodger,' said Coffin.

The dressing table was tidy and unused except for a comb with hairs in it.

'Careless fellow,' said Coffin. 'You should always take your hair with you.'

A cupboard covered both walls, but it was empty except for a tweed jacket.

'Not mine,' said Stella.

'Belonged to the chap who left his hair and probably his blood behind. Forensics will tell us.'

'Pip.' Stella was clear. 'The blood isn't mine, I didn't touch a towel. The towel belongs to the flat, though.'

'Good,' said Coffin lightly. 'Something established.'

Stella sat down on the bed. 'Wait a minute, I've been thinking, I was a fool not to see it. You didn't need me to lead you to this flat, you knew. You knew that as well as the rest. You probably had a key.'

'No key and I didn't know which flat, just the general neighbourhood, but I did know you had something here... Lodge doesn't know, nor Archie Young.'

'That's a comfort,' said Stella bitterly. 'But then they are not privileged with your confidential, special information. I mean, they are not in your game, are they?'

Coffin had bent down to look under the bed, his foot had caught on something. He drew out a carrier bag.

'What's this?' He drew out a crumpled cotton shirt stained with blood, pale blue jeans, and a jacket, also bloody. There was a bright cotton skirt and toning blouse as well.

Stella looked. 'Those are mine, I recognize them. How did they get here?'

'How indeed?'

'I gave them to Maisie to give to the charity shop she works in.'

'Then we shall have to have a word with Maisie, shan't we?' said Coffin, his voice grim. Somehow he did not make it a question in which she could share. 'Do you trust her?'

'Yes, and yes.' Stella sounded bewildered. 'She's been my dresser on and off for years. We're friends.' She paused. 'More important, do you trust me?'

'Always and for ever,' said Coffin. He held his arms out. 'And you have to trust me. We may have a bad time, both of us, but we will get over it. No promises, but I think so.'

Stella lifted her head. 'Kiss me.' She sank slowly backwards under the pressure of that kiss on to the bed.

'I can think of better beds,' he said. 'What's happening here?'

'Always a tendency to fall in love with your leading man—in films more than in plays; the script demands it,' she said nervously.

'Are we playing lovers because the script demands it?'

'No. You know that.'

He raised himself. 'Then let's go home, we have a better bed there.' Besides, forensics would be all over this one. Even in a moment of love he remained the policeman. 'You will have to take those clothes off, in case they have traces, and I am afraid they will want to go over all your stuff, things you might have worn or brought here.'

'I don't like that.'

'It will happen. Mine today as well, I expect. Nothing can be overlooked.'

Stella realized once again this time with an even sharper pain, what she had done to him. 'We are both in it, aren't we? I have dragged you in… I'll do anything you want.'

'Just co-operate. And don't try to be clever. Remember, they're clever too.' He added: 'I'll ring for a car to collect us.'

'No, let's walk. I would rather.'

'Not too tired?'

'No.'

Coffin hesitated, then said: 'There is something for me to say. I owe it to you to tell you something of what I've been involved with these last months.'

Stella looked at him without speaking.

'I was a member of a committee vetting security. Top-level stuff. Spying on friends and colleagues. Treat it as a game, I was told.'

'And who were you watching?'

'I can't name names even to you.' Especially to you, because you were one of them. I was to watch Inspector Lodge and Sir Fred, who was no doubt watching me, Pip Eton—yes, his name came forward because of you, I knew about him, Stella. Also one person who managed to stay in the undergrowth and is a murderer.

'Not a nice game.'

'No, well, that's it? Still want to walk by my side?' Stella nodded. 'Thank you.'

As they emerged into the street, Stella said: 'I've remembered something… There was someone else here besides Pip. I heard another voice… There was a woman.'

What a lot was packed into that period when you were drugged, Coffin thought sadly.

ELEVEN

NOTHING IN COFFIN'S life ever went as planned, a process he had long learnt to expect but was often surprised by all the same.

Even before he and Stella got to St Luke's, while they were still walking towards it, a police patrol car stopped and hailed him with relief.

'Sir, sir, they're trying to get you. I was told to look out for you...thought you might be walking the dog,' here the driver saw Stella and gave her something between a bow and a salute. 'Afternoon, ma'am.'

Stella smiled and took a step aside. It so happened she knew the driver because his wife worked in the theatre box office and he was a regular attender with surprisingly highbrow tastes.

He held out his phone. 'Do you want to use it, sir?'

Coffin looked at Stella with a smile and shrug, before picking up the phone. Paul Masters answered at once, relief in his voice.

'Glad to get you, sir.'

'I wasn't out with the dog.'

'No, sir, of course not, the dog's here, you left him with me, lying on my feet this minute.' In fact, he had had the pleasure of the dog's company all the morning. Briskly, he went on to report that there was a riot down at the Spinnergate Docks.

'Well...' began Coffin.

'Of course, it's being handled by Inspector Dover of B unit, but I knew you would want to know.'

'How big a riot?'

'Mini, sir. However, the media are there.'

'Damn!'

'Yes, sir, but it's not why I wanted to make contact.'
Paul Masters drew breath. Distantly, Coffin could hear
him politely requesting Augustus to get off his feet,
please. 'Sir Fred is on his way for a meeting with you,
he will be here in about twenty minutes.'

'Ah,' Sir Frederick Mantle was a prominent figure on
the secret committee on which Coffin served. In fact,
Coffin had the idea that Sir Fred was a member of the
even smaller committee which controlled the larger one.
There were always rings within rings, in his experience.

Paul Masters was not privy to all the secrets of Coffin's life, but he certainly knew something of the part
played in life and circumstances by Sir Fred.

'What about Inspector Lodge?'

'On his way too, sir.'

'I'm on my way,' Coffin assured Paul. 'Keep Sir Fred
happy if he gets there before I do.' A last thought: 'Get
hold of Chief Inspector Astley and tell her I want a
word.'

'Will do. She was asking for you earlier, sir.'

Was she? Coffin thought. What had she got about the
death of Pip Eton or possibly the earlier victim, the one
with fingers cut off and no name?

Coffin refused a lift in the patrol car, and turned back
to Stella.

'Crisis?' she asked.

'A small one. Nothing to worry about.' Or so he
hoped, although one never knew with Sir Fred. 'But I
shall have to go straight back. Can't linger.' And he gave
her the smile she loved most: gentle, full of humour and
self-knowledge.

She slid her arm through his. 'Let's enjoy the walk back.' She asked no questions, she had been his wife long enough to know that was something you did not do. 'Tell you what: I'll try and have a word with Maisie. Find out what she knows about the clothes under the bed. Can't believe there is any harm in her, she's such a good old thing.'

'I won't forget what you say about hearing a woman… If we get the chance, I will ask you to identify a voice. But think about it…as a professional used to the nuances.'

'I shall. I think it was a woman.'

Coffin nodded and kept quiet his conviction that good old things like Maisie could get up to a surprising number of little wickednesses if they felt like it.

They parted at the corner of Madely Street near to the police headquarters and within easy distance of St Luke's.

'I won't come any further with you,' said Coffin to his wife.

Under the interested eyes of several of his colleagues driving past in a van—on their way, he supposed, to the small riot—he gave her a brief kiss, then followed this up with a much longer kiss. A relieved and happy Stella responded with an enthusiasm that further delighted the happy band en route to subdue their fellow citizens of Spinnergate. Stella, of course, knew exactly what she was doing. While not always acting, she was never quite not acting. She waved her hand to him and strolled away, making a good exit.

She thought to herself: I will have a straight talk with Maisie and sort things out. She had never yet been in a situation where she could not 'sort things out' and it had not occurred to her that this time perhaps she would not be able to. She would telephone and let Maisie know she was coming. Yes, that would be wise.

She looked ahead to St Luke's and the theatre complex which lay just around the corner.

COFFIN CALLED first into the viewing room where banks of screens showed the live pictures from the cameras set on the tops of roofs over the Second City. They commanded all the main streets and street corners. He looked at one street corner which was crowded with moving figures, on their way to the riot, no doubt. A van was turning the corner, the cameras were swivelling to follow.

The sergeant in charge of the room said that they had been asked to keep a check on that van.

Coffin watched for a while, then went away to the meeting in front of him.

COFFIN FOUND Inspector Lodge already waiting for him in the outer office, with Phoebe Astley lounging in a chair by the window. Phoebe was in jeans and tweed jacket—as Stella had once said, 'She has the legs for it'—while Inspector Lodge was darkly clothed in anthracite grey. Both of them stood up as he came in.

He acknowledged them with a nod and a wave towards his own room. 'Go through, I'll be with you.' Then he turned towards Paul Masters. 'How's the riot going?'

'Pretty nearly tidied up, sir. But you can see for yourself on the TV.' He pointed to one of the screens across the room, where, the sound off, a figure could be seen against a background of men and women waving flags demanding ACTION AGAINST THE ENEMY.

Coffin winced. 'No, thank you. And Sir Fred?'

'Telephoned through. His car is held up in the traffic—the riot, you know, but he will be here shortly.'

It was always the way with Sir Fred. He was always arriving shortly and leaving shortly after that. A man of high motives and much mobility.

'Buzz when Sir Fred touches ground here.'

'Right, sir.' Paul Masters was wearing one of his brighter suits that day, he was never one for the dark outfit, his spell in the uniformed branch must have been a severe trial to him, and today he was in cream and tan. Coffin had named it his defiant suit and wondered whom his efficient, ambitious, but aggressive young assistant was battling with today. Probably Coffin himself, he thought, as went into the other room.

He sat down quickly at his desk, tidy as usual, with all papers neatly stowed away. The problems to be dealt with were there, though, even if hidden in the drawers or in files.

'Phoebe, glad you are here. I want you to do something for me.' He sat down and scribbled an address. Linton House, Fish Alley. 'Check over this place. Take a team in—forensic, the lot—and see what you get. Come back to me. Quietly.'

Phoebe stood up. 'Right, I'm off. Can I have a bit more information?'

'When you discover the name of the owner you will understand.'

She looked at him, frowning. 'You know.'

'I know.'

He's dumping me into something, Phoebe decided, he's done it before. But fear not, friend, I will fight my way out.

'I want you to come at it cold, form your own impression. You may get a surprise.'

'Shock is the word that comes to mind,' said Phoebe. 'I wonder why?'

'What did you want to see me about?'

Phoebe considered. 'You know I've been working on the copies of *The Stage* that were used to wrap up the corpse? They match with those left behind in the theatre. The fingerprints on those found on the corpse were very smudged. But one or two were clearer…they matched with those of Miss Pinero.'

Silence. Inspector Lodge kept his face expressionless.

Coffin did not quite manage this, but he was calm.

'How did you get her fingerprints?'

'She supplied me with them yesterday.'

'Very sensible of her.'

'Not surprising to find them on the newspapers, they were from her office.'

Coffin sat in silence for a second, then he said: 'You have the address. Go to the flat on the second floor.'

Phoebe nodded. 'I'll be off then. Sounds like work. Don't tell me you've got a body waiting for me.'

'No body, but there may have been one there. I'm not sure about that.'

She raised an eyebrow. 'Our boy dressed up in paper clothes?'

'Could be. Find out for me. And nothing, as yet, for the media.'

So it has to be Stella Pinero again, Phoebe decided. 'I'll be on my way.'

She slid through the door as a buzz and a noise in the outer office announced the arrival of Sir Fred.

Grey-suited, small, plump, almost smiling all the time but never quite making it a broad grin. Stella, on meeting him once, had said that she would cast him as Dracula any day.

'Apologies for being late.' Sir Fred set great store on being punctual. 'Came through a bit of trouble on the way here,' he announced with satisfaction.

'Under control,' said Coffin.

Sir Fred continued looking at him, eyebrow raised.

'Two rival football teams, basically.' With added elements from all over the Second City, but he was not going to mention that. Coffin was reluctant to explain at all.

'Bad, bad.'

Coffin could feel his teeth grinding together as he bit back his irritation. He understood that the ability to create this irritation at will and thus weaken a protagonist was a valuable skill of Sir Fred's, but he did not relish being the victim.

So he smiled. 'Let me give you a drink. Whisky?'

Sir Fred was well known to like a certain malt whisky, so his answer would be revealing. If he said no, then that would be a very bad sign indeed.

There was a pause. It was ended by Sir Fred: 'Thank you, Jack.' No one called Coffin Jack. 'A little, thank you.'

Coffin got up to go to the armoire which Stella had picked up on a tour of France and brought back (at vast expense) for him.

'Neat,' said Sir Fred. 'Never water malt. Ice yes, water no.'

'I haven't any ice. But I could send for some.'

'No matter, no matter.'

Coffin turned to Inspector Lodge: 'The same for you?' Lodge did not refuse. Finally Coffin poured himself a drink, making it a careful, small one; he needed all his wits about him with this pair.

Then he sat down to study the two men; he was pretty

sure that they had been discussing him already. It would
be in character for Sir Fred to do this and for Lodge to
listen, nodding sagely. Coffin found he was getting
crosser with every minute that passed. He ranked much
higher than Lodge, but it seemed that in the different
world of security, Lodge had the pull.

So Coffin drank, kept a still tongue and waited for Sir
Fred to utter. That gentleman was taking his time, which
again irritated the Chief Commander, who was thinking
of Stella.

Sir Fred put down his glass. 'I have admired you,
Coffin, you know that.'

Do I? Coffin asked himself silently. I hadn't noticed
it. Aloud, he said: 'Thank you.'

Obviously Sir Fred was getting ready to add a rider
to his last remark of praise.

'But,' he began, 'you are too close to all this...your
wife, you know. I think you should step back.'

Coffin did not answer. He was not surprised, but even
angrier. He took a drink, offered some more to Sir Fred
who accepted and to the Inspector who refused. Coffin
leant across to fill the glass. If he trod on Sir Fred's toe
to do so, he did not care.

'I understand what you're saying.' Coffin paused in
pouring the whisky. He saw with pleasure that Sir Fred
was sweating. Lodge looked cool enough, damn him.
'But I don't think I can, and for the very reason you
suggest that I should: my wife.'

He put down his own drink, largely untouched, and
stood up. It was a spontaneous movement of protest, no
threat intended, but Sir Fred pushed his chair backwards
quickly. Lodge coughed.

'Now, now,' Sir Fred said. 'Don't take it amiss what

I say. It's in your own interest, my dear fellow. And Stella's. Keep out. Let others take over.'

Coffin looked straight at Lodge.

'No, no, not necessarily our friend here.'

'Inspector Lodge is involved too,' Coffin pointed out coldly. 'He has Peter Corner. Missing.'

'He's been in touch.' Lodge spoke up quickly.

Coffin decided it was his turn to stand on his dignity. 'Has he now? I was not informed.'

'You would have been. I tried to contact you today, this very afternoon, but you were out of touch.'

Coffin briefly admitted the truth of this to himself while still not forgiving Lodge. Then he saw a flash of expression on Lodge's usually impassive face... He cares for that man, Coffin told himself. God, how could I not have seen that about Lodge? He and Corner, not a relationship, almost certainly not, but he is attracted. Well, I never.

Lodge swivelled in his chair, then took out a hand-kerchief to blow his nose. He had given himself away, and he knew it. Sir Fred was watching, no surprise there. So he knew. There were no secrets in the world they both moved in. No doubt this side of Lodge was used.

'We will talk about this later,' said Coffin, in a voice that offered no promises.

He turned to Sir Fred. 'I think there is something else, sir, isn't there?'

Sir Fred finished his drink, carefully setting down the glass so that it should not mark the polish of the table at his elbow. 'Clever of you to see it. Always knew you were a clever chap.'

Coffin waited.

'It concerns the first dead body. Di Rimini, or Bates as he was rightly called. By this time, did you or did you not know that he was a police snout?' Coffin nodded, unwilling to reveal what he knew or did not know. Keep Sir Fred guessing. 'No doubt you are surprised about my part in this, but I am obliged to have contacts here and there.' He did not glance towards Lodge, who was sitting still. 'Even if it flushes out people like Bates, the snout. Not much used and not much use either, as far as can be ascertained. He was not a man over-blessed with friends who confided in him, but he was a drinker. Mostly, I believe, he drank on his own.' Sir Fred looked a little sly, as if he knew that Dennis Garden counted as a friend. 'But he picked people up, or sometimes was picked up himself.'

Come on, Coffin muttered, get on with it. Don't swither.

'You know we can't choose the contacts we work with.' Sir Fred gave a seraphic smile.

'What are you working round to?'

'A person who drinks in the sewers of Spinnergate— joke, dear boy, one of our contacts, but we can't use the best people—informed us that di Rimini, also known as Eddy, had said he knew that a terrorist was at home in Spinnergate and was very close to the top man himself. I quote.'

Coffin said: 'Who is this man who passes all this on?'

'Did I say man?' said Sir Fred smoothly.

'From all I have learnt of Bates or di Rimini, call him what you like, he was not the sort to confide in a woman.'

'Well, frankly, our contact seems to fit either sex.'

'Two drunks talking together,' said Coffin. 'What reliance can you put on that?'

Sir Fred stood up. 'Look, it's no good us quarrelling,

we won't get anywhere that way. I pass it on to you to think about what it suggests.'

Coffin stood up, too. 'Oh, I see all right: that di Rimini—I prefer that name, I think—was not just picked up off the street as someone who could be killed, dragging in my wife, but was killed because he had dangerous knowledge.'

Sir Fred nodded. 'It's worth thinking about.'

'Did he have names to offer as well?'

'No names.'

Coffin turned to Lodge, who had risen also. 'And what about your man? Has he got this story too?'

'No, or if he has then he hasn't reported it. He simply says he is working on a good lead.' Lodge sounded uneasy, which Coffin noted. Everyone was uneasy in this bloody case.

He turned to Sir Fred. 'Thanks for coming, thanks for telling me, but as you can see I am not going on holiday to the South of France. I am not getting out.'

'Never thought you would.'

'It may be taken out of my hands, of course. I see that. But the story about my wife knowing a suspected terrorist was passed on to me some time ago, so I have had time to think about it. Stella did not kill either di Rimini or Pip Eton. And for that matter, neither did I.'

'Never thought it for a moment.'

'Or had him killed.' Which is what you might have done yourself, you old sod, in a similar position… Except that Sir Fred would never get into any position of personal peril. That you could count on.

Sir Fred was actually smiling, although Lodge was as grave as ever, the perfect secret servant.

Coffin suddenly felt good. I got the better of that round, he thought.

Such moments can be dangerous, because that is often when life wipes out the joke.

As he got himself through the door, Sir Fred said: 'For what it's worth, I don't think Miss Pinero was meant as the contact.'

'MESSAGE FROM Miss Pinero, sir,' said Paul Masters, through the open door. 'She can't talk to her dresser, Maisie, the woman isn't there.'

Coffin sat at his desk, silent, troubled. You're never where you think you are, he thought to himself. The ground moves beneath your feet.

Because he had his secret, he had his own game, one he had entered into—what was the word?—obligingly.

He thought about it with sadness.

Get back to thinking about Stella, he told himself. Poor Stella was part of the game and she did not know it. He had used her, which was one of the reasons he must forgive her for Pip Eton.

He thought about the Production Room in the basement of his own police building, the room in which were stored all the artefacts which had had a place in crime: a blood-stained jersey, a six-pack of Coca Cola, and rows of radios and clocks. Each item, neatly packaged in a plastic bag, labelled and recorded in a register, lay on the steel racks which rose to the ceiling.

The copies of *The Stage* that had covered Pip Eton would be there, stored away in safety, like the clothes from Francesco di Rimini. Unless Phoebe had kept out those newspapers which had Stella's fingerprints on them.

Unlucky Stella, he must get her out of this trouble, although at the moment he was unsure how to do it. It would come though, because it had to. A bell was ringing faintly in his mind, which was a good sign because a physical symptom often accompanied a genuine idea, he had noticed.

He had found that he got ideas from a study of the objects which had figured in a crime. Somehow the mind was acted upon by the touch of a piece of cloth, a leather bag, a dried bloodstain on a shirt. It was as if you had been there yourself at the scene of the crime. He never expressed this idea to his colleagues, who would have found it fanciful.

But he knew what he had to do first: go to see Maisie and ask her a few sharp questions about the clothes she was supposed to have given to a charity shop but which had turned up under Stella's bed in the flat. 'Maisie as a priority, then the Production Room.'

The clothes themselves would end up in their plastic bag on one of those steel racks in due course, no doubt. The whole room was a bit like the property room in the theatre, only here all the plays were over. Dead and done with.

Before setting out, he rescued Augustus from his hiding place under Paul Masters' desk, put on his leash and walked him to the car. 'Sorry to see him go,' Paul said, watching them. 'I like the little chap, and I think he's beginning to like me.'

Augustus obligingly wagged his tail, although Coffin knew well that this meant nothing more then a general pleasure in being a dog.

Coffin appreciated the company of Augustus because he could talk to him and get no answer back, and he enjoyed this in a world which so often returned a reply he did not want.

'Get in the car, boy. You're coming with me on a

visit. We won't be taking Stella, and yes, that is where she sits, and you won't be getting out of the car.'

Augustus settled down on the front seat. He was too short to see out of the window, but he liked the motion of the car. He was aware of Coffin's voice droning on in his ear, but he paid no attention since none of the magic signals like walk or food were coming through.

Traffic was heavy as the evening dark drew on. It was getting dark earlier now, summer was over, autumn well advanced, you could feel the distant march of winter.

He spoke to Stella on his car phone. 'I'm on my way to speak to Maisie. She may be home by now.' She had better be there. 'How are you?'

'Better for the afternoon with you. But busy. Letty is in control, more or less. She's marvellous with money.'

'As we know.'

'As we know. Letty is cross but working fast; Jane is trying to make me build up her character, which I won't do, it would throw the play out, and Fanny is being sweet. Alice has migraine and is away. Everything pretty much as usual.'

She did indeed sound happy. It was wonderful the way she bounced back. Theatricals had to, probably, with such an up-and-down life.

There was one more call to make. 'Archie? How's the riot?'

'A load of nonsense.' The Chief Superintendent was tired and irritated. 'Someone just wanted some publicity. Got it, too. We shall all be on the TV news.'

'I want you to go to Linton House in Fish Alley. It's off Arrow Street.'

'I know where Fish Alley is.'

'Flat on the second floor. I think it may be where Pip

Eton was killed. I have sent Astley there, but it's for you, too.'

Archie Young grunted a reply. 'We have the Ferguson and Giner Eccles fraud tidied up. Two arrests; the courts may muck it up, but we've done our bit.' The Chief Superintendent had not been involved in the riot at the docks, that had been handled by the uniformed branch, B unit, and CD (Crowd Control and Disperse) unit in particular, but he had his own problems of which this big fraud case was one. The di Rimini and Pip Eton murders were just another case, even if an interesting one.

'I hear there's a floater turned up by the Great Harry Dock,' he said. 'But the word is that it's suicide, so not one for us. Right, I'll get down to Fish Alley, but Astley's efficient, she'll have it all organized.'

'I want your eye on it.'

'Right, right.' Young was well up on the saga of Stella Pinero, as indeed were all his colleagues. As one wag had said, you'd have to be living up a tree in Greenwhich Park with the birds not to know. Stella was admired and liked, but was also the subject of intense speculation and gossip.

'The place belongs to my wife, long lease, dates back to the days before St Luke's. Keep it as quiet as you can.'

Young said, 'Right, right,' again. He hung on to his telephone until Coffin broke the link. Bugger all, he thought, he deserves better.

TWELVE

COFFIN HAD DRIVEN to where Maisie lived. He was studying the house with some interest. This time round he wanted to see what Maisie had made of the place. You could tell a lot about a person from what they did to their home, and he needed to understand Maisie. He could see that she cared for the place, the paintwork on the door and on the window frames was red and white, and looked to be new. Or if not new then washed recently. The curtains on upper and lower windows hung crisp and fresh. Yes, Maisie was a good housekeeper. He hadn't taken that in last time, now he did.

The house also looked mildly prosperous. How much did dressers earn? Not a great deal, he imagined. Possibly Maisie had other resources. It was worth thinking about. In Coffin's sad experience money was always worth thinking about. The most unlikely people had their little secrets here. In his own family, his sister Letty probably had more than one secret and not so little either. He had none, partly as a matter of professional ethics, but also because he had never had any money to speak of. He did not despise money-makers like his half-sister Letty, but it was not his style. Or luck, he might have said. He did not despise money-makers, he just was not one.

He walked slowly down the narrow garden path, pausing to study the door with its brass knocker and brass bell. The trace of blood was still there, by the door bell. Coffin rang the bell.

No answer.

He waited, then rang again. He could hear the bell ringing in the hall, but no one came. So he tried the knocker; experience had taught him that householders often came to a hearty series of knocks because the neighbours could hear it.

He knocked several times more, then drew back to look at the house.

All right, Maisie was out. She might be at the theatre, but Stella wasn't performing, so it was not one of her nights and Stella had not been able to find her there. As always now when the image of Stella appeared, he felt anguish. Since she had come back into his life, he had known great joy, but he seemed to have become sensitized to other emotions; happiness, misery, he felt them all more keenly. It was as if being with Stella had peeled a layer of toughness from him.

He shook himself like a dog (had he picked this up from Augustus?—a sardonic underthought) and went back to hammer on the door. If the bloody woman was there, he would flush her out.

This time he rang the bell and banged on the door all at once. It made a satisfying noise but did not produce Maisie.

But the front door of the adjoining house opened and out popped a woman. She stood on her doorstep and demanded to know what was going on. 'Enough to wake the dead. My husband works nights and he needs his sleep.'

As if to support this, a tousled head appeared at an upstairs window. 'Bloody noise. Shut it, will you.' He left his wife to carry on.

'It's no good banging on the door like that. If Maisie doesn't want to open the door, she won't.'

Coffin explained mildly that he needed to talk to Maisie. Had she gone away?

'No, not her, she always gets me to look after the cat when she goes away. Anyway, she's there. I saw her come back from shopping and go inside.' The woman marched back to her door.

From above came a shout: 'Bang again and I'll get the police in.'

'I am the police.'

The woman swung round, walked over and stared at him. 'Yes,' she said after consideration. 'You could be, you've got the look. Bit old though, aren't you, to be on street work?'

'We don't all get the promotion we should do,' said Coffin.

'That's true enough,' said the woman. 'Look at my husband: twenty years in that place and nothing to show for it except a bad back.'

A voice from the window called out: 'Stop gassing, Ena, and come back in. I want my tea.'

Ena gave a shrug and turned away. 'Try the door,' she said, over her shoulder. 'Maisie doesn't always lock it behind her.'

'And you ought to know, you cow,' called the irate voice from above before drawing the window down with a bang.

Lovely man, thought Coffin, as he returned to the front door with whose appearance, down to the last scratch on the paint, he now felt thoroughly familiar. Still, who knew what Ena was like to live with?

He hesitated for a minute, then took hold of the brass handle. It turned, the door opened.

Coffin stepped inside. He was careful and had not made much noise but no one shouted, 'Who's that?' at him. He looked around him: a small hall carpeted in red, a door to the left, and another at the end of a short corridor. A staircase rose sharply in front of him. Break your neck on that if you didn't step carefully, he thought.

'Maisie, are you there?'

He opened the door on the left, put his head round the door, and stared in to a tidy sitting room with a round table in the window, four upright chairs covered in red velvet and a sofa of the same. There was a television set against the wall.

All ordinary and quiet enough.

Only one odd thing: the television was on, but with the sound turned down. Coffin stared at the mouthing face of a woman with a froth of bright red hair. He thought he knew the face, which was that of the hostess of a chat show. The camera moved to take in the ranks of the audience, some whom were laughing: the red-haired lady had made a joke.

People did leave the television on with the sound off; he had done it himself if the telephone rang or someone called unexpectedly.

There was a teacup on the little table by the sofa; Coffin touched it: cold.

It was hard to be sure on this carpet, but that looked like a stain by the door, a drop, a blotch. He bent down to touch it, one delicate flick with a forefinger.

Blood.

Perhaps it was already too late to be calling Maisie's name.

He walked down the corridor to the kitchen, only to find it empty. There was a milk jug by the kettle which still had a trace of warmth in it. Hot not so long ago, he thought.

Moving more quickly, he went up the stairs. The door

was open to the bedroom. A chair was turned over and the telephone pulled from the table to the floor, where it lay quietly, no longer making the scream some telephones make when disturbed in their sleep.

He must find out how long it took for a telephone to go quiet after it had been knocked from its hook.

Without realizing he was moving, he found himself standing in the bathroom.

There was blood on the floor, blood in the bath, blood where Maisie lay with her head backed against the wall. Blood on a small bundle of tabby fur.

They needn't have killed the cat as well, he thought.

He looked down at Maisie's body, then he bent for a closer look, being careful not to touch. She had been stabbed in the throat, that was where all the blood had come from. It was all over the bath and over the carpet. There must have been blood on the killer and hence downstairs.

It looked as if Maisie had been stabbed either in the bath or dropped into it, and that she then struggled out and got as far as the window.

It looked, at first glance, as though Maisie had not fought her killer. She was a sturdy, strong woman who could have put up a fight, of which there was no real sign.

Coffin walked down the stairs and out to his car where he used his telephone to call Paul Masters.

'Paul, get hold of Archie Young. He's probably in Fish Alley with Phoebe Astley, but he'll have his mobile on.' And curse him if he hasn't. The Chief Superintendent had been known to turn it off. 'And get him down here. There has been another murder.'

He gave the address and asked for the back-up crews of SOCO and forensics as well as the police surgeon.

'I will be here.'

He got out of the car, to find Ena and her husband on the pavement waiting for him. They advanced side by side, shoulder to shoulder, towards him. He was surprised to see that Ena was younger than she had seemed, while her husband, now wearing jeans and a white shirt, was not such a rough as he had looked when shouting out of the window.

'It's Maisie, isn't it?' Ena was fierce. 'What's happened? She's dead, isn't she?'

'Now, you don't know that,' said her husband, putting his arm round her.

'Shut up, Stan.' Ena turned her head to get a look as the first police car swung round the end of the road. 'Something is up, anyway, and I think it's Maisie.' She began to march towards Maisie's house. 'I'm going in to have a look. Maisie was a friend and I want to know.'

'Don't go in,' said Coffin, putting a restraining hand on her arm. 'Leave it.'

Ena swung round. 'She's been murdered….done in.' She had tears in her eyes. 'Poor cow.'

Her husband came up to her and took her by the hand. 'Come on, love, back into the house.'

'I want to know.'

'You'll know later,' said Coffin. 'I shall want to ask you some questions.' It was amazing what different faces people could put on. A few minutes ago Ena had been aggressive, angry, with a husband who had seemed surly and ill-tempered, but now here was a woman mourning a friend, being comforted by the sympathy of her husband.

What an old fool I am, he thought to himself. I ought to know that by now. Don't I do it myself, change my face to suit the circumstances.

Two more police vehicles had arrived. From the first, a white van, came the forensic team, and from the second, the tall figure of Archie Young.

Coffin took a pace towards him. 'You made good time.'

'Got the message, came straight away. Left Astley doing her stuff in Fish Alley.' He looked at the Chief Commander with well-contained curiosity, wanting to know how Coffin had found the bloodstained clothes in the flat, and what was to be made of it all. How did it fit with the double murders? He was assuming that the two killings were connected; that was the working assumption of the investigation. Could be wrong. And now there was this new death. And, once again, there was Coffin, discovering it. 'Another body?'

'Yes, Maisie Evans. She is, was, dresser to Stella. I came round to ask her about the clothes…' He stopped talking.

Archie Young waited, before saying: 'Would I be right in thinking you mean the bloodstained clothes in the flat in Fish Alley? And before we go any further, let me say: the accepted opinion is, yes, Pip Eton was killed there. Fingerprints and traces of old blood that can be matched with his, or we hope it will. Also on the clothes which you mention.' He was brisk and businesslike; this was a difficult situation for him.

'Yes, Stella was there with me when I found them. I had got Stella to admit that this was where Pip Eton had held her.'

'It's her place, isn't it? So you told me,' asked Young, bluntly, his eyes on the front of the house where a stream of police officers were now passing in and out.

'Yes, I know it and you know it. Stella thought it was a kind of secret. She had lived in it once; now…' he shrugged. Let Archie think what he liked. 'She let friends use it in a casual kind of way.'

'Casual,' nodded Young thoughtfully, stopped by a sharp look from the Chief Commander's blue eyes.

'Damn you, Archie. I am speaking to you as a friend.'

'Hearing it as one,' said Archie.

'But you are police as well, I know that. I just don't want Stella prejudged.'

'I like to think I am a friend of Stella's,' said Young with dignity.

'Her flat, her clothes, with blood on them. That's not so good. She told me these were clothes she gave to Maisie to take to a charity shop. I came round here to talk to Maisie myself—and found her dead.'

'Right. I've got the picture.' And a nasty one it is, thought Archie Young. All this, and her fingerprints on the copies of *The Stage*, it was beginning to mount up.

Coffin nodded. 'Whatever you are thinking, so am I. And I'm even more disturbed, you can believe that.' He moved towards the house. 'Let's take a look inside.'

SIDE BY SIDE they moved into the narrow hall. They were both big men, so that there was not much space. Coffin's shoulder knocked at a picture on the wall which fell to the floor.

Young picked it up, a romanticized picture of a cat family, mother and three kittens. 'Nice picture. She liked cats.'

'Yes,' said Coffin shortly. 'There's a cat upstairs in the bathroom with her.'

Young gave him a sharp look.

'Yes, dead too. The killer was not a cat lover.'

The police surgeon had finished his examination of the body. He stood up, took off his white rubber gloves, and nodded. 'Stabbed in the throat. Tore into an artery, accounts for all the blood, must have come spurting out.'

'How long dead?'

'Not long, matter of hours. Could be less. Rigor only just setting in. She's hardly cold.'

Coffin nodded. If he had been a bit quicker, then he would have met the killer.

'Looks as if she was stabbed in the bath, where she may have been pushed, and then managed to stagger to the window.'

'Does look like that. So she didn't die straight away?'

'No, although the killer may have thought she had. Who found her?'

'I did, less than an hour ago.'

Dr Marriot, the police surgeon, who knew Coffin, pursed her lips. 'This is pure speculation, and I wouldn't like to go into court without a better check, but I think it was not much before.'

'And the cat?'

'I haven't inspected the cat, and I'm no vet, but I make a guess it died soon after. Poor beast, just got in the way, I suppose.' He knelt down to take a look, prodding the little corpse with a gentle finger. 'Stabbed, like the woman.'

Dr Marriot prepared to depart. 'I've done my bit: it's for the pathologist and the forensic lads to get on now…' He looked round the room. 'She struggled a bit, I guess. Not a lot, though. Think she knew who killed her?'

'Very likely,' said Coffin, who did think so.

'What was the motive? All right, don't answer. You don't know.'

The doctor got himself out of the room in a good-humoured way.

'So why do you think she was killed?' Archie Young

asked Coffin. Any real motive, he was asking himself, or just some nasty murdering bugger?

'I think she was going to tell me who she gave the clothes to that we found. I don't know how the killer knew she was going to do this, but I think that was the motive.'

'Maisie may have warned the killer herself.'

'Wish she could speak now.' Coffin moved towards the telephone which was still on the floor, awaiting the full attention of the photographer, who was still busy with Maisie, and the forensic team who were looking for scraps of this and that and dusting for fingerprints. He looked at the bedtable. 'I see she has an answerphone.'

Archie Young studied it. 'No calls waiting.'

'Sometimes you can hear an earlier call if she hasn't wiped it off but just let the tape run on. I've done it myself.'

'Haven't we all?'

'Let's listen.' Coffin put a handkerchief over his hand to tap the buttons.

Quietly, a voice was speaking. Coffin felt his neck stiffen.

There was a certain amount of noise from the comings and goings of the SOCO outfit and the forensic team gradually working their way round the house.

'Turn it up louder,' requested Archie. 'I can't hear.'

A moment later, for the Chief Commander's sake, he regretted having asked.

Stella's voice could be heard speaking softly. Coffin said, without much expression, 'I'll turn it back.'

Stella said: 'John will be coming round to speak to you, Maisie. I won't be coming myself, but you know what to say.'

There was a pause while Archie Young first looked away out of the window and then straight at Coffin.

'She couldn't have done it better if she'd tried for years, could she?' said Coffin, in a no-expression voice. 'But it was spontaneous. I wonder if we have it all? Didn't quite finish.'

'It doesn't mean anything, you can ask her.'

You bet I will, thought Coffin. Before I strangle her myself. 'Let's see what Maisie's last call was.'

'She may not have the last call check on her phone.'

'She has,' said Coffin. 'And guess where she dialled? The theatre.'

He met Archie Young's embarrassed gaze, and shook his head. 'Let's go downstairs.'

I suppose I could always shoot myself, he thought, and then he began to laugh. Oh Stella, Stella. What am I going to do with her?

Archie Young heard the laugh. He was glad the boss felt like laughing.

In the hall, Archie saw that the picture Coffin had knocked down was on the floor again. Two of the forensic team were there, Jem Sider and Al Jansem, he knew them both.

'Oh that's down, is it? I knocked it down earlier. It's awkward, seems to stick out.'

'Yes, and I know why. You didn't look at the back.'

Jem showed the two men the back of the picture on which was taped a large brown envelope.

'Get it off,' said Coffin, 'and see what's inside.'

'Might be a bomb,' Jem was a joker. He had it off and handed it to the Chief Commander. 'Wait a minute, sir.' He held out a pair of white rubber gloves.

Coffin put on the gloves, and opened the letter. It

might very well be a bomb, but if so it was likely to be of an emotional nature.

Inside was a thick wad of twenty-pound notes.

'Not a bad place to keep your savings,' said Jem, 'when you live round here where you might be broken into. Who'd think of looking behind a picture?'

Outside in the street was Jack Lowerly, the local CID inspector who would be handling the case. He looked awkward, if not surprised (since he had been well alerted), to be confronted with the Chief Commander and the Chief Superintendent. Both men were liked and respected, but rank told. You watched out, and checked how you were doing.

A darkened ambulance was waiting at the kerb to take Maisie's body to the mortuary where it would be given a careful examination by Dennis Garden. Since this seemed a safe observation, he said: 'Be getting the deceased off, sir. The Prof will be taking a look, but I don't suppose he will have much to add. Clear enough how she died.' Lowerly allowed himself to go on as his audience seemed to be listening. 'A real tragedy, a nice lady. My wife worked in the theatre for a while, in the office, and saw a bit of Maisie.'

Coffin nodded.

Lowerly, always a talker, went on: 'We're trying to locate the next of kin, but no luck so far, a solitary lady, her life was the theatre. Would Miss Pinero have any idea?'

'I'll ask her.'

'There will be a bit of money, I expect. My wife said Maisie liked to turn an honest penny.'

'Robbery doesn't seem to have been a motive for her murder.'

'So I gather, sir.' A foxy look came over Lowerly's

sharp-featured face. 'There will be money in it some-where.' He decided he had done well, and was moving away before he fell into trouble.

'You're a philosopher, I can see, Inspector,' said Coffin. 'But with murder there has to be something else as well as money.'

Lowerly left wondering whether he had done well or badly after all.

Coffin and Archie stood by the Chief Commander's car; Coffin shrugged.

'All the same, he wasn't far wrong,' said Young. 'Not always a straightforward motive for a murder, however much we try to show there is.'

There's no need to listen, he said to himself, watching his chief's withdrawn eyes. I'm only talking for the sake of talking, as I guess Lowerly was too—and making a better job of it than I am.

Coffin had heard him, because he gave him a wry smile. 'You and I know that sometimes there isn't a motive for murder—not a credible one—and that all we have is a killer and victim.'

'More than one killer, do you think?'

'Forensics ought to be able to utter on that... fingerprints.'

'If any.'

'If any. Body traces, fibres... There's always something if you look hard enough.'

Archie thought that you sometimes had to look mighty hard, but he kept quiet.

'I think just one killer, but that's a guess.'

'You're usually a good guesser.'

'Thank you. Experience, really, I suppose...' He paused. 'I have had a high-level warning to keep out of it.'

Archie, to whom all things were soon known, had heard about Sir Fred's visit.

'Stella will have to make a statement. And I would like her to make it to you, not Astley. Lodge will have to be present, I suppose. It's his territory.'

'Right.' Archie Young recognized that in certain circumstances Inspector Lodge had to be accepted as important. He did not much like the man, but he understood that it was not Lodge's game to be liked.

Coffin said quietly: 'If Stella is seriously involved, I shall have to go.'

Archie was later, when he talked about this to his wife, to feel ashamed that his first reaction was where would it leave him? He had had John Coffin's support all the way through his career. They had worked together as a team, with Archie respecting the flair and intuition (not to mention plain luck) of his boss. With him gone, what would happen to Archie? His wife, robust and practical as ever, had poured him a large whisky and told him to grow up and be a big boy. He had not been quite sure what she meant by that, except a strong feeling she supported the Chief Commander, but women were always on the side of John Coffin.

Except possibly the one he had married. What was Stella Pinero up to?

He said goodbye to the Chief Commander and went back into the murder house. Then he rang Phoebe Astley on his mobile to tell her what was going on and to ask her about Fish Alley. He listened without comment to what she had to say and then, without mentioning this to Phoebe Astley, went off to take a statement from Stella Pinero.

John Coffin, meanwhile, drove back to his office, with a sleeping Augustus in the back of the car. He envied the dog his tranquil peace of mind. Then Augustus gave a tiny, muted growl from the depths of a dream. You too? thought Coffin.

In the office he checked with Paul Masters on all the matters that concerned them both in the day-to-day running of the Second City Force. No more riots, no more bombs and no armed robbery to take his mind off his own problems.

And then: 'There's a message from Chief Inspector Astley.'

The careful way of handing it over suggested to Coffin that it was not a message he was going to enjoy.

'How does she manage to get a fax out of Fish Alley?'

'Don't know, sir.'

Coffin grunted, reading what Phoebe had to say.

'The Todger is round here in Fish Alley,' Phoebe began without preamble, 'he has with him his young man, Pete Corner, the one we thought originally had been murdered, and who was the Todger's hidden man to check on the bombmakers. Not naming any names, but claims to have been following an interesting suspect from the theatre complex to Fish Alley over several days. Again naming no names, he says the evidence he has from the Anti Terrorist unit is that a group of six was responsible: four outsiders and two locally based. Pip Eton was one of the second lot. The feeling seems to be that he was killed by one of his colleagues. Apparently, this is not unknown in the business, so Pete says. Some connection with the old KGB, no doubt, trained there perhaps. Joke.'

But only half a joke, thought Coffin.

As an extra, Phoebe added: 'Found a lot of blonde hairs around, likewise fingerprints.'

Stella owns the bloody place, Coffin muttered, you

know that. My fingerprints must be there, too. And it's pure chance that hair from my head is not all over the bedclothes, not to mention what are known as bodily fluids.

Phoebe could be very irritating.

'And we have what looks to be the murder weapon. I'm linking up with Archie Young, just in case.' A characteristic Phoebe Astley parting comment: 'Pete's a lovely lad, I can see we could work together well.'

Damn you, Phoebe, thought Coffin. For God's sake keep out of Pete's bed.

THIRTEEN

CHIEF SUPERINTENDENT Young was sympathetic. 'What I have to ask you,' he began, then hesitated. He never knew how to address Stella in a formal way—when they met for drinks or dinner, that was easy but now... Should it be Miss Pinero or her married name? So he kept it professional, Miss Pinero. It did distance the Chief Commander a fraction. 'Just some questions about today.'

Stella looked at him, wide-eyed and apprehensive. 'But I've already answered—' she began. Her face was very pale.

'I have your earlier statement about Pip Eton and your involvement with him.'

He could see from Stella's face that she had begun to take in that this was a new and serious inquisition. She was an actress, of course, and knew how to milk a situation. He had to take that into account.

A picture came into his mind of all four of them at a police dance, and how lovely Stella had looked in a plain black dress with pearls at her throat. All real, too, by the look of them, his wife had said with envy. And how, when he had told Stella a few days later how beautiful both of them thought she looked in black silk and pearls, she had laughed and admitted the pearls were real but borrowed.

He hadn't wondered then if that was true, but he did now. And then he remembered how, on another occasion, she had comforted his wife when their eldest son was in a coma after a road accident. No silk and pearls then, just a little cotton dress. She had been more help than his own mother, who had sat there weeping; more help than he had given himself. And she had looked after the other child, then cooked an evening meal for the lot of them (well, microwaved, but who said you had to be a cook?) and stayed the night so the two of them could go back to the hospital.

No acting there.

'Miss Pinero,' he said, 'we can take the statement here or we can go the station, as you prefer.'

He had brought with him the youngest and mildest of the detectives, Teresa Behr, known, as might be expected, to her colleagues as Teddy Bear. He had thought that Teresa might make Stella feel relaxed. Instead, he saw that Stella was casting uneasy glances at the pretty young woman with her air of quiet competence. Inspector Lodge had been busy in Fish Alley and unable to attend. Good.

The Chief Superintendent had passed Letty Bingham and Alice Yeoman on his way through the corridors, the first of whom he knew by sight and the second he could not fail to know by name since Letty was shouting at her angrily for not being around when wanted. 'But who is, in this place?' she had ended. 'Actors!'

Alice had broken away from Letty to ask the Chief Superintendent what he wanted, then made a good guess and told him Stella could not see him.

He ignored this advice. An interesting woman though, with good deductive skills; they could do with one like her on the Force. He did not fail to notice that she threw off Letty, no mean feat in his opinion, and slid into the room behind them, stationing herself near Stella.

Guard or protector?

'I will talk here,' said Stella, her voice unsteady.

Alice spoke up. 'Can't you see she's crying?' she said fiercely.

'You've heard about Maisie?'

'Of course she has.'

'Let Miss Pinero speak for herself,' said Archie Young.

'Yes, I know,' said Stella quietly.

'Who told you?'

'Word gets round quickly here,' said Stella.

It was no answer so Archie sat there, waiting.

'I told her,' said Alice. 'It's all over the place, everyone knows. We're not dummies here, you know.'

Archie Young took action. He stood up. 'I think we will talk down at the station, Miss Pinero.'

Stella did not look at Alice. 'Hop it, Alice,' she said wearily. 'You mean well, but leave me to it.'

DC Behr held the door for Alice, thus tacitly passing her judgement. Archie nodded his thanks to her. She'll go far, that Behr, he thought. Mind you, the other one might, too; a fighter.

He turned back to Stella.

'She's a protégée of my husband, he got me to give her the job,' Stella said as Alice disappeared. 'I have wondered if she was his daughter, but he says not, says she is the child of a colleague, now dead, whom he owed... They don't look alike, so I believe him. She's not a theatre person at heart, but she makes herself useful.'

Archie was not sure if Stella was making a joke about Coffin's daughter or not. Probably not, he thought, so he allowed himself a smile, a soft-duty answer for everything, then took her through the story of Fish Alley.

She explained, with a good grace, that yes, the flat

belonged to her, that she had suppressed this fact when she first told her story. Yes, she knew now that Pip Eton had been using it, but she had not realized it straight-away. Yes, she had been imprisoned there, or felt she was, even though in the end she had escaped with ease. She skirted round the nature of her relationship with Pip Eton, but managed to say she had heard a woman's voice, and Archie let her leave it there.

For the moment.

Then they talked about the bloodstained clothes, the jeans and so on. Stella seemed quite willing to discuss this matter. He moved on.

'You knew that the Chief Commander was going to visit Maisie about the clothes, your clothes, that were found under the bed in Linton House?'

'Of course, I knew. He told me. I wanted to go myself, I would have done, but I got caught up with things here.' She looked around here. 'It's always like that in the the-atre, set one foot inside and the tasks descend on your head... I expect it's the same in your job.'

Archie agreed that it was.

'Did you make a telephone call to Maisie?'

Stella said: 'If you ask that, then you know that I did. I don't know how you know.' She considered. 'The an-swerphone, I suppose, she had it on, although she an-swered.' She shrugged. 'Oh, well, you know what it was about: the clothes.'

But we only know the tail end of the conversation, the bit that didn't get wiped. Erased, that's the word.

'What did you mean when you said to her: "You know what to say?"'

Stella studied her hands. 'Ah well, you see, I had told my husband that I passed on clothes that I no longer wore to Maisie for a charity shop. That was not quite true.'

'What was true?' He was aware of DC Behr quietly taking notes.

'I sold them. Some of my clothes were expensive and not much worn, and you know the theatre…we never have any money, a lot of us sell clothes, shoes and handbags even… Maisie did it for me. She took a rake-off, of course.'

Of course, she did, with knobs on, more than you knew, probably, hence her hidden money.

'And you didn't want the Chief Commander to know?'

'No, he has to know now…but I wanted Maisie to handle it tactfully. He's so generous himself, I didn't want to seem mean.' Stella shrugged. 'Oh, I don't know. I was all mixed up.'

'I see.' He wasn't sure that he did, nor if he believed her. 'And did she make a telephone call to you?'

Stella shook her head. 'No.' She shook her head again. 'No, I never spoke to Maisie again.'

She hesitated. 'How did Maisie die?'

'We think she let her killer in, and then was killed.'

'How was she killed?'

'She was stabbed,' he said reluctantly.

'So is there a connection with the other deaths?'

'It seems likely, doesn't it? But we don't know yet.'

This time, the tears that sprang to her eyes were real.

The Chief Superintendent asked a few more routine questions about times and so on, more to keep the interview going while he watched Stella than anything else.

Finally he said, 'Well, thank you.' He looked at DC Behr, who stood up, smiled at Stella, and walked away.

Archie followed. At the door, he paused and looked back.

'Sorry I had to make it so formal, but it seemed best.'

'Oh, sure. I understand. I'm glad it was you asking the questions and not someone else.'

Archie nodded. Like Phoebe Astley, for instance. She wasn't out of that wood yet, though she didn't know it. There was a going over from Inspector Lodge ahead of her, one of his specials, with his own particular brand of questioning. He would be there asking about Pip Eton and also about the first death of all, that of Francesco di Rimini.

He longed to light a cigarette and offer one to Stella, but he was a dedicated ex-smoker who still had hankerings when under pressure, as now: he was walking a tightrope here between loyalty to Coffin and loyalty to the job. And there was his own career to consider. He was beginning to see that they might sink or survive together. Tonight he would talk it over with his own wife and benefit from her advice; he trusted her judgement more than his own, which seemed to him the right way round in a marriage.

She admired John Coffin while being slightly envious of Stella's glamorous career. His wife had a career of her own, she did not mind being outshone by Stella, but she had once admitted rather wistfully that she would have liked those clothes!

He left Stella then, thanking her again for her help.

'Is that the end?' she asked nervously.

'Probably a few more questions, but don't worry.'

'That's what doctors say when there is everything to worry about.' But she said it with spirit and did not attempt to detain him.

He admired her for that: she was a fighter. On the way

out, he passed Alice, also a fighter, he judged. A hefty young woman, too; he couldn't see her playing Ophelia, but perhaps there was a place for everyone in the modern theatre.

As he took in the aggressive tilt of her square shoulders, he allowed himself a passing wonder about her sexual stance. If she preferred women, that explained her manner—half-protective, half-hostile—to Stella Pinero. Not likely to get any change out of Stella, who was enthusiastically hetero. He knew that performers could be any which way, but not Stella, not the Chief Commander's wife.

Archie Young nodded politely to Alice and moved on; he had a very straightforward attitude to sexual matters. Too straightforward, his wife had once hinted. A hint Archie did not take and, in fact, hardly recognized for what it was.

Archie's wife was herself a policewoman, currently chairing a committee on pornography and women, so she was a very knowledgeable lady. It might be a good idea to get her to take a look at Alice.

He turned back for a last word with Stella. 'Work on remembering the woman's voice,' he said. Wondering if there really had been a woman.

Stella gave him an opaque look.

JOHN COFFIN, with Augustus once again firmly attached to him, was working in his office, checking through reports with Paul Masters. If he himself was destined to be a life peer when he retired, as had once been sourly predicted, then he would see that Paul was promoted. Archie Young, so long his friend and ally, would have to be included in the pantheon somewhere, but he was a detective pure if not simple and without the administrative skills the top jobs demanded. And Inspector Lodge could be moved on.

But I am not going yet, Coffin told himself. Those who think so can wait and see.

Before he did anything else, he had to telephone Stella. She was in her office, so she answered promptly.

'You might have told me you were sending a great big dragon round breathing fire and asking questions.'

'I don't believe that Archie breathed any fire.'

'I admit he is a nice friendly dragon at heart, but he tried. He did a little bit of puffing and huffing. He sends out rather nice smoke for a dragon.'

'You're making me jealous.'

'No, need, but you might be jealous of Alice, she's been eyeing me a bit.'

'Has she?'

'You don't sound surprised. But don't worry, I'm not really her style and she is certainly not mine.'

'Glad to hear it.'

'I think I know who is: Letty, judging by the way Letty was shouting at her. Angry.' Stella managed a laugh.

'Letty?'

'Yes, she picked it up and reacted. Energy was crackling through her.'

'You said anger.'

'Often the same thing with Letty.'

That was true enough.

'I've dropped you in it, haven't I?'

'We will talk later,' he said gently. 'In fact, I ought to apologize to you.'

'What do you mean?'

'I will explain, but later.' Not a superstitious man, he kept his fingers crossed.

They ended there and he returned to Paul Masters.

'I'm off to Fish Alley.'

Paul Masters nodded.

'The Chief Superintendent is talking Stella through various episodes.'

Masters gave another nod. He knew; he was the man who knew everything.

'I believe she will have to speak to Inspector Lodge… I shall see him myself.'

'He's at Fish Alley,' said Masters. Phoebe Astley would not like that.

'I know.' Phoebe had told him. Coffin asked: 'Anything further on the riot?'

'A white van was tracked to a house in Dedman Street, just beyond the Spinnergate tube station…the ring leaders were inside. They've been brought in to be questioned. Inspector Dover is well pleased.'

'Good. It was an arranged thing then, not spontaneous?'

'No, there was a bank robbery planned for the same time…didn't come off. The new CCTV cameras tracked three men in a stolen car on their way there… They have been brought in too.'

A busy day, but a commonplace in the Second City, and not without its successes.

This time he did not walk but drove himself to Fish Alley, where the kerb in front of Linton House was lined with police cars.

Inspector Lodge was standing on the stone steps to the front door, deep in thought. He looked up to see Coffin park his car. 'Thought I would find you,' said Coffin. 'Had a chance to look round yet?'

'A bit. I've been talking to Peter Corner.'

'Oh yes, he's the man you had planted with the building firm.'

'Yes, a building firm is always a good place to put a man, a sleeper, which is what Pete was more or less. Builders move around, get to know all the gossip.'

'So they do.'

'To tell you the truth, I had had my doubts about the firm I got him into. They had been doing some work on contract in Belfast, I thought they were worth watching.'

'And are they?'

'The Archers seem to be clean enough, although when Pete went missing I did wonder. And the dead man being found in a house they were working on...' Lodge shrugged. 'But nothing has turned up that incriminates them. Astley's got a nose for that sort of thing,' he said admiringly, 'and she would have smelt anything there was. She says not. I could do with her on my team.'

Coffin said nothing. He knew well that the men and women who worked with Lodge were a group of individuals who followed their own line, investigated in their own way, and although loyal to their mates were not team workers. It was not always safe to think of yourself as a team in their questionable world. Phoebe might do well in it, he granted Lodge that much.

The flat was quiet, but not empty. You could feel the presence of the police all over it.

Phoebe Astley was in the sitting room with Peter Corner. She was pouring coffee from a tall carton into white plastic mugs.

'Like some coffee, sir?' she said as she handed a mug to Peter Corner, a tall, dark-haired young man with bright blue eyes. Coffin could see straightaway that she was giving Corner one of her more flirtatious treatments. It was a treatment, sometimes you felt the better for it and sometimes much the worse. Corner looked unmoved, which Coffin judged to his credit.

'Have a sandwich.' Phoebe held out a plate. 'We were so hungry that Pete kindly went along to Max's and brought grub back. Cheese and chutney, ham and salad, and smoked salmon. Try the salmon, Peter, it is said to be stimulating.'

She was deliberately baiting the Todger, who stayed expressionless but was probably chalking it up.

Coffin drank some coffee, black. Max made the best cup of coffee in the Second City. Even a plastic mug could not spoil it.

The whole feel of this room had changed since he had visited earlier that day with Stella. A forensic team, a clutch of photographers and several detectives had been through it, probing and looking, and changed the scent.

He stood in the middle of the room and demanded bluntly: 'What have you got?'

Phoebe took it upon herself to be the voice: 'In the first place, the clothes, the bloody bundle. From the nature of the bloodstains down the front of the T-shirt, all down the leg of the jeans, and on the arms and front of the denim jacket, we feel sure that the killer was wearing them at the time of the killing. Forensics have taken them off to match with the blood of Pip Eton.'

'Right.' Coffin nodded. 'What else?'

Phoebe hesitated. 'No name tags, but they are good Italian jeans and denims…you say Stella thought they were hers.'

'Thought they could be,' he said tersely. 'She hasn't missed them. She keeps working clothes at the theatre.'

Phoebe spared a passing thought for a woman who could keep expensive clothes which these were, as spare working clothes. 'Quite. Easily purloined.' She was rather pleased with her use of that word, put her in the Wilkie Collins or Edgar Allan Poe class as a commentator on crime.

'I want to look round.' He made a silent tour of the flat, followed by the others; he went into the bedroom where the clothes had been found, and looked under the bed. There was a fair amount of dust, which told him nothing he did not already know about Stella and housekeeping. He moved on to the bathroom, where he paused, studying the hand basin, the bath and the lavatory.

'Any traces of blood here?'

'Forensic took samples and will be coming back to us.'

Coffin nodded, and went on to the kitchen. He stared at the floor, which was carpeted. 'Looks a bit wet.'

'Forensics took a scraping.'

'And the sink?'

'From there too.'

He made no further comment, until they all came back into the sitting room.

He sat down and picked up his unfinished mug of coffee.

'That will be cold.' Phoebe seized the carton and shook it. 'Still some here, feels warm, let me give you a drop more.'

Coffin finished what was in his mug. 'I don't mind it being cold.' He turned to Peter, who was standing with his back to the window. 'Before we talk about anything else, what about those underpants of yours?'

There was silence. 'Is this important?' asked Phoebe.

'I think it is, I think it is very important. I wouldn't be surprised if Inspector Lodge did not agree with me.

These were the ones found on the dead body in the bombed house in Percy Street.'

'How do you think they got there?'

'I thought it was pure chance.'

'Did you? Why was that?'

'The reason I have my name inside is partly because the unit like us to be labelled in case we turn up dead— that's the hidden message for knowing eyes only—but I have my name written in marking ink because I use a laundry and they do get lost. I have lost several pairs. Other clothes too. If you have your name inside, the laundry is willing to refund you the loss.'

'And have they refunded you for these?'

'I haven't made a claim yet. I've had other things on my mind.' He had left them, of course, when he last visited di Rimini. They probably knew. Lodge must have guessed.

'You did not address your mind to how and why they turned up on a murdered man? I can see from Inspector Lodge's face that he has been wondering.'

Lodge moved his hands in front of his face, then drew them down as if he was wiping it.

'I had other things on my mind, you know, sir. I was following up a lead which led me here. I've been working as a temporary handyman in the local school, and doing the furnace here. It was my way to keep an eye on things here. But yes, I was out of touch, we don't always keep in touch in this game.' He was definitely defensive; ambition, rivalry with Lodge had driven him. Sex—unluckily he really liked di Rimini—had been a spur also. He wanted to avenge him.

'I think you knew where they could have been...not who used them, because that would mean you knew the killer,' said Coffin carefully. 'But certainly where they might have been so the killer could use them.'

Peter looked at Lodge, then at Phoebe, who was giving him a careful scrutiny.

'Well, I never,' she said. 'I never would have put you down for one of di Rimini's pick-ups.'

'I was working a line, you often have to do things you don't like, act in way that is alien, when you are on a job.'

'That's true,' said Inspector Lodge.

Peter shrugged. 'When the matter came up, when the question was asked, I would have said. But other clothes of mine have gone missing, including underwear.' To Phoebe's amusement, he spoke the words prissily, like a woman referring to her knickers. 'What do we call them now?' she asked herself, repressing her mirth. 'Briefs, bikinis?'

'Oh, Pete,' she said, shaking her head. 'How you disappoint me. And I expect you are breaking Inspector Lodge's heart.'

'Cool it, Phoebe.' Coffin stood, drawing himself up to his full height. 'Did it never occur to you that you were compromised? That your work and status was known?' He turned round. 'I can see it occurred to Inspector Lodge.'

'Of course it did,' said Lodge irritably. 'I thought you were dead.'

'I came across Francesco—I called him Frank or Ed sometimes—at a pub down at Spinnergate. We chummed up, I thought he was worth working... And he was, it was something he said that put me on to Fish Alley and to watching this place here. I was already eyeing Miss Pinero. All right, I did keep mum and drop out, but we do in our business, and it was worth it. I got a strong lead on Pip Eton.'

'A strong lead,' said Coffin again. 'So what was it?'

Peter looked at inspector Lodge, then made his own mind up. He was, so Coffin decided, fully the same rank as Lodge, and in the world in which both men moved, possibly his superior. How much of an act his mock repentance had been was not clear. God what a crew, Coffin thought. I wish I had never got mixed up with it all, but I couldn't keep out.

Briskly, speaking coolly and with command, Peter Corner said: 'We knew about Pip Eton, of course. He had been identified as a member of a small cell, associated with the bomb makers. He was a recruiting officer and the one with the money, but up to whatever he was asked to do, you can take that for granted. He may have helped place the second bomb, he may not. Not sure.'

'Was his unit responsible for the bomb outside the shop in Spinnergate?'

'As I say, we can't be sure as yet. The main team came from outside. This lot were a reserve team, but they would have played their part. I've been watching them for some time, it's why I am in the Second City. Pip Eton hung around with some locals and was trying to make time with Miss Pinero. He was the paymaster, the money man, but also the professional soft man of the unit, the one that went out to make friends. He may also have been their M man, the one who got the transport, but his main use was to get a local contact. Well, he had one ready made, close to you.'

'So he did,' said Coffin. 'We know that.'

'But I didn't know about the house in Fish Alley, whereas Frankie did. He had a foot in the theatre world and these things get passed around. The woman Maisie knew, and she knew Frankie, they drank together.'

'She's dead,' said Coffin thoughtfully.

'Yes, now. And so is Pip.'

'So he is,' said Phoebe.

'Now, one school of thought says he was killed by a member of his cell for talking. Or for spending their money. I favour that view myself. I lived opposite for a week…sometimes I slept in my car, sometimes I didn't sleep at all. I watched Linton House. I was inside the place doing odd jobs, I watched Pip Eton go in the day his body was found. I didn't see him leave, but there is a back entrance where you could park a car. He may have left, dead.' This was the fullest statement the man had made so far.

'Any other comings or goings?'

With some reluctance, Peter admitted that a local bus ran past Fish Alley once an hour, that the stop was not far away from Linton House. No, he could not see who got on and off.

'So Pip could have got on it?'

'That is so. He wasn't a man who liked going on a bus. Public transport was not his preferred way of getting about.'

Coffin ignored this.

'But he could have done?' Phoebe was not about to ignore anything.

'It's possible.'

'Anything else?'

'The second day I was watching, I saw Miss Pinero going into the house. Pip Eton had his arm round her, he might have been pushing her. Two days after that, I saw her leaving, on her own, she was walking fast. Running.'

'She herself has told me,' said Coffin.

'I confirm it, then.'

Score to you, Coffin thought, but did not like him any the better for it. 'You can confirm the days, can you?'

'If I'm not bullied. I get confused if I am bullied.'

'The Chief Commander will ignore that,' said Lodge quickly.

'All right, I didn't say it. Wipe it out, due to my absence of mind, when I forget where I am. But there is something else which might be of interest to you about the house.'

'What is it?'

'I went back to watch. There was another person there.'

'A woman?' Coffin asked quickly, remembering what Stella had said about hearing a woman's voice beyond the door.

'A woman, or a man? No, I can't answer. I only got a glimpse through the window, but it looked like a man.'

Coffin held out his beaker. 'Any more coffee, there? Thank you, and no, I won't have a sandwich.' There was a tension in his stomach that was not hunger.

He drained the coffee, lukewarm now, and put the mug on the table.

'I don't think Pip Eton was killed here. I can see no real evidence. The only blood was on the clothes, which could have been brought in.'

'The carpet in the kitchen—' began Phoebe.

'It was washed. If traces of blood appear, fine, let me know, but otherwise, I think we have to look for another killing field.'

He walked to the door. 'Keep me in touch, Inspector.'

Lodge nodded assent, and got up to follow him out.

'Peter,' Coffin made his voice gentle, 'next time you

have to leave anywhere in a hurry, take your under-clothes with you.'

Phoebe closed the door quietly but firmly behind them. She and Coffin looked at one another.

'He's a clever fellow,' said Coffin thoughtfully. 'I could almost fancy him for the killing myself, but he's too sharp for that.' Oxford-trained, he thought, probably got a degree in philosophy. Or even theology, they were the really formidable outfit, weren't they? The real vultures, ready to pick the flesh off the bones.

'Shows you how they work, doesn't it?' said Phoebe. 'Turds.'

'Watch it, Phoebe.' She was letting her anger show.

'Oh, I get like that sometimes.'

She watched the Chief Commander go out to his car. The lovely Pete has made an enemy there, she thought. Good, and I'm another one.

'Sir,' she said, going up to the car. 'We found traces of a sedative in a bottle of wine, more in a teacup… Miss Pinero was probably doped. She may very well have lost track of time. In case you wondered.'

'Thank you.' He was grateful, he had wondered and never asked how it was that Stella had been imprisoned for several days without getting out. A sedative, she had mentioned that herself and I was sceptical even if I did not show it.

I know better now.

'Thanks, Phoebe,' he said again.

FOURTEEN

ONCE IN THE CAR, driving out of Fish Alley, he realized that Augustus had been with him, perhaps had been so all the time. No, that was not likely, Augustus was a dog who took his duties seriously, who would probably have snapped at Peter and snarled at Inspector Lodge.

No, not at Lodge, there was a man more deserving of sympathy than a snarl.

'Besides,' Coffin addressed Augustus, 'I snapped for both of us, didn't I?'

Off to the office to tell Paul Masters that the Chief Commander was still around, and then off to find Stella.

The best place to look for Stella seemed to be the theatre.

STELLA HAD decided that the theatre was a democracy in which every player, even those whose employment was temporary, should have a voice. Her own was loudest, of course, but the others were allowed a shout or two.

The local university supported the theatre with funds, so that some intellectual input was demanded. Out of every five plays, one might be an Ibsen or a lesser Albee even if the audiences were thin. She could rely on good reviews for these plays, however, in the university newspaper and in *The Stage,* even if their own dear *Spinnergate Herald* was hostile.

The democracy of the theatre was gathering in the bar to develop ideas for new productions. Stella was expected to look in later. She was admired for her skill as an actress and her ability to keep the whole show going. Letty Bingham was admired for her financial acumen, recognized to be vital, yet feared for the axe she could wield. But Letty, swift as ever, had sped away on a Concorde bound for New York. Checking her investments, one school of thought said, buying new clothes said another. No one disputed that while Stella was a lovely woman whose looks could survive slopping around in jeans and trainers, Letty had the best clothes, the sort you did not see and certainly could not buy in the Second City. This naturally did not increase her popularity.

Present that evening were Jane Gillam, Fanny Burt and Irene Bow. They had all three been in *Noises Off,* while Jane and Fanny had survived *An Ideal Husband.* They had started off with some scorn for the Wilde play but ended with an appreciation of Wilde's skill as well as his splendid jokes. As they worked they saw, contrary to what they had first thought, that most of his best jokes were at the expense of men. They had all enjoyed the Frayn, but agreed it used up a lot of energy because you were always on the move.

Jane went to the bar, returning with white Italian wine for them all. 'I would like to do a couple of the new, small Pinters, two together. One before the interval and one after.'

'I don't know. Thanks for the wine.' Fanny took a sip and considered. 'Would we get an audience round here?'

'From the university,' said Irene Bow. 'Not everyone round here wants light comedy.'

'Most of them do,' said Fanny. 'Or that's what Stella will say.'

'What about a Sam Shepherd? He's very strong.' Irene admired the American.

'Not for us,' said Fanny. 'Can't see it filling the seats, and you know what Letty can be like.'

Irene sipped her wine. She was happy to be in work, when so many of her friends were not. 'Just a suggestion.'

'You could put it up,' said Jane. 'Stella doesn't knock everything down.'

'Especially if there's a good part for her.' Fanny was a cynic.

'Oh well, you can't blame her, she invented this theatre.'

'So she could go on acting till she dropped.'

They were, all three, very young.

'She has turned down some good parts to stay here with us,' said Irene in support of Stella. 'Films, too.'

For a moment they sat in contemplation of a future in which they, too, might turn down a film offer. Except I never would, said Fanny inside her head. Not if the money was good.

'Do we actually count? I know it's a democracy and we have a voice,' said Fanny, 'but do they listen? Does Stella?'

Michael Guardian and Tom Jenks appeared through the door. 'I know who does listen, girls. We do, especially if you're buying us a drink.'

'Buy your own,' said Fanny. 'You earn as much as we do.'

'It is true,' agreed Tom, 'that the money is equally meagre for us all, taking no account of the extra weight we men bring.'

'Which is considerable, in your case.'

'True.' Tom was complacent. He was a large young man, not handsome but pleasant to look at. He intended to be the sort of character actor, always in work, who ends up with an Oscar for playing himself.

'So what were you talking about?' Michael had brought some drinks over.

'Plays, productions, casting—what else do we talk about?' This was Jane, in one of her sharper modes. 'I wondered how much notice Stella takes of what we say.'

'A bit,' said Michael, who had been with the company longer than anyone else. 'I have known her to do a modest late Pinter. You're jealous of her. But she did set this place up.'

'I've always wondered where the money came from,' said Tom.

'She had a series on TV and a film or two, and I daresay someone put money in. Anyway, it's run on a shoestring.'

'Yes, but it's her shoestring and we all dance to it.'

'Oh, Tom,' said Fanny. 'You're jealous.'

'Aren't we all?' Jane asked.

'Yes,' said Tom. 'Fault admitted.' He drew his mouth down. He could look baleful when he chose. Or perhaps, Jane thought, when he did not realize that he was giving himself away. He does suck up to Stella, she thought, but what's underneath eh? 'I'm jealous,' he went on, 'because you women have it easy, compared to men in the profession.'

Irene said, 'I'd like to try *The Women*, it has some wonderful parts...of course, it's period now, but that would be part of the fun, all thirties clothes.'

'Big cast,' pointed out Jane, who could see herself in it, possibly as the injured wife who wins out in the end. 'Some strong parts.'

'All for women,' said Michael, with emphasis. 'This isn't a girls' club, you know.'

Tom gave a groan. 'No, take pity on us and the audience.'

'Most of our audience are women,' said Jane. 'Especially at matinees.'

'They like to see a man, you know that, I know it, and you can bet Stella knows it.'

'True,' said Jane, the realist.

'Talking of which, our esteemed Stella has not been around much lately.'

There was a pause.

'She's in today,' said Irene quietly. 'She looks white, though. Still, she's working as usual. Alice is doing props with her, the ones that were borrowed from the university. She said she would be along.'

There was another pause; they had all heard about Maisie.

'She must be upset about Maisie.' Jane looked sad. It was one of her best expressions, her features suited it, as she well knew. 'They've worked together for such a long time.'

'I can hardly bear to think about it.' Fanny shook her head.

'I'm frightened,' Irene admitted. A nervous look suited her also.

Tom said: 'I was nervous before, I don't mind admitting it. My digs got a blast in the Spinnergate bomb. I still haven't got glass in my window.'

'It's the third murder,' said Irene. 'Stella must feel safe, being married to top brass.'

'I suppose.' Jane was thoughtful. 'I think he's quite alarming himself.'

'Attractive, though.'

Michael said in a firm voice: 'I'm as sorry as you are

about Maisie, she was a great old girl, part of the theatre, the old theatre. But the murders can't touch us.'

They were silent.

When Stella walked in, Alice by her side, they all started to talk at once.

'We're talking plays,' said Tom, blithely.

'Talk away. Now, I have consulted my six-month schedule—you know I try to work to it, although sometimes fail—' her turn to smile. 'And I see we voted to do *Night Must Fall*.'

So much for our right to choose, thought Tom. His expressive face showed his thoughts which Stella read.

'Of course, none of you except Alice was with me then, but I assure you it was a democratic decision.'

There was silence.

'Yes, you're thinking what I'm thinking: not suitable at the moment.' She looked down at the list she carried in her hand. 'We had Bill Barton pencilled in for the killer, but, as it happens, he's involved in a TV series so he probably wouldn't have been free, although I believe he would have tried to honour his promise. So, no problem there.'

With a bit of make-up, I could have played the old lady in that play; there was one, wasn't there? thought Irene. Then she remembered Maisie and decided, maybe not such a good idea.

Stella went over to the bar to order a bottle of wine for them. She was talking as she went. 'I thought of Shakespeare, you always feel safe with Shakespeare, the play supports you, but I decided against; any Shakespeare needs more time, even though all of you will have done your stint in him. So I wondered what suggestions you have?'

Alice carried the wine over to the table, pouring it with a steady hand.

'Ayckbourn?' This from Fanny.

'Done him a lot here,' said Tom, who had been studying past productions at St Luke's. 'In fact, there's a school production of one in the Experimental Theatre next month.'

'True,' admitted Stella, who had already made up her mind though she had no intention of showing her hand yet. 'But something light yet serious is a good idea.'

'*An Inspector Calls?*' Michael had played the inspector once, knew the part to perfection.

'Priestley is a good idea,' said Stella with conviction. 'I seem to remember we talked about it.'

'*When We Are Married,* then?'

'Now, that is bang on,' said Stella with even more conviction, grateful that she had not had to suggest the title herself. She had had the other play in mind if necessary, some tribute must be paid to democracy. But cheerful, rumbustious comedy was the thing.

She drank some wine before discussing parts. I really need a strong brandy, she thought. I should have left all this till later. But no, I wanted to get on with things, cling to normality, whatever and wherever that is.

'I think you are marvellous,' said Irene, 'when you must be so miserable.'

Stella did not answer. I am that, and more, said a voice in her head.

'I don't suppose I've taken it all in yet. First the bombs, then the murders.' I am well acquainted with unnatural death, she reminded herself, being married to a man whose work it is.

'Shall we be questioned about Maisie?' asked Jane.

'Yes, I expect you will.'

'I wonder what they will ask?' Jane sounded nervous.

What petty crime has she got on her conscience? Tom asked himself. Bet she's got a little stash of Ecstasy or such stowed away somewhere. Destroy it, dear, before they come.

'Oh, they will just poke around,' said Stella, vaguely.

'Answer up promptly and don't worry.' Alice, the child of a policeman, was firm. 'They aren't gods, you know, they can't see through you.'

Stella looked down at her hands. Sometimes I think my husband can do exactly that. Not because he has some extrasensory power, but because he is sharp, observant and clever.

'Don't be too cocky,' said Tom. 'I had an accident on my motorbike last year and they weren't nice at all.'

'I expect you were drunk.' Jane knew her friend Tom.

'Well, only a bit tipsy. All I did was to crack a shop window, but I broke my own nose.'

'Life's very unfair,' said Jane.

Suddenly, Michael said: 'I think Maisie was worried about something. She used to talk to me a bit—she liked men, liked a gossip with what she called her boys—and she let out to me that she was worried. She knew my father was a solicitor, so I suppose she thought I might be a good source of legal advice if she needed. "I could be in trouble," she said; she'd made me a cup of tea, she often did that. "Someone I knew years ago, an actor, as a young chap, I think he's got me into something I'd rather not be in. It could be big trouble."' Pip Eton, thought Stella at once.

'And he wasn't the only one. Maisie seemed more worried about what she called "the other one". I couldn't make out if she meant man or beast, then she laughed it off. "Take no notice of me." I didn't much at the time—she did go on sometimes—but now I wonder. Should I mention it to the police?'

'If they ask,' said Alice. 'Otherwise don't.'

'I think you should,' said Stella gently. Suddenly, she felt sick. The picture of Maisie, anxious and worried, melded with the picture of the dead Maisie, covered with blood. She put her hand to her head.

'Are you all right?' That was Alice. Even when she was being sympathetic she sounded steely.

'Yes, I'm fine, but I think I'll get off home. We'll have another work talk tomorrow.'

STELLA MET Coffin and Augustus in the corridor outside her office.

She embraced him eagerly. 'Take me home, I want out of here. Just let me collect my things.' She gathered up her coat and briefcase.

Augustus gave a small, excited bark and leapt up towards her.

'Right, boy, right,' said Coffin, holding him back. 'She's coming with us.'

From the door, Alice said: 'Can I help?'

'I think she's all right,' said Coffin. 'We're on the way home.'

'She's not well, look after her.' Even a benediction from Alice could sound like a threat.

'I will be in tomorrow,' said Stella. Augustus was growling softly. 'Be quiet, boy. Quiet, all of you. I'm all right and I will be back at work tomorrow, Alice. We will go through those property boxes and cupboards.'

Alice gave a nod.

STELLA AND COFFIN let themselves in through the door at the bottom of the tower in which they lived. Not a convenient way of living with rooms on every floor and a winding staircase, but the rooms were large, full of light and had a curious charm. The belfry where the bells had hung was their attic. The bells themselves, damaged in the Blitz, had been repaired in Whitechapel, where they had been made, and now lived in another church, so they had not been silenced.

'Poor old Alice,' said Stella, over her shoulder as she ran up the stairs. A drink was foremost in her mind, then something simple but delicious to eat. She would probably ring Max's restaurant to get something sent over. He did a very good chicken dish. 'She'll never make her way in the theatre unless she learns how to move. She likes the life, I think, although I am never quite sure of that, but she's got to handle her appearance better.'

'She is a bit on the plain side, like her dad. He wasn't bad-looking as a man, but it won't quite do in a girl.' Coffin was carrying Augustus, who had decided that the stairs were too much for his short legs.

'There's a place for a woman who's not a beauty; probably a good place but you have to convince, not be hangdog about it.'

'Is she?' Coffin put the dog down as they reached the kitchen. 'Positive sort of character, I'd say.'

'Perhaps I see a different side of her.' Stella was reaching for the telephone. 'Pour me a drink, while I ring Max's.'

Coffin poured out some claret. 'I meant to be across to collect you earlier, but I got held up in the office.'

'You always do.'

'True.' Somehow he always did. Tonight, there was a report from London to skim through and yet another savage crime in the Second City about which he must be alerted: a double killing, the murder of a wife and child by the husband, who then tried to burn the bodies but only succeeded in giving himself third-degree burns. This terrible event might make the national press but would probably not figure on the television news, even locally. Coffin had noticed that the media liked an extra bizarre twist that they could get their teeth into, a domestic murder, even a vicious one, could be passed over.

'Let's not talk about what's going on until we've eaten,' said Stella. 'I know Maisie was up to something, I've caught that much today in the theatre. Stupid of me not to have noticed before. I thought when I threw myself into her house after being shut up in Linton House that she was...not exactly reluctant to take me in, but hesitant in a way I would never have expected of her. I didn't mean to stay, after all, just tidy up and settle my nerves.'

'We might as well get it over.' Coffin wondered whether brandy would be better than wine, or strong tea as good as anything. You could never tell with Stella: wine for celebrating, she had said once, and tea for support. 'Maisie was involved with Pip Eton, probably over a long period. He may have been blackmailing her. I suspect that her life was not unspotted.'

Stella nodded. 'Yes...plenty of life, I daresay. Oh, how sad.'

'She must have taken money from him. She may have let him have the bag and the clothes that Francesco di Rimini wore, she may have been the voice you heard in the flat.' I say 'may', he thought. 'Or she might have sold your things elsewhere. The good clothes probably did not see a charity shop.'

Stella frowned. 'Could be.'

'She didn't kill Pip; not clear yet where he was killed.'

'And he couldn't have killed her; he was already dead,' Stella said quickly.

'No, nor did he kill Francesco di Rimini, although he might have wanted to.'

'He was violent.'

'I believe you there. You certainly had a struggle. Can you remember more now? Your arm, for instance, how did that happen?'

Stella looked down at her arm, and ran her hand down it. In a hesitant voice, she said; 'You know, I think the idea of biting was a fantasy... I was hurt or I hurt myself, I seem to remember something, but it is too much of a blur now, and getting more so with every day that passes, like a nightmare, so clear at first, then fading. I think I picked up a knife... I remember a serrated edge, like a bread knife.'

'That would explain something of the nature of the wound.'

'He got it off me...' She shook her head. 'I am sorry. It's gone again.'

'OK, so he didn't kill Maisie, he was dead himself then. I don't think he killed Francesco di Rimini either. Eton wasn't an irrational killer, he was a terrorist. These deaths bear another mark.' He was talking half to himself.

But Stella was listening. 'I bet there is a school of thought, and not so far away either, that thinks it must be me.'

'You can rule out Phoebe Astley. She told me that forensic had found traces of a sedative in a glass at the flat, and she thinks this was given to you. Which would explain why you didn't notice the passage of time.' He was not going to let her know how much this had troubled him. 'And also how confused you were.'

For a while there was silence. Stella got up, went to the window to look out. It was a fine, bright evening with a clear sky and a full moon. A cloud passed across the moon as she stared out. The cloud was long and angular, with what could be a tail. Sometimes I see a cloud that's dragonish, she thought…was that Shakespeare? Was it even true? That cloud looked more like a bird. Or Superman, she thought, with a hint of a giggle. She was coming to life again, she could tell.

'You said you would be apologizing to me,' she said, still looking at the moon.

Coffin said nothing for a while. 'That will come,' he said, at last.

I wonder if I could tell her, he was asking himself. Dare I do so? He poured her a strong brandy, and as he handed it to her, he said: 'Piece of advice, don't go into the theatre tomorrow.'

Can't she see that there is a strong personal element of hatred for her in this?

FOR ONCE THE telephone did not ring. Max's van delivered a hot meal of chicken and salad which they ate together, with Augustus receiving his share. They chatted idly of this and that: whether they should get another cat and what would Augustus make of it, whether Stella should get her hair cut. It was quiet and peaceful.

'I'll make some coffee,' she said.

'Don't bother.' He held out a hand to stop her. Standing, she smiled down at him, then they walked up the staircase together.

Augustus hesitated at the kitchen door, then made a decision. He turned back to his basket.

Bed was indicated.

THE DELAYED pleasures of the afternoon were performed, perfected even, in the night. They were almost

silent, pleasured and friendly as only lovers who have
been together for years can be.

'I expect those kids in the theatre think we are too old
for this.' Stella rolled back upon her pillow.

'I'm quite sure Paul Masters does, I can see the look
in his eyes.' Phoebe Astley did not, she knew better; a
slight touch of guilt there, quickly repressed. After all,
their relationship, if you could dignify it by that name,
had been over before Stella came back into his life.

'I miss you terribly when you are away,' he said
sleepily.

'So do I. Let's retire and live on a desert island.'

'Why not.' Sleep was deliciously close.

Except, thought Stella, I have had an absolutely marvellous offer of a thirteen-week contract from the
BBC—these things have to be considered.

She raised herself on one elbow to look down at her
sleeping husband with affection. He wouldn't come either, there would always be another crime, another crisis
before he could leave, and he never would leave.

He was lying on his back, with his mouth slightly open.

Any minute now, you are going to snore, my darling,
she thought. Now that is something that the crew down
at Spinnergate Central HQ would never think of you.

Only I know that.

IN THE MORNING, they breakfasted quietly in the kitchen,
drinking strong coffee and eating toast which Stella had
burnt, then scraped clear. 'Still, it's crisp,' she said. 'And
I expect the carbon is good for you.'

'True.' Coffin slid a bit down to Augustus, who liked
charcoal.

'I'm going in to work,' said Stella. 'I heard what you
said last night, but I want to go.'

Coffin nodded. 'Take the dog with you, will you? He

may not have very big legs—' Augustus looked up and
wagged his tail— 'but he's good little fighter.'

Stella did not believe in any threat to her, so she prepared for work without concern.

Coffin, anxious for Stella, was not worried about himself because he had not seen where the real threat was
directed.

As they set off, Augustus was just happy to be going
out with the two people he loved most.

At the door of the big theatre, a stone's throw from
their own front door, they said goodbye with a kiss. Coffin patted Augustus and walked away.

Stella sailed into the foyer, followed by Augustus,
tethered by a lead. She checked all was as it should be,
she hated it when the theatre looked untidy, as if last
night's audience had only just moved out.

But no, she was proud of it. Her office was tucked
away in a corner of the building, strategically placed
near the new young woman installed by Letty to manage
money and accounts, but equally near the backstage cit-
adels of costume and props.

There was a neat pile of letters on her desk prepared
for her by her secretary-cum-assistant, a middle-aged,
stage-struck local matron who worked for the minimum
wage because she loved drama. Mrs Brighton was an
ally and a friend, the more so because she never intruded. The spirit of Letty Bingham hung over them all.

Indeed, there was a fax from Letty on Stella's desk,
with the message, threat even, that she would be back
next week. Stella worked on, referring at intervals to her
six-month schedule in which forthcoming productions
were pencilled in, possibly more firmly than she allowed
the democracy of the theatre to see.

In mid morning she needed to check the properties of
the last production but one, some of which had been

rented and should have been returned. She walked down the short corridor; Augustus, freed from his lead, came with her. He had the swaggering roll of a peke in good condition and fine humour. Together they entered the room where Mr Gibbs, he was always called this, was talking with Alice and an assistant. Working, too, Stella hoped, but she noticed long ago that work in the theatre involved much conversation. Coffin said it was the same with the police.

While she discussed the problem of the missing props with Mr Gibbs, the other two wandered off to the far end of the room and Augustus strolled around investigating. Had the missing items—one small chair and a pretty desk—gone back but not been recorded? If so, why not? Or were they still here, hidden behind other furniture?

oAugustus was at the other end of the room, sniffing at a double door behind which was a large, walk-in cupboard. He was making a noise which attracted Stella's attention. Then he began to scratch at the door. Stella walked over to stop him. This made him go at it even harder, looking at her as he did so.

'Probably got a rat,' said Mr Gibb.

'I hope not.' Stella opened the door, switching on the light as she walked in. 'Bit stuffy in here.'

She took several paces into what was really a small room lined with shelves.

In the bright light hanging from the ceiling, she could see that the floor was stained.

For a moment, she hesitated, looking back at Mr Gibb, but Augustus pushed forward and snuffled at the floor, his body shaking with excitement.

An old brown stain of blood. A big old brown stain of blood. Perhaps someone had tried to wash it away, there were signs, but this blood was there to stay.

Augustus raised his head and began to howl.

FIFTEEN

COFFIN SAT AT his desk staring at the assembled mass of letters and reports all demanding his attention. He did not find this side of his work boring or something to be deplored, he liked a tidy desk. He liked the feeling that he was in charge. If he could have run the whole Second City Force from one great computer, he might have been tempted to try.

Paul Masters came in with the internal mail which he had already read and initialled, making his usual sharp comments here and there.

'Sir Fred's been on the line.' He kept his voice neutral.

'Thought he might be. He's our action man.' He raised his head. 'And what did Sir Fred want?'

'He's coming down to see you.'

'Not today, keep him away from me today.'

Paul Masters considered the possibility of keeping out that commanding figure before deciding that it could not have been meant seriously. 'I'll try.'

Coffin laughed. 'We'll set Phoebe Astley on him, shall we? I think he is frightened of her.' And Inspector Lodge certainly is. But he did not say this aloud; one does not make too many jokes about a colleague. Or Coffin didn't. 'Take these reports with you, will you? Cast your eye over them and let me know what you think.'

Paul Masters took a brief look. 'About recruitment, is it?'

'That's right, we will have to talk it over.'

As Masters left the room, he looked around for that small figure he knew so well, and whose white hairs he had so often brushed off the edge of his trousers.

'Not got Augustus with you today?'

'No, he's with Stella.'

There was nothing in Coffin's tone to breed alarm, but for some reason, Masters felt uneasy. He closed the door behind him with extra care.

Once on his own, Coffin let his mind run over the picture he had formed of the three deaths.

Pictures were coming up, clear and sharp, in his mind.

The first one, the body in a bombed house in Percy Street. The dead body of a man who was dressed as a woman, and that woman, his wife, Stella Pinero.

No accident there, he told himself, Stella had been selected with deliberation, as had the victim, di Rimini— or Bates, to give him his proper name. They were both victims.

Stella was meant to be involved. Her jeans, her handbag with a few possessions in it. Coffin felt he could say now that all these had been appropriated, stolen, by Maisie, certainly with no idea what they were going to be used for, but either sold or given to some person who had a hold over her.

Pip Eton might have been that person. His figure was there in the story, but his own murder suggested to Coffin that there was a shadow behind him.

Coffin found himself pacing the room. You know who the killer is, he told himself, you have known for some time. Well, guessed, and you did not want to face it.

A colleague, investigating a terrible death, had once said: 'Don't you hate the human race?' At the time, Coffin had been able to say, no, there was always hope. But now, he felt a black depression. Guilt, you could say,

because he had the idea that he could have prevented
these deaths.

Hubris, perhaps, that dangerous pride to which we all,
except the genuinely humble—and not many of them
around in the police, he thought—succumb at times.

All my fault, you say, and quite enjoy the self-
flagellation.

After Francesco, that shady character (though not
without his attractions, if Dennis Garden was any judge),
was the murder of Pip Eton himself. A lot still to un-
cover there.

Coffin paused in his perambulations: Why did I say
'himself' like that, as if he was the fulcrum on which all
balanced? As far as my poor wife is concerned, he certainly was that central figure. She knew him, she had a
relationship with him, and she gave him a key to the
place in Fish Alley.

He gritted his teeth at the thought of the flat in Linton
House. Stella could be a fool sometimes, in a way that
only the theatre, and possibly politics, added a cynical
undertone, seemed to bring out.

The first victim had been killed, without too much
blood loss, by a deep stab wound. Then his face had
been beaten to bits. The received opinion was that he
had died where he was found, that he had walked there,
prettily dressed, to meet his killer. You could see his
walk on the video.

Right, that was murder one.

Murder two: Pip Eton. Stabbed.

He was not killed where he was found, obscenely
dressed in a kilt and hat made of back issues of *The
Stage*. He was dead when he was propped up there.

Coffin moved to the window. From where he stood
he could make out the roof of St Luke's Theatre. If he

turned his head he could study the roofs of Spinnergate near to Fish Alley, but he could not pick out one house from another. A bird might do, or possibly a wandering cat with a good knowledge of the rooftops, but he could not.

Anyway, Pip Eton had not been killed there, either. In Coffin's opinion, the bloodstained clothes were a plant. Where had he been killed?

It was probably crucial to finding his killer. Location was important here. Because a dead man is heavy, no easy object to transport into a public place.

You are telling yourself where he was killed, said Coffin, moving away from the window. Obvious. In or near the theatre.

Once again Stella Pinero walked the stage.

He moved away from the window while his assessment moved on to the next death.

Murder three: Maisie.

No doubt where she had been killed: at home. Murdered by someone she knew, whom she had let into the house, and to whom she had spoken on the telephone. You might say she had summoned her own killer.

Which suggested the motive: she was about to name that person to the police.

Coffin wished he had either Phoebe Astley or Archie with him to hold a dialogue, but he had his own reasons for talking to himself.

He was still a player in his secret game, as Sir Fred, no doubt carrying Inspector Thomas Lodge in his train, would be arriving to remind him.

He put his head round the door to ask Paul Masters if Sir Fred had said exactly when he would come.

'No, he left it open. He said he would ring when he was on the way.'

'And he hasn't rung?'

Paul shook his head. 'Not yet. I would have been straight on to you.'

'Good.' Coffin went back to his desk where he drew towards him the file on the death in Percy Street.

He took from it the shot from the video of the dressed-up figure of di Rimini walking down Jamaica Street towards his death. His killer, it was thought, was there before him.

But Coffin's eye was drawn to the blurred figure on the edge of the picture. He laid a magnifying glass over it to bring out what detail he could.

It seemed to be a man. A man dressed in dark trousers and a loose jacket.

He took it to the window to study it in the best possible light. Yes, swinging round the corner of Jamaica Street was the killer. He was following his victim, not waiting for him.

Those clothes, dark and neutral, reminded him of something.

Coffin put out his hand to the telephone, then withdrew it. No, he would take himself down to the Production Room where he would look for himself.

'I'm nipping out for a minute or two, Paul. You don't know where I've gone.'

'Just as you say.'

'If Sir Fred turns up, give him a drink and keep him happy.'

'I'll do what I can,' said Masters, watching the Chief Commander's retreating back.

On the staircase, Coffin met Phoebe Astley. 'Just coming to see you.'

'Good. Come with me on this call, then you can tell me what you think.'

'I don't know what to think about,' observed Phoebe mildly.

'You'll find out. Tell me, I suppose the usual teams went over the theatre after the body was found?'

'Still doing it, I think. It's a big job.'

'Not found anything?'

'Not yet, as far as I know.' Phoebe did know, but loyally said nothing about the fact that the forensic and SOCO teams had enjoyed the theatrical company so much that work had gone slowly. She herself had delivered a sharp kick to them only that morning.

'What's all this about?' She was moving fast to keep up with him.

'We're going to the Production Room.'

Phoebe raised an eyebrow, but followed without a word. When the Chief Commander was in this mood, it was best to do as asked, without fuss.

One lone figure, Sergeant Bailey, was in the Production Room. He looked up in surprise as the Chief Commander came in.

'Morning, sir.' He stood up.

'I want to see the register.'

Every artefact connected with any crime, great or small, was bundled up in a plastic bag, entered in the register, together with the name of the officer who brought it in, the date, and a few identifying details.

Silently, the sergeant handed the book over. 'It's all on the computer as well, sir. We've never lost anything yet.'

The joke was ignored as Coffin studied the register.

'I want to see Number 33741.'

He waited while Bailey checked the shelves, brought a step ladder, and climbed up to search the top shelf.

'Here you are, sir. Brought in by Sergeant Miller.' He

pointed to the signature and the date. He was a man who liked everything authenticated, well suited to the job he did, which many considered dull. He found a certain romance in these objects once touched by a crime, so never to be let loose in the world again. Kind of sacred, in a way.

Coffin took the bundle to the long trestle table in the middle of the room where, under the centre light, witnessed by Phoebe and the sergeant, he opened the parcel.

A dark pair of trousers, and a very loose black jacket.

'These were found in the house in Percy Street. Thought to have been left there before the bomb fell.'

'So?' said Phoebe.

'I think they were worn by the killer over the killer's own clothes.'

'Is that just a guess, sir?' Phoebe was careful to be formal.

'No, if you study the video of the street scene you can see a figure dressed like this following di Rimini.' A wolf after his prey. Coffin was spreading the clothes out on the table. 'Did they ever come under forensic study?'

'No, they were not thought to be connected.'

'Sloppy thinking.' He stretched out the jacket and then the trousers, examining both inside and out. He was slow, taking his time. There was a stain at the crotch, to which he pointed. 'Now that is an interesting stain.'

'It's on the inside—' protested Phoebe.

'Yes, think about that. Get a proper forensic study done for me, and sooner than soon. I want to know about the blood.'

'I'll see to it, sir.' She looked at Sergeant Bailey, who moved towards the telephone, muttering about a messenger. 'But sir…no blood analysis is much good to us, without a suspect to match it to.'

'Use your mind, Phoebe,' said Coffin briskly. 'You are a woman.'

'So you've noticed,' Phoebe muttered under her breath.

He marched out of the room. 'Come on, the sergeant can get on with that, I want you with me.'

'Going where, sir?'

'To the theatre. You had better drive, I want to think.'

THE ENTRANCE TO St Luke's was blocked by two police cars. Phoebe double-parked her car beside them.

'Something's up,' she said. As she did so, her phone began ringing. She picked it up. 'Sir,' she called out, as she listened. 'Sir—'

But Coffin was out of the car before her, moving rapidly into the foyer. A uniformed constable greeted him with a surprised salute.

'What is going on?' demanded Coffin.

The constable was about to answer that he didn't know much but he knew that traces of a lot of blood had been found and that Miss Pinero—

He was interrupted by the appearance of a detective sergeant who seemed surprised at the arrival of such a high-level visitor, but also relieved.

'Sergeant Lomas, sir. We had a call about a lot of blood—' He in his turn was interrupted by the sound of barking. 'That's the dog, sir,' he began.

Coffin was off, through the swing doors behind the box office, through the darkened theatre, following the sound of the dog. 'Thought you had a team going over the theatre,' he called over his shoulder.

'Must have got called elsewhere,' said Phoebe as she

followed. Curse them, she thought, I'll have their lights and livers, or Archie Young will. 'There are about three cases on the go at the moment, sir.' Excuses, excuses, she was muttering, I will kill them regardless.

There was a WPC at the door of the property room. Inside, Stella, Alice, and Mr Gibb stood grouped together at one end of the room before the opened doors of a big cupboard. Nearer the door, and huddled together, were a frightened group. Coffin recognized Jane Gillam and Irene Bow, and there were a couple of young men whom he did not know, except by sight.

Augustus was barking and whining, rushing between Stella and Alice. When he saw Coffin, his barking increased in fervour but he did not move away from the women.

Coffin walked up the room, nodded to Stella and Alice without speaking, then went through the double doors.

There were indeed traces of blood; stale, dried blood, and plenty of it, even though an effort to scrub it away had been made. A bucket with bloody water in stood at the end of the little room. There was more blood here. A trolley of the sort used to move props around stood, blood on it.

'Well, well,' said Coffin, coming out. 'So this was where Pip Eton was killed.' And how his body was moved. Cover it up with a sheet or blanket and you could move through the corridors with some impunity.

Stella began to say something.

'Be quiet,' ordered Coffin, his voice stern. 'And keep the dog quiet.'

Stella picked up Augustus, who kept up a low grumble.

In a low voice, he said: 'So this is where you killed your fellow conspirator.'

'No,' Stella cried out. She tried to take his arm.

'Not you.' He moved away. 'You, Alice, you.'

He was aware of Phoebe Astley, together with the detective sergeant, moving quietly up the room towards Alice. She was shaking her head from side to side.

'Keep away, you lot,' she called, without turning to look. 'Or I won't answer for who gets killed.'

'Oh, I daresay you have a knife up your sleeve,' said Coffin. 'But you won't use it.'

'I won't need to, everyone knows it's all her,' she nodded at Stella. 'Your lovely wife. All her doing.'

'No, that won't wash. Stella is in the clear. You are not. We can prove you were in the house with di Rimini.'

'The old transvestite? Oh, big deal.'

'The clothes you wore to kill him, you left them behind and went home in jeans and a sweater. We will probably track that down on the video.'

'You'll have a job proving they are my clothes,' she laughed. 'What rubbish!'

'We will track you at every street corner till you got back to the theatre: picture of a killer. And we will examine the clothes; there is blood inside the trousers...'

Alice shrugged. 'So what?'

'I'm making a guess it's menstrual blood, Alice. You were bleeding yourself when you stabbed him. Are you always worse at those times?'

'Stop it, stop it. I hate that talk. You're all doing it, shouting. The walls are shouting at me. I can hear them all the time.' She was still moving her head, then a steel blade had appeared in her hand. 'I may not be able to kill your wife, but a slash or two down her face won't improve her looks.'

Stella made a small noise.

'I don't want to harm her, it's self-defence. It was you we were after all the time. Orders, you know. Get close to you, compromise you, get you out. Pip was to do the job with help from Stella.'

'And he didn't get it right, so you killed him. Maisie knew it was you. She had sold you some of Stella's clothes and was about to say so. Pip, first, then her.'

'It was me or him. I think he liked Stella, he was going to tell her everything.'

'Thank you for putting it into speech. There are witnesses.'

She did not bother to look round. 'Stop shouting at me. I won't be here. No one will touch me while I have this knife... And I have friends who will get me away. A pleasure to go... I hated you, you know. You would play the big benefactor, the kind man, but you are selfish and cold. A proper careerist. Because of you, my father died. I knew that and I knew it would be a pleasure to drag you down. You think Pip Eton recruited me and Charles Mackie? No, I was looking for someone like him. I couldn't get in fast enough.'

She put out a big strong hand which gripped Stella by the shoulder. The knife, long and bright, was in the other hand. 'I'll take her with me for safety. Touch me and I will drag this knife down her face.'

Coffin drew back.

Alice began to push Stella towards the door. 'Let me pass, you lot.'

But at the door, Augustus wrenched himself out of Stella's arms. As she staggered backward, free, the dog went for Alice. She kicked him away as she pushed into the group at the door and through them, Augustus following.

'Don't bother touching her,' called Coffin. 'A woman

running through the streets with a peke pursuing her will be picked out on every camera in every street. Let her go. I'll warn them. She may lead us to the centre control she must have had, if not, a patrol will take them in whenever—Astley, take over.'

He walked towards Stella. 'Bloody you,' she said angrily, rubbing her elbow where she had fallen.

'I said I would have to apologize and I will...but later.'

FOLLOWED BY THE cameras, Alice was picked up some forty minutes later entering a house to the south of Spinnergate Tube station. Augustus was still with her, footsore and weary.

The house was later raided by a special police unit; three men were arrested in connection with the recent bomb. Bomb-making material was found in the garage.

'They aren't the whole unit,' said Coffin to Tom Lodge later, 'but a good part of it. Some others blew themselves up.'

'Good work,' said Sir Fred, even later. 'I congratulate you, Chief Commander.'

LATER STILL, Coffin made his peace with Stella. Over a special dinner at Max's restaurant.

'You aren't really as angry as you act, are you?'

'Yes, I am. Furious.'

He looked her in the face and smiled.

'You can pour me some more champagne. We might need another bottle. I hope it costs.'

With a sigh, he said: 'I apologize, I repent, I confess—will that do?'

Stella considered. 'A bit more detail is required.'

Coffin buttered one of Max's special bread rolls.

'Even now, I can't tell you some things. I knew about you and Pip and the place in Fish Alley, I've told you that. I was to get you out of it all... I know how dicey Alice was, her father had told me. I knew I was in the game, but I shouldn't have asked you to give her a job. For that I apologize.'

'Apology accepted.'

'I didn't know how much she hated me. I should have thought about it long before Edinburgh. But my game was to get Alice...unluckily, her game was to get me.'

Stella considered. 'Pip's dead... She can't have done all that on her own. She must have had help.'

'Yes, I think Maisie helped. Not in the killing—I don't see Maisie as a killer—but afterwards—in the tidying up, in the transport of the body on that barrow, skip—whatever you call it. And keeping watch while the body was moved. Yes, she could have helped there, but I guess that was also the time when she took fright and thought about confessing. And so Alice killed her.'

Stella shook her head. 'And Maisie did all this for money?'

'Alice had her hooks well and truly in by then, but Maisie liked her, strongly.' Coffin studied his wife's face. 'Just guessing. You never noticed anything? I think one or two of the cast did.'

'I knew about Maisie, we all did, but she kept that side of her life from me, she knew I wasn't that way.'

'Money and sex,' said Coffin. 'They come in everywhere.'

Stella was considering what she had heard. 'And is that all? Was anyone else involved?'

Coffin decided that honesty was best. 'I expect so, my dear. You have to face it. This is not the end, there is more to be found out. But my guess is that the theatre will be in the clear. I wonder about those builders, though.'

Stella sipped her champagne. 'Let's take the rest of the bottle home. Max won't mind. We mustn't leave Augustus alone any longer. He is exhausted, poor boy.'

'He deserved a medal. I hope you aren't too tired?'

Stella looked at him under her eyelashes. 'Let's see, shall we?'

The Case of Alice Yeoman

WHEN THE CASE came to court, a plea of abnormal menstrual tension was put forward by the defence. This plea was rejected by the court, which accepted the Crown's medical assessment of manic depression leading to a psychotic state.

The prisoner was committed to a secure mental hospital for the duration of the Queen's pleasure with the provision that if she responded to treatment she might be released into the community.

COFFIN VISITED her in hospital, he being her last friend, or unfriend, in the world. She seemed normal, but probably was not.

She wanted to discuss the affair and her involvement with the bombers. 'Blew themselves up, didn't they, so I've heard.'

'Yes,' Coffin said. It had been in the papers. 'By mistake, as they were packing up to disband. They had rented an empty garage down by the river.'

'I know. I put them on to it.'

'I'm surprised they let you into their group.'

'I had a passport,' she said gleefully. 'You.' Then she

added: 'And a lot of local knowledge—streets, houses, garages, that sort of thing.'

'I wonder that they trusted you.'

'Oh, they didn't, not a lot. Kept me on the edge, but I enjoyed it, because I meant to drag you in through Stella and see you go down, down, down.' She kept on repeating 'down, down'. Then she said: 'I expect they would have killed me, too, in the end.'

So they might, thought Coffin. You were hardly the ideal terrorist. A one-woman terror campaign.

'I was determined to soil you, degrade you.'

Thanks, he thought. 'Why did you leave di Rimini's finger in a handkerchief belonging to Stella?' Ask a silly question, get a silly answer; but no, what came out was rational enough.

'It implicated Stella in his death, like dressing him up in her clothes and using the other chap's underpants—well, I didn't think of that; Corner left them behind, I suppose,' she sounded shocked. 'Di Rimini must have put them on. As for me, I paid him, I knew his ways from that place we both drank in. He thought we were making a film, so he dressed himself up, he did a bit of porno posing for dirty pictures. I knew the chap who did them, that's how I got the picture of Stella faked, do anything with a camera, that man could. Give you his name, if you like.'

'We found it out,' said Coffin grimly.

'So?' She was disinterested. 'Di Rimini didn't have to do any acting, just lay there as asked, and then I stabbed him and hit him. Stabbed him first. He squeaked a bit; I reckon he owed a fingernail—and he didn't miss it, he was dead. Moribund, anyway,' she added thoughtfully. 'It does take time for some people to die. Then I went away. No one takes any notice of what you do in

Spinnergate if you look as though you are working, as if you have a purpose.'

'You certainly had that. What about the other deaths?'

She shrugged. 'Oh, you know how it is. I had to kill Pip Eton, he knew it was me. I even went to the hospital with him to jolly him along. I thought he might kill Stella for me, but all he could do was to try to threaten her, and through her get at you. I went to Linton House and suggested he might kill Stella, but he wasn't up for it, and he was beginning to threaten me. So I did him. I fancied to by then. Maisie, of course, had to go, and she knew it. She knew I bought clothes off her and she soon knew why. Couldn't trust her to keep quiet.'

'A lot of killing in a short time.'

'I am nimble—you can do it if you are nimble.' She leaned forward. 'Don't tell them here, but I might be nimble enough again.'

Alice fell silent, no more to say.

All gone, Jerry, Andrew and Charles. And her victims.

And her father whose death she blamed on Coffin— had she really loved him so much that only a string of deaths could exorcize his memory?

AT CHRISTMAS, Alice Yeoman sent a card from Bishoptown Hospital, Surrey, to John Coffin with the message:

SEE YOU WHEN I GET OUT.

kiLLinG tHyme

PETER ABRESCH

A JAMES P. DANDY ELDERHOSTEL MYSTERY

Take a few ambitious chefs, a handful of amateur cooks on
a week-long tour of Baltimore's greatest restaurants, season
with a bit of competition for a spot on a new TV show,
"A Dash of Thyme," throw in a ruthless killer and voilà,
a perfectly seasoned dish of homicide.

Amateur sleuths James P. Dandy and his ladylove
Dodee Swisher embark on a culinary caper as delicious
as it is deadly—with a clever killer who's eager
to serve them just desserts.

Available August 2000 at your favorite retail outlet.

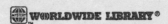

WORLDWIDE LIBRARY®

Visit us at www.worldwidemystery.com   WPA356

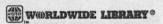

MURDER FLIES LEFT SEAT

JACKIE LEWIN

A GRACE BECKMANN MYSTERY

Grace Beckmann would prefer solid ground any day to the glory, freedom...and sheer terror of riding shotgun in her husband's beloved Piper Turbo Arrow. So when the couple arrive at the airport to find their plane stolen, Grace breathes a silent prayer of thanks. Unfortunately, the small aircraft is found crashed in the Rockies, with the body of a good friend inside, a victim of sabotage.

Was is supposed to be them? Was the crash carefully planned to ground the Beckmanns...permanently?

Available August 2000 at your favorite retail outlet.

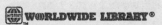 **WORLDWIDE LIBRARY®**

Visit us at www.worldwidemystery.com   WJL357

WINNING CAN BE MURDER

BILL CRIDER

A SHERIFF DAN RHODES MYSTERY

It's been a while since Sheriff Dan Rhodes's football days, but things haven't really changed. But the excitement of the upcoming state play-offs is short-lived when coach Brady Meredith is found shot to death.

His murder leads to rumors concerning illegal betting and black-market steroids. Then the sheriff's old nemesis, a biker named Rapper, reappears, causing too many coincidences for Rhodes's comfort.

Another corpse makes it a second down for a killer determined to lead Sheriff Rhodes into a game of sudden death.

Available July 2000 at your favorite retail outlet.

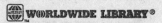

WORLDWIDE LIBRARY ®

Visit us at www.worldwidemystery.com   WBC354

The Second Sorrowful Mystery

JONATHAN HARRINGTON

A DANNY O'FLAHERTY MYSTERY

Having traded his native New York for his Irish roots, Danny O'Flaherty is teaching school in Dublin, and making frequent visits to the small close-knit town of Ballycara, where fishing and a lovely redhead capture his attention.

But here in this picturesque seaside town, a shocking murder draws him into the secrets, sins and sorrows of its most colorful inhabitants. Danny never anticipates the tragic web of deceit and vengeance behind Ballycara's darkest secret....

Available August 2000 at your favorite retail outlet.

Visit us at www.worldwidemystery.com   WJH358